A Pebble Tossed

MARK LEE TAYLOR

Cover design by James Geckle

ISBN: 1495945774
ISBN-13: 978-1495945779

DEDICATION

This book is lovingly dedicated to
Brianna and Melissa,
my inspirations.

1

Tim Raither is asking for trouble. He's gotten it into his head that he's the luckiest man alive, and anyone who does that has forgotten a basic truism: the universe has a way of balancing the books.

It's hard to blame him, though. He has a summer morning of exhilarating beauty all to himself, and there is, after all, no better time for bike riding.

Beneath a pastel sky adorned with a single scrap of pink cirrus, he hurtles downhill, slicing through the air like a razor on two wheels. The sun, an oblate disc perched on the crest of the next hill, casts its light full in his face. Mailboxes whip by him at regular intervals, while the lawns on either side, still wet from last night's rain, sparkle in the shifting hues of daybreak. Lingering in the air is a faint hint of ozone and earthworms.

Tim takes it all in with savage joy. It's a perfect day for the start of the Great Treasure Hunt.

He's been planning the event for a solid year, working day and night to create an experience that Lindsey and Amanda will never forget. Now the day has finally arrived, and it's hard to say who's more excited, Tim or his daughters. It's kind of like Christmas Eve, when all the decorating is done, and the house is clean, and the presents are wrapped, and all you have left to do is … watch it happen.

All he has to do now is hide the treasure, get back home by eight o'clock … and watch it happen. That's it. What could go wrong?

By that time, he should be in his Adirondack chair with a glass of iced tea, waiting. He may even have time for a quick dip in the pool before the festivities begin.

As he rides, he goes over his mental checklist one more time.

He put Station 2 in its hiding place a couple of days ago. Stations 3 and 4 have been ready for two weeks. Station 5, secreted last weekend. Stations 6 and 7, just yesterday. The last Station, #8, was the first one he hid, a month back. Puzzles, gadgets, red herrings; all squirreled away in various places around the house, the yard, and the neighborhood, places that his daughters will only find by solving the earlier clues, in sequence.

And the first clue, the one that'll get the big ball rolling, is in an envelope that Tim left next to his sleeping wife, before embarking on his morning ride.

Yeah, everything's ready.

Everything, that is, except the treasure itself, which is safely stashed in his bike's saddlebag, and now on its way to its final destination.

He's past the bottom of the hill now, with the gauzy light of dawn giving birth to a day of shattering brilliance. He pumps the pedals hard, straining to maintain his speed as he works his way up the next hill, feeling the delicious burn in his thighs, and the nagging discomfort of the old lacrosse injury in his right knee.

For a thirty-nine-year-old recovering alcoholic, Tim is reasonably fit. Determined not to squander the second chance he earned himself when he beat his addiction, he now devotes himself to a healthy lifestyle. Diet, vitamins, exercise. Family. These are his new addictions.

He's done with self-destructive behavior. He has too much to live for now.

He reaches the top of the hill and begins another descent, picking up speed as he hunches over the handlebars to lower his profile.

Tim's mind turns to Kate, of how sexy she looked as he left her, with the thin summer blanket clinging to her form in the watery pre-dawn light. Of the affection he felt for her at that moment, in spite of the argument they'd had last night. Or maybe because of it.

It was long overdue, he thinks. *Cathartic.*

Indeed, the first real quarrel of their two-year marriage had broken the tension that had been building between them for months. The sudden absence of that tension adds yet another dimension to Tim's high spirits this morning.

Hell, we even made love afterward. I am the luckiest man alive.

When he reaches the bottom of the second hill, he straightens his back, shedding velocity as he coasts past houses that are so close together, he feels like Luke Skywalker bombing the Death Star. It saddens him that all this rampant suburbia was once part of his father's farm. Mentally subtracting the gauntlet of yuppie starter homes, he can see a ghost image of the cornfield that was.

Back in those days, the hill he just came down was known as The Sleddin' Hill, and right here at the bottom of it was where he and his brothers would often come in the spring, sifting the freshly tilled earth for Native American arrowheads.

He once had a Maxwell House coffee can full of those arrowheads, but he hasn't seen it since high school. He has long suspected that his brother Greg emptied it into his own collection years ago.

Tim feels the first sweat break out in the center of his back. *Must be pushing eighty degrees already.*

As he exits the housing development through its broad main entrance, he can see the playground equipment across the road, its angular shapes and bright primary colors standing out against the dark green of the forested area looming behind it.

He cruises into the parking lot, and dismounts. Only a twelve-foot border of unmown grass separates the playground from the wooded area. Guiding the bike beside him with one hand on the seat, he makes his way along this grassy strip, with the playground to his right and the woods to his left. As he walks, he hears a sudden rustling and crackling in the brush at the edge of the woods. He turns to see what animal he might have spooked, but whatever it was— groundhog? deer?—it's already gone.

He moves on until he sees the sign reading "NATURE TRAIL—NO VEHICLES" (in letters barely legible through the rust and the flaked paint), then turns left and delves into the forest.

After leaning his bike against a tree, a few steps behind the undergrowth surrounding the trail, he takes three long swallows from his water bottle, replaces it in the rack, hangs his helmet on the handlebar, and finger-combs his thick dark hair back over his head. Then he opens his saddlebag and takes out the towel-wrapped mason jar containing the treasure.

Not even Kate knows what the treasure is, or where it's headed.

In sudden alarm, he pats at his pants pockets. "Damn," he says. "Forgot my cellphone again."

Now he wishes he'd told someone where he was going. If he were to, say, fall and break a leg, he'd be in real trouble.

He chuckles. *As if that could happen to the luckiest man alive.*

He resumes his trek into the forest. It is like a large airy room, a dappled place of graceful arches and green light, still damp from the rain. As he strolls, he breathes deeply of the earthy smell permeating the area.

The music of the forest surrounds him. The wind in the trees is the melody. The persistent patter of water dripping from the leaves defines the rhythm. Birdsongs and the dizzy droning of insects are constant counterpoints.

A couple of squirrels chase each other up and down tree trunks, making a staccato scritching sound.

3

While his feet take him deeper into the forest, his mind takes him five hundred years into the past, to a time when only Native Americans lived here. Some of them may have even been Tim's ancestors. His father has often told him the legend of a Susquehannock princess way back in the Raither family tree. What evidence exists is murky at best, but if the legend is true, it certainly appeals to Tim's sense of romance ...

He soon reaches a point where the ground drops away to a lower plain, with a rickety wooden stairway resting askew on the slope, like a sunken galleon. Fearing that the stairs won't support his weight, Tim slip-slides down the muddy incline instead.

As he continues on his journey, his excitement mounts, and he has to make a deliberate effort to slow himself down to a safe jog. He keeps up that pace until he rounds a bend in the trail and stops, numb with amazement.

The rows of towering trees growing on either side of the woodland hollow form a great arch, beneath which the valley's floor is a vibrant green sea of ferns, mayapples, and skunk cabbage. Billows of early-morning mist rise wraith-like from a meandering stream.

My God, he thinks. *It's like a visual symphony.*

As if on cue, brilliant lances of sunlight stab into the valley, illuminating the mist in parallel bands.

Overhead, the canopy tosses in a restless breeze, sending water droplets earthward. The droplets flash bright pinpricks of light as they pass through the sunbeams, and then disappear. Tim barely has time to appreciate this spectacle before it's over, but that only enhances its beauty, and the afterimage is burnt permanently into his mind.

He crosses the stream on a wooden footbridge. His feet make hollow thumping noises as the bridge quivers under his weight. The stream beneath him, swollen with runoff water, makes a sound like laughter.

Past the bridge, a hollow stump squats on the right side of the trail. The stump is the landmark where he (and his daughters, if they understand his poetry) must leave the trail and strike off to the left.

Off to the left ... where he now hears the loud snap of a stick breaking. He turns his head in time to catch sight of something he hadn't expected, or wanted, to see.

He curses under his breath. "You gotta be kidding me. *Now?*"

That he wants to be back before the treasure hunt starts is only one of the reasons he's out so early. The other is that he wants to be alone, and unobserved, when he hides the treasure. Who would expect to find another human being, on this forgotten nature trail, at this hour?

Yet there, not more than fifty feet away from him, is a man. Wearing long sleeves and long pants, all dark in color, the stranger scuttles away from Tim in a half-crouch. As the man reaches the top of the opposite ridge and melts into the undergrowth, Tim frowns and lowers his eyebrows.

"Groundhog, my ass," he says. "It was that guy."

Stranger in dark clothing. Lurking at the edge of the woods.

Near the playground.

A sick feeling of revulsion and dread creeps over him.

"Aw, hell no," he says. "Not in *my* neighborhood."

He considers his options. He could simply go on about his business and pretend he never saw the guy. After all, he's on a strict timeline. There's not much wiggle room for diversions like this.

But no, he can't do that. Suppose this scumbag harasses a child. Would Tim be able to live with himself if he knew he'd passed up an opportunity to stop it?

Worse still, what if that child were one of his own (both of whom would be here in this very forest in a matter of days)?

That can't happen, he thinks. Much as he hates to admit it, the Treasure Hunt is cancelled, at least for the time being. Until Scumbag is out of the picture.

So much for options.

Officially abandoning caution, the luckiest man alive sets off after the stranger.

He leaves the trail and begins wading through a large colony of bracken. The tall fronds brush his hips, soaking his pants and all but obscuring his feet from view.

Reaching the top of the ridge where the stranger disappeared, he sees the remains of an old stone building. It is broken, crumbling, returning to the earth. Of the original four walls, only one remains, and that one is broken off at mid-window level. Composed of stacked flat stones, the two corners of the building and the section of wall between the two window holes resemble three jack-o-lantern teeth.

In this remnant of a wall is a loose stone that can be easily removed to expose a small cavity, in which Tim, up until a few moments go, intended to hide the treasure.

He's reminded of the day, a month ago, when he first came to this area, scouting for potential hiding places. At that time, he had no idea what had drawn him here. He was just following a hunch. But as soon as he saw the wall, with its three "teeth" jutting up out of the ferns, he felt the tug of a fragmentary memory. He'd been here before. But when? He couldn't place it.

No matter. He'd found a wonderfully mysterious and evocative place to hide the treasure. Lines of poetry were already coming to him. This place was perfect, and that was all he cared about.

Later that night, a dream came to him in which the wall figured prominently, and he realized that it was not the first time he'd had this dream. It was a recurring nightmare that had plagued him for years.

In the nightmare, he is very young, and he and a companion are running, terror-stricken, and in their flight they come across this fascinating relic from another century, but are in too much of a hurry to stop and investigate. His companion has only a blur where his face should be, and the threat from which they flee is equally shrouded in mystery.

Each time this dream comes to him, he awakens in cold sweat.

Never mind all that.

He pushes on, hoping to get a good field of view on the far side of the wall, and maybe pick up the trail of the escaping stranger.

Past the foundation, he finds a narrow, weed-choked lane that was once intended for vehicles, but has obviously not been used for decades. This lane is familiar to him from his recurring dream, as well. He and his companion run along this route each time, as if the devil himself were on their tail.

Tim now sets foot on it once more, but in the opposite direction this time. Reasoning that the stranger probably hightailed it when he hit this open corridor through the trees, Tim begins to run as well.

The road bends to the left, and he skids to a halt when he rounds the corner, his mouth open in disbelief at the glaring anomaly in front of him.

A parked car, in the middle of the woods. A gleaming, blue, recent-model Chevy Malibu with a Hertz license plate frame on the front bumper.

Must be Scumbag's ride. But where the hell is—

A wrecking-ball impact to the center of Tim's back knocks him off his feet, and then several things happen in rapid succession: a splintering sound as he hits the ground, a moment of vertigo, a bright lash of pain, an involuntary clenching of all the muscles in his body, and a glimpse of darkness reaching out to engulf him.

2

ONE YEAR AGO
2:15 PM

"Honey, are the cheeseburgers up yet?" Kate yelled from the kitchen.

Outside by the grill, Tim said, "No, I'm still working on the shish kebabs. Do you need cheeseburgers now?"

"The kids are starving."

Tim, with great show for effect, turned his gaze toward the pool. "What are you talking about? Isn't that them in the pool?"

"They told me they were hungry before they got in the pool," she said, stepping to the back door so she wouldn't have to yell.

"They don't act hungry to me. *Kids, are you hungry?*" he shouted.

He received a chorus of yeas in reply.

"Can you just get on it, Tim?" Kate said, an I-told-you-so smile on her face.

"Yes, dear," he sang. "I'll get right on it."

It was a typical July day in Sycamore, Maryland. The sun's heat pulsed down from the hammered-pewter sky like God's thumb squashing a bug. This wasn't the dry oven-door heat of the desert southwest. This was the eastern seaboard, with its accompanying humidity that makes the air feel like soup and keeps sweat from evaporating.

Three men lounged on the deck at Tim and Kate's house, celebrating a friendship that stretched back more than twenty years. Charged with overseeing the kids in the pool, they were also drinking beer, discussing women, and blackening various foodstuffs on the gas grill. And sweating.

"I wonder who wears the pants in *this* family," said Tim's friend Brian. His eyes took in every twitch of Kate's behind as she left the scene.

"Yeah, P-Dub. You shoulda said, 'How high,'" added Darryl.

"On the way up," Brian added.

Darryl snickered.

"Jealous?" asked Tim.

"Me? And be tied down like you are? I don't think so," Brian replied.

Tim and Darryl laughed. Tim knew that Brian would never admit it, but he *was* jealous of what Tim had. Brian, who had been the best man at both of Tim's weddings, was still single. During their twenties and thirties, when his friends were getting married and starting families, Brian had been focused on acquiring money, rationalizing that women would be more likely to hop in the sack with a rich guy than a pauper. He'd spent the days building his home improvement business into a small empire, and the nights moonlighting as a bouncer at various bars. As he amassed his fortune, he did indeed get laid with remarkable regularity, but lasting attachment had somehow eluded him.

Now, at thirty-eight, Brian was a wealthy, successful, world-traveling businessman, but still single. With each passing year, he had become more and more vocally cynical about the prospect of marriage, and Tim feared his friend had virtually given up on finding the happiness he secretly craved. Instead, Brian professed devotion to bachelorhood, as he plowed through an endless parade of bar bimbos.

"On the other hand," Brian continued, "she's smart, she cooks, and she's got a great ass. Which, by the way, looks to me like it might be wearin' a thong. Is that true, Kate?" he asked, raising his voice so Kate could hear him in the house.

Kate, standing at the blender with her back to them, turned to Brian, grinned, and turned back to the blender. Then she stuck her thumb into the top of her shorts and lowered them enough to show off the north end of the thin strip of fabric bisecting her backside.

Tim smiled and shook his head in resigned amusement.

"Ouch," Brian said. "The sight that drove Clinton off the deep end."

"You gonna let the big guy ogle your woman like that, Tim?" Darryl asked.

Tim took some shish kebabs off the grill. "He can look all he wants. She's going to bed with me tonight, right?"

"That's my point, exactly," Brian said. "She goes to bed with you *every* night. It's boring. You should share. And I'm gonna see if I can talk her into it."

Tim laughed. "She likes hair."

"I ain't bald," Brian said, rubbing his scalp. "This is shaved. Women love it."

"Go ahead and try, then, Kojak," Tim said.

"Nahhh," Brian said. "It's hopeless. You two were made for each other."

Tim settled for a thoughtful, self-contented smile.

"Yeah, we do see that, dude," Darryl said, fixing his perpetually half-lidded gaze on Tim. "Believe me, man, we're just glad to have you back. We thought we'd lost you when you were married to Paula."

"Yeah," Brian said, "you don't know how often we all talked about you back in those days. It was like you were dead or somethin'."

Darryl nodded. "And since you've been with Kate, it's like the old Tim is back. It's good to see you happy, man." He raised his bottle in a toast, a gesture that Brian immediately mirrored. They took healthy pulls off their beers, then set them down on the table in unison. A beat behind, Tim joined them, the potency of the ritual diminished not a bit by the fact that his swallow came from a glass of sweet tea.

"Hey, P-Dub," said Brian, then paused to belch. "How 'bout a refill?"

Brian could drink more beer without seeming to become intoxicated than anyone Tim had ever met. His metabolism, like his body, resembled that of a bear.

"Another round?" Tim asked, and turned toward the cooler, but nearly collided with his oldest brother Greg, who had stepped out of the house just in time to assert his square-jawed authority.

"I got 'em," Greg said. "Don't make Timmy do that, guys. Have a heart."

"It's okay," said Tim, who was long past the point where seeing others drink was a danger to him. Hell, there was a bottle of Captain Morgan in the pantry that had been there since the day he quit drinking, and he walked past it every day without answering its call. Passing out beers to his friends was nothing in comparison. The urge to join his friends lurked like the nagging discomfort of a dull headache, and always would. But it would not make his decisions for him. Not today.

He pulled a fresh Corona out of the ice for Brian, and a Sam Adams Summer Ale for Darryl, who refused to drink "Mexican piss-water." "Greg?"

"Sure, okay."

Tim grabbed another Corona and passed them all out.

Watching as Brian stuffed a lime wedge into his Corona, Darryl said, "How good can a beer be if you have to add lime to it just so you can tolerate it?"

"Whatever, Deadhead," Brian answered. "It's better than that stew *you* call beer. At least I don't have to chew mine."

"Actually, this stuff is pretty light," Darryl said, scratching his beard. "It ain't Guinness, that's for sure. You should give it a chance."

"Not today, buddy. I'm on a roll. Can you drink six of those as easy as I just drank six Coronas?"

"Six? How can you be on your seventh beer already? I'm only on my second."

Brian shrugged. "It's Corona. Besides, I got here before you did."

"How much before?"

Brian shrugged again. "Five minutes."

Tim, shaking his head at his friends' good-natured bickering, turned to his brother. "You're late, man," he said. "Where've you been?"

"Sorry, Timmy," Greg replied. "I was at church, setting up for the bake sale tomorrow."

"And the wife?"

"Still there. She might make it later, but probably not."

"Sorry to hear that." A lie. Privately, Tim was relieved. His sister-in-law, who had been close to Tim's ex, habitually treated Tim with thinly veiled contempt since their divorce.

Tim and Paula's marriage had started out fine, as they all do.

They met in the ninth grade, dated for three and a half years, and broke up when Tim went to college. Five years later, their paths crossed again, and they rekindled the old flame. In another two years they were married, and managed to keep it together through the birth of their two daughters.

What happened after that was open to interpretation. According to Paula, Tim's drinking drove her over the edge. If you asked Tim's friends, Paula became such a bitch that Tim had to drink to escape her.

Tim preferred to think it was a little of both.

Regardless of who was at fault, Paula moved out, taking Lindsey and Amanda with her. Tim and Paula each handed their lives over to their respective attorneys. It took two more years for the divorce to become final.

Financially and emotionally eviscerated, Tim then allowed his demon to take control. He began missing work, and when he did show up, he would sometimes take long lunches and come back smashed.

He soon learned that one of the best things about being unemployed was that he had more time to drink. His bank account ran dry, the bills piled up, and the repo man got his car. He was lucky to have been living in one of his father's three rental properties, or else he might have lost his home as well.

Since Tim seemed unable to support himself or even behave like a rational adult, Paula was left with little choice. With the backing of the courts, she stopped allowing him to see his daughters.

Perhaps that was what Tim needed, his proverbial rock bottom. Losing his daughters accomplished what losing his wife and his job and his car could not. At last he found his own bootstraps and said, *Enough*. He simply stopped drinking. Right then and there, all at once. Not another drop.

After three days of complete wretchedness, during which his body rejected anything he tried to put in it, he found the nearest AA meeting. He'd never been sure how he felt about all of that higher power mumbo jumbo; he believed that, in the end, the power to take control of his life ultimately had to come from himself. Still, the meetings helped him in many ways. For one, through his sponsor, he was able to get a fresh start as an account analyst at a large trucking company.

After he proved himself "cleaned up," Lindsey and Amanda came back into his life.

Positive change led to positive change, reversing what had happened to him two years earlier. He put all of his energy into building a new life for himself and his daughters, and he realized that he could be content with this new life until the day he died, even if it was just the three of them.

What little dating Tim did during the early stages of his recovery seemed awkward and contrived to him, and led nowhere. He wasn't looking for love, so when it came, it ambushed him.

He could still remember the first time he laid eyes on her. He'd been working at G&L Trucking for three months. She was a journalist working in the PR department, and he would've had to be dead not to notice her. She was small, blonde, blue-eyed, and the focus of a lot of speculation among the male employees (and not just the single ones). Tim knew her name was Kate Burgess, but he didn't think she had any idea what his was. She was out of his league.

That changed when she needed help from someone in accounting for a project, and he drew the long straw. During their week of working closely together, he found out that, in addition to being easy on the eyes, she was also witty, outgoing, and intelligent. A year younger than Tim, she was a divorcee like him, but childless. She seemed not to know how pretty she was, a quality that drew him more than any other.

When the project ended, their relationship continued. Over the next few months, it grew in an incremental progression of chances taken and bridges burned. What had started out as strictly professional became friendship, and at some point made a smooth segue into love.

When he looked into Kate's blue eyes, Tim found it hard to understand how anyone could have let her get away, but thanked his lucky stars that someone had.

A year ago, they'd been wed, putting a cap on the extraordinary turnaround of Tim's life.

"By the way," said Greg. "Are Mom and Dad coming?"

"A little later, they said. But they won't stay for long. You know how Mom is."

Greg nodded at what remained unsaid: to put it politely, Tim and his mother did not always get along.

Greg was "the rock of the family," the one on whom everyone leaned when in need of spiritual or moral guidance. Middle brother Randy could do no wrong in his mother's eyes, wherever his muse took him (Silicon Valley currently, a college drop-out making an annual salary five times that of Tim's).

But Tim could not seem to win their mother's approval, no matter what he did.

A high-pitched squeal of terror shattered the air, jolting Tim and Greg out of their conversation. The men on the deck turned their heads toward the pool, where they saw two panicked kids clambering out of the water. Two other youngsters stayed behind, jeering.

"Shark?" said Darryl.

"Naw. Crocodile," offered Brian.

"A bee, a bee! Uncle Tim, a bee!" screamed Greg's daughter, Abbie.

"Christ," said Brian. "All that for a bee?"

"You think that was bad?" Tim said. "Wait'll the bats come out later."

Lindsey and Abbie flew up the steps onto the deck, spattering water everywhere. "Uncle Tim," said Abbie, "there's a bee in the water, buzzing his little wings. Can you get it out? Please?"

Tim handed towels to the dripping girls. "The skimmer'll get it. Now, since you're out of the pool, why don't you go get yourselves some plates and rolls and I'll have these cheeseburgers off the grill for you in a few minutes. Sound good?"

"Hey, Uncle Tim," Darryl's son, Jerome, yelled from the pool. "We got the bug out. It's not a bee, it's just a Japanese beetle."

Tim turned back to the pool, where Amanda and Jerome (who owed his name to the purported fact that he was conceived at a Grateful Dead show) held up their prize in a dipper net, still laughing at the other two. Amanda, at eight years old, claimed that she couldn't stand boys (and usually emphasized the statement with simulated gagging or some other expression of disgust); yet lately, she sought out Jerome's company above all others whenever the opportunity presented itself. Lindsey, four years older, was past that stage, but now refused to talk about boys at all, deflecting the subject whenever it arose. That alone aroused suspicion.

Tim sighed. His little girls were growing up so fast.

With a significant chunk of their childhoods already irretrievably lost to him, he was determined not to miss a single day from here on out. That resolve, more than anything else, represented Tim's "higher power."

It was amazing to him how different his two daughters were in some ways. Lindsey, the dancer, the fashion princess who never went outside the house without brushing her hair, was normally the leader. She now stood shivering and dripping on the deck, frightened out of the pool by a

Japanese beetle; while Amanda, the lover of horses and climber of fences, who could pull a tick out of her own skin without a flinch, laughed at her older sister for her squeamishness, yet idolized her at the same time.

He supposed it might have something to do with how they'd been raised, or more to the point, *by whom* they'd been raised. Lindsey was in grade school while Tim was at his lowest. Hence, she was a product, for the most part, of Paula's rearing. In contrast, by the time Amanda had reached those formative years, Tim had righted himself. He'd become more of an influence on her life than he'd been on Lindsey's, and so had his father, who had recently retired after selling the farm. It was Ed Raither who had been responsible for fostering Amanda's equestrian bent.

Their disparate strengths made them a tough team to beat when they were getting along, but sometimes these same differences generated friction. They were each other's staunchest supporters, and most annoying antagonists. They were, in every sense of the word, sisters.

"All right, thanks, guys!" Tim yelled back to the two in the pool. "Come on up here and grab some burgers!" Turning back to the two on the deck, he said, "Are you guys *kunumunu*, or what?"

Kunumunu was part of the internal lexicon of the Raither family. Tim had picked it up from a Trinidadian truck driver at work. It meant, depending on the context, either a lovestruck fool or a complete idiot. When Tim and Kate said it to each other, it could mean either of those, but it took on a different meaning when the girls were involved. With them, it was just a fun way to say "silly."

"Sorry!" they answered together, and scurried into the house, wearing identical grins.

Jerome and Amanda, rolling their eyes, soon followed.

The ladies were in the family room, where the temperature was more civilized and the seating more comfortable. Kate sat on the couch with her sister Donna. Kate's best friend Selena occupied the love seat across from them. They were sipping margaritas and discussing how hard it was to cook for Tim, now that he'd virtually given up red meat. "I mean, how many different ways can you cook chicken?" Kate asked. "It's driving me crazy. It seems like I just alternate chicken cacciatore and chicken parmesian. I'm sick of 'em."

"Too bad Mom's not around," Donna said. "She knew a few ways." Donna, two years younger than Kate, shared her blue eyes, but wore her mousy brown hair long, in contrast to Kate's blonde bob.

"Do you know any I don't know?" Kate asked.

"Probably not, but we could call Dad. He still has her recipe book."

"No, I'll pass on that, thanks," Kate said. "I don't need it that bad. But I need some ideas. Tim's killing me with those two dishes over and over."

"If you don't want him, I'll take him," Selena said with a theatrical wink.

Kate laughed at the long-standing joke. In high school, dark-eyed Selena, with her perfect tan and perfect teeth and spectacular body, had once stolen Kate's boyfriend. Time had brought the matter into perspective, but that didn't mean that Kate would ever pass up an opportunity to remind Selena of it, or vice versa. It was part of the fabric of their friendship.

The back door opened, and four chattering kids came into the kitchen. Kate could hear them from a room away, even over the noise of the blender.

"Hey, Lindsey and Amanda?" Kate yelled. "Can you two come in here a minute, please?"

Tim's daughters shuffled to the family room door, wrapped in towels and holding plates. They stopped, shivering and dripping while they waited for their stepmother to continue.

Kate was often struck by how similar the two girls appeared at first glance. Both girls had blonde hair and their mother's blue eyes. But on closer examination, the differences became apparent. Lindsey had straighter hair, a longer face, and her father's dimples when she smiled. Amanda had smaller teeth, a bit of wave to her hair that never went away, and a dusting of freckles across the bridge of her nose, a trait she shared with her mother.

Because of their hair and eyes, the girls looked more like Kate than like Tim, an irony that rankled them (Lindsey in particular) whenever strangers assumed that they'd sprung from Kate's loins. That probably wouldn't last. The girls would never have Tim's brown eyes, but they would soon grow to be tall like their natural parents, surpassing Kate's petite stature. In time, their hair might darken as well, to more resemble their father's dark mop.

Pointing at two partially consumed cans of Dr. Pepper on the computer desk, she asked, "Whose are those?"

The girls looked at each other. "Ours, I guess," Lindsey said.

"Can you get rid of them, please, before Widget gets an idea?" The cat was notorious for knocking over open containers, apparently for no other reason than to watch them spill.

"Sorry," they said, shuffling across the room to pick up their cans. Kate could have picked up the cans herself, but what would the girls have learned from that?

As they left the room, Lindsey turned and said, "Kate, can we go to the mall tomorrow? We wanna spend our gift cards."

"I suppose so," Kate answered. "Your father and I've not really had a chance to talk about it yet, though. We weren't prepared for you guys to finish your treasure hunt so fast. I think he's going to make it harder for you next time."

Both girls gasped. "There's gonna be another one?"

"Sweet!"

"Now, wait a minute," Kate said. "He hasn't said anything. I was just thinking out loud."

"Yessss! Let's go ask him!" Amanda cried. The girls whirled and vanished into the kitchen.

Kate put a hand to her brow. The damage was done. *Poor Tim*, she thought with a smile. *He's in for it now.*

"What was that all about?" asked Donna.

"Tim made up a treasure hunt for them," Kate said. "You know, they had to follow clues from place to place until they found the treasure?"

"Yeah, of course," Selena said. "Kirk did one for me on my birthday a couple of years ago."

"Oh, yeah?" Donna said. "What was the prize?"

Selena smiled. "Well ... there were rose petals all over the bed, and—"

"Okay, we get the picture," Donna said.

"He hid stuff all over the yard," Kate said, "and all over the house. We hoped it would last them all week, but those little stinkers, they finished it all in one day. The grand prize was a hundred Mall Bucks, and now it looks like we'll be shopping all week instead of relaxing."

"I know Tim's gotta hate that," Selena said.

"Yeah," Kate said, "and I think I just committed him to doing another one. He's gonna kill me."

Side by side, Lindsey and Amanda tried to exit the house and get onto the deck, each seeking a positional advantage over the other. They were on a mission.

"Daddy, Daddy!" Amanda said. "Kate said you're gonna do another treasure hunt for us!"

"Is it true?" Lindsey asked.

"*What?*" Tim said. "She did? Well, I was thinking about it, but—"

"Yayyyy!" Amanda cried.

"When, when, when?" Lindsey asked. "How 'bout next week?"

"Next week? No way. It took me a month to put that one together, and it was too easy. The next one ... *if there is a next one* ... is going to be a lot harder. It'll take more time to get ready. Next year, let's say."

The girls' jaws both dropped. "Snap!" Amanda said. "A whole year?"

"Yeah, Daddy," her sister said. "Can't you do it maybe next month?"

"No. Next year. And I'm not even promising that. Okay?"

"All right," they said, pouting.

At their crestfallen faces, Tim relented. "Okay, I promise. In fact, let's set a date. One year from this very weekend, okay? Do we have a date?" He held up his hand for high fives, and both girls gave them.

"Good," he continued. "I love you guys."

"Love you too!"

"Before you two wander off," Tim said, "come here a minute." He crooked his finger at them. "Closer."

Both girls drew near to Tim.

He mock whispered, "Run in the house, please, and tell your stepmother that I'm going to kill her."

Giggling, the girls grabbed burgers and ran off to join the others at the picnic table.

"What was all that about?" Brian asked.

"I made them a treasure hunt," Tim said. "I thought there was no way they were gonna have as much fun solving it as I did making it, but man, you should've seen 'em yesterday. They had a blast. My face still hurts from smiling."

"So now they're makin' you do another one," Darryl said. "That'll learn ya."

"I was just givin' 'em a hard time. I already decided I'd do another one. Once I saw how much fun they were having, it was a no-brainer. But next time, it's gonna be bigger. A *lot* bigger. I was afraid to pull out all the stops this time, 'cause I wasn't sure how they were gonna take to it. Now that I know ... oh, man, I can't wait. Treasure Hunt II is gonna rock."

"How'd you get the idea in the first place?" Darryl asked.

"From a children's book, *Key to the Treasure*, by Peggy Parish. It's about three kids that spend the summer on their grandparent's farm. See, their great-grandfather left a treasure hunt for *his* kids when he went off to the Civil War, but he never came home. His kids couldn't find the first clue so everyone forgot about it. Then the three great-grandchildren come along a hundred years later and solve the whole thing. I read it when I was a kid, and I never forgot it. When Lindsey was six, I got my old copy out and started reading it to the girls. And you know what I found out? It's just as good now as it was when I was a kid."

"You still had the same copy?"

"Yeah, I saved it. I only saved three books, and that was one of them. Anyway, the girls love the book too, and once I saw that, I've been thinkin' about recreating that experience for them ever since."

"What were the other two books?" Darryl said.

"*Treasure Island* and *The Phantom Tollbooth*."

"Wow," Darryl said. "Pretty good company."

"Shit," Brian drawled. "The only books I took out of my parents' house were *Playboys* and *Penthouses*."

"Why doesn't that surprise me?" Tim asked.

Over the next year, Lindsey and Amanda asked about the treasure hunt at least once a week. Whenever asked, Tim replied that he was working on

16

it, and *yes*, it would be ready in time.

He spent the first few months brainstorming. By September he had a sheaf of papers in his briefcase, all with notes that he'd jotted whenever an idea had occurred to him. He spent a rainy October Saturday afternoon getting them organized into a rough outline.

By January, he had put the clues into code, or concealed them in poetry.

In February, he worked on the last clue, putting it into the most intricate, stylized font he could find and stretching it so it covered an entire page. Then he reversed the image and printed it on a jigsaw puzzle transfer sheet, separated the pieces and mixed them up. The girls would find the pieces a few at a time, from the first station to the next-to-last. They would not be able to decipher the final message until they had collected all the pieces and assembled them.

By April, he had decided that the challenge still wasn't hard enough, so he added one more clue at the end; and that concluded the mental phase of the job. With summer coming up fast, Tim knew it was time to get dirty.

He planned his excursions for days when the girls were with Paula, hiding one or two clues a week over the last month leading up to the treasure hunt. Occasionally Kate would ask where he was going with that shovel, or that drill motor, but Tim refused to share. She couldn't blab what she didn't know.

By the Friday before the treasure hunt, everything was ready but the treasure itself, which he would hide at the last possible moment. He'd get up early, go to the old wall in the woods, put the treasure in its hiding place, and be back home before anyone else woke up.

That was the plan, anyway.

3

Kate rolled onto her side. Something from the real world had just touched her, impinging on her dream. Maybe it was a sound. Either way, she didn't like it. She hoped it wouldn't happen again, so she could go back to sleep, just for a few more minutes. The air conditioning chilled her and she tugged the blanket up over her shoulder. She began to drift back ...

Again, something touched her shoulder. And then a voice. "Kate. Wake up."

She opened one eye, and saw four other blue eyes gazing into hers.

Lindsey and Amanda smiled at this first sign of wakefulness from their stepmother.

"It's time to get up," Lindsey said.

"Treasure hunt!" Amanda said. "Where's Daddy?"

"Umm ..." She paused to yawn. "He got up early and went for a ride." She craned her neck to steal a glance at the clock. "He's back by now. Outside, I guess. Reading, probably."

"Hey, what's this?" Lindsey said, eyes wide. She picked up the sealed envelope from Kate's side. "This is the first clue, isn't it?"

Dimly, Kate remembered Tim having given her the envelope before he left. "Gimme that," she ordered, reaching for it. "Eight o'clock, remember?"

With obvious disappointment, Lindsey handed the envelope to her stepmother.

"Well, come on then, Kate. We want pancakes."

"All right, all right. I'm coming. Could you do me a favor and go start

18

the coffee pot while I get myself up? I'll be out in two minutes." They were gone in a flash.

"While you're out there," she added in a louder voice, "tell Daddy to come inside."

"Okay!" they chimed.

The room was bright with sunlight. The storms had ended sometime during the night, and that was good news. It meant the Treasure Hunt could go on as scheduled.

She tossed the covers off and stood, naked. Unable to locate the underwear she'd discarded with such haste last night, she pulled on a pair of light pajama pants, and topped off with a Mountain Dew t-shirt that Tim had left lying on the floor.

The shirt smelled of him: his cologne, his body. The soft fabric whispering across her skin sparked a replaying of the previous evening's amorous nightcap, a warm delicious gush of sensuality. She crossed the room to the window, hoping to catch her husband in an unguarded moment.

It was so bright outside that it hurt her eyes. She had to squint at first, but she could see that Tim was not in his hammock. Nor was he in the pool. *Hmmm.*

Oh, well. The girls would find him.

She went to the bathroom window and looked out on the unoccupied deck. That left the magnolia tree, casting its shade over two Adirondack chairs in which Tim would often sit, reading the paper or sipping a glass of iced tea.

Then she saw the girls come back up onto the deck from their own backyard search. They were not smiling. She heard the slider open and the girls come inside. Lindsey yelled, "Kate! Daddy's not here!"

Damn, she thought. *He's not back yet. Unbelievable. How could he be late on this day, of all days?*

"Kate, did you hear us?" Lindsey asked from the hall. "The car and the truck are both here, but Dad's not."

"Yes, I heard you," she answered from the bathroom. "I told you he's on his bike. I'm sure he'll be back any minute. He'd not miss this treasure hunt for a million bucks."

She washed up, then met the girls in the kitchen.

"I'll just get started on these pancakes and I bet he'll be back before you two finish eating."

Lindsey and Amanda wolfed the pancakes down as quick as they came off the griddle, practically choking themselves in their zeal to get started on the treasure hunt.

When they were finished, Tim still had not returned.

"Can we start now, or do we have to wait for Daddy?" Amanda asked.

"Yeah, can we please start now?"

Kate hesitated. "Let's wait just a few minutes. I know he'd want to be here when you start. It's not yet eight o'clock, anyway."

The girls groaned.

"Tell you what," Kate said. "Why don't you clean up here, and then go brush your teeth and get dressed? If he's not back by the time you're done, then we'll talk."

The girls washed their dishes and put them in the drying rack, then scrambled for the bathroom. Kate could hear them in there, jockeying for space at the sink, getting in each other's way, and becoming, if she wasn't mistaken, a mite testy with each other.

When they'd moved to their bedrooms and finished getting dressed, the sounds of squabbling coming from the hall confirmed her suspicion.

"Do you always have to wear the exact same thing I wear?" Lindsey said.

"I'm not wearing exactly what you're wearing, I'm just wearing what I wanna wear," Amanda replied.

They came marching back into the kitchen, both dressed in flip-flops, spaghetti-strap tanks, and black shorts that said "SPOILED" in pink letters on the rear.

"Kate," said Lindsey. "Can you tell her to put on something different? Look at us! Every time I put something on, she tries to copy it. I don't wanna go out looking like this."

"There's nothing wrong with you two looking alike," Kate said. "I think it's kind of cute."

"Fine," Lindsey said, "*I'll* change. I should've known I wouldn't get any help from *you*." She stalked off into her bedroom, slamming the door behind her.

"Well, this is a nice way to start," Kate said. "Amanda, don't worry. You wear what you want to wear. She'll be okay. I'm gonna go talk to her, do you mind waiting here?"

Amanda sat down without a word.

Kate sometimes worried about the way Amanda held things in. Whenever she was angry or sad, she clammed up; you couldn't get a word out of her.

Lindsey was the opposite. She had no internal filter; whatever she felt came out of her mouth. And all too often, what she expressed was mistrust of Kate, sometimes verging on open hostility.

She wished Tim were here. Then again, maybe it was about time she handled a crisis without him.

She went back to Lindsey's bedroom door, steeled herself, and knocked softly.

"*What*," Lindsey said from inside.

"Can I come in?"

Pause. "I guess."

Kate entered the room. "You shouldn't get so mad at Amanda," she said. "She's younger than you, and she looks up to you. She tries to be like you because she idolizes you."

"Whatever."

"That's not a bad thing, you know. I have a younger sister myself, so I know what you're going through. I know it can be irritating sometimes. But whenever it gets that way, just try to remind yourself that you're a role model."

Lindsey blew out a breath. "Sometimes I just want to be my own person, you know?"

"And there's nothing wrong with that either. I understand. Just change into something different now, and I'll make sure Amanda stays in what she's wearing. Tomorrow you can switch up. Does that sound good?"

"Yeah, I guess," she said, gazing at the floor.

Kate left Lindsey alone to change clothes, savoring her small victory. She checked the clock when she got back to the kitchen: 8:05. *Come on, Tim,* she thought.

"Lindsey will be out in a minute, Manda," she said. "She's going to change into something different. It's just part of being a teenager, I suppose. I think you guys look cool when you dress alike."

Amanda smiled. "Me too."

"Well, it's not gonna happen today, kiddo. Maybe another day, right?"

Amanda didn't answer.

Kate let out an exasperated sigh. It was so hard for her to hold a conversation with Amanda. The girl acted like she was afraid to get too close.

Thanks to Paula, Kate thought. She suspected Paula made her loathing of Kate quite clear to the girls, so they couldn't have positive feelings about Kate without feeling like they'd betrayed their mother. So far, that had been tough for Kate to overcome. Paula had all the power.

Lindsey came out of her room, still pouting. "Can we start now?"

"Let's give Daddy until 8:15, okay? If he's not here by then, we'll start without him."

"But, Kate," Lindsey said, "you know how he gets when he's out on his bike. He prob'ly got distracted, looking at a tree or something."

Amanda giggled. "Yeah. Or a flower."

Kate couldn't suppress a smile. "All right, then. As soon as Lindsey cheers up, you can start."

Lindsey pasted a phony-looking grin on her face. "Is this good enough?"

Kate sighed. "Okay," she said. "I guess it's time." She went back to the bedroom, retrieved the envelope, and brought it out to the girls.

They grinned as their eyes met, and sat down at the table together. Lindsey ripped the envelope open, pulled out a sheet of paper, unfolded it, and read aloud:

"Dear Lindsey and Amanda,
"Welcome to the Second Annual Treasure Hunt! This is your chance to become truly great detectives. I won't tell you what the treasure is, but I *will* tell you that you're going to like it a lot more than last year's."

At this, Lindsey and Amanda stopped to look at each other. Both their eyes and their smiles grew wide.

Lindsey continued:

"This treasure hunt is not nearly as easy as last year's. You will have to really use your heads. There are a lot of puzzles to solve. You will have to go inside and outside the house, and around the neighborhood.
"Along the way you will find some objects with the clues. You may not understand what they're for right away, but don't lose them, no matter how silly they might seem! You can solve this mystery without all the objects, but you won't know which ones you need until you need them.
"Let's get down to it. Here's your first clue. It's an easy one.

"It's just a picture," said Lindsey. "Can you tell what it is?" she asked Amanda.

Amanda took the page and studied the picture. "It's a close-up of something."

Kate stole a glance over their shoulders. It was a photo, and Amanda was right, it was a close-up of some embroidery stitching, all black and orange and white.

"It looks like a sweatshirt," Lindsey said. "See the stitching?"

"It's an oriole," said Amanda. "Oh, it's Daddy's Oriole hat. This is part of the bird."

"You're right!" Lindsey said.

"The closet!" They ran to the hall closet, where Tim kept all of his baseball caps. Kate used the opportunity to walk over to the window and check for any sign of her husband. Nothing.

The girls started throwing caps out into the hall: Terps, Ravens, UnderArmour, Nike, Key West, Martha's Vineyard, Outer Banks, South Park, Star Wars, Discovery Channel, Grateful Dead, Ocean City; you name it, Tim had a hat that advertised it. At the very bottom, they found the orange and black Baltimore Orioles baseball cap.

"Here it is," said Lindsey.

If only Tim were here to watch this, Kate thought, seeing the joy on their faces.

They found a plastic ziplock sandwich bag taped inside the hat. Amanda opened the bag and shook the contents onto the dining room table: a folded sheet of paper, a coil of orange mason's string, and three or four jigsaw puzzle pieces.

Lindsey inspected the string and set it aside, then picked up the piece of paper, while Amanda studied the jigsaw pieces.

"It's a code!" Lindsey said. The paper read:

EG6DIRB ES3ROH KO8OL EC2NO
RED7NU N1AR NO4RI E5REHW

"It looks hard," said Lindsey. "Let's check out the puzzle pieces first."

They laid out the four pieces, each white with an abstract pattern of black blobs and lines. "This one's an edge piece," said Lindsey.

"And this one's a corner," said Amanda. They tried all the combinations they could imagine, but none of the pieces connected to each other.

"This is hopeless," said Lindsey.

"We need more pieces."

"A lot more pieces. Let's go back to the code."

They smoothed the paper out on the table between them.

"It's all letters and numbers mixed together," Amanda said.

"It's separated into groups, like words. And each group only has one number, and the rest are letters."

They both studied the code for a few minutes, coming up with nothing.

Kate, watching the girls work, couldn't help but smile to herself, in spite of her growing concern over her husband's whereabouts.

She checked the clock again. 8:20.

"Hey, I think I found something," Amanda said, breaking the silence and snaring Kate's attention.

"What?" said Lindsey.

"The second one here spells 'horse' backwards, if you leave out the three."

Lindsey looked. "Yeah, it does," she said. "How did you notice that?"

Amanda shrugged. "I like horses."

"Maybe they're all backwards words, if you leave out the numbers. Let's see ... yeah, look, this one spells 'bridge.'"

"Let's do all of them! I'll get a pencil."

Amanda got a pencil and a note pad from the junk drawer, and gave them to Lindsey. Amanda read as Lindsey wrote. Dropping the numbers and reversing the order of the letters, they came up with:

BRIDGE HORSE LOOK ONCE
UNDER RAN IRON WHERE

"They're mixed up," said Lindsey.

"Maybe the words are in backward order, too," said Amanda. They both looked.

"No, that doesn't work," said Lindsey.

Amanda gasped. "Hey, we forgot about the numbers!" she said.

"Oh, that must be it," said Lindsey. "I bet we have to rearrange the words to put the numbers in order."

Amanda nodded.

Putting pencil to paper again, Lindsey wrote:

RAN ONCE HORSE IRON
WHERE BRIDGE UNDER LOOK

"Snap! It still doesn't make sense."

"Yes, it does," Amanda said. "*Now* read it backwards."

"Look under bridge where iron horse once ran," Lindsey read. "At least that's a sentence. But I still don't get it. Do you?"

"No, not really. What's an iron horse?"

"I don't know. You're the horse lover."

"I've heard of lots of different kinds of horses, but I never heard of an iron horse. Maybe it's a horse that carries iron. Or maybe Iron Horse is somebody's name. It sounds kind of like an Indian name. There used to be Indians around here, didn't there?"

"You mean Native Americans."

"Yeah, them. Dad says they used to live all around here. I bet there's some place where they used to run. Like an old trail."

"It could be that, I guess. Kate? Ever heard of a Native American named Iron Horse?"

Kate, remembering that Tim had admonished her not to give anything away, bit her tongue and shrugged. "Google it," she said. As the girls ran to the computer, Kate did another window check. She felt an emptiness growing inside her, an insistent need to know where her husband was, but she forced herself to remain calm in front of Lindsey and Amanda.

"There's nothing here about Native Americans," Lindsey said. "But there's some other meanings. 'Iron Horse Tavern?' I don't think that's it."

"How about 'A rock band formed in the late 1970s by Randy Bachman of Bachman-Turner Overdrive fame,'" read Amanda. "Do you think that's it? I know where Daddy keeps his old albums. Maybe the next clue's inside of one of 'em.'"

"Maybe, but here's a Wikipedia article. Let's try that," said Lindsey. She clicked on the link. Up came a picture of a steam locomotive. They locked eyes, and Kate could see realization dawning on both of them.

"The bike trail!" they exclaimed together.

Kate hadn't been there to witness it, but she'd heard the horror story countless times from Tim and other longtime Sycamore residents: how the county had gone to hell in recent years. Once an undulating patchwork quilt of fields and forests, creeks and country roads, fieldstone walls and barbed-wire fences, cattle and corn, the county had been swallowed whole by suburbia, they said. Gone were the farms, the local markets, the mom-and-pop hardware stores, and the small crossroads communities; all buried under highways, new schools, big box stores, and convoluted clusters of cookie-cutter homes.

To the natives, one of the few *good* things to come out of the county's slow and painful destruction was the Mason-Dixon Rail Trail.

Up until the late 1950s, a rail line had run from Baltimore to York, Pennsylvania, the Mason-Dixon Line. Tim was an ardent student of its history, and Kate had absorbed it by osmosis. When it ceased operation, it left behind a system of rails and bridges cutting through the hilly countryside. Allowed to fall into disrepair over the next couple of decades, it had become almost completely overgrown in places. With the arrival of the suburban invasion, the rail line had been converted into a walking and biking trail, the rusty rails and rotted ties replaced by a bed of gleaming white crush'n run, lawsuit-proof bridges of yellow treated lumber erected to span the many creeks and gullies. Passing through what remained of the region's unspoiled forests and tiny hamlets, the trail offered a quiet and bucolic trip into history, and was now frequented by walkers, joggers, and bikers from all around.

Tim loved the trail, not only for its serenity, but also for the leftover relics of the age of steam. Old bridge abutments, railroad signals, discarded spikes, and the remains of buildings all fascinated him.

The trail passed just a quarter mile north of their house. The girls were quite familiar with that section of the trail.

"It must mean that big bridge that crosses the swamp," Lindsey said. "Remember, right before you get to the train station?"

"Oh, yeah," said Amanda. "'Look under bridge where iron horse once ran.' Daddy must have hidden the next clue under that bridge."

"Kate, can we go?" asked Lindsey.

"All the way down there? I don't know. That's a long way to go by yourselves."

"Oh, come on. Please? Daddy must have thought it was okay."

"Well, all right. But not by way of White Horse Road; it's too dangerous. There's no shoulder, and the cars just fly on it." Unbidden, an image came to her mind, of Tim being struck by a speeding semi on White Horse Road and thrown into a ditch like a bloody rag doll. "Go through Belle Forest. It's safer. But be careful, and take your cellphone."

Belle Forest was a new housing development that had sprung up on one of Ed Raither's former fields. By car, one entered it from the west, by Griffith Road. But the girls, who had friends living there, often cut between the houses and entered at the southeastern corner, right across the street from their house.

The rail trail passed directly behind the row of townhomes that formed Belle Forest's northern edge. The girls could get there without the use of any main roads at all.

"Thanks, Kate," Lindsey said. She ran to her room to get her cellphone. As the girls bustled out the back door, Kate said again, "Be careful."

Lindsey rolled her eyes. "You already said that. And we're always careful." And she closed the door between them without another word.

Kate sighed. She watched out the window as the two girls got bikes out of the shed, then crossed Garland Drive and went between the houses into Belle Forest, chattering the whole way.

She looked at the clock. 8:33.

Come on, Tim. How late are you gonna be? You'd better get back before one o'clock, because I've got to leave then, whether you're here or not.

Then she winced, having caught herself breaking a promise *in flagrante delicto*. That was just the kind of thinking that had gotten her in trouble with Tim last night.

She was beginning to wonder if this real estate thing had ever been such a hot idea in the first place.

Kate and Tim had run into a financial bind shortly before they were to be married, when Tim's parents had decided to divest themselves of their three rental homes on Garland Drive. Since Tim had been living in one of them at the time, the soon-to-be-newlyweds had used Kate's name and good credit to buy it.

With the new mortgage added to Tim's maxed-out credit cards, both of their outstanding legal bills, and money owed for some unavoidable improvements on the home, they'd barely been able to make ends meet. Around the same time, Tim's old truck crapped out, the refrigerator was on its last legs, and they'd already promised the girls that the four of them would go on a cruise in two years. They had virtually no savings, and two daughters nearing college age at an alarming pace. It became obvious that, barring a hit on the lottery, they would need to supplement their income in the near future. Somehow.

It happened that Selena's father-in-law, Charles, had a real estate business. There was a housing boom going on, and he convinced Kate that it was a good way to make some extra money. In fact, he hinted that she might just end up quitting her day job, once the money started rolling in.

"I'll warn you, though," he said. "This business is hard on marriages. It'll take up a lot of your free time."

Kate shrugged that off. She'd nothing to worry about on that account.

After taking the required classes and passing the exam, she started working out of Charles' office in January.

She sold her first house in late February. Kate got almost six thousand dollars as her commission. One check, *boom*, in the bank.

Tim and Kate were hooked.

As winter passed into spring, the real estate market warmed up along with the weather, and Kate sold two more houses in short order. Energized by her success, she began to devote more time to her new business. She was often absent at dinner and on weekends, for these were the times when her clients were most available. Sometimes she was able to give advance notice to Tim, but other times not. He never said anything, but she knew, in the back of her mind, that these unscheduled disappearances irked her husband.

However, her willingness to devote herself to her clients translated to great success in her business. Tim and Kate caught up with their bills, took care of some of the things they needed, and then watched their bank account swell as the money continued to come in.

In May, Tim and Kate created a home office for her expanding business, a private nook off of Tim's basement den, and it became her haven. She spent more of her waking hours in there than she did with Tim and the girls.

She had conflicting feelings about this. It was as much about pampering her ego as it was about the money, and she knew it. When she stopped to think about it, it made her feel, somehow, unfaithful. She told herself she was being silly, but that nagging sense of guilt made a nuisance of itself, vexing her from time to time like the smell of a dead mouse in the walls.

She brushed off the signs of Tim's building resentment, rationalized that he was simply annoyed at the amount of pure drudgery involved in running a family household; a gripe for which she had little sympathy. Besides, it wasn't like she was just hiding. She was working, and she was bringing in money, which they needed.

Eventually, Kate began to see that Lindsey and Amanda had picked up on their father's attitude, and begun to express frustration in their own ways.

A few times, Kate had to break family plans to meet with one of her clients or to show a house. Tim forgave these transgressions to a point, but when she missed Lindsey's dance recital, she could feel the tension coming from him in waves. Kate tried to make up for it by buying each of the girls an iPod. As far as the girls were concerned, that went a long way toward repairing the damage; but no word of encouragement or absolution came from Tim.

It wasn't until last night that her husband's seething silence had come to a head, giving Tim and Kate barely enough time to resolve their differences before the start of the big treasure hunt. It was a testament to their strength as a couple that they had done it without spoiling the day for everyone.

Now the day itself had arrived, with Tim and Kate's relationship arguably stronger than ever. The girls, having forgotten that anything was ever amiss, were fully engaged in the treasure hunt. Everything was perfect.

Or would be, if only Tim would come home.

She checked the time again. 8:38.

"Come on, Tim. This is getting ridiculous."

4

Kate picked up her cellphone, tried to speed-dial Tim, fumbled the keys, and called her sister instead. "Shit!" she said. "Calm down."

The next time, she got it right. She listened as the ringing came over the line, then lowered the phone and turned her head toward the hallway.

She ran to the bedroom, hoping against hope that she wasn't hearing what she thought she was hearing. But when she opened the bedroom door, the strains of Steve Winwood singing "Gimme Some Lovin'" came to her loud and clear. Tim's ringtone for calls from Kate. And there, on Tim's dresser, danced his phone, vibrating in a circle on its third ring. She pressed the disconnect button on her phone, and Tim's fell silent as she watched.

Of course, she thought. *That would have been too simple.*

She felt a flash of irritation at Tim for having, once again, forgotten to take his cell. Then one at herself, for not having been awake enough to remind him.

Something is wrong. No way he would have missed all this.

On her way back to the kitchen, she ransacked her mind for explanations.

Maybe he just forgot. He stopped to talk to somebody and lost track of time.

By the time she completed the thought, Kate had grabbed the house phone and started dialing Brian's number. It rang twice, then Brian picked up and answered in the gravelly voice of someone still in bed.

"Hey, P-Dub. A little early, ain't it?"

In a flat voice, Kate said, "It's me, Brian."

"Oops. My bad. What's up, Bunny Buns?"

Kate cringed.

Ever since she'd flashed him her thong, he'd acted as if he was entitled to have his own personal pet name for her. He would never let her forget that mistake.

Swallowing a retort, she said, "By any chance have you seen my husband today?"

"Nooooo ... should I have?"

"No. I'm grasping at straws, I guess. He's out on his bike and he's been gone a while now. If you see him, could you get him to call me please? Tell him I'm starting to worry."

"Will do, sugar. But I wouldn't worry. He's probably in his own little world out there."

"Yeah, I know. But today is the treasure hunt. It's weird for him to be missing it.

"I'll keep an eye out for him."

"Thanks."

"And, hey, Kate ... If he doesn't come back, do you think you and me could—"

"Goodbye, Brian." She hung up, smiling and shaking her head ruefully. The man was so offensive that you couldn't allow yourself to be offended by him. It was just Brian being Brian.

Next place to rule out: Tim's parents.

Kate balked at the idea of calling Tim's mother.

She didn't mind talking to her father-in-law. Selling the three hundred eighty-eight acre farm that had been in his family for generations might have made him a millionaire, but he still dressed in faded jeans and flannel shirts from WalMart, still acted like a hardscrabble salt-of-the-earth farmer (albeit one with nice wheels and a lot of free time). Amiable in a vague sort of way, he grew distant after the first few words of any conversation not involving horses or fishing, yet he always had a smile and a cheerful greeting for Kate. She liked him, and believed he liked her.

However, with Ed currently on a fly-fishing trip in Simmons Creek, Wyoming, that left only Dottie at home. Dottie, unlike her husband, seemed to revel in the trappings of wealth. Kate tried to be nice to the woman, but it was a hard thing to do with Dottie continually looking down her nose.

In Dottie's eyes, Kate's first mistake had been in hailing from Towson. Like many longtime Sycamore residents, Dottie harbored a resentment toward "snot-nosed rich kids from the suburbs." Dottie also looked at Kate as a two-time loser, no more likely to succeed at her third marriage than she had been at her first two attempts.

These things Kate knew, although Dottie would deny them. Dottie never said anything overtly insulting or rude, but the oblique slurs and sneering condescension that peppered her speech made her opinions quite clear, while at the same time making it difficult to call her on them.

Kate sighed. Dottie had been married to the same man, a good man, for more than forty years, the perfect yin to her yang. She'd never had to make the terrible decisions Kate had been forced to make, could never understand what Kate had been through.

Kate and her two younger siblings had been raised in Towson, lower middle class kids stuck in an affluent school district. Kate's father had been an egregious drinker, and one of his favorite things to do when drunk had been to abuse his wife. The three children were never victims of his violence, but were often witnesses.

Kate's mother, a child of Italian immigrants, accepted the abuse with meek equanimity. She had dinner ready every night when her husband came home from work, she kept the house up the way he liked it, and she did her best to forestall his violent outbursts by avoiding all situations that might set him off. She walked on eggshells her entire life, trotting out her well-worn excuses for her husband's behavior—*Your father's under a lot of pressure ... works hard to put food on our table, we must respect his wishes ... has a hot temper, but he means well / is a good man ... has a different way of showing his love ... has a right to be angry, it was my fault.* That last one was her favorite.

It must have worked for her, because she stayed with him until the day she died. It took Kate years, and lots of therapy, to understand that through all that time, her mother was making unwitting accomplices of her children in these self-deceptions, and in doing so, she instilled these disastrous survival strategies in them.

Kate's escape from an unbearable home life was in academic achievement. She graduated second in her high school class and earned a full scholarship to Towson State University. She thought she was free at last, that she would break the cycle of abuse. She was mistaken.

Without clear understanding of the reasons for it, Kate found that she was most comfortable when she could employ the survival strategies she had learned from her mother, translating into a predisposition to choose abusive mates.

She met her first husband in college. He lasted two years. She thought he was still in jail, but she wasn't sure and didn't care.

Her second husband, Phil, was an explosive control freak who lasted almost seven years. He gave her two miscarriages and a shattered psyche, but not much else. Although she threatened to leave him numerous times, he convinced her to stay each time through tears (genuine) and promises (empty). The first time she went as far as to pack her necessaries and move to her sister's house, he got her attention by the only means left to him: a suicide attempt. It was unsuccessful, and probably staged, but it had the desired effect. Kate flew to his side.

After Phil was released from the hospital, spouting platitudes about his newfound focus and his love for her, she moved back in with him, failing to grasp the obvious truth that pity was a weak foundation upon which to build a relationship.

Things were better, for a while.

The next time Kate left, it was for good. Phil raged and threatened, cried and begged, all to no avail. When he started stalking her, she took out a restraining order. That didn't work, so she enrolled herself in self-defense classes. Still the stalking went on, and didn't stop until Phil found a new obsession and moved on. Kate never had occasion to defend herself, but she found an outlet in her new abilities, and kept on with her classes for several years.

Her best friend Selena was the one who first suggested that Kate might benefit from a relocation. She and Kirk had moved to a neighboring rural county a few years earlier, and had grown to love it there. Now, at Selena's urging, Kate followed her friend. She got an apartment, landed a job at the local newspaper, and started afresh.

For the next four years, she lived alone and did not go on so much as a single date. Many a knight in shining armor attempted to storm her castle, only to find that her walls were too big and too strong.

Until she changed jobs, and Tim came along.

Kate and Tim were both, understandably, wary of new relationships. At first theirs was distant, professional, but it didn't take long before elements of friendship crept into it. Tim was kind, gentle, funny, and supportive. He offered friendship and asked for nothing more in return. That alone attracted Kate, and her wall came down in tiny stages. At some point in that asymptotic process, she fell in love, but looking back, she could never pinpoint the exact time that it had happened.

Their first kiss was almost an accident, an impulsive act by Kate for which she immediately apologized. Tim's reply was, "It's okay. Could we do it again? I almost missed that one."

The second kiss lasted a bit longer, and from that point they could not turn back.

Besides being an out-of-towner and a two-time loser, Kate was now a real estate agent, which, in Dottie's world, put her at the very bottom of the food chain with lawyers, nematodes, and women who smoke while they're pregnant.

But Kate had an idea that even if she'd been a farm girl from Sycamore, she'd still struggle to find acceptance from Dottie, simply because Tim had chosen her. Tim could do nothing right, so Kate had to be just another of his mistakes.

Enough.

She took a couple of deep breaths to calm her nerves before placing the phone call. She tried to anticipate some of the things that might come out of Dottie's mouth, and to rehearse how she would respond to them without being confrontational.

When she was ready, she dialed Dottie's number. She listened to four rings, and then the answering machine kicked in.

She hung up. *Well, that answers that question,* she thought.

Call the cops? No. Not yet.

Kate forced herself to sit down and relax. She picked up a paperback and tried to read, but it was hopeless. She put her book down on the end table and drummed her fingers on the sofa arm. She was unable to keep her mind from conjuring images of Tim, having suffered any number of gruesome fates: crushed by a truck, bounced off a windshield into a ditch, stung to death by yellow jackets, drowned in the swamp, fallen from a bridge, bitten by a snake.

But no, any of those things would have resulted in someone in a uniform knocking on her door to give her the news. Wouldn't they?

Tim was safe. He had to be.

Lindsey and Amanda pushed their bikes across Garland Drive, up Mrs. Johnson's driveway, and across the edge of her back yard. Back-to-back with Mrs. Johnson's yard was a house on Foxwood Drive that happened to be one of the few homes in Belle Forest without a fence. They were always nervous crossing this yard, and stayed close to the neighbor's fence. Mrs. Johnson didn't care about the neighborhood kids using her yard as a thoroughfare, but the couple in the house behind her was quite concerned about the greenness of their grass and had been known to berate the kids for "wearing it out."

They made it to Foxwood Drive without incident, then pedaled down to Fernwood Drive, and cut straight across onto the sidewalk running between two townhouse buildings. Behind the townhouses they made a right turn onto the bike trail, following it as it passed behind the townhouses and into an open field. They exchanged greetings with the people they passed: a few kids riding bikes, a few adults strolling. The fine gravel crunched under their tires as they rode side-by-side toward White Horse Road.

"Kate gets on my nerves so bad sometimes," Lindsey said as they rode.

Amanda didn't answer.

"Doesn't she get on your nerves?" Lindsey pressed.

Amanda shrugged. "I guess. Sometimes."

"I mean, it's like she's trying so hard to be our mom. And she's *not* our mom."

"She's our stepmom."

"Exactly. And she can't *ever* be our mom."

Amanda didn't answer.

"Don't you have anything to say about it?" Lindsey asked.

"Not really."

"Why not?"

"I don't know. Do we have to talk about it?"

"I guess not."

They reached the place where the trail joined the dead end of Myrtle Drive, with a yellow line on the blacktop separating the trail from the almost non-existent vehicular traffic. Small fifties-era bungalows dotted either side of the little street. At its end, to the girls' left, tangled brush concealed the charred ruins of a fieldstone farmhouse, the oldest house on the street, for which Myrtle Drive was once just a long driveway. Only two blackened brick chimneys were visible, jutting out of the thicket like rotten teeth. Where the weed-choked driveway met Myrtle Drive, a length of steel cable, stretched at hip-height between two stout posts, blocked access. A NO TRESPASSING sign hung suspended from the center of the cable.

"Wanna go see the haunted house?" Amanda asked as they approached.

"Yeah, right," Lindsey replied. "Dad would kill us. Besides, it's not haunted."

"Is, too. Deanna's brother Grayson says at midnight you can still smell smoke down there, and it's been, like, twenty years since the fire. He said he saw a ghost down there, too. A real one."

"Grayson Watters is a lyin' little punk."

"Yeah, I know. He's mean, too. But still … doesn't it make you wonder?"

"Not as much as what Lexie's brother's best friend said. He went down there at midnight one time, too. He said he heard two people screaming, a man and a woman, even though nobody was there but him. He says all the lightning bugs blink red down there, for blood."

"Cool! You think it's true?"

"I don't know and I don't plan to find out."

Both shivering, they left the ruins behind.

"I do know one thing," Lindsey continued. "That place creeps me out in *daylight*. There's no way I'd go down there at midnight."

"I thought you said it wasn't haunted."

Lindsey shrugged. "Just in case."

They fell silent until they reached the road entrance of Myrtle Drive, where it came to a T at White Horse Road. A painted road crossing led to the opposite side of White Horse, where the trail plunged into forest. They stopped, checked for traffic, and crossed.

The trail was shady and cool on the other side of the road. They said nothing for a bit, enjoying the respite from the sun, and then Amanda picked up the earlier conversation. "I guess I liked it when it was just me and you and Daddy."

"Me too."

"We were like best friends."

"Yeah."

"It's different now, with Kate there."

Lindsey snorted. "You could say that."

"Kate has different rules than Mom," Amanda said.

"Totally."

"Like, she makes us clean our rooms."

"Yeah, and do dishes! All that nasty stuff on the plates, ugh! It's so disgusting. Mom never makes us do that."

Amanda laughed. "Mom has a dishwasher, you gooseberry."

"And then she smiles at us like she's trying to be our friend. It makes me sick sometimes."

Amanda grew quiet again.

The trail threaded its way between a hill rising on the left and a large swampy flood plain on the right. All across the lowland, the stripped remains of drowned trees clawed for the sky as if gasping for release from the waterlogged soil. Their father said the area was once a big beaver lake. The stream that ran through the center channel of the swamp was called Bottleneck Branch, and from here it wound its way into the woods behind the girls' grandparents' house, where it emptied into Sadler's Run.

No sign of human habitation spoiled the scenery. They saw a couple of joggers, and one man whizzed past them on a mountain bike, but they had the trail largely to themselves.

"Mom doesn't like her," Lindsey said.

"Nope. But Daddy sure does."

"Yeah. Sometimes I think Daddy loves her more than he loves us."

"That's not true," Amanda said. "Daddy loves us different."

"How do you know that?"

"'Cause I asked him once, who he loved more, me or Kate."

"You asked him that?"

"Yeah. I wanted to know."

"You're crazy, Manda," Lindsey said, amazed. "So what did he say?"

"He said it was a different kind of love, and you couldn't compare it."

"Yeah, right," Lindsey said. "I hope you know what *that* means."

"Then he asked me what was my favorite kind of food, and I said pizza. Then he said what was my favorite song and I said 'Pieces of Me.'"

"So? What does that have to do with anything?"

"I'm trying to tell you. Then he asked me, which do you love more, pizza or 'Pieces of Me?'"

"What did you say?"

"I said I couldn't decide. What would you have said?"

"That question reminds me of my Language Arts teacher. You can't answer it. Pizza is food and 'Pieces of Me' is music. How can you decide which one you like best?"

"That's just what Daddy said. He said how he loves Kate and how he loves us is just like that. Like food and music."

Lindsey was silent for a few moments.

"Aren't you gonna say anything?" Amanda asked.

"I'm thinkin'."

"So, don't you think what Daddy said makes sense?"

"I told you, I have to think about it. I'm not sure right now."

"Well, when will you be sure?"

"I don't know, Amanda! Later."

They traveled upstream for a while with the swamp to their right, and then came upon a bridge that crossed it. The original trestle, from which, many years ago, their Uncle Greg had fallen and broken his arm, was long gone, replaced by a sturdy new bridge, complete with safety rails.

The girls pulled their bikes off the right side of the trail just short of the bridge. They leaned their bikes against the guardrail, and stepped over it onto the white riprap that sloped down to the swamp. They looked in both directions on the trail and saw no one else, so they clambered across the stones to stream level, then turned upstream to pass under the bridge, with the abutment on their left and the stream itself on their right.

Although springtime typically brought a twenty-foot-wide creek rushing under the bridge's span, in summer the flow of water was usually confined to the three-foot channel in the center. On days following serious rain, such as this one, it might double its normal width, but no more.

Being careful not to step in any of the numerous rivulets of sluggish water, the girls made their way across the squishy floodplain to the edge of the main channel, checking behind rocks and under logs, keeping their eyes open for any object that might conceal the next clue.

They came up empty.

"Hmm," Lindsey said. "Maybe it's on the other side of the stream."

"There's no place to cross here," Amanda said.

"We'll have to go back to the bikes and ride across the bridge." They were about to turn around and retrace their steps when Lindsey chanced to look up.

"There it is!" she said, pointing. Attached to the underside of the bridge, between two joists so it was hidden from anyone not standing directly under the bridge, was a glass jar with a screw-on lid. Two metal straps, the ends of which were screwed into the underside of the bridge decking on either side of the jar, secured it. It was on its side, with the bottom facing them.

The sun reflected off the surface of the water and made shifting projections of light over their heads, lending a magical quality to the air.

The girls went to the water's edge. The jar was still out of their reach, right over the center of the stream.

"Do you think that's it?" Amanda asked.

"Has to be," Lindsey said. "There's a piece of paper in it. And something else."

"Puzzle pieces!" Amanda said.

"Yeah, I think you might be right. And there's something red in there, too."

"How are we gonna get it down?"

"It's not that high. We might be able to reach it if we could get right under it."

They regarded the stream, which ran brisk and opaque after the previous night's storms and contained small masses of black matter that may have been rotting vegetation ... or anything else. It was a swamp, after all.

"I am *so* not getting in that water," Lindsey stated.

"Me neither," Amanda said.

Lindsey began scanning the area around them. "What we need is a long stick, about—"

"About as long as this one right here?" Amanda asked. She flourished a five-foot-long, wrist-thick branch she'd just picked up from the ground.

"Yeah, that's perfect. Pass it here."

"Daddy must have left this here for us."

"Maybe," Lindsey replied. Then she heard a sound from above them and froze in alarm. "Shhh!" she said in a harsh whisper. "Somebody's coming!"

They lapsed into silence. Over the sound of the water flowing, they could hear feet crunching on the gravel path above them, approaching the bridge from the far side.

"Why are we being quiet?" Amanda whispered.

"Because we're not supposed to be under here."

Amanda's eyes got big. "Are we gonna get in trouble?"

"Not if you shut up."

They heard a loose board creak as a person stepped onto the bridge. The first foot made a dull clunk as it hit the wood, the next one scuffed. The person was limping or very tired. *Clunk, scuff. Clunk, scuff.*

"Lin," Amanda whispered urgently. "The bikes are up there!"

Lindsey clapped a hand over her mouth. She'd forgotten that.

As the stranger passed over them, they looked straight up through the cracks between the boards. They glimpsed a man with a full black beard and wearing a black t-shirt. The man's pace slowed, then stopped, as he stood in the middle of the bridge, muttering to himself.

After a moment, Amanda whispered, "What's he doing?"

Lindsey shrugged.

"I have to pee really bad."

"Me too."

The sound of ducks clattering and cavorting came to them from the large pond downstream. From somewhere in the opposite direction, they heard a bullfrog's croak.

The man mumbled something.

He moved from the center of the bridge to the rail on the upstream side and stopped again, still talking to himself. Looking in that direction, the girls could now see his shadow where it fell on the marsh. He leaned on the rail, seemingly just taking in the sights. Then the shadow crouched, stood again. Its arm came up, whipped out, and the girls watched a pebble arc out over the grasses and plunk into the middle of a still backwater. They watched as the ripples spread.

The figure on the bridge stood still.

"Lin, I'm scared," Amanda whispered.

"Me too."

Amanda drew in a sharp gasp, her hand flying to cover her mouth. She stared wide-eyed upstream. "Did you see that?"

"He's gone," Lindsey said.

"He's not just gone. His shadow … it just disappeared!"

"He walked away."

"No, you don't get it, Lin. Didn't you see it? It *just disappeared*. Just like that," she said, snapping her fingers. "Besides, if he moved, we woulda heard him."

They remained still for a few moments, listening and watching.

Ducks quacked.

"He must have tiptoed," Lindsey said. She bent, picked up a rock, and hurled it upstream, where it splashed into the water.

"Lin!" Amanda said.

They waited some more. From somewhere came the cry of a seagull.

"See? He's gone," Lindsey said, feeling safe to speak aloud.

Amanda sighed. "I guess you're right. Who was he talkin' to?"

"Himself, I guess. Unless he had a cellphone. Either way, that dude was weird, that's all I know, and I'm just glad he's gone."

"Me, too," said Amanda. "Let's get out of here."

"Not without the jar," Lindsey said. "Gimme that stick. I'm gonna try to push the jar out of those two hoops with it."

"But it'll fall in the water," Amanda said.

"That's okay," Lindsey said. "It won't leak because it's a Mason jar, and the air inside will make it float."

"How do you know that?"

"I know things. I'm almost an adult, you know, Manda."

"You're not an adult. You're thirteen."

"Well, I'm a teenager. I have more experience than you."

"So? I'll be a pre-teen next year."

Lindsey rolled her eyes. "As if. By then I'll be fourteen, silly. I'll *always* have more experience than you. Now please give me the stick."

Amanda complied.

Lindsey checked her footing and stretched the stick out before her, pointing it at the jar as best she could.

"Wait!" Amanda said.

Lindsey let the end of the stick drop. "Now what?"

"It's gonna fall in the water."

"I know that, Manda. I already told you it wouldn't leak. And there's no rocks under it so it won't break either."

"But, Lin, how're you gonna get it *out* of the water?"

"With this stick, doofus!"

"But it'll go that way," Amanda said, pointing downstream.

She was right. Lindsey had forgotten about the current. Following the stream to the right with her eyes, she said, "See where it gets real skinny down there? We'll have to go down there and catch it."

"How fast do you think we can get there?" Amanda asked. "It's kind of far."

Lindsey considered the bank between the bridge and the spit of land jutting into the marsh where she wanted to intercept the jar. The way was studded with grassy hummocks, fallen logs, slippery rocks, and scummy pools. The jar would get there long before the girls could, and then it would be gone. Beyond the point was a large, still pool where the ducks swam, occasionally dipping their heads for a choice morsel from the bottom. If the jar made it out there, they might never get it.

"Okay," Lindsey said. "We're gonna have to do this as a team. First, you go out there and get ready to catch it, then I'll knock it down."

"No way. I'm not goin' out there by myself. What if that guy's still around?"

"He's not. But let's go check first."

Together, they came from under the bridge, climbed the riprap, and checked up and down the trail. They saw no trace of the man.

"Lin, why can't you go catch the jar?"

"Because you're not tall enough to knock it down. I have to do that part. You have to go down there. It'll be all right, nobody's around. See?"

"Okay," she said glumly.

Lindsey went back under the bridge and watched as Amanda went downstream, picking her way from rock to hummock to rock to log, until she reached the semi-solid peninsula that constricted the stream to a narrow channel at its tip. She continued out to the end, then called to Lindsey, "Okay, I'm ready."

Lindsey stood on tiptoes and extended her arm full length, reaching with the stick, trying to butt it up against the bottom of the jar. The stick missed, and Lindsey lost her balance. The end of the stick fell into the water as she leaned forward, so she jammed it into the bottom to keep from falling in herself. She pulled the stick free, aimed and poked again, and this time hit the jar, which moved only slightly. "It's tight," she called. "I may have to hit it a few times."

She poked the jar twice more, scoring two more hits, and freed the jar of the first strap, leaving it hanging askew. "I think one more'll do it!"

She reached, poked. A miss. Her foot nearly slid into the water, but she caught herself, readjusted her stance, poked again. A hit!

The jar fell.

Splash. Both girls gasped as it disappeared for a moment. Then it popped to the surface and floated in place. A few seconds later, it began to spin slowly and move downstream as the current caught it. The jar picked up speed, clinked against a rock, shot through a tiny rapid, and headed directly for Amanda, bobbing and twisting its way past underwater obstructions.

Lindsey watched as Amanda squatted, both feet planted on a patch of muddy bank only inches from the rushing water, and reached her arms out to poise them above the center of the stream.

The jar was halfway there. "Get it, Manda!"

When the jar was ten feet away from Amanda, Lindsey realized she was going to miss it. It hugged the far bank, out of her reach.

"Oh, snap," Amanda said, and Lindsey saw her put her left hand directly into the water to give herself purchase for a longer reach.

"Ewwww, gross!" Amanda said. "The bottom's all slimy." But she reached out and grabbed the jar as it passed her, and lifted it high into the air.

"Lin!" she said, "I got it, but I'm stuck! I can't get back up!"

"I'll be right there!" Lindsey answered. She began moving as quickly as she could toward her sister.

"Hurry, Lin! I'm sinking!" Her voice was tinged with panic.

"I'm coming as fast as I can!" Lindsey's left foot slipped off a rock into the mucky water. She kept going.

Amanda emitted a sharp squeal. "I felt something move!" she said. "There's something alive in here!"

Lindsey reached her, took the jar from her upraised hand, and placed it behind her on safe ground. Then she crouched behind Amanda, grabbed her by both armpits, and hauled with all her might. Amanda's left arm came out of the mud with a sucking sound, and both girls fell to the ground, Amanda sitting in Lindsey's lap.

"Yuck! Nasty!" Amanda said, holding her arm well away from her body. It dripped water and loose clumps of mud and rotted vegetation. "Oh, it stinks! Get it off me, get it off me!"

"Manda, get up, you're dripping all over me. OMG, it *does* stink. Get it away from me!"

Amanda dipped her arm back into the water, which was brown and muddy, but an improvement over what clung to her arm. She rinsed it, then wiped it on a patch of grass as best she could, and sat down with Lindsey to study the jar.

Inside were a couple of pieces of paper, four or five more puzzle pieces, and a pair of red-tinted glasses. Lindsey wrapped her hand around the lid and grimaced, straining every muscle as she tried to twist the lid. "I can't open it," she said.

"Try tapping it on that rock."

Lindsey tapped the lid on the edge of the rock a few times and tried again. Still, it was too tight for her. "I guess we'll have to take it home," she said. "Daddy can open it for us. He was the one that put it on that tight."

"Good," Amanda said. "Let's go. That guy might still be around here somewhere. Plus I *really* have to pee."

They climbed back to their bikes.

"Whew!" Lindsey said. "It's hot. I'm so getting in the pool when we get home."

"We better hurry, then," Amanda said. "It's gonna rain."

"No, it's not. The sky's perfectly blue. Look at it."

"Yeah, but the leaves are all upside-down. Check out the trees. Poppy says when the leaves turn all silver like that, it means—"

"I know, I know. It means it's gonna rain. You and Poppy and your *things*."

Amanda made her eyes as big as she could and stuck her tongue out.

"Whatever," Lindsey said. "I totally don't think it's gonna rain. But let's hurry, just the same. After we swim, we can solve this puzzle."

They mounted their bikes and turned toward home.

Madison Kingsmore didn't believe in monsters any more. She was too old for that. Madison was in second grade now. Well, not quite, because it was summer, but when school started in September, she would be a second grader, and that was close enough for her.

She knew her cousin Ashleigh still believed in monsters, but that was because Aunt Bonnie was a worry-wart. Aunt Bonnie worried so much that she made Ashleigh afraid of monsters. That's what Mommy said, anyway.

"Fifteen minutes, now," Mommy said to her. "Okay?"

Madison nodded. "Okay, Mommy."

"Have fun." Mommy opened the back door for her, and Madison

walked down the concrete steps and ran for the gate in the back yard fence as the back door slammed shut, BAM!

Madison was a lucky girl. Her school was right next door to her house. She didn't ever have to ride one of those big stinky yellow buses. On school mornings, Mommy would hold her hand and walk her to the school's front door. After school, Mommy would be right there waiting for her. On Saturdays, unless it was raining or too cold, Mommy let Madison cut through the back yard and go to the playground. Now that it was summertime, *every* day was Saturday. Mommy usually let her go play while "The Price Is Right" was on. Mommy loved "The Price Is Right." Madison thought it was a stupid show.

As she crossed the narrow strip of lawn between her yard and the school playground, she could see that no one else was playing there. She frowned. There almost *never* was. Madison's house was the only one on the same side of the road as the school. She knew some kids lived in the houses across the road, but Mommy wouldn't let her go play over there. She said there was a lot of maniacs on that road. Mommy always said, "Stay away from the road, Madison." And she meant it.

None of those kids on the other side of the road ever came to Madison's side either, she guessed 'cause their moms knew about the maniacs, too. All moms knew stuff like that.

Anyway, the playground was empty today. Madison didn't mind playing by herself, but having a friend with her was ever-so-much more fun.

The playground had a fence around it, but the gate was never locked. Madison slipped through and went straight to her favorite swing. She kicked off the ground and began to swing, laughing as her hair blew first one way, then the other, then back again.

So far, summer was boring. It was always just her and Mommy. Daddy was always at work except for at nighttime. Daddy worked a lot and he worked really hard. She was pretty sure her Daddy was the bestest man in the whole world. She knew he loved her, but he had a really important job and he had to make money so he could get the things Madison and Mommy needed. So she only got to see him for dinnertime and after dinner and on Saturdays and Sundays. The rest of the time it was just Madison and Mommy. She loved her Mommy, too, but Mommy liked to watch TV a lot, and Madison didn't like the same shows Mommy did. Sometimes her and Mommy would go to the Mall together. Not today.

Next week, swim camp would start. That was going to be fun. But until then, nothing to do, no one to play with …

"Oh, yeah!" Madison said aloud, eyes wide with delight. She had just remembered that Ashleigh was coming over to spend the night tomorrow night. She could hardly wait, 'cause she'd just gotten a My Little Pony game for her Game Boy, and she wanted to show it off. And then on Sunday, her and Ash could go to the playground together!

She got bored with swinging, and skipped over to the brightly colored steps that led up to the catwalk. Once on the catwalk, she could come down by the straight slide or climb up to the next level and come down by the twisty tube-slide, or she could just hang out in the sky fort and play with the steering wheel.

Too bad Madison wasn't going to Ash's house instead of the other way around, because Aunt Bonnie always had the bestest food. Sometimes she would give Madison and Ash hot dogs for lunch. Madison loved hot dogs. Mommy and Daddy never let her eat hot dogs, or pancakes either, unless they were hole wheat. She didn't know why they were called hole wheat, because they didn't have any holes in them. She asked Mommy about that one time, so Mommy picked a pancake up off Madison's plate and folded it in half and took a bite out of it. Then she put it back and said, "There, now it's got a hole in it." Mommy and Madison both laughed, but Madison didn't ask about the holes anymore after that.

She walked around in a circle in the sky fort for a while, going around and around the steering wheel in the center (steering wheels were for boys, anyway), singing that song by Selena Gomez that they played on the Disney Channel all the time. She loved that song. When she got tired of that, she used the twisty slide to come back down to the ground. As she skipped toward the sandbox, she kicked at the mulch. It was fun to watch the stuff bounce around. Miss Osteen said it was made out of old tires. It sure didn't look like tires, but Miss Osteen was a first-grade teacher and she was probably right. On the way by, Madison grabbed at the lowest set of hanging rings and swung back and forth a couple of times before moving on to the sandbox.

At Aunt Bonnie's house, she usually-almost-always got pancakes for breakfast and hot dogs for lunch. One time, Mommy and Aunt Bonnie got mad at each other over it. Later, Mommy explained to Madison that she still loved Aunt Bonnie. Sisters were just like that sometimes.

Madison wondered what it would be like to have a sister.

Sifting sand through her fingers, Madison wondered if Aunt Bonnie would ever let her play in the playground by herself like this. She'd say there might be a monster in the woods right next to it. Madison laughed out loud. There was no such thing as monsters.

Was there?

There *was* a monster lurking in the bushes. It was motionless and nearly invisible as it kept a silent vigil over its hunting ground. It was relentlessly focused and patient, perfectly designed for its niche in the ecological milieu.

The monster had a mind driven only by its most basic instincts: hunger, greed, carnality. It had no use for such things as pity, compassion, empathy, remorse.

The monster had many names. To his current employers, he was known as Jerry. He was watching the playground this day because it was both his hobby and his profession. Not many are so fortunate in their choice of career as to be permitted to make money doing something they love. Jerry was one of the lucky ones.

This morning's hunt was not for pleasure; he was on a job. He had been commissioned to kidnap two to three blonde females between the ages of six and twelve. A lot of money waited for him if he should come through, and he *would* come through. He was very, very good at his job.

That didn't mean he couldn't enjoy himself at the same time.

Jerry had been staking out this playground, and one other, for several days. He had chosen the two playgrounds for their convenient arrangements with respect to the surrounding landscapes. This one was behind the school, thereby shielded from view by passing motorists. Near it was a wooded area in which he could hide. A short walk to the other side of the woods brought him to his nondescript rental car, which he had left parked on a tractor trail. This trail ran along the edge of the forest and across several fields, eventually leading to a narrow country road that was in dire need of resurfacing, more than a mile away from the school as the crow flies, three miles by road. All he had to do was lure his prey into the trees, and they could be in the next county before anyone knew she was gone.

The other playground had a similar arrangement, although that one was lost to him now.

As was often true in rural areas, this community had yet to sufficiently safeguard its children from predators such as Jerry. In less provincial areas, one would never find a playground so close to such an easy snatch-and-grab route. Playgrounds like this might soon cease to exist here as well, once he had done his work, but he cared not. By that time, he would have moved on to another community, another state.

He knew his prey's routine. She always started on the swings, moved from there to the stairs leading up to the crow's nest or whatever it was, spent some time up there, came back down by one of the slides, hit the sandbox, and went back to the swings before heading home. Her home was right next door to the playground.

Her mother probably felt it was safe for her to go to the playground unattended, since she was within sight of the house. *Foolish, foolish woman.*

Ordinarily, Jerry was the epitome of patience. Today, tomorrow, the next day, next week … there was no hurry. He found the uncertainty of it delicious. It heightened the pleasure of anticipation.

But today, Jerry was a bit disconcerted. The incident at the other playground this morning had changed his timetable. He felt the need to get the job done and vacate the area as soon as possible.

He checked the contents of the shoebox next to him. All was in readiness. Madison headed for the swings just as Jerry had known she would, climbed up onto her favorite, and began to kick.

She was beautiful. As Jerry admired her pretty blonde hair, tanned skin, and sleek legs, he licked his lips. Sweat broke out on his brow and he felt flushed.

He would take her as she moved from the catwalk to the sandbox. That was when she passed closest to his hiding place.

Madison finished swinging and headed toward the stairs to the catwalk, singing to herself. Jerry lifted the lid of his shoebox and set the small black and white kitten free in the woods behind him. The kitten looked around, took a few tentative steps. Jerry had no worries that the animal would escape, for it was undernourished and exhausted.

Madison came down the slide. She kicked at the rubber mulch as she moved toward the sandbox.

Jerry fished a bottle of Visine from his pocket, and put three drops in each of his eyes, allowing the excess to run down his face. He stood, took two steps to his left onto a game trail, and stepped out of the wooded area.

"Excuse me, Madison?" he said.

Startled, Madison regarded him warily. "How did you know my name?" she asked.

"Why, don't you recognize me? I'm Jerry. Your mom knows me. I live right over there," he said, pointing vaguely to his left. "I don't mean to bother you, but I seem to have lost my kitten. Have you seen her? She looks like this." He took out his wallet and opened it to a picture he'd put there this morning. "May I show you?" He leaned across the fence, extending his wallet toward her so she could see the black-and-white kitten in the photo.

"I guess so," she said. She leaned toward him without moving her feet, to look at his wallet without getting any closer to him than she had to. *Smart girl!*

Jerry put his wallet away. Then he sniffed and made a show of blowing his nose and wiping his eyes.

"Where did you lose her?" Madison asked.

"She ran into the woods right there," he said, pointing at the game trail.

Madison peered into the shade of the trees. "Hey! I think I see her!" she said.

"Oh, you do? Where?"

"Right over there. See?"

"No, I can't see her."

"She's *right there*. She's not moving."

"Oh, my eyes are so bad. I can't see her, honey. Would you mind getting her for me? I'll wait right here."

Madison shrugged. "Okay." She ran to the gate, exited the playground, and walked into the forest, saying "Here, kitty, kitty."

So cute, he thought. They all said that.

Jerry smiled, licked his lips, and walked in after her.

5

Kate paced between the front door and the back, like a tiger in a cage. Occasionally, just to break up the monotony, she'd peer out the family room window that looked down the length of Garland Drive, or go out on the deck and check the driveway.

Within the past hour she had gone from worry to anger and back to worry, and was now verging on panic. She couldn't imagine him being this late if it was within his power to be here; he must be in trouble.

He'd better *be in trouble, or he's sure as hell* going *to be in trouble when he gets home.*

An idea struck her.

Excited, she raced to the basement, to the magazine rack right next to Tim's favorite reading chair. Heart thudding in her chest, she plopped into the La-Z-Boy and searched amid the sea of magazines and folded sports pages for the bright yellow folder, the one in which Tim kept his notes for the treasure hunt. There it was!

She withdrew the folder and opened it with trembling fingers.

In the folder was a single sheet of lined notebook paper, with Tim's message in his even block printing, all caps:

> DID YOU THINK IT WOULD BE SO EASY? HAHA! I
> BURNED IT ALL! CLEVER OF YOU TO LOOK HERE,
> BUT SHAME ON YOU FOR TRYING TO CHEAT!
>   LOVE, DADDY

Kate's heart sank into her feet. She got up, dropped the folder onto the chair, and trudged back up the stairs.

If she had any idea where he'd gone, she might have gotten in her car and taken to the roads to look for him. No. She couldn't do that anyway; she needed to be here when the girls returned. Her eyes stung as she reached the kitchen. Her lip trembled.

I refuse to cry, she thought.

Speaking of the girls ... what was keeping them? They'd been gone for nearly two hours. She squeezed back the tears and channeled her frustration into that problem, one she could do something about.

She called Lindsey's cellphone. It rang five times, then went to voicemail. "Oh, no," she said. "Not them, too." She disconnected and started to put the phone down, but it rang before she got it to the table, sending a jolt through her like the touch of a live wire, and she gave a little yelp before answering it.

"Hi," came Lindsey's voice.

"Why didn't you answer?"

"The phone was in the kitchen and I couldn't get to it in time. Is Dad home yet?"

"No, not yet. What kitchen? Where are you? You've been gone for almost two hours."

"We're at Lexie's house. Don't worry," Lindsey replied in a slightly defensive tone. "Daddy hid the clue under the bridge and we had a hard time getting it. Plus Manda got wet and dirty, and we both had to pee real bad, so we stopped at Lexie's house to use the bathroom. But why isn't Dad home yet? Shouldn't he be there by now?"

"I'm sure he'll be here soon. But I want you two to get home right now."

"All right, we're coming."

They hung up.

Kate paced some more.

She wondered if it was still too soon to call the cops, and decided that it was. She imagined that the minute she made that call, Tim would come cruising down the driveway on his bike, whistling "Dixie Chicken." She'd die of embarrassment.

Maybe I'll just call Alan, she thought. *Unofficially. He'll know what to do.*

Walter Alan Curtis III was a captain in the Sheriff's Department. Known by his middle name all his life, he was also a friend of the Raither family. He and Tim's brother Greg had been best friends since grade school, and his father, Walt Curtis Jr., had gone to school with Tim's father. Alan wasn't particularly close to Tim, but Kate had met him on two occasions and knew that she liked and trusted him (in spite of his association with Greg). She felt comfortable calling him to ask for personal advice.

She'd give Tim ten more minutes. No more.

Tim, where are you?

I'm walkin' the tracks with my brothers. It's October, and I wish I'd wore a better jacket, 'cause it's pretty chilly out today. The trees are real pretty though. When there ain't no wind, like today, the duck pond has all the same colors as the trees, only upside-down, and it looks like a painting by one of those famous guys like they hang in the doctor's office.

We just crossed White Horse Road, on our way to the trestle. Mom don't let me cross White Horse by myself, 'cause I'm only eight, but if Greg and Randy are with me she don't mind.

We ain't allowed to climb on the trestle since Greg fell off it last fall and broke his arm, but I don't care 'cause I never wanted to anyways. I tried to go acrost it once, but lookin' down between the railroad ties and seein' the creek down there about made me sick to my stomach. Some of the ties are missin', and you have to take big giant steps just to get from one to the next. Greg and Randy, they do it all the time even though Mom said not to, and they laugh at me when I don't wanna do it.

When we get to the trestle, Greg says, "Hey, Timmy. Me and Randy are gonna keep walkin' until we get to the old station. We're gonna meet Alan over there. You don't have to come along if you don't want."

Now maybe I'm only eight, but I know when I been uninvited. I can tell when Greg means what he's sayin', and when he means just the opposite, and when he means somethin' in between. I know if I say I wanna go along, they'll come up with some reason why I shouldn't. And if I still go, they'll be mean to me the whole way until they get their way.

Sometimes I can't stand my brothers. Especially Greg. He thinks his shit don't stink.

But this time, I don't care, because I already decided I wanna go over to the duck pond and skip some stones.

"Nah," I say. "I'm gonna go skip stones for a while."

"Okay," Greg says. "We won't be long. We'll pick you up on the way back."

Now, that might be true and it might not. This ain't the first time they've ditched me, and I know they might come back and get me and take me home, or I might get tired of waitin' for 'em and wander on back home by myself.

It don't matter. Either way, I'll get home.

So they go on without me, and I slip-slide down the slope right next to the trestle until I get to the—

He becomes aware of two things. The first is that he has just emerged from a dream. The second is that he is in excruciating pain. The pain drives out the memory of the dream, scours it into nonexistence as as a hailstorm might do to a butterfly.

After a few minutes, or eternity, he begins to become aware of other sensations.

Wetness. Cold.

Confinement. He feels cramped, restrained. He is wet and cold and in pain and he cannot move.

Where am I? he thinks.

Never mind. Tired.

Blackness.

—swamp at the bottom. This here whole area is nothing but a big swamp. Must be a hundred little streams goin' this way and that, and a zillion little islands, but ain't none of 'em ever in the same place twice. All the little streams combine into one big one under the bridge, then they start to split up again, but pretty soon they all dump into the duck pond. We call it the duck pond 'cause, well, there's always ducks swimmin' around in it, but really it's just part of the swamp. You have to be real careful gettin' over to the duck pond from the tracks, so you don't get a foot stuck in the mud. Sometimes a spot that looks like dry land turns out to be so wet you sink right into it, and sometimes those spots are hard to get out of. Once, my foot sunk down to my knee, and when my foot came back out it was without a shoe. I had to reach my arm way down in the hole and grab ahold of my shoe and drag it back out.

Boy was Mom pissed that day.

Anyways, so I get to the bottom of the slope and I start walkin' alongside the creek toward the duck pond, and I hear a squelchin' noise like you hear when you step in the wrong spot. But it didn't come from me, it came from behind me, so I turn around to see what made the sound, and there's this kid I know from school. He's comin' out from under the trestle like he's been hidin' there the whole time while me and my brothers was talkin'.

I don't really know him too good. I seen him around school, but this year is the first year he was ever in my class. I can't even remember right now what his first name is. Everybody just calls him Lynch.

"Hey, Lynch," I say.

"Hey, Timmy."

"Whatcha doin' under there?"

"Just hangin' out," he says.

"Do you live around here or somethin'?"

"Yeah," he says, pointin' back down the tracks. "I live over there on Myrtle Drive."

"No shit? I musta just walked past your house then."

"Yeah. I've seen you walkin' past it other times, too."

"How come you never said 'hi' or nothin'?"

He shrugs and says, "I dunno. Just didn't."

He don't seem very friendly, really, does he? But then, goin' by the look on his face, maybe he's just downhearted or somethin'. Come to think of it, I just now remembered that his Dad passed away last summer. When it happened, Mom asked me if I knew him, 'cause she knew we were the same age and all, and I told her no, but she said if I was to ever be around him, to be nice to him, 'cause his Dad just died.

"I was gonna go over to the duck pond and skip stones," I say. "Wanna come along?"

He looks at me a second or two, like he's gonna say no, which wouldn't bother me, 'cause I done my part, but then he says, "Sure. I don't know how, though."

"You gotta be kiddin' me. Everybody knows how to skip stones. What are you, a girl?" I shouldn'ta said that. It just popped out.

"I ain't a girl. Just 'cause you can skip stones and I can't don't make me a girl. Can you fish?"

"Yeah."

"Can you hunt?"

"Yeah. Well, my dad says I'm too young. But I know how."

"Well, I've done it. Can you fix cars?"

"No," I say. "Why, can you?"

He nods, smiling. "Yup."

"Wow. What else do you like to do?"

"I read a lot."

Pain wakes him again. How much time has passed? There is no way to tell.

What happened? Am I dead? Is this Hell? Is this Heaven?

Blackness.

Uh-oh. He reads a lot? Now, he had me with the huntin' and fishin' part, and especially the fixin' cars, but now he's losin' me. Still, I need to come up with somethin' else I like to do besides skip stones, 'cause he's way ahead of me now, so I tell him, "I collect arrowheads." Which is kind of a lie, 'cause I only have two arrowheads that I found in the field at the bottom of the Sleddin' Hill after Dad plowed it last spring. Two arrowheads don't hardly amount to a "collection," but I had to say *somethin'*, didn't I?

"Max cool," he says. "Real ones? Can I see 'em?"

"Maybe, someday."

"When?"

"Tell ya what," I say. "I'll show you how to skip stones, and maybe someday I'll show you my arrowheads, but you hafta show me how to fix cars. Deal?"

"Deal." He comes over to me and we shake hands.

"Not like that," he says. "I know a secret shake." And he shows me how to do the secret shake. First we grab like a regular handshake, but with the first two fingers stretched out along the other guy's wrist. Then we let go, slap palms, slap the backs of our hands together, and last we link our thumbs together.

"Cool," I say. "Where'd ya learn that?"

"I made it up."

"Who else knows it?"

"Nobody," he says. "Just me. And now you."

So we make our way over to the duck pond, without losin' any shoes, and we stop where there's this little strip of bank that has some flat rocks on it, and I pick one up and whip it across the pond. It barely touches the water once, twice, three times, then it curls off and hits about five or six times so fast you can't tell between 'em, and then it slows down and sinks.

"Jesus Christ on a pogo stick," Lynch says, his eyes all wide. "How'd you do that?"

At first I can't really say anything 'cause I'm thinkin' about the Savior on a pogo stick, but when I stop laughin' I say, "That one wasn't even all that good. One time I threw one that skipped eighteen times."

"You're lyin'."

"Am not. Ask my brother Randy. He was there."

"All those little skips at the end don't count. They should only count as one."

"The hell you say. If I can see 'em, I can count 'em."

"All right, I wanna try. Show me how."

"First," I say, "you got to have the right rock. It has to be shaped like this." And I show him a nice, round, flat pebble.

Lynch reaches down and finds one for himself.

"Hold it like this," I say, and I curl my finger around the edge. He does it, too. "Now get your arm down close to the water and flip it sidearm, like this." I toss mine, and it skips clear across to the other side of the pond.

Lynch, he tries to copy me, but his rock goes straight into the water like a bullet, and I bust out laughin'.

"Don't throw it *into* the water," I say. "Try to throw it *onto* the water, so it bounces. And make it spin. When you let go of it, flick it like this with your finger. So it spins, see?"

He tries again, and this time it skips twice, real high and tumbly, and then it kinda flops into the water and disappears, and it was about the awkwardest-lookin' piece of work any boy ever threw, but still ... it skipped.

I never seen a kid so happy to make a stone skip twice.

We skip stones for a while, takin' turns, and pretty soon Lynch is gettin' the hang of it. Ten more minutes, and he's gettin' halfway decent at it. Not as good as me, of course, but not bad for a rookie. We toss pebbles until we both get tired and sore, and I say I'm gonna chuck one more and quit, and I do that. Then the two of us take a breather and we watch the ripples spreadin' across the pond, and Lynch, he says he wonders if there wasn't no banks to stop 'em, would the ripples just go on and on, all around the world, and forever and ever 'til the end of time.

I never heard anybody talk like that before.

And I look at this kid, and I think to myself, *You know, he ain't that bad. Maybe we could be friends.*

Pain. *God! It hurts!*

It's so dark. Where am I?

Tim tries to open his eyes. One opens, but the other refuses to come unglued. Through the open one, the left, he perceives only darkness all around him … except right over there to his left, where a circle of light blinds him with its brilliance. It makes his head pound to look at it.

I need to get there …

He closes his eye.

Wet … cold … so cold.

So much pain … I need help.

Blackness takes him again.

"We're home!" said Lindsey as she entered the house, with Amanda right behind her.

"Thank God!" Kate said, and got up to give the girls a hug.

The girls beetled their brows at each other. "Wassupwiddat?" Lindsey asked.

"Nothing, girls, I'm just glad to see you. But you stink! What happened?"

"The swamp," said Lindsey. "The mud got all over us."

"Is Daddy home yet?" Amanda asked.

"No, not yet."

"Still? Can you open this for us then?" Lindsey asked, showing Kate the jar.

"Sure," Kate said. "Bring it in the kitchen."

"Daddy should have been home by now," Amanda said.

"He's probably having fun riding his bike," Kate said. "Here, give me the jar. Hey, this is one of my old canning jars!" She tried to open it with her hands. "Umph! It's sealed tight, all right. You can tell a man did it."

Kate took the jar into the kitchen and applied her Pampered Chef Lid Gripper to it. It opened easily, and she handed it back to the girls, who turned it upside-down over the kitchen table. Out fell two folded pieces of paper, a small key, a pair of red-tinted sunglasses, and some more jigsaw pieces.

Amanda went straight for the glasses and put them on; Lindsey was more interested in the key.

"How do I look?" Amanda asked, smiling.

"Like a hippie," Lindsey said. "Like Uncle Darryl. Take a look at this key, Hippie Girl."

Lindsey showed her the key. It was small and silver, not the kind of key that would fit in a door or a car, but more like the kind that goes in a padlock or a locker.

"This must open up the treasure chest," Amanda said. "Now all we have to do is find it. Do you think that means we're close?"

"No," said Lindsey. "I doubt it. He said this one would be really hard, remember? He's just teasing us."

"Yeah, I guess you're right. Daddy can be like that sometimes," Amanda said. "Let's look at the puzzle pieces. What did we do with the old ones?"

"They're right here on the table where we left 'em," Lindsey said. They put the new pieces on the table with the old ones. Of the nine pieces they'd found so far, four could be connected into two pairs. Still, they could make nothing of the design.

They got a ziplock sandwich bag out of the pantry, put all the pieces into it and sealed it. Then they moved on to the clue.

A helicopter passed over the house, low enough to rattle the windows. They all looked up, then at each other.

"Whoa," Amanda said. "That was gi-hugic."

Kate's heart thumped in her chest, and the room swam around her. A low-flying copter usually meant a serious accident somewhere nearby.

"Girls," she said, "I need to run out to the store for a couple of minutes. I want you two to stay right here until I come back. Understand?"

"Now?" Lindsey asked.

"Yes, now. But I won't be more than ten minutes, okay? I have to get some milk."

"Okay. We'll work on this clue until you get back. Or we might go swimming for a while. Is that okay?"

"You know better. Wait 'til I get back. I won't be long."

"All right," Lindsey said.

Kate walked into a pair of flip-flops and slipped out the back door.

As soon as Kate was gone, Lindsey jumped up from the table and strode to the refrigerator. She opened it, reached inside, and pulled out a gallon milk jug … three-quarters full. She held it up for Amanda to see, with a little mocking half-smile on her face.

"Oh," Amanda said. "Why did she really go out, then?"

"I don't know. But I know she lied to us."

"She was still in her peejays."

Lindsey's eyebrows shot up. "She was, wasn't she? And Daddy's t-shirt."

"I bet she's going to meet Daddy. It's got something to do with the treasure hunt."

"Yeah, that could be. They must be up to something. Or else Dad would be here," Lindsey said. "Let's get to work on this puzzle. When Kate gets home, we'll take a dip. Otherwise, I don't think I can hang around you all day, the way you stink."

Kate could still hear the helicopter, and see it occasionally over the trees to the southeast, but whatever it was doing, it couldn't involve Tim. It was too far away.

Since she was out anyway, she swung through the Wawa parking lot, keeping an eye out for Tim's bike. She did the same thing at Corner Video. Then, on a hunch, she cruised behind the old Ringgold's building. There was a door in the back of the abandoned market that looked like kids had broken into it, but she was sure that had nothing to do with her husband. She moved on. She checked the bank, the post office, both churches, and the school. In desperation, she even checked McDonald's.

Where else? she wondered, waiting for the traffic light to turn green.

Tim Raither, when I find you, you'd better be ready to do some fast talking.

As she turned onto Route 128, a Sheriff's Department blue-and-white came screaming toward her from the west, lights blazing and siren wailing. The siren's pitch dopplered down as the cruiser passed her. In her mirror, she watched it turn right onto Route 5 and disappear southward. *Must be something big going down,* she thought.

She couldn't put it off any longer. She had no choice now but to call Alan, as soon as she got home. But as she slowed to make the right turn onto White Horse Road, Cappie's Bar came into view beyond the intersection, and an idea that had been crouching in the back of her mind suddenly pounced. She frowned in momentary indecision, then flipped off her right turn signal and blew right past White Horse.

Just to rule it out.

She pulled into the parking lot of Cappie's and drove around the building, feeling like a turncoat. Especially when—as she should have known—Tim's bike was nowhere to be seen.

He'd be devastated if he knew she'd done that.

She got back onto 128 and headed for home.

———

Two pieces of paper had tumbled out of the jar. One was small, only three inches square, and had a three-question quiz on it. The girls set it aside and moved to the larger one, a sheet of notebook paper that had been torn in half crosswise. It was labeled "CLUE #3 (Part 1 of 2)," and had a list of phrases on it, each phrase followed by a series of numbers.

"This looks hard," Amanda said. "Let's get changed, so we can hop in the pool as soon as Daddy and Kate get back. We can work on it after we swim."

"Good plan," Lindsey said.

With that, they both marched into their bedrooms and changed into swimsuits. When they came out, they were still alone, so they went to the family room and turned on the TV.

They'd been watching Nickelodeon for about ten minutes when Kate startled them by bursting through the back door. They'd been sucked into the tube and hadn't heard the car pull up.

"I'm back," Kate said without inflection.

"Where's Daddy?" Amanda asked.

"Well, if I knew that, then I wouldn't be—" she stopped and started over. "I'm sorry. Your father is still out on his bike somewhere, I suppose. He should be back soon."

When the girls were safely in the water, Kate dialed the sheriff's department. The phone rang three times before an icy receptionist answered. Kate left a message for Captain Curtis, who was not currently at his desk, to call her back about a matter that was "kind of important." She assumed that would earn her a return call sometime tomorrow, or at best, today at the end of the shift.

She hung the phone up in its cradle and started toward the refrigerator. She needed a Diet Coke, *now*.

The phone rang. She picked it up before it had time to ring a second time.

It was Alan Curtis. Kate thanked him for the prompt reply, and he said, "No problem. What's up, Kate? I prob'ly don't need to tell ya that we're real busy here today."

"I don't want to bother you too much. I was hoping for a little personal advice. I sort of have a missing person here."

"One of the girls? How long?" he said with surprising urgency.

"No. Not one of the girls. It's Tim. Since six o'clock this morning."

"Oh, Timmy?" he said, seeming to relax. "Since this mornin'? That's only four hours. It's a mite early to get worried about it, ain't it?"

Finding herself irritated by the question, Kate said, "He left on his bike and he was supposed to be back in a half hour. And today is a really special day here for us; I'm sure he'd be here if he could. So I'm worried that something might have happened to him."

"You say he took off on his bike?"

"Yes."

"Well, at least he ain't behind the wheel. Have ya checked with your in-laws?"

"They're not home. Ed's in Wyoming, Dottie's somewhere else. Probably shopping."

"What about Greg?"

"Tim can't stand Greg." *Oops.* She'd forgotten Alan and Greg were close.

"How 'bout friends?" Alan asked, either failing to notice Kate's *faux pas*, or affecting not to notice it.

"I checked."

"All right, good. Now, listen to me, Kate," Alan said. "Timmy's a big boy, he can take care of himself. I'm sure he'll be strollin' in any minute now. Don't you be worryin' yourself. If he don't show up by, say, bedtime tonight, then it might be time to start worryin', you foller me? I mean, this is Timmy we're talkin' about, right? And I guess you musta heard about what's been goin' on here today, so—"

"No, I've not heard. What's been going on?"

"You ain't heard? It's been all over the news."

"I've not had the TV on today at all."

"A little girl's gone missin'. This mornin', not too far from your house. And this place has gone pure ape-shit, pardon my expression. But with that situation keepin' the whole department busy, we just can't afford to put any manpower on lookin' for your husband right now, Kate. I'm real sorry to have to tell you that."

"I understand you're busy, but can't you at least check out the roads around here, see if he's had an accident or something?"

"Now, Kate, if he had, we'd already know about it because your whole area is just crawlin' with units right now. But I'll tell ya what I will do. I got to come over your area in a few minutes, in fact I was fixin' to step out the door when you called. So what I'll do, I'll stop by your house and on the way there I'll keep an eye out, you hear?"

"Thanks, Alan, that'd be nice."

"No problem at all. I'll see you in about twenty minutes."

She hung up the phone with weird vibes. She understood that the department was fully mobilized to find this missing little girl, but Alan's air of nonchalance seemed to go beyond that. She would take it up with him when he arrived.

She heard the distant sound of a helicopter again and looked out the window. The chopper came over the houses to the southeast, made a loop, and disappeared behind the trees.

A missing child. How horrible that must be for the girl's parents.

She decided to turn the TV on to learn what she could about the situation, and went to the family room. With remote in hand and thumb on button, she stopped as Lindsey and Amanda came back into the house.

"Is there anything to eat?" Lindsey said. "We're hungry."

Kate dropped the remote on the sofa unclicked, reversed direction, and followed the girls back into the kitchen. "Sure. What do you guys want?"

"How 'bout grilled cheese?" Amanda said.

"No prob. That good for you too, Lin?"

"Wicked good. We're gonna get dried and dressed."

"All right. I'll have the sandwiches ready in about ten minutes."

As she buttered bread, she thought about the unspoken rule in the Raither house, the one that said, since Tim was too absent-minded to be held responsible, it was Kate's job to remember all the little things when they left the house. Little things such as wallets and keys. And cellphones.

Damn it, she chided herself. *I should have gotten up with him this morning. Then maybe all of this could have been avoided.*

The grilled cheeses were gone. Lindsey and Amanda were ready to get back to work on the clue.

She'd been expecting it, but the knock on the door still startled Kate. She went to answer it.

"Hi, Alan," she said. "Come on in." Alan was a short, blocky man in his early forties, with reddish-brown hair starting to go gray.

"Hello, Kate. I can't stay but for just a minute, now. Hello there, ladies," Alan said as he saw the girls with their wet hair. "You look like you been doin' some swimmin'."

The girls nodded.

"You remember me, Mr. Alan? I'm an old friend of your dad's and your Uncle Greg's."

"Hi," they said together. Amanda offered a sheepish wave.

"Girls," Kate said, "would you mind going back into one of your bedrooms to work on your puzzle? I have some things to talk to Mr. Alan about."

"Why can't we stay?" Lindsey asked. "Is it about our Dad?"

"Why?" Alan asked. "Did he rob another bank?"

Amanda giggled. Lindsey's mouth was set in a straight line.

"Girls," Kate said, "could you please do as I ask, just this once?"

"Come on, Manda," Lindsey said, and they slunk back the hallway, casting curious glances over their shoulders.

Turning to Alan, Kate said, "I guess you didn't find him." She noticed his eyes taking in her attire before they snapped up to meet hers, and she thought she detected disapproval in the set of his mouth. Knowing Alan, it was probably nothing more than his professional habit of cataloguing details; but nevertheless she felt self-conscious, and folded her arms in front of the thin fabric stretched across her chest.

I really should get dressed soon, she thought. *As soon as he's gone.*

"No, ma'am," the deputy replied. "I didn't see any sign of your husband. I asked around, too, and so far nobody's seen hide nor hair of him. Now, could ya tell me what Timmy was wearing today?"

"I don't know. I was asleep when he left."

"I see. And what kind of bike does he have?"

"I don't know. Blue. I have a picture of him. Would you like it?"

"No, that's all right. I know what he looks like. Ain't a man in the department, except maybe some of the newbies, that *don't* know what he looks like. Meanin' no disrespect."

"It's a picture of him on his bike."

"Now, that might be useful," he admitted. Kate handed him the picture and he tucked it into his shirt pocket. "All right. That's not much to go on, but then again, all of us know him. We'll do what we can, y'hear? Well hello, there!" he said, looking down at his feet. The cat had come in to inspect him, rub her jaw against his pants leg.

"Widget!" Kate said. "Leave him alone."

"It's all right," Alan said, stooping down. He stood, holding the cat in his left hand and scratching her behind the ear with his right. "I'm a cat person, myself."

"You are?"

"Yeah, I know what you're thinkin'. Cats are for women, right?"

"I didn't—"

"It's okay. I get it all the time. Truth is, since Lana and I never had kids, the cats are kinda like our family."

"How many do you have?"

"We had three up until last week. But ol' Jasper, he was gettin' up there, foller me, and his kidneys sorta gave out on him. We had to put 'im down. So we're down to two now."

"Oh, I'm sorry to hear that."

"Thanks. Lana, she's still gettin' over it. Misses ol' Jasper bad. I reckon we'll have to get us another one if she don't snap out of it soon. Now whaddya call this here color pattern?"

"Tortoiseshell."

"Yes, ma'am, I believe you're right. Tortoiseshell, that's what it is. Right friendly, ain't she?"

"She seems to like you."

"Most of 'em do. Widget, I guess you ought to get down now," he said. He put the cat back on the floor and watched, smiling, as she sauntered into the kitchen.

"What about this little girl?" Kate said. "Is there anything I need to worry about? I mean, should I keep the girls indoors?"

"Well, now, we don't know for sure that it was a kidnappin' at all. Could be the child is just lost in the woods. Sometimes kids hide on purpose, even. Maybe her Ma just whooped her or somethin', you foller? We just don't know yet. For now, I'd say it'd be a good idea to keep an eye on your girls, at least until we know somethin' for sure."

"I'll do that."

"Now like I was tellin' ya earlier, Kate, we're real super busy right now. And I can't lie to ya, everybody's lookin' for that little girl. We even got a chopper up there, you mighta noticed. Now if we find her today, or tonight, why then, that'll free up some of our men and maybe we can put a few of 'em on Timmy."

"If that's the best you can do, I understand. I appreciate your being honest with me."

"Well, lemme be honest with ya about somethin' else. Like I was sayin' earlier, it ain't really time to start lookin' for Timmy anyways. Tomorrow might be more like it, do ya foller me?"

"But don't you have to start searching for somebody that's been missing for so many hours?"

"Well now, there ain't really a hard 'n' fast rule about that. It's sort of a judgment call. A missin' kid is more urgent than a missin' adult, you foller?"

"Of course," said Kate.

"We can't just go hyin' off to find every adult that's gone missin' for a couple of hours. Suppose you and Timmy decided to take off for a weekend getaway and not tell nobody, and then somebody noticed you were gone. Would you want the cops to come lookin' for ya?"

"No."

"Course you wouldn't. And folks do that all the time. But then we have to keep in mind that if somebody really *is* lost or hurt or kidnapped or somethin', then every minute we waste, it gets harder and harder to find 'em, you foller me? So we hafta balance your privacy against your safety. And there's other things to consider, too, like if the missin' person is old or mentally handicapped, or has a history of runnin' away to Atlantic City for a week. All these things are important."

Kate was silent. She thought she knew what was coming.

Alan took a breath. "The reason I'm tellin' ya all this, Kate, is that I want ya to understand and I don't want ya to take it personal. Because in Timmy's case, we hafta keep his past in mind."

"Tim's not had a drink in over three years," Kate said, fuming.

Alan held his palms out toward her. "I'm sure he ain't, as far as we know. But these things have a way of croppin' back up, ya know what I'm sayin'? Now, I'm sorry to have to ask you this, but how've you two been gettin' along?"

"Wonderfully. Well, I mean, we had a little spat last night, but—"

6

The girls were so bubbly they could barely eat.

"Daddy, can we start now? Pleeeeeeeeeeeeease?" begged Amanda. "We can't wait another whole day!"

"What's the rush? You have all week. Could you pass the salt, please, Lindsey?"

"But, Dad, what difference does it make?" asked Lindsey. "If we can start tomorrow, why can't we start a few hours early?"

"Because."

"Because why?"

"Girls," Kate said, spearing a chunk of chicken with her fork, "I think we've already discussed this. It's tomorrow. Tonight we're going to relax and watch a movie together, as a family, and go to bed and get some decent rest."

"That's right," said Tim. "You're going to need it. And tomorrow, as soon as you get up and have breakfast, the treasure hunt begins. Now, could I please have the salt?"

"How long do you think it'll take us?" asked Lindsey.

"Nine days," he replied without missing a beat.

"Why?" asked Lindsey. "Is it that hard? What's the first clue? Can't you give us a hint?"

"It's very hard, and no, you can't have a hint. What do I have to do to get some salt?"

"Kate? Will you tell us?"

"I'm sorry, honey, I can't. Your father won't tell me anything."

"That's because you'd spill it," said Tim.

"No, I'd not," she replied with mock offended dignity.

"Yes, you would, wouldn't she, girls?"

"Yeah, she would," said Lindsey.

"You were smart not to tell her, Daddy," added Amanda.

"Manda!" Lindsey said. "Whose side are you on?"

"Sorry."

"What's the prize?" asked Lindsey. "Is it the same as last year?"

"You know, it's cholesterol I have a problem with—"

"Is it more than last year?"

"—not my blood pressure."

"Kate! Dad won't answer us."

"I can't help you," Kate said.

"I hope it's more Mall Bucks," Amanda said.

"Yeah," said Lindsey. "I need to get some more bras."

Tim smiled at Kate. Lindsey never passed up an opportunity to talk about the fact that she now wore a bra.

"Are the clues gonna be only in our yard, or are they other places, too?" asked Amanda.

"That I can answer. They're not all in our yard."

"How far away are they? Are we gonna have to go somewhere in a car?"

"No, you can get to all of them under your own power."

"Are there any clues as far away as, like, McDonald's?" asked Lindsey.

"I think that's enough," said Tim, reaching across in front of Lindsey to get the salt himself. "I'm not answering any more questions. All questions will be answered tomorrow when you get your first clue."

"What time?" asked Amanda.

"After breakfast."

Lindsey pounced on that. "You mean, *whenever* we eat breakfast? Like, can we get up at four o'clock and have breakfast, then will you give us the clue?"

Rolling his eyes, Tim said, "No. No four o'clock. Eight o'clock, okay? At eight o'clock, if you've already had breakfast, you can have the first clue. No earlier. Got it?"

They got it.

After dinner, the girls took off to ride their bikes over to Lexie's house. Kate told them to be back in an hour so they could go pick out a movie. When they were gone, Tim and Kate began to clean up dinner.

Kate chuckled. "Think they're excited?"

"They sure seem to be."

"Have I ever told you what a wonderful father you are?"

"Lots of times. But I don't mind hearing it again."

Kate placed both of her hands on Tim's chest and looked up into his eyes. "They adore you. And so do I."

Tim smiled and put his arms around her. "Goes both ways."

Kate smiled back at him and rested her head on his chest. *Enough with the buttering up*, she thought. *Tell him.*

She separated herself from Tim and turned away from him, making a show of doing dishes while she worked up her courage.

"I have to tell you something," she said.

Pause. "Okay."

"Tomorrow I may have to go out for a while."

"Kate," he said. "You promised to clear your calendar for these two days."

"I know, but—"

"How long of a while?"

"I don't know. Maybe a couple of hours or so. It depends."

"Depends on what?"

Kate spoke in a rush. "See, I've got this couple, they're really ready to buy. I've already shown them three houses that didn't quite fit what they wanted, and they say they want to give me one more chance. Charles showed a lot of faith in me to give me a chance with this account."

Tim exhaled loudly and walked a few steps toward the family room, stopped in the doorway with his hands on the walls on either side. He stood there, facing away from her.

"Tim?"

"I can't believe this," he said.

"I'm sorry, Tim. There was no way around it. And it's only for a couple of hours."

"It wasn't enough, I guess, that you missed the dance recital that Lindsey prepared for all year. Now you've found a reason to miss the treasure hunt, too."

"That's not fair. You know it killed me to miss the recital. If I hadn't gone to that settlement, it would have cost me … cost *us* … four thousand dollars. I *had* to go."

Tim turned around to face her. "Four thousand, huh? And how much is tomorrow worth to you?"

Kate paused. "Worth to *us*, Tim. And the house goes for a million five. A million five. Think about that."

Tim's mouth was compressed into a straight line. "So you're selling the Taj Mahal. Am I supposed to be impressed?"

"Don't you understand? That would be twenty-two thousand dollars for us. It takes me *six months* to make that much at G&L. I can't pass that up. If I miss this one, they'll get another agent. I'll lose the chance."

"Yeah, there's always a reason. Every time. You're really pushing me, Kate. I asked you to clear one weekend, and you can't even do that. *One weekend!"*

"But what was I supposed to do? All that money—"

"Money, money, money! Is that all you can think about? To hell with the money! What do we need it for? I'm sick of this. You're never here anymore, or if you are, you're in your little cave. This business, it's sucked you in like a Chinese finger puzzle. The deeper you get into it, the more it tightens its grip on you. I feel like I've lost my wife, and I want her back. I want you to give up this little fantasy of yours."

Kate puffed up. "Well, without 'this fantasy of mine' we'd not have this nice new fridge here. We'd not have the pool paid off, and you'd not be driving that fancy F250. We talked about all this already."

"I know, but I didn't realize how hard it was going to be. I thought we could handle it. I was wrong; my priorities were all screwed up. If that truck costs me you, it's not worth it. I miss you. The girls miss you."

Kate snorted. "Oh, please. *They* don't miss me. They'd be just as happy if I disappeared for good."

Tim lowered his eyebrows. "That's not true. And I resent you saying that. I think they're adjusting very well."

"They don't have any respect for me, Tim. They always look to you when I tell them to do something. As if it doesn't really count that I said something unless you rubber-stamp it."

"That's because you're never around when they're here. It's just the three of us most of the time, and they're dealing with it the only way they know how. You have to *earn* respect, Kate, and you have to *be* here to earn it."

"They act like they don't want me around. They make me feel like an outsider in my own home. So, yeah, I schedule a lot of appointments for times when they're here. Do you blame me?"

"They disrespect you, so in turn you disrespect them? You think that's gonna work? Somebody has to step up and stop the cycle. Somebody has to be an adult and say, 'enough.' They want a relationship with you, but they sense you shutting them out, and this is how they deal with it. If you won't quit for me, do it for them!"

Kate's jaw fell open. She could feel herself quivering with repressed rage. When she resumed talking, her voice fairly crackled. "How *dare* you? How dare you use the children to try to control me?"

Tim flinched. "Control you?"

"Yes, control me! Because that's exactly what this is all about, isn't it? You don't like it that I have my own life and make my own money. Maybe you want me right under your thumb where you can keep your eye on me. Is that what it is? I'll tell you one thing for sure; I've spent enough time in my life being controlled by men. You'll not see me turning into my mother."

"Whoa," Tim said, holding his palms out to her, "this is getting way out of hand. All I'm saying is—"

"I know what you're saying, Tim. You're saying you don't like it when you're not in control. So how can I help you, m'lord? Your humble servant awaits her orders."

Now Tim's face reddened with fury, and he spoke with quiet menace. "Do whatever you want, Kate. Forget about me. Live your life. Go make your money. Do what you have to do tomorrow. Go have lunch with your real estate buddies. Go to dinner, too, while you're at it. Have a few drinks if you want, I don't care. But I won't let you spoil our day tomorrow. The girls are too excited about it, and so am I. We don't need you."

Tim turned his back on Kate and walked out the back door.

Silence fell over the house. Kate filled the vacuum by calling her husband a few choice names, then collapsed on the love seat and let herself cry. She blew her nose and held her hands to her eyes, moaning wordlessly.

What had just happened? She'd never spoken to Tim like that before, nor had she ever heard that tone of menace in Tim's voice. Why was he being so stubborn?

But his point did strike home with her. She'd been feeling guilty for some time about the amount of time she spent away from the family. Why did she so often try to make it up to them, if she didn't feel, in her heart, that what she was doing was somehow wrong?

So if Tim was right, why am I digging in so fiercely?

She heard what she thought was thunder, worried that a storm was blowing up, and wondered where he'd gone. And where the kids were.

Oh. He'd brought up the kids. In that moment, it became clear to her what had triggered her rage. Poor Tim, there was no way he could have understood. He must have felt like he'd been hit by a truck.

Tim walked down Garland Drive toward White Horse Road, his eyes focused on the pavement a yard in front of his feet. For the first few minutes, with his emotions running so high, he was unable to string two logical ideas together. The only thing he could think about was how quickly and inexplicably the conversation had gone south.

The temperature had dropped a few degrees in advance of the thunderstorm building in the west, and Tim's head cooled off with it as he walked. With each step he took, he seemed to leave a bit of anger behind.

Mrs. Cagle, an elderly neighbor to whom he'd spoken a handful of times, was outside pulling weeds, and greeted him as he drew near. He gave her a perfunctory wave and kept walking. Unavailable for small talk.

With his thoughts settling down, he replayed the discussion with Kate in his mind. By the time he reached White Horse Road, five minutes after leaving the house, he'd figured out where he'd hit a few conversational hot buttons, unintentionally ramping up the emotional component at the expense of the rational.

Also, he had to admit that some of Kate's comments contained an underlying truth.

He turned around at the stop sign, began to retrace his steps. Thunder rumbled.

Still, he was missing something. Sure, he'd screwed up, but Kate's reactions to his gaffes had been way out of proportion. Why?

He'd have to talk to her to find out. And now he felt like he *could* talk to her, this time with a clearer head. He picked up his pace.

Caliginous clouds blotted out the western sky with roiling darkness. It wouldn't be long now. Passing Mrs. Cagle's home, he noticed that she had apparently gone inside, as had anyone with a lick of sense.

As he neared his house, a few scattered raindrops fell around him, making quarter-sized splats on the pavement. He jogged the last few yards back into his driveway, leaped up onto the back porch, and opened the door.

Seeing Kate sitting on the couch, cheeks blotchy from crying, he stopped where he was.

Kate glanced up at him, then her eyes flitted to the window, the floor, back to the window, and finally settled on her hands resting in her lap. She picked at the nail of her right ring finger.

Tim closed the door behind him, cleared his throat.

She met his gaze again briefly, so briefly, and turned her attention back to her hands. She sniffed.

"Um … we just had our first argument," he said. "Didn't we?"

"Yeah, I guess we did." She looked up at him. Her face was so familiar to him, and yet, at the moment, so foreign.

This time it was Tim who looked away.

"I've gotten control of myself now," he said. "No pun intended."

The ghost of a smile crept onto Kate's face. "Me, too."

"I'm really sorry for some of the things I said to you."

"I was just as bad, Tim. I'm sorry, too."

"I'm also sorry that … well, I think maybe you were at least partially right in what you said about me."

"I understand why you're frustrated with me, though. And I need to explain something to you. I'm not saying I was right, but there's a reason why I reacted the way I did."

"Okay. I'll listen. But can I hold you first?"

Kate nodded, stood up, and rushed to him. They met and enfolded each other.

Then, as the rain came with a sound like a thousand gnomes tap dancing on the roof, the back door opened to admit Lindsey and Amanda, dripping and laughing.

"OMG," said Amanda. "That was close!"

"Dad!" yelled Lindsey. "We're—"

Both girls froze, staring at the scene before them.

"—home," she finished in a small voice. "Is everything okay?"

"Yes, honey," answered Kate.

"What happened?" asked Amanda.

"We're having a discussion, Squirt," said Tim. "It's nothing to worry about."

"You weren't fighting, were you?" asked Lindsey.

"Do we seem like we were fighting?"

"No, actually," said Lindsey, "you seem like you were kissing."

"That's exactly what we were about to do, but you guys interrupted us. Now would you mind giving us about five minutes' privacy so we can finish what we were talking about?"

"Okay, if you're gonna kiss, I don't wanna see it," said Lindsey. "Are we still going to get a movie?"

"Yeah, if you want. But we might wait for this rain to let up a little first."

"Okay. Manda, let's go watch TV in my room." The girls left the room.

When she heard the bedroom door close, Kate said, "Think they bought it?"

"I dunno. Maybe."

"Talk about timing."

"I'll say."

They were both silent for a moment.

"I didn't expect you back so soon," Kate said.

"Me neither. My first impulse was to go out and find me a drink. I decided to take a walk instead. Clear my head."

Kate nodded.

"The storm was really coming up fast," he continued, "so I turned around at White Horse and came back. Besides, I was ready."

"I'm glad you're back. I need to unload this before I lose my nerve."

"Okay," Tim said. "Wanna sit down?"

"Yes, let's," she replied, and they both sat on the love seat, facing each other. Kate reached over and grabbed both of Tim's hands with both of hers.

A flash and a crash came from outside, nearly simultaneous.

Kate took a deep breath, expelled it. "You know my dad was a drinker."

Tim nodded.

"He was also a really bad control freak, when it came to Mom. Especially when he was drunk, which was almost every night. The only time he let her out of the house was if he was with her, because he said other men always looked at her because she was so sexy. He said if she went out without him, that one of them would probably rape her and he couldn't live with that. So he kept her with him at all times. She was like his arm ornament. And he'd always be looking around when we were out, trying to catch other men staring at her, and if he did, he'd glare at them until they looked away, and if they didn't look away he'd say something. A couple of times I remember he almost got into fights because of it, but Mom would drag him away and we'd have to get in the car real fast and Daddy would peel out of there, burning rubber. And in the car all the way home, Daddy would holler at Mom and blame her for it, and say she must have been looking back at the guy or something. Sometimes he'd smack her face or punch her in the arm."

The rain pounded on the roof without mercy. The gutters overflowed, unable to keep up with the sudden deluge.

"There was only one thing Mom was allowed to do by herself, and that was go to bingo on Tuesday nights. Daddy figured that was okay because the only men there were 'just a bunch of wrinkled old fucks.'

"My Dad was not a nice man," she continued. "He's better nowadays, because now *he's* one of those wrinkled old fucks, and Mom's gone; but back in those days he was … impossible. When I think about Mom dying first and him living on, I just … I can't …"

She paused to blow her nose and wipe her eyes. Tim handed her a fresh tissue.

Thunder rolled, rattling a vase that sat too close to the glass in the bay window. They could feel its bass rumble in their abdomens.

"Daddy was a happy drunk, at least on the surface. He'd get real friendly and laugh a lot and tease us kids and tousle our heads and call us his 'little farts' and give us candy. But there was a real bastard underneath, just waiting for something to provoke him. If anything happened that challenged his idea of what the world should be like, then he'd get really pissed.

"This one night, it was a Tuesday, so Mom planned to go to bingo. I must have been about ten. I try not to think about that day, but I remember it like it was yesterday. Mom had this lavender sweater that Daddy gave her for Christmas one year, and she loved that sweater. She wore it all the time. She looked good in it, too. It was probably the only thing he ever gave her that she liked, but I don't think he even remembered that it came from him. Anyway, on this night everybody was happy, especially Daddy, but then Mom started putting her lavender sweater on, and Daddy said, 'Where the hell are you going?' And I knew the happy Daddy was gone.

"Mom said she was going to bingo, and Daddy said, 'The hell you are,' and then he went on and on about it, how she was always going to bingo and leaving him and us kids there alone, and didn't she care about her family? And I remember him pointing at us and saying, 'The kids are tired of you disappearing all the time. Look at 'em! They're scared! They're scared you're gonna leave 'em again!"

She paused.

"I don't know why I did it," she continued. "I was certainly old enough to know better. Daddy had us all well trained by then.

"I guess it seemed so simple to me and Daddy didn't understand, and somebody needed to explain it to him, and then everything would be okay. So I tried to explain it to him."

"Tried to explain ... ?"

"That we didn't care if Mom went out; it was *him* we were afraid of."

Tim's eyebrows shot up.

"Yeah, big mistake. He didn't hit me, but he looked at me so mean, and he came flying across the room with his arm cocked over his shoulder like he was going to backhand me, like I'd seen him backhand Mom so many times, and I was *so sure* he was gonna hit me ..." She swallowed.

"Kate, I think I get it. You don't have to go on."

The rainfall outside had slacked off a bit. They could hear water gurgling through the downspout at the corner of the house, but the sound of it falling on the roof was now much more subdued. The diminishing sound of thunder now came from the east.

"I was so scared. I couldn't stop it. I peed right there on the floor. Daddy saw that and he got all red in the face and I thought he would explode. Then he screamed at Mom to clean up the mess she'd made me make, and Mom right away ... she ... sh-shhhhe, um ..." Kate paused to get control of her emotions. She wiped her eyes and cleared her throat a couple of times, then continued: "She took off her sweater, her *favorite sweater*, and threw it the floor and used it to soak up my pee. Then she sent Donna and Louis off to their rooms, and put me in the tub."

"Jesus."

"After that, I never again spoke up to Daddy when he was drinking. That was the first time and the last. And as far as I know, Mom never went to bingo again."

For a moment, Tim stared at her. Then he pulled her into his arms. "Kate, I'm not your father."

"I know that, and I'm sorry."

"I'm sorry, too. I'm not your father, but I was wrong using the girls to try to manipulate you that way. And I don't want you to quit your job. That was just emotion talking, frustration. I know how much the job means to you. It's not just the money, it makes you feel good about yourself, and that's important, too."

"Yes, but I don't want you to be afraid to say what you feel. That's my fault. I don't blame you for being frustrated with me, and please don't bottle it up inside. If you can't say what you mean to me, then I'm as bad as my father."

Tim nodded. "Okay. So we were both wrong. Let's try to get back to the real problem, and I'll try to avoid mentioning the girls at all when I present my argument." At this, Kate smiled. That was encouraging. Tim took a deep breath and began: "Look, you're very good at your business, and you have a lot of work. The problem is you don't know when to quit, and that's not all your fault. Every time a conflict comes up between your family and your work, there's thousands of dollars at stake. So taken individually, of course you're going to go with the money, every time. I can't blame you for that."

"But taken as a whole, I've basically sold my family for money."

"I wouldn't have put it that way, but ..."

"It's true. And I can't keep doing it, I see that now. But at the same time, I don't want to give up my business."

"You don't have to. Can't you just ... cut back a little bit?"

"Well ... I guess I could take fewer clients. We're caught up with our bills now, so we should be able to afford it."

"So that would mean fewer evenings? And weekends?"

"Theoretically. We can iron out the details later, but I know we can reach some sort of compromise. The point is, I'm willing to work on it. Are you?"

Tim let his smile be his reply.

They kissed. Their first fight was over.

"I think this rain's about done," Tim said. "Ready to go get a movie?"

They watched the latest Disney/Pixar masterpiece, and ate three bags of microwave popcorn. Tim's was butter-free, and he groused about it until all three girls asked him to please shut up.

After the movie, the girls trooped off to brush their teeth. They decided to sleep together in Lindsey's room.

"Goodnight, my princesses," Tim said to them. "Get some sleep. Tomorrow's the big day."

"We're too excited to sleep," Lindsey said.

Tim chuckled. "Try."

Tim and Kate went to bed immediately thereafter. As they lay down on their backs side-by-side, Kate said, "Tim."

"Yeah?"

"I'll cancel my appointment tomorrow if you want me to."

"You don't have to. It's not in the morning, is it?"

"No, it's at one-thirty."

"That shouldn't be a problem. As long as I have you in the morning. But it means a lot to me that you offered."

"What do you need me for in the morning?" she asked.

71

"I have to go out early and hide the treasure. It might take me a half hour or so. I'm going to leave the first clue with you, so if the girls wake up before I get back, you can give it to them."

"Why can't they just wait until you get back?"

"That wouldn't be fair. We made a big deal about them not starting early, so it wouldn't be right for me to make them start late. I'm as bound by the schedule as they are. Besides, it shouldn't be an issue. I should be home way before eight."

"Okay. What time are you getting up?"

"Six o'clock," he said.

"Whoa! On a Saturday? It's almost midnight. You better get to sleep."

"Not just yet," he replied. Rolling toward her onto his elbow, he planted a soft kiss on her lips. Her arms came up and encircled him as her mouth opened like a flower.

They made slow, gentle love to the sound of distant thunder. Another storm was on the way.

As they finished, rain began to fall again, and the soft rhythmic sound of it lulled them to sleep in each other's arms.

7

Kate found herself drifting, lost in the remembrance of that blissful, torpid post-coital cocoon. And what a wonderful, tender lovemaking it had—

"Now, you say you two had an argument *last night?*" Alan asked, startling her out of her reverie.

"Yes. Sorry. Yes, but we made up. We're okay now."

Alan did the facial equivalent of folding up his notebook and putting his pen back in his shirt pocket. "Kate, I'm sorry, I don't mean to insult ya, bein' Timmy's wife an' all, but I've known Timmy all his life, and this is what he does. Every once in a while, he goes off on a bender. Usually after somethin' bad happenin' to him. A fight with his wife, for instance. He don't hurt nobody other than himself, and in a day or so, he comes right on back."

"But he'd not! You don't understand, he was so excited about today, he'd not've missed it for anything! He could be lying somewhere dying or dead and you're going to stand there and tell me that he's off on a *fucking bender?*"

"Now, just calm down. I told ya what the situation is here, and I told ya not to take it personal, an' that's exactly what you're doin'. It's procedure, Kate. It's not my call. Now I got to get out there and find that little girl. I'll put the word out for the fellas to keep an eye out for Timmy, you hear? And if he don't show up by tomorrow mornin', you gimme another call and we'll take it to the next level, you foller me?"

Kate nodded, numb with shock.

"Have ya told anybody else to keep an eye out for him? Family and all?"

"Only his friend Brian. As I said, his parents aren't home. And if it's all the same to you, I'd like to keep them out of it."

Alan smiled. "Can't say as I blame ya there. We both know how Miss Dottie can get. We'll keep it between ourselves for now."

"Thanks."

"I got to be goin'. You take care now."

"You too, Alan." As Alan stepped out, she closed the door behind him and whispered, "Bastard."

She sank into the armchair, rested her forehead in her hand, her elbow on her knee, and fought back tears. She heard Lindsey's bedroom door open, heard the girls come pattering down the hallway and stop in front of her. She turned to face them, and whatever expression she wore must have tipped them off, because they both blanched.

"What's wrong?" asked Lindsey.

"Is it about Daddy?" Amanda asked.

They both looked at Kate, expectant. "Don't worry, girls," she said, "I'm sure Daddy's all right; we just don't know where he is right now. All I know is he went out this morning to hide the treasure and he didn't come back. But we're going to find him. And when we do, we're going to give him a talking-to for scaring us like this, aren't we?"

Amanda nodded.

Lindsey stared at Kate like she knew Kate was holding something back. Kate flashed a smile at her to show courage, and Lindsey gave her the same weak smile back. "Are the cops going to look for Dad?"

"Well, it's complicated. They say it's too soon; they'll not start searching for him until tomorrow."

"Tomorrow!" said Lindsey. "Are they crazy? We can't wait that long. What if he's hurt or something?"

"They've a lot to do today," Kate said. "They said they can't spare anybody. But in the meantime, it's up to the three of us to do something. And I, for one, don't plan to sit around here like a bump on a pickle. I'm going out and look. I'll keep driving until I find him. Do you want to ride along, or wait here?"

"We're coming," said Lindsey.

Amanda nodded her head.

They left Tim a note to call Kate's cell if he came home, then piled into the car, the treasure hunt forgotten.

The rear parking lot at Maple Hills Elementary was now a command center for the search. Captain Alan Curtis got out of his car and threaded his way past the police cruisers, rescue vehicles, and news vans with their telescoping booms. He stepped under the yellow crime scene tape. There were a lot of deputies and other people milling about, but exactly what they were doing was a mystery to him. Certainly nothing constructive. He canvassed the area until he found George Booker, a deputy who'd been in the force even longer than he had, and waved him over. Booker came to meet him, all legs and elbows, twirling the ubiquitous toothpick with his tongue.

"Book, whadda we know?"

"The girl lives with her mom and dad right over there. Dad was at work; Mom let her come over here to play. Says she does it all the time, and the girl's very responsible."

Alan snorted.

"Yeah, that's what I thought too," Booker continued. "Anyway, Mom says she went into the living room to watch TV for five minutes, no more, and when she came back to the kitchen to look out back, the girl was gone. That's all she knows. Said nothing unusual happened lately, no family trauma or anything, and the girl is not the type to play a trick like this. She was wearing blue shorts, a yellow t-shirt, and brand new white Nikes with a pink swoosh."

"Any cars comin' in or out?"

"Not according to Mom."

"Neighbors?"

"Nobody saw anything."

"What was Mom's state of mind?"

"She was a goddamned mess, but she was lucid, if that's what you mean."

"Any exes in the picture?"

"Nope. Mom and Dad been married ten years."

"Miracle."

"Yep."

Alan took a deep breath, exhaled it with cheeks puffed. "All right, I gotta go take charge of this clusterfuck over here. Have any of these prettyboy sumbitches looked in the woods yet, or are they all scared to get their shoes muddy?"

"Correlli's in charge, Cap, and he had us walk around the perimeter of the woods, calling the girl's name. There's not much the crime scene guys can do at this point. They're dusting all this playground equipment for prints, but it's probably a waste of time. We're hoping the chopper will bring us some good news, and meanwhile waiting for the Nerps and the bloodhound to arrive."

"The perimeter." Alan shook his head with disgust. He thought about mentioning that the chopper couldn't see anything in the woods, and that they were wasting precious time while they waited for the Natural Resources Police, but he knew that Booker was well aware of these facts. Booker was a good cop, but he wasn't in control here.

"I'm sorry, Cap. Correlli said—"

"I don't care what Correlli said. Correlli is about to be relieved. In the meantime, I got somethin' else for you to do."

"What's that, sir?"

"Get in your unit and go find Timmy Raither. He's gone off again. Check over at Cappie's, the Fireside Inn, and Basilone's, ya foller me? And over to that other place, down there on Orenzo Mill, Robin Hood's or somethin'."

"Friar Tuck's."

"Yeah, that's it. Hit that one, too. He's on his bike; it's blue. Wait, here, I got a picture of it." Booker took the photo, glanced at it, and stuck it in his breast pocket.

"You know Timmy," Alan continued. "He ain't gone far. When ya find 'im, wrassle 'im into your car and take 'im on home. His wife's worried, she thinks he's dead somewhere. But make it quick, Book, 'cause I need somebody here with balls besides me, foller me?"

"Will do, Cap."

"Get outta here. I'll handle this mess for now."

Booker turned, flicked his toothpick onto the ground, and got into his cruiser. As he took to the road, Alan walked over to the group of deputies busily doing nothing. "Correlli!" he said.

"Yes, sir."

"Come with me. We're gonna walk this friggin' game trail here for a few minutes. The rest of ya stand here and play with each other's dicks like ya been doin'."

"Ouch!" I holler. "That one got me. Damn, shit, son of a bitch!" I clap my hand over the back of my neck, where a pissed-off wasp just stung me.

Can't say I blame him. We were throwin' rocks at his nest. I guess I'd be pissed off too.

I was bored this mornin', and my brothers were gettin' on my nerves, so I walked down the tracks to Lynch's house, steppin' on the ties where there still was some and walkin' on the rails where there wasn't. I pounded on Lynch's door until he came out, and then me and him decided to go across White Horse Road and keep on goin' down the tracks, and we crossed the old trestle where we met a couple years ago, and then we crossed Orenzo Mill Road too, and got to the old fallin'-down train station, which was as far as we ever been before. Then we thought, hell, it's as good a day as any to set a new record, and we kept right on goin'. We kept goin' 'til we saw this big old building off to the left of the tracks, and that's where we stopped. Bein' normal ten-year old boys, we just had to see what was in it.

What a cool place we found. Stone building, almost as long as our school, with most of the doors and windows knocked out, and vines growin' all over it. Big brick smokestack stickin' up from one end. Inside, it's full of wasp nests and snakes and bats up in the rafters and all kinds of old stuff lyin' around that ain't been touched for years. The floor's all wood, and there's this one place where it's real soft and it sags when you walk on it. There's a basement, too, and we wanted to see what was down there, but we both took one look at how dark it was down them stairs, and we decided to throw rocks at wasp nests instead.

We run until we're out of that cloud of ornery wasps, and when it's safe we stop to catch our breath. Lynch is laughin' so hard, his face is all red. "You shoulda seen your eyes when he stung you!" he says. "You looked like a girl gettin' ready to scream."

"Shut up," I say. "I don't guess you'd make a funny face if one of them fuckers stung you, huh?"

"Not me. I don't feel pain."

"Yeah, okay. Ten years old and you're a big man now. Take a look at this thing, will ya?" I turn around and show Lynch the back of my neck.

"Damn, Timmy!" He says. "It's all swollen up already. Wait, hold still. Let me pull the stinger out of it for you."

I try to keep from squirmin' while Lynch pokes at my bee-sting with his dirty fingernails. I yell "Ow!" a few times, and Lynch just laughs at me and keeps telling me to hold still and calling me a wuss.

"There," he says, and flicks the ass-end of that wasp onto the floor.

"Whew!" I say, rubbing the back of my neck. "Burns like fire!"

Lynch is laughing again.

"Will you shut up?" I say, 'cause now I'm gettin' annoyed.

"I can't help it," Lynch says. "You were so funny!"

"And you're supposed to be my best friend," I say. "You think I'd be laughin' if it happened to you?"

"Damn right, you would. And I *am* your best friend." And he holds up his hand for the secret handshake that we been doin' almost every day for two years now. "Sorry, buddy. I won't laugh no more, I swear."

I give him the handshake, and right away I see he's about to bust from holdin' in some more laughin'. I stare at him, and finally he does bust, and the giggles come flyin' out of him like air out of a popped balloon. Now I can't help it, and I start laughin', too.

I guess it *was* kinda funny.

"Let's head on home," I say. "We been out here all day. Mom's prob'ly wonderin' where the hell I am."

"Yeah. Okay. I'm hungry, anyway."

We leave the building by the same door we came in through, and walk through the bushes and stuff until we get back to the old railroad tracks. We turn right and head back toward home.

"You know he's gonna die now, right?" Lynch asks me.

"Who's gonna die?"

"The wasp. Wasps have barbs on their stingers, so when they sting you, they can't pull it out. It breaks off and they die."

"So?"

"Just thought you'd wanna know. He got you, but you got him back. At least you ain't gonna die. Hornets and yellow jackets don't have barbs, so they can sting you over and over. And they don't die. But wasps do."

"How do you know so much stuff like that?"

Lynch shrugs. "Read it somewhere, I guess."

I act tough, but damn, that bee sting hurts, and I can't wait to get home and put some ice on it. Home is like, what, about a half-hour's walk? No way I'm gonna cry in front of Lynch. I'll just have to hold it that long.

"Next time, let's see if we can get downstairs," I say as we're walkin'.

"I dunno," Lynch says. "It was really dark down there."

"Now who's the wuss?" I say, 'cause, you know, I been called one already, and now I gotta prove I'm not one.

"Not me," Lynch says.

"Then swear you'll go down there with me next time," I say.

"Okay. I swear."

"On what?"

"On your ass."

"No way, Jose. That ain't good enough. Swear on your mother's life." Which ain't exactly fair of me, but I ain't worried about fair right now, I'm just worried about gettin' back on top.

"All right, all right. I swear on my mother's life I'll go downstairs with you next time."

"All right then. Shake." And we do the secret shake thing again.

I'd say me and Lynch are like brothers, but me and my brothers don't get along too much, so I guess we're not anything at all like brothers; but I *do* think we were born to be best friends. We been in the same class at school for the last two years, and we spend most of our free time together too, 'cause Lynch don't really like to go home, so he spends a lot of time at my house. And when we ain't at my house, we're off on a hike or a bike ride or some adventure somewheres.

Me and Lynch, we're a lot alike, except Lynch is a whole lot smarter than me, and I guess you could say I'm better at sports. But that don't seem to get in our way. We usually know what each other is thinkin', and we don't hardly ever disagree about anything. He knows all my secrets and I know all his. Well, most of his.

There was that one time when we butted heads, and that was when that new girl came to class, Francine something-or-other, and she found out that Lynch didn't have no dad and she asked him what happened to him. And Lynch, he told her, without even stoppin' to think about it, that his dad choked to death on a hot dog. Straight up.

Well, I knew that wasn't true, 'cause everybody knew, I mean it was even in the papers and everything, that a car fell on his dad and crushed him, and I shoulda kept my mouth shut, but like a dummy I piped up and said somethin' about it.

That was the one time I ever seen Lynch get really mad. "Timmy, what do *you* know about it?" he said to me. "Were you there?"

"No, but everybody knows—"

"Nobody knows," Lynch said. "You don't know 'cause you weren't there, and neither was anybody else. I was there. I know what happened to my dad, 'cause I saw it with my own eyes. My dad choked on a hot dog. It was an accident."

And then he turnt and walked away from me and he might as well have smacked me in the face, 'cause that's what it felt like. And he went straight home after school, and he didn't talk to me for a couple days. It was the only time we was ever apart for that long.

After that, I never brought up his dad no more and I ain't about to, ever again. If he wants to believe his dad choked on a hot dog, then that's fine with me. I don't know why he felt like he had to tell me it was an accident, though, 'cause nobody chokes on a hot dog on purpose. Somethin' don't square up about that whole story, and that's the one secret of Lynch's that I ain't in on.

We walk for a while without talkin', and after we cross Orenzo Mill, Lynch says, "Hey, Timmy."

"Yeah?"

"We *are* best friends, right?"

"Sure."

"I mean, 'cause I know you got your brothers and all, but I don't have nobody, and—"

"Are you kiddin' me, Lynch?" I say. "You're more of a brother to me than my brothers are. What the hell's the matter with you? We're best friends now and we'll be best friends in twenty years, when we're thirty-year-old geezers. We're best friends for life, okay? Don't ever bring that up again."

Lynch don't answer.

We cross White Horse onto Myrtle Drive, and when we can see the chimneys of Lynch's old farmhouse, the last house on the right, he asks me if I wanna come in for dinner.

"Naw," I say, not just 'cause his mom gives me the creeps (I think even he knows that), but mostly 'cause of my bee sting. "I gotta get on home."

We shake one more time, and Lynch goes inside, and I keep on goin' toward my house. Already, I'm plannin' for tomorrow. I'm gonna get up early, like around ten o'clock, and come get Lynch, and we're gonna go back to that old building. This time I'm gonna take my BB gun and we're gonna shoot some bats. I love summer.

Jesus, what is that smell? Oh, man, I think I'm gonna be sick. There must be a dead animal down over the side of the tracks there. Smells like rotten hamburger in a hot garbage can.

This bee sting really hurts. I mean, the pain, holy shit. It's moving. Spreading. It started at my neck, but now it's all over. My head, my arm, my back, my legs, oh man, everything hurts. Oh, Jesus, what's goin' on? Hey, wait a sec. Am I ...? Oh, no, no, don't wake up!

The tattered rags of his dream flutter in his mind and dissipate like so much smoke. Except for the smell. And the pain.

It was a dream, he thinks. *A crazy dream.*

No. Not a dream. A memory. All that stuff really happened. Years ago. When we were kids.

He hasn't thought about Lynch in years. Why now?

He tries to turn his head, but it hurts too much. He stops. He tries to move his right arm. Same thing. Every time he makes even the smallest motion, it causes him such intense pain that he has to freeze in place. But the tension of remaining immobile also brings pain. He tries to relax.

That hurts, too.

Where the hell am I?

He rotates his eyeball. That doesn't hurt. He looks to his left, squinting into a perfect circle of light.

No. That's not left. That's up.

The circle of light is on the ceiling, not beside him.

All around him, to the left, right, before, and behind him, there is darkness. His head whirls in confusion as he reorients himself.

He looks away from the light, and concentrates on the darkness beside him until his eye grows accustomed to it. Details emerge. He finds that he is in a tiny circular room walled in stone. So tiny that he could not stretch out both his arms, even if he could move. Perhaps five feet in diameter.

He sees a flicker of movement on the wall. Perched in the crack between two rocks is a small wet creature, a newt or salamander, staring back at him.

His legs feel so cold. He rolls his eye down to see why, and finds that he can't see them. He can only see a reflection of the ceiling light. The lower half of his body is separated from the upper by a plane of some reflective substance.

He twitches a finger. The reflection wavers, ripples as if ...

It's water. I'm standing in water up to my waist.

No. I'm sitting. I'm leaning against the wall, sitting on the floor. In a pool of water.

Letting his eye drift back toward the bright light without looking at it, he finds that the room is much higher than it is wide. *Much* higher. He is not in a room at all. He is in a tube. A stone tube with water at the bottom and a light at the top.

That's not a light on the ceiling. There is no ceiling. That's daylight.

Jesus Christ on a pogo stick. I'm at the bottom of a well.

The sickening smell of rotten meat is so thick it is like liquid going into his lungs.

He shivers.

Something sharp and hard is digging into both of his shins. He tries to shift his legs to alleviate the discomfort, but this results in searing jolts of agony through so many places in his lower body that he is unable to differentiate them. His mouth opens to scream, but only a dry croak comes out. He's never dreamed that this level of pain was possible.

Oh my God it hurts.

He passes out.

Some seconds or minutes or hours later, he comes to. He will not try to move his legs again. He has learned his lesson. *I've broken my leg,* he thinks. *Both of them, probably. Maybe my hip, too. And something's wrong with my right eye.*

He tries to move his right arm, and is greeted with another blast of pain. His arm is trapped between the wall and his body, twisted behind him at an unnatural angle. He is unable to lever his body away from the stones enough to free it. Sharp stabbing pains in his chest let him know that he also has some broken ribs.

His left arm is lying in his lap, and he is gratified to learn that it is relatively uninjured. He lifts it out of the water. The shoulder is sore, as if it has been badly bruised, and a long ugly gash runs from his elbow to his wrist, but he can move it.

He reaches up to touch his right eye. It is encrusted with something gluey that holds his lid closed.

Blood.

His fingers move up his face onto his forehead, then past the hairline where he finds an area about the size of the palm of his hand that is nothing but sticky, half-clotted clumps of hair and tissue. And bone. His skull is exposed. A flap of his scalp has come loose and is hanging down over his ear. The entire right side of his face is covered with semi-congealed blood.

"Fuck," he says aloud, startling himself when the sound of his voice reverberates in the tubular chamber.

How the hell did I get here?

The last thing he can remember clearly is picking up the girls from Paula's house. And then ... yes ... on the way home, asking them about how their week with their mother had been. Amanda's reply: that they'd spent the day before at Hershey Park, and Lindsey had lost a flip-flop on the Great Bear. And he'd asked, Why was Lindsey wearing flip-flops on a suspended coaster in the first place?

After that ... a vague recollection of dinner, of not being able to get any salt. Then ... nothing. It is as if he'd fallen asleep at the dinner table—how long ago? Hours? Days? —and awakened here in this well. This hell.

He knows there must be some interconnecting events he's not remembering, so he puts all his limited powers of concentration into trying to recall anything that may have happened after dinner.

Walking. He remembers walking, trying to get over his ... (anger/confusion), while lightning ripped the sky all around him. A storm coming ...

Another image, almost subliminal in its brevity, of Kate's face, twisted by emotion, her eyes brimming with tears. Had they argued? What about? Was this after dinner, or before? Did they part in anger?

Fragments. Puzzle pieces. Vignettes from the past. He's not even sure about the proper sequence of the few events he remembers.

In time with his heartbeat, his entire body pulses with pain, concentrated mostly in his head, right shoulder, and everything below his hips.

His lips and throat are parched, the inside of his mouth sticky with half-dried saliva. He needs water. That's one problem he can do something about.

He dips his good hand into the water to bring some up to his lips, but then notices something floating in the water.

What is that?

He is not alone in the well. Two empty eye sockets have him fixed in their gaze, from their position in a half-submerged mass of bones, hair, and glutinous tissue that was once a small animal, probably a raccoon or an opossum.

That explains the smell.

Tim feels his gorge rise. His stomach spasms and all his sphincters relax simultaneously. Tim cries out with the pain caused by his body's heaving, and fresh tears spring from his eyes. In spite of the cold, he breaks out in a sweat as he vomits.

In addition to the rotting carcass, the water is now fouled with his own bodily waste.

So much for drinking the water.

The direness of his predicament comes crashing in on him. He has only one limb that works, is bleeding from several wounds that have been immersed in foul water, is possibly bleeding internally as well. He almost certainly is in shock and probably has a concussion. He has no food, no water, no idea where he is, and no way of climbing out. Unless someone finds him first, he will die here slowly, of blood loss or blood poisoning or dehydration, alone and in pain.

He hasn't heard a single human voice since he awoke, either. *Why not? Why hasn't anyone shown up to help me?* The answer: *Because no one else knows where I am either.*

I'm gonna die here.

He begins to imagine all the things he'll miss. Graduations, proms and weddings, dance recitals and horse shows, grandchildren—all these will happen after he has died. His wife and daughters might never know what happened to him.

"*Hello?*" he yells hoarsely. "*Is anybody there? Anybody!*" In desperation he yells again, "*Helllllllllllllllp!*" but his voice breaks and only the driest whisper is left. He can make no more sound.

Defeated, his body shakes with silent sobs as despair takes him. Then, mercifully, the blackness comes again.

Alan Curtis was beyond angry. He was brimming with a nuclear rage.

Not fifteen steps into the forest, he'd found six-year-old Madison Kingsmore's footprints. Mingled with them, a set of larger footprints, those of a man. They were on a game trail. He'd followed it through the forest and out the other side. There he'd found the farm road that the state boys in the chopper had reported seeing. A car had been parked there several times over the last few days, leaving clearly visible tire tracks. The last set of tracks was not rain-softened. It had come after last night's storms. Today.

If someone had gone through the forest before he'd gotten there, they could have saved precious time. While Madison Kingsmore got farther beyond their reach with each passing minute, they hung around the playground. They had no idea who the kidnapper was, what he looked like, what he was driving, or what direction he'd taken. And instead of trying to learn these things, they'd been standing around here waiting for the Nerps and the bloodhound. The crime scene techs were busy, taking pictures and measurements of the footprints and tire tracks now, and trying to lift fingerprints from the shoebox Alan had found in the woods, but all that should have been done a long time ago. It wasn't much, but it was all they had.

Alan had just finished blistering the personnel at the command center when George Booker's cruiser pulled back into the lot. Alan turned from the men and went to meet Booker at the car, carrying the kitten he'd found in the woods.

"Didja hear about this fubar?" Alan asked.

"I heard it on the radio," Booker said, donning his Stetson as he got out of his car. Alan saw that Booker had noticed the kitten, but hadn't asked.

"I found it back there. Looks a lot like ol' Jasper, don't she? Only good thing that's happened all day, if ya ask me. This little sweetie might perk Lana right up."

Booker nodded, chewing his toothpick thoughtfully. Alan's soft spot for animals was well known in the force. "I'm sorry, Cap. I knew we were handling it wrong. I should have spoken up."

With a flip of his hand, Alan waved off the comment. "You were under orders. Didja find Timmy?"

"Nope."

"Damn," Alan said. "I thought for sure …"

"I could keep looking, you know, spread out a little, but I thought you'd rather have me here."

"Way it turns out, I don't really think any of us are needed here anymore. I think that little girl is long gone." He expelled a lungful of air and stared at the sky. Thunder rumbled from the northwest, the second such peal he'd heard in the last ten minutes. Another storm rolling in.

"Uh, Cap …" Sweat trickled down from Booker's hatband into his buzz-cut gray hair. He took off his Stetson, wiped his scalp with a handkerchief from his pocket, and replaced the hat.

"What is it, Book?"

"Well … I know this Timmy Raither thing is sort of off the books, right?"

"So far. I'm just doin' a favor for the family."

"I know that, and that's why I hesitate to bring this up."

"Bring *what* up?"

"Well … I was just thinkin' … somebody grabbed this little girl this morning, right?"

"What's your point, Book? I ain't got all day."

"And Timmy disappeared on the same day."

"We'll get to him. The little girl's more important right now."

"That's not what I'm gettin' at, Cap."

"Well then, for Christ's sake, what *are* ya gettin' at?"

"Hell, I'm sorry, Cap, but if I don't say it, somebody else will." He paused for a beat. "Are we sure it's just a coincidence?"

Alan stared at him as comprehension dawned. "No. Oh, no. I don't believe that for a second, Book. I've known Timmy all his natural life. He's a fuckup, but he ain't no child molester."

"Alan, I don't want to believe it either, but coincidences bug the shit out of me. And you know as well as I do that these kinds of guys can live under the radar for years. How can we know for sure?"

"No, Book. Get it out of your mind right now. It'd be a waste of our time to even think about it, when we could be thinkin' about the *real* kidnapper. I'm tellin' ya."

"Yes, sir."

Alan paused, and made an attempt to corral his swirling thoughts. Could it be? Could he have missed something so obvious? Was he letting friendship blind him to the truth?

No. There were ... "Tire tracks."

"What's that, Cap?" Booker said.

"The kidnapper was in a car. Timmy was on a bike. Both his cars were in the driveway."

Booker nodded. "Okay, that makes me feel better. But even so, it coulda been a rental. If this gets out, you know people are gonna start asking questions. They're gonna want to talk to his wife and they're gonna want to ask his daughters ... he has two, right?"

"Yep."

"They're gonna want to know if there've been any ... incidents." He sucked the toothpick into his mouth, snapped it in two, and spit it out.

"Yeah," Alan said. "Yeah, you're right about that, Book. It could get ugly for 'em." He sighed. "All right, ya got a point. We gotta look into this. I can't believe Timmy would be involved, but it'd be wrong of us not to at least check it out. I'll handle this myself, foller me? In the meantime, you forget about Timmy. I want ya to get on over to where that farm road comes out on Redbird Road, and see if ya can tell which way the sumbitch went, before this storm hits an' starts wipin' stuff out."

"I think we should turn around," Lindsey said. "He wouldn't have come this far."

They had passed Sycamore's unofficial northern limit into an area generally accepted as part of Kalmia. Ahead of them, the sky was the color of slate, shot intermittently with white ribbons of lightning.

"I suppose you're right," Kate said. She turned the car around and headed back toward Sycamore. "Let's go back down Route 5 the other direction for a little ways. We'll turn around at the John Deere dealer, then we'll come back and check down Orenzo Mill as far as the railroad station. Then after that, we'll come back through Virginia Street and Summit Circle to get back to White Horse. Sound like a good plan?"

Both girls murmured their assent as they gazed out the windows with worried frowns. They had elected to sit together in the back seat, both spurning the opportunity to ride shotgun with Kate.

Kate's cellphone rang. "Tim!" she blurted. Frantic, she fished the phone out of her purse, looked at the display. "Oh, shit. It's Charles." In a sudden flash of realization, it came to her that she'd missed her one-thirty appointment. "Hello, Charles."

"Kate. Is everything okay?"

"No, not really. Charles, I've got a little problem."

"No, Kate, you've got a big problem. I just got a phone call from Mr. Maloti. He says you didn't show for their appointment."

"Yes, I know, and I'm trying to tell you—"

"I got them to go for another appointment at three. You can make it if you leave in the next ten minutes. Get out there now, Kate. I don't have to tell you how important—"

"Charles!"

"Yes?"

"I quit." She hung up the phone. She glanced in the rearview, and saw Lindsey and Amanda looking at each other, too stunned to speak.

The phone rang again.

She answered it, said, "Yes, Charles, I meant it, please don't call me back. I'm very busy."

She hung up and dropped the phone into the console cubby between the front seats.

They crossed Route 128, passed the McDonald's and the Wawa, and continued south, watching for signs of Tim's blue bike.

Safe in his hotel room, Jerry removed his shoes and flopped down on the bed. He took the clothes he'd been wearing in the woods, now freshly laundered, out of the duffle bag. He needed a shower badly, but remembered that he had told his employers he'd call in today. He got his cellphone and placed the call.

"Yes?"

"It's Jerry."

"I know who the fuck it is, asshole. Do you have good news for me?"

"There's no need for profanity. It offends me. But I do have one for you. Just the kind you asked for."

"One? The commission was for two or three."

"One is better than none, is it not? I could've had another one yesterday, but she had brown hair. I can't be blamed for your narrow-mindedness. She was perfectly lovely."

"The script calls for blondes. I didn't write it. I'm just doing my job, just like you."

"She would have been so easy to take. It was a disgrace to leave her behind."

"Oh, I *bet* you wanted to take her. Didn't you? Hmmm? Was she hot?"

Jerry felt warm from the memory. "Yes. She was quite juicy."

"How about the one you did get? You didn't touch her, did you? You know the script calls for untouched."

"No. I didn't. You made that clear."

"Because we've had trouble with you in the past on that account. You didn't even sneak a peek?"

Jerry was uncomfortable. "Whether I sneaked a peek is irrelevant. You asked me not to damage her physically and I did not." He licked his lips. "Do you want this one or not? Because if you don't, I *am* going to touch her. More than touch her."

"No, I don't," was the reply. "I told you, the commission was for two or three. One does me no good. Call me back when you have what I need."

"It's not safe for me to remain in this area, you imbecile. Not only are the authorities on high alert because of the child I took, but also I accidentally killed a man this morning. It would be prudent for me to move my operation somewhere else. So you need to come pick this one up now."

"Did you say you *killed* a man?"

"Yes. It was an accident, I assure you. I was merely trying to knock him down so I might escape, but he landed directly on top of an old well cover and fell through it."

"Are you sure he's dead?"

"If he's not, then he will be in due order."

"If he's in a well, then he's not likely to be found for a while, dead or alive."

"That's probably safe to assume."

"Did anyone see you, or your car? After you killed the guy, or after you took the child?"

"I don't think so, but I haven't had a chance to watch the news yet."

"Then stay there until you get me what I need. Then, and only then, will I send someone to pick up the merchandise."

"This is unwise, but you force my hand. I suppose I could stay one more day."

"All right, good. Is the merchandise stored safely?"

"Yes."

"Where is it?"

"Nice try, my friend. I won't be sharing that information with you. Rest assured that she is safe and comfortable, and nowhere near my present location."

"Fine. I'll be expecting better news from you."

With each oscillation, the passenger-side windshield wiper made a squealing noise that was driving Kate out of her mind, but in this rain, turning the wipers off was not an option. It was coming down so hard that she struggled to see well enough to keep the car between the lines.

She was tired and dejected. They'd covered all the roads they could think of, cruised up and down every dead-end street, driven through every development of cookie-cutter homes, searched in every parking lot. Wherever Tim was, he was not visible from the road, nor was his bike. He must be lost somewhere in the forests or the fields. He couldn't be more than a couple of miles from home, but that still encompassed a lot of territory.

Kate supposed she shouldn't be surprised. Considering that he'd been hiding the treasure, he was not likely to be in a place that was easily seen from the road. But she'd had to try.

"Let's go home, girls. The way it's storming, I don't think we're doing any good out here. We'll not be finding him this way."

Amanda, who had been keeping a stiff upper lip during their ride, began to sniffle.

Kate saw it in the rearview mirror. "Don't worry, Amanda. Everything is going to be okay." She knew it was a ridiculous thing to say, but what else could she tell her?

"I'm scared. I want my Daddy."

Kate watched as Lindsey pulled Amanda closer to her and whispered something in her ear, and saw Amanda look up at her sister with a hopeful expression.

A few minutes later they pulled into their driveway and made a mad dash through the downpour to the shelter of the awning over the back door.

They shed their wet shoes just inside the door, then came into the kitchen, where Kate stopped dead in her tracks, staring at the dining room table.

"Damn it!" she said. "Widget's been on the table again. Look at this mess!" There was an open can of Dr. Pepper lying on its side on the table. Brown liquid pooled around it and ran off the edge of the table, forming a wide splatter pattern on the floor.

"Amanda, how many times have I told you not to leave open cans on the table like that?" Kate said.

Amanda gazed at her with big, shining, blue eyes.

"It was my fault, Kate," Lindsey said. "I left it there." She got several paper towels off the roll and got to work sopping up the mess.

Amanda broke out of her trance and followed behind her sister with a wet dishrag. They wiped the table clean, then moved to the floor.

"Thank you, girls," Kate said. "I'll take over."

"We got it," Lindsey said. "It's okay."

Kate stood for a moment, watching the girls work. It wasn't like her to snap at the girls like that. Her nerves were shot. She closed her eyes and massaged her temples with both hands.

When she opened her eyes, Lindsey and Amanda had stopped what they were doing and were looking at her. Lindsey said, "We're gonna clean it up, Kate."

"No," Kate said, waving the comment off with one hand. "It's not that. It's just ... I don't ... I'm a little rattled, that's all. I'll be okay. I just need to ..." She lifted her face to them with a pasted-on smile, saying, "How 'bout something to eat?"

"I am kinda hungry," Lindsey admitted.

"You, too, Amanda?"

Amanda nodded.

"Okay. All right. Let's see," Kate said, rising, hands fluttering, eyes darting around the kitchen. "Let's see what we have in the fridge."

She opened the refrigerator and said, "Hey, here's some leftover spaghetti sauce I can heat up. That work?"

"Yeah, that sounds good," Lindsey said, as they finished their cleanup. "We're gonna go to my room and watch TV. Can you let us know when it's ready?"

"Sure thing. Amanda, you okay?"

Amanda nodded. Kate hugged her and said, "Sorry I jumped on you about the soda. It's not you, okay? Forgive me?"

Amanda nodded again, then said, "Kate? Is Daddy …?"

"Daddy's fine, honey. We just have to find him. And we will. I don't know how, but I know I won't rest until he's back home safe. Try not to worry, okay?"

"Okay."

"Come on, Manda," Lindsey said. "Let's go *watch TV.*" She grabbed her sister by the elbow and dragged her back the hallway.

Kate sighed. It was getting harder and harder to keep up her facade. She'd just come very close to breaking down in front of the girls. That simply couldn't happen.

She had a brief moment of confusion in which she took several tiny half-steps in alternating directions, then she put the sauce in the microwave and set it for three minutes.

She was having trouble thinking straight. It was as if she were trapped in a maze with no exit, only a series of dead ends. The dead ends were named Dread, Anger, Despair, Prayer, Denial, and Blind Panic, and her mind had fetched up against all of them at some point or other over the last few hours. She was currently at Despair, and searching for the next stop.

She'd never felt so helpless in her life. She wanted to scream, pull her hair out, pound on the walls, break windows, throw dishes. Her body ached for some form of expression, some conduit of release for the bottled up hysteria within her. A large part of her wanted to curl up in fetal position and wait for it all to go away.

Keep moving, she told herself. *Stay on task.*

She crossed the room and opened the pantry door. As she reached for a box of spaghetti noodles, a bottle of amber liquid on the top shelf caught her eye, and she froze.

Now that *might be just the ticket.*

She grabbed the bottle of Captain Morgan, got a glass from the cabinet, some ice and cold Diet Coke from the fridge, and seconds later let the first swallow of Captain & Diet slide down her throat. She gave the alcohol a second to both chill and warm her, felt the icy bite of the spiced rum suffuse her innards, rise up into her sinuses to tingle her nose. Then she took the rest of the glass at once, three long swallows, and immediately felt a small pinprick of remorse.

Ah, what the hell. Tim's the alcoholic, not me. Maybe this'll help settle my nerves.

As she made the second drink, she came back to Denial. Leaving her drink on the counter, she marched toward her bedroom, with each step growing more and more certain that she was right. "I know you're here, Tim," she called, and opened the basement door. It revealed only a yawning silent darkness. "Where are you? Enough, Tim! This isn't funny anymore!"

She continued into their bedroom, where she threw back the comforter. Nothing. She bent and looked under the bed. Dust bunnies, shoes, and the underwear she'd lost last night. She rose then, and peeked behind the door. A tall shape behind it gave her heart a tiny lurch before she realized that it was only Tim's bathrobe, hanging on a hook.

"Tim, please!" she called. "Please come out. I mean it, Tim. The game's over. Are you in *here?*" She opened the closet, and looked behind the hanging clothes. Nothing. In frustrated rage, she began yanking shirts off their hangers and flinging them onto the floor, punctuating each spike with a guttural roar, until the closet was all but empty.

Spent, panting, she stared at the pile of maltreated clothing as if it were somehow to blame for everything that had gone wrong this day.

Then, furtively, like she was sneaking up on prey, she let her gaze slide over to Tim's dresser, where she found a more suitable focus for her ire: the cellphone he had left behind. She stared at it through narrowed eyes. If she could have shattered it with the power of her mind alone, she would have done so, right there and then.

But why blame the phone? The phone was an inanimate object. Nor could she blame Tim, who was, in his absentmindedness, akin to an inanimate object. He could no more remember to bring the phone with him than the phone could remember to jump into his pocket of its own volition.

Time to admit it, Kate, she thought. *The blame is yours, and yours alone.*

Because she'd wanted an extra hour's sleep, she'd let Tim leave the house without making sure he had his phone. That was a very costly hour's sleep.

She eyed the organized litter of the objects on top of Tim's dresser. The cellphone, his keys, his wallet, his deodorant, a "Fear the Turtle" hat, some spare change, a receipt from Target, a comb, a Michael Crichton paperback, and a Philips head screwdriver. His cologne. She hesitated, then picked up the bottle and spritzed it on her wrist. She inhaled the scent, and was immediately sorry.

So intense was her yearning for her husband that a dull discomfort, a visceral knotting like a menstrual cramp, awakened in her abdomen.

Thunder boomed outside, and she looked out the window at the crashing rain.

This is my mess. It's my responsibility to clean it up.

She returned to the kitchen, picked up the phone, and called Selena.

"What was that all about?" Amanda asked, rubbing her elbow. "You didn't have to drag me."

"Yes, I did," Lindsey replied, closing the bedroom door behind them. "You were about to get into a conversation with her about finding Dad. I *told* you I have an idea."

"Fine. So what's the big secret?" Amanda asked.

"It's not a secret, really. I just don't think we should involve Kate. We can handle it without her."

"We can save Daddy? Us?"

"Yes. You and me. We can do it, without anyone's help. Actually, we're the only ones that *can* do it. The police don't care, and they couldn't find him if they did. Kate's coming unglued. Only you and me can do it."

"How?"

"Kate said Daddy went out this morning to hide the treasure. That's what he was doing when he got lost. Whatever happened to him, wherever he is, it's between here and the last hiding place." She handed Amanda the jar they'd retrieved from under the bridge. "All we have to do is finish the treasure hunt."

Amanda stared.

Lindsey waited.

Amanda's eyes grew wide. "We find the treasure, and we find Daddy!" she said, brightening.

"Exactly. And I need your help with this; I can't do it by myself. Dad made sure that we'd have to work together to find the treasure. Now we have to work together to find *him*. Are you ready for it? Dad's depending on us."

"You're right. Let's do it. But why can't we tell Kate? She could help us. She really does care about Daddy, you know."

They stopped talking as they heard Kate's plaintive cries, along with several crashes and thumps, coming through the wall from the next room, the one shared by their father and Kate.

Lindsey looked at her sister with eyebrows raised. "See?"

"She's losing it," Amanda said.

"I know, right? And even if she wasn't, you know how she is. She doesn't trust us. She won't even let us try."

"Yeah, I guess you're right. It'll have to be our secret."

Lindsey nodded her head. "Partners?" she asked, and extended her hand for a shake.

Amanda took the hand, and said, "Sisters." She paused, and said, "By the way, why did you take the blame for me? I was the one that left that Dr. Pepper there."

Lindsey shrugged. "I just get so tired of the way Kate picks on you all the time. It's like, what's the big deal? Who cares who did it, just clean it up, you know? Besides, it's not our fault that stupid cat is psycho."

"I could've handled it myself, Lin."

"Yeah, right. You weren't sayin' anything. You were just takin' it."

"Because it *was* my fault. She was right."

"Whatev, Manda."

"Well … thanks. I guess."

"You're welcome. I guess."

The girls smiled at each other.

A few minutes later, a knock came at the door.

"Come in," Lindsey said.

The door opened. "Girls," Kate said. "I'm going to be leaving in a couple of minutes."

"But we just got here," Lindsey said.

"I'm sorry about dinner, but I've got to go back out and look for your Dad," Kate continued. "I can't sit still. I want you two to stay here, though. Selena's coming over to stay with you. She'll be here in about fifteen minutes, and she's bringing movies and a pizza."

"But why can't we come with you?" Lindsey asked.

"Look, it's miserable out," Kate said. "I really appreciate you guys helping me earlier, but in this weather I want you at home and safe. I have things I have to do. And don't worry about your Dad, okay?"

Lindsey wanted to argue further, but she refrained. She saw something in Kate she'd never seen before, grim determination with a slight touch of depravity, a wild, don't-mess-with-me look in her eye. It was a Kate that would brook no opposition, and Lindsey recognized it without understanding how.

Besides, she had her own agenda.

"Okay," Lindsey said. "When are you coming back?"

"As soon as I can."

Amanda sniffed.

"Don't cry, Amanda," Kate said. "I told you I'm going to find him, and I will. I won't rest until I do. If we're not both home by morning, then I'd love for you two to come out and help me some more. But for now, it's my job to look, and it's your job to get some rest. Deal?"

"Okay," Lindsey said. Amanda nodded.

"Good. I'll be back soon. I love you both."

"Love you, too," they responded automatically.

Kate stepped out the door and closed it behind her.

8

I guess you could say me and Lynch sorta grew apart this past year. We were in eighth grade, and it was the first time since we were seven that me and him weren't in any classes together. I started hangin' around with a different bunch of kids, ones that had the same teachers as me and all, ones that were more like me. Lynch, he don't hang around with much of anybody anymore.

Back in the fall, Lynch still used to come over my house every once in a while, but Greg was always so mean to him. Pretty soon Lynch just stopped comin' over, and to be honest, I was kinda glad.

A lot of kids made fun of him for the rest of the school year. Kids just naturally can't stand other kids that are different, and boy is Lynch different. I guess, for one thing, 'cause he's so smart. I mean, he knows a lot of useless stupid shit, like all the Presidents, in order. He knows their birthdays, the exact dates they held office, everything. The Vice Presidents, too. He reads all the time, everything from world history to science fiction; even poetry! No math problem is too hard for him. Rubik's Cube? One minute, max. And like a lot of brainiacs, he sucks at all sports. So bad.

But it's not just that. It's also 'cause he's got long greasy hair and bad breath and nasty teeth, and his clothes are always old and out of style, and they smell like mildew. Behind his back, people say he's a mama's boy, and say if his slut mom wasn't such a drug addict, he might have enough money to buy some decent clothes, and shit like that.

I try to stay out of it. He's still my friend and I don't like it when people are mean to him, but I don't wanna get lumped in with him, either. So I don't say nothin' when kids start talkin' like that.

Anyways, school's out now, and when it starts up again, me and Lynch will be in high school. Not that I'm ready for summer to end or anything, but I've already started callin' myself a ninth-grader.

So out of the blue, Lynch calls me up this mornin' and asks me if I wanna do somethin' with him today. Just like old times. I figured, what the hell, it's summertime, we can hang out in the woods or somethin', nobody'll see us. What's the harm? Hell, it might even be fun.

And that's how we ended up here, sittin' on top of Thinkin' Rock, catchin' up with each other. There wasn't nothin' uncomfortable about it at all. We picked up like we just saw each other yesterday, and I'm startin' to remember why I used to think he was like more than a brother to me. Dad says you can always find truth at Thinkin' Rock. Maybe that's part of it.

But I'm not sure what Dad even meant by that. He say's I'll know it when I find it. He believes all that Indian crap. He thinks this was some kinda Indian holy place, but all I get up here is a feeling like a good coffee buzz, and I think that's just because of the height.

"Thought you might like to eyeball these," I say to Lynch, and I hand him the can of arrowheads I collected with my brothers over the years.

He opens it up, looks in, looks back at me, and says, "I thought you were lyin' when you said you collected arrowheads."

I shrug. "I was, kinda, back then. Only had two at the time. Got some more after that, though."

"How come you never showed 'em to me before?"

I shrug again. "Not sure. I think maybe 'cause it was somethin' I did with my brothers, and when I was with you I didn't wanna think about my brothers."

He nods. "I get that."

He reaches a couple fingers into the coffee can, and he picks one arrowhead out and holds it up real close to his eye. "It's chert," he says. "Yeah, this is the real thing, all right. Look here, where these notches are. That's where they tied it onto the shaft."

I just listen. I figure chert is a type of rock, but I don't know chert from a ham sandwich.

"You found all these on the farm?" he asks. I nod. "There must've been a camp around here somewhere. That's so cool. Can I take these home tonight?"

I hesitate. It took me years to collect all those. "I don't know ... ," I say.

"I have some books at home. I can figure out who made 'em, and when. I'll bring 'em back to you tomorrow. I promise. Timmy, look at me: I promise."

"What if I don't see you tomorrow?"

Lynch rolls his eyes. "Okay, here," he says, and pulls an old book out of his jacket, and hands it to me.

"What's this?" I say.

"It's Tennyson. Poetry. You can hold it until I bring the arrowheads back, okay?"

"Poetry?" I give the book a once-over, frowning.

"Not just poetry, Timmy. It's Tennyson. There's some real powerful stuff in there. My favorite is 'Ulysses.' I know it by heart. Listen: 'Come, my friends / 'Tis not too late to seek a newer world' / Push off, and sitting well in order smite / The sounding furrows; for my purpose holds / To sail beyond the sunset, and the baths / Of all the western stars, until I die.'

Finally he stops, lookin' at me with this big dopey smile on his face. "Isn't that cool?" he says.

I shift my legs, uncomfortable. "I don't know, Lynch. You know I can't stand this stuff. You were the one that ate it up in seventh grade."

"You loved that class, too, dipshit."

"No. I just had the hots for Ms. Pullen. I faked it."

"Well, whatever. What counts is that it's important to me. That book is as important to me as the arrowheads are to you. It's collateral. You get it?"

I frown. "I guess so."

"Good. It's a deal, then." We do our secret shake like we used to do in grade school.

Lynch sets the coffee can down and says, "Hey, Timmy. Look what I got." Then he reaches back into the pocket of his CPO jacket (he wears that thing every day, no matter how warm it gets) and pulls out a leather sheath, and out of that he draws the goddamn wickedest knife I ever saw. It's long and it's polished like a mirror and it looks dangerous as hell. The handle, or the hilt, I think they call it, is made out of bone or somethin'.

"It's a deer antler," Lynch says, like he musta read my mind. "My Dad shot the deer himself. He had the knife made especially for me."

I'm not sure how much of that I believe. I believe that his dad shot a deer, 'cause his dad shot lots of deer, everybody knows that. But Lynch was only eight when his ol' man died. Who would give a widowmaker like that to an eight-year-old?

I keep that to myself and I say, "Damn, Lynch! Can I see it?"

"Sure," he says, and he hands it to me, hilt-first. One side of the blade has teeth on it like a saw, but I can tell by lookin' at the opposite edge that I don't wanna drag my thumb acrost it like they do in the movies. It'll bleed me for sure.

"Nice," I say, 'cause I don't know what else to say, and I hand it back to him.

He resheaths it and puts it back in his jacket. "I got something else, too," he says. Then he pulls out a black tube-shaped thing about as long as my little finger. At first I don't know what it is, then I realize it's a lighter, a new one, not like the one he used to carry that made that "ka-chink" sound when he opened it. This one is the kind you throw away when it's out of fluid.

"What, again with the fire? What you wanna burn this time?"

"This," he says, and he brings out a plastic sandwich bag from the same pocket. There's something in the bag, and it looks like—

"Oh, no, that ain't pot, is it?" I ask him.

"No, it's even better. It's flakes."

"Flakes? What's flakes?"

"You don't know what flakes are, you dumbass? It's oregano, sprayed with PCP. Phencyclidine. It's a horse tranquilizer. It interferes with receptors in the brain—"

"I know what PCP is, Lynch. I mean, I didn't know all that, but I know what it is. Where'd you get it?"

He frowns, and his eyebrows draw down toward the bridge of his nose. "Why do you want to know?"

"I don't," I say, to make him feel better. "But what are you doin' with that shit? It's dangerous." I say that, but in my mind, I'm thinkin', *How does a kid who lives alone with his mama, who's so poor that he's never even been to the dentist in his whole fuckin' life, get hold of PCP?*

"It's not dangerous if you know what you're doing," he says. "And I know what I'm doing. You should try it, Timmy. You see the most incredible things. I'll share it with you if you want."

"That's all right," I say. "I think I better be gettin' home soon. My mom's gonna be lookin' for me."

"You're chicken."

He's right, but I'm not ready to admit it yet, not even to my best friend. Maybe *especially* not to my best friend, who lately is startin' to seem less and less like the guy I grew up with, between the knife and the PCP and the lies and all kinds of other weird shit I can't put my finger on. Somethin's just not right about him these days. So I say, "I'm not chicken. I just don't have time. I'll smoke with you next time."

"You never know, Timmy. There might not be a next time."

"There better be," I say. "You got my arrowheads. I'm serious, I gotta go."

"Okay. See ya," he says.

"You stayin' here?"

"For a while."

"Okay. Been nice talkin' to ya." So I stick the old book of poetry in my pocket and climb down from Thinking Rock and turn toward my house. As I'm walkin' on the Crossing Log, I look back up at the top of Thinking Rock and wave at Lynch. He waves back, then picks up a loose rock and tosses it into Sadler's Run. I watch it hit, then I turn and head for home.

Something drips on my head. I open my left eye, the only one that still works, and look up to see where it came from. There's a hole in the sky. *What the … ?*

Like frost melting on a windowpane, the fabric of dream slowly dissolves, and reality reasserts itself in the stark colors of darkness and pain.

What is happening to him? Why do these lost fragments of his childhood, repressed for more than twenty years, keep crowding his brain *now*, when all he wants to remember are the events of the last couple of days?

One good thing. After all these years, he knows what happened to his arrowheads. Lynch never kept his promise. Most likely they're at the bottom of a pile of ashes in what's left of Lynch's house. For a brief moment, Tim considers the idea of going to the property at the end of Myrtle Drive, the "haunted house," and sifting through the wreckage in hopes of finding some or all of his precious arrowheads; but he is then forced to admit to himself that he will most likely never get the chance.

The circle of sky is not as painfully bright as it once was. He can see movement up there, things swaying back and forth.

It's trees, blowing in the wind, he realizes. And beyond the trees, he sees low gray clouds rolling and twisting across his narrow field of vision. It is raining. Rain is falling on his face.

How can rain be falling straight down the tube with the wind blowing like that? It should be rolling down the walls.

Ah. There it is. Studying the well wall above him, he can see a place where water shoots into the air from between two stones about halfway up. This little jet of water, about as big around as his finger, disintegrates into spray on its way down, and falls on his face as rain.

Tim opens his mouth as wide as he can, ignoring the protesting pains from the battered infrastructure of his face and head. Some of the drops fall into his mouth and he swallows, eager to ease his burning thirst. Bright light flashes in the sky, and thunder follows closely behind.

It's not a very efficient way of getting water, and it takes a while, but he keeps at it until his thirst is satisfied. Then he uses the water that has fallen on his face to clean some of the crud away from his right eye. With his left hand, he gently prods and massages the lid, peeling off gooey chunks of clotted blood until he is able to pry it open. He blinks a few times, rubs some more rainwater into his eyelashes, blinks some more, feeling relief at this small improvement.

He examines his new friend Rocky Raccoon for the first time, fighting the urge to gag. Some of its flesh has sloughed off, but its skeleton is intact, held together by greasy-looking masses of connective tissue. Clumps of hair and decomposing flesh still cling to it in various places.

He wonders how long the animal has been dead. A couple of weeks? He is no expert on the stages of decomposition. One thing he can tell is that the animal's claws are all broken or worn down to the nub. How many times did it try to climb these walls and fall, only to get up and try again, mindlessly striving for survival until it simply drowned?

Grimly, he reflects on the urge to survive that is so powerful in all creatures, himself included. As hopeless as his situation is, still he struggles to get water. His body fights to survive to the very end.

A memory flashes by, like a butterfly at the edge of vision. Coming down the Sleddin' Hill on his bike, the wind tearing at his sleeves, cookie-cutter houses flashing by on either side.

Recent? Maybe. He can't recall the context, and that alone makes him think it comes from the missing chunk of time between dinner and ... here. Maybe more memories will resurface if he just lets his mind wander instead of trying to focus on it.

Lynch was right about one thing. There was no next time.

Tim remembers now that after that day on Thinking Rock, the next time he saw Lynch was after school started in September, and by that time, the Lynch he knew was gone. Sometime during the summer, he'd had a psychotic break. Tim only talked to him a couple of times that autumn, and it was like talking to a stranger. A crazy stranger.

No one ever said if the PCP pushed Lynch over the edge, or if he just crossed that blurry boundary between genius and madness, but to Tim, the timing was ... suspicious. A twinge of long-forgotten remorse worries at the back of his mind.

I should've stopped him.

A series of rapid-fire images comes to him now, like single frames inserted into a movie reel: a beautiful morning, the shadows long and cool ... the smell of earthworms ... a kiss from Kate ... the wind in his hair, in his face, his shirt fluttering on his back ... a sealed envelope ... a playground. Snapshots, points on the continuum between Friday night and now ... whenever *now* is.

If only he could connect the dots. Finish the puzzle.

What was in the envelope?

He feels that if he could remember that, then the rest of the puzzle pieces would fall into place. The envelope is the key.

The key. The key.

Lightning flashes above, casting the well wall in blinding bas-relief for a fraction of a second, and tripping the return of another wayward memory. An image, bereft of context, but with similar lighting. Kate, lit briefly from the right side by a flickering burst of light coming through their bedroom window. She is naked, straddling his hips as he lies on his back, her elbows locked as her hands pin his to the mattress on either side of him. With her rocking motion, her blond hair sways gently around her face, the left half of which is cast in shadow; the right half, caught in an actinic freeze-frame of passion, the eye closed, the moist, luscious lips slightly parted, the tip of her tongue visible as it rests on her bottom row of teeth.

It happened. Perhaps the last moment he shared with his wife before falling into this well. He hopes so.

He needs more water, opens his upraised face again. As he collects the falling water in his mouth, another flash of lightning comes from overhead. The stroboscopic backlighting gives the drops of water the appearance of diamonds falling in stop-motion, spurring the return of yet another memory. The stream, the bridge, the white bands of mist, the shower of brilliant little stars. He remembers standing and watching the drops of water fall into the sunlight, and thinking how beautiful it was.

He tries to put himself in that place, with the mist and the falling stars, see what he saw, feel what he felt, think what he was thinking ...

Wait ... what's this ... something in my hand, wrapped in a towel.

Like the sun bursting over the horizon, it comes to him. His memories come back in a flood.

The treasure hunt! I was on my way to the wall, to hide the treasure. This well ... it must be somewhere around there.

The trees he can see far above him, tossing in the storm, would seem to corroborate the idea that he is in a forest, at least. But it could be any forest. How can he verify that it's the same patch of woods where he'd intended to hide the treasure?

He gropes around in the black water with his good hand. Around his legs, which are now numb to the touch, he finds several rocks, bricks, sticks (or were they small bones?), and a few pieces of lumber from what he assumes must have been the well-cover that broke under his weight. And one strangely shaped package, tucked partially under his left leg. A cylindrical object, wrapped in cloth. He pulls it forth, grimacing in pain at the necessary jostling of his leg, and holds it before him, dripping.

The treasure.

Through some crazy chance, the jar didn't break in the fall. Its contents should be safe.

He knows where he is.

Now if only someone will come and help him. Surely they must have missed him by now. They would realize something has happened and they will come after him.

No. They won't.

The gravity of his situation settles on him like a great crushing weight. *He* may know where he is, but no one else does. Not even Kate. He's in the middle of nowhere, somewhere near a nature trail no one knows about. He's far from any road, and his bike is hidden. It could be days or weeks before anyone uses the nature trail again, and even then, what's the chance they'll stumble across this well by accident? It would take a miracle.

Unless ...

Kate gripped the wheel with both hands, leaning forward to peer through the windshield. The rain came down in sheets.

She could feel a rum buzz coming on. She held a hand up in front of her face, and was pleased to see that it no longer trembled.

She put her flashers on and slowed the car to a stop where White Horse Road crossed Sadler's Run. The surface of the ground fell away from her on either side of the road, sloping down to the level of the streambed. A man on a bike could easily have been knocked off the edge of the road, over the guardrail, and be lying down there out of sight. While at home, she'd come to realize that she and the girls had driven right past many places like this.

She hesitated, listening to the rain pound on the car's roof and hood, watching the windshield wipers sweep back and forth, each time making that annoying squeak on the upstroke. She saw no traffic before her or behind her.

With one hand on the door handle, she realized that she hadn't thought to bring an umbrella. She was going to get very wet, very quickly.

It wasn't only the rain that made her hesitate. She hoped to find Tim, yet was terrified that she might. What if he were lying at the bottom of the slope, broken and bleeding, a twisted bicycle inextricably intertwined with his body? Could she bear to see that?

What if he were lying there in the rain, dying, waiting, hoping against hope that someone would find him. Trusting that, even if no one else did, *his wife would come looking for him?*

In one fluid motion, she sprang from the car. She ran around in front of it, ignoring the rainfall pelting her.

She stood at the guardrail and peered over it, down the slope. She held her hand over her eyes to block the rain.

Nothing but weeds and bushes.

The rain lashed her face. Her hair was plastered to her head and the back of Tim's t-shirt was already soaked. She swiped rainwater from her eyes and crossed the road to check the opposite side.

No Tim. No bike.

She darted back into the frigid shelter of the car. Shivering, she moved the temperature control up a bit.

She pushed wet hair away from her face in irritation. "This'll never do," she said to herself. She fished in the console and found a scrunchie, the perfect thing. She pulled her hair back into a loose pony. Then she checked in the back seat, and wonder of wonders, there was one of Tim's hats. She seized it and turned it around to see the front. Her lip curled in disgust.

The hat read "Surf Naked." She'd asked Tim to get rid of that hat several times, but he insisted on keeping it. It embarrassed her to see her husband wearing it, and she thought even less of it on her own head, but it would keep the rain and her hair out of her face. She pulled her ponytail through the back and settled the brim over her eyes.

She took a pull from the travel mug she'd brought with her from the house. Then she put the car in drive, popped the flashers off, and moved on.

She'd done it, she'd checked one place. She knew that dozens of similar places within biking distance of their house remained to be checked out.

She would check each and every one of them if she had to. No one else was doing it, so by God she would.

She came to the stop sign at Route 128 and turned left.

The pizza was gone. The girls were helping to clear the table when Selena excused herself to go to the bathroom.

As soon as she was out of earshot, Amanda whispered, "Why'd you keep kicking me under the table like that?"

"Because you kept pestering her to take us out to look for Dad. If we're out there, we can't work on the clues, and we need to do that. In case Kate doesn't find Daddy, we're next."

Amanda was still pouting. "But she wants us to watch movies. How stupid is that? How can we help if we're watching movies?"

"I know. But if we tell her what we're planning, she'll tell Kate. There's nothing we can do but wait until we get a chance."

"We could say we're tired and we wanna go to bed."

"It's too early. She'll know we're up to something. We gotta pretend like everything's normal until we get to our regular bedtime. Then we can work on the clue. Maybe Daddy and Kate'll be home by then, and we won't have to worry about it."

"How can we pretend like everything's normal? Everything is *so* not normal today."

They heard the toilet flush.

"Listen, let's just watch one movie with her and then we'll say we're tired and we'll go to my room. Then we'll stay up late and solve the clue, and we'll get up super early in the morning and go find Daddy."

"You make it sound so simple."

"It *is* simple. Just chill."

"Okay. But I'm worried about Daddy."

"I am, too. But let's pretend we're not."

Jerry weaved through the trees, carrying an umbrella with one hand and pushing aside wet branches with the other. Under his arm, the one with the umbrella, he carried a plastic sack of food.

He had parked, as was his habit, on a different road from the one on which his destination was located, and cut cross-country to get to it. He came out of the woods and crossed the short access road to the loading dock of the abandoned supermarket where he'd stashed little Madison, his darling. He scanned the area. No one was around. He climbed up onto the covered loading dock, closed his umbrella and leaned it against the wall, and jimmied the door he'd broken into last week. Inside, dim emergency lights cast a flickering maze of shadows across the deserted stockroom.

In a small alcove off to the side, Madison was handcuffed to a water pipe. She sat on a small mattress, her knees pulled up under her chin and her free arm wrapped around her legs. Near her, the small television that Jerry had thoughtfully provided for her chattered away. He had removed one of the emergency light bulbs and screwed a receptacle fitting in its place to supply power for the television.

It was beastly hot in the stockroom, and Madison glistened with sweat. Her blond curls hung in limp clumps around her face. Her face was tear-streaked and red. When she saw him, she moaned and struggled against the cuff restraining her.

The sight of her moist body and the smell of her fear excited him. It was all he could do to keep from touching her, caressing her tiny form. As it was, he had to content himself with visual gratification. His eyes drank in the sight of her, her terror-stricken face, her thin arms and legs, her tiny pink toes. Pity this one was not to be for him, else he would have undressed her for an even more delicious time.

"Please," she whimpered. "Please let me go. This thing hurts my wrist real bad."

"I'm afraid I can't do that, darling. But don't worry, I'm not going to hurt you."

"I want my Mommyyyyyyyyyyyyyyy!" she cried, and then began to make the most annoying sounds.

"Please don't cry, darling, I promise you everything is going to be fine. I've brought you some nice food. Do you like hot dogs? Yes? Mac 'n' cheese? I thought so. I've hit the nail on the head, haven't I? I thought when I first saw you that you were a hot dogs and mac 'n' cheese girl. And I was right, wasn't I?"

"Yes," she said in a quiet voice. She sniffed. "But Mommy and Daddy say they're not good for me. They hardly ever let me eat them. Especially hot dogs. Mommy says they're made of pig's ears and eyes and tails."

Jerry sat down on a folding chair and opened the sack. He withdrew a Styrofoam plate, a hot dog wrapped in foil, a plastic fork, some packets of ketchup, and a tiny container of macaroni. As Madison watched in silence, he opened the hot dog and decorated it with ketchup. He peeled the foil top off the macaroni and cheese container, arranged the food on the plate, and put the plate on the mattress in front of her, where she could reach it with her free hand. "Now wait just a minute," he said. "What did I just hear you say? Your parents won't let you have hot dogs? Or macaroni and cheese?"

Madison shook her head no, picked up the hot dog, and took a bite.

"I put ketchup on it for you. I hope you like ketchup."

Madison nodded.

"Ahh, I thought so. It seems to me I know you better than your parents, no?"

Madison pouted. "My parents love me very much."

"I'm sure they do, darling. But they treat you like a child, do they not? Why won't they let you make your own decisions about what to eat? You're old enough to know what you like, aren't you?"

Madison nodded, ate some macaroni.

"Oh, I'm sorry, you must be thirsty, too. I've brought you some Yoo-Hoo. Do you like Yoo-Hoo?"

Madison's eyes fairly popped out of her head at the sight of the bottle.

Jerry chuckled. "I'll take that as a yes." He opened it and held it out to her. She reached for it, and he moved it away, teasing.

"Just kidding, darling," he said, smiling, and handed her the bottle. He watched her lips and tongue working as she took liquid from it.

"It seems to me," he said, "that if your Mommy and Daddy really loved you, they'd let you make your own decisions, like the grown-up girl that you are. Do you agree?"

"Well …"

"I realize that might be a hard thing for you to understand right now. But I think you'll begin to, once you're with people who really and truly love you. Tomorrow you will get a new Mommy and Daddy, and they will truly love you and give you whatever you want. And they're even going to let you be in movies! Would you like to be in movies, darling Madison?"

Madison's eyes had grown wide as he spoke, this time in shock. "No!" she said. "I mean yes. I mean, I'd like to be in movies, but I don't want a new Mommy and Daddy. I want *my* Mommy and Daddy."

"But why, Madison? You've just told me that they treat you like a child. Why would you want to go back to them if you can have *better* parents?"

"My Mommy's going to be really worried. And my Daddy's going to be really mad if I don't get home soon."

"But why would your Daddy be mad at you?"

"Because I didn't come home in time and made him worry."

"And what will Daddy say to you?"

"He won't say anything. He'll just punish me."

Jerry feigned shock. "What? Why, that's horrible! You say your Daddy

103

loves you, yet he would punish you for being late? Madison, I know you may not believe me, but what you describe is not love. I promise you, Madison, your new parents will never do that to you. They will teach you what true love is, and they will never punish you, for any reason."

Madison sniveled. "I wanna go home."

"And you will go home, Madison darling. Tomorrow. Are you finished eating? Some more Yoo-Hoo? Here you are. Mmmmmm, good. How is your water supply? Oh my, you've barely drunk any water."

"I don't like water."

"But Madison, darling, in this heat it's dreadfully important to stay hydrated. You must drink some of this water if you get thirsty. There are six bottles here. You should drink at least two a day. Do you understand?"

She nodded, her lip trembling.

"Tomorrow when I come back, I'm going to bring you some clean new clothes to wear when your new parents come to meet you for the first time. Would you like that?"

"No, no, no," she wailed. "I wanna go home to *my* Mommy and Daddy."

"I've explained that to you, darling," Jerry said. "And now I must be going. I have a bit of shopping to do, then I have plans for tonight."

"*Nooooooo!*" she screamed. "Don't leave me, please don't leave!"

"Don't worry, darling, I'll be back tomorrow. I'll leave the light on, and you have your TV for company. I'm sorry there's no cable here, but I'll leave it on Channel 13 for you since it seems to come in the best. Goodnight, darling Madison. Sweet dreams."

"Noooo! I'm afraid of thunder! Come back, come back. Please, please, please don't leave me! Please, please, please! Come back!"

As Jerry walked to the back door, her words degenerated into a meaningless shrieking babble. He exited, and pushed the door closed on the sound, leaving it behind him. He opened his umbrella, went back into the trees, and headed for his car, adjusting his pants with his free hand. Darling Madison had gotten him aroused, even with her clothes on.

Kate dashed back toward the waiting shelter of her car.

Acting on a hunch that had become more like a compulsion, she had just checked the vicinity of the railroad station for the second time today, only to be disappointed again.

She slammed the door behind her with a thunk. Then, shivering, she started the engine to clear the windshield of fog, and maybe, just maybe, warm up a little while she thought about her next course of action.

With the rain pouring down and the windshield wipers off, the interior of the car was a like bubble of reality floating in a fantasy of wind and water.

She was running out of ideas. She was at the limit of what she considered to be a safe distance from home for the girls; besides, the only things between here and Route 5 were Friar Tuck's Tavern and a whole lot of trees. Nowhere to hide anything, even if Tim had gone that far from home, which she doubted.

As the windshield began to clear from the bottom up, she thought she caught a suggestion of movement near the railroad station. A fugitive shape, a shifting of patterns of light and dark. Maybe it was wishful thinking, but she was sure it was a human figure, walking between the station and the public restroom building next to it. Her heart did a flamenco trip-hammer beat in her chest.

"Tim?"

She flipped the wipers on and hunched down to peer through the semicircle of clear glass at the bottom of the windshield. She cleared some fog away with the edge of her hand. The wipers wiped ... and an involuntary yelp came out of her as she jumped back in the seat, startled. There he was, standing in the rain, less than twenty feet away. Not Tim, but a man with wild bedraggled black hair and beard, wearing an old seventies-era Kiss t-shirt. Staring at her.

A wild gust of wind rocked the car on its springs and blew a sheet of water across the windshield, and by the time the wipers cleared it, he was gone. Like he'd never been there. She hadn't seen him dash away. It was more like he ... evanesced. There one moment, gone the next.

Had she imagined him?

She turned the wipers and fan up to high, and through the windshield she scanned the entire area.

Nothing.

Briefly, she considered getting out of the car to track the man down. Then she decided against it. What would be the point? It wasn't Tim. What did she care if someone wanted to stand out in the rain on a night like this?

But she couldn't escape the feeling that her seeing him here was no coincidence. The way the man had stared at her, as if he knew her. As if he had something to say.

She thought about it for a moment, and then chided herself, "You're losing your mind, Kate. Seeing ghosts. There's no one out there. Ridiculous!" She gave a little laugh at her own capacity for self-deception.

The more she thought about it, the more convinced she became that her mind was playing tricks on her. She was cold and wet and exhausted and upset, and so frantic to find Tim that she was seeing things that weren't there.

Already she found she couldn't remember what the man had looked like.

Time to move on.

The rain suddenly diminished to an insistent drizzle. On the western horizon, the sky turned brighter, as if the sun was trying to break through.

She picked up the travel mug and shook it. Nothing left of the rum drink but a bit of ice. She frowned, made a decision, and put the car into drive.

Better check in with Selena and the girls before I get to where I'm going.

Selena answered on the second ring. "Did you find him?"

"No. Not yet. How are the girls?"

"They're fine now. We went through a rough patch during dinner, but after dinner they straightened right up. I think they're scared, but they're being real troopers. We just finished watching the first movie, and I was going to put the other one in, but now they say they're tired and they want to go to bed."

"Really? What time is it?"

"A little after eight."

"That's odd. But then, I guess they did have a rough day."

"To say the least. How're you?"

"At the moment, a little spooked."

"How come?"

"I thought I saw somebody. It turned out to be nothing. But listen, I've checked every place I can think of within ten miles of the house. I've looked in every ditch, under every bush, under every bridge, down every embankment. I've been through high grass and under low-hanging trees. I must have put a hundred miles on this car, and I'm wet and filthy and freezing. I'm telling you, there's no way he was involved in a bike accident unless he was off road. And he'd not go off road on that bike."

"Maybe he was on foot."

"Maybe. Parked the bike somewhere where we can't see it, and walked. If so, though, I don't know how we'll ever find him."

They were both silent for a moment.

"Well, how 'bout some good news?" Selena said. "I talked to Kirk earlier, and he told his father what's been going on. Charles says you still have your job if you want it. He says take as long as you need, and he'll cover for you."

"Whatever. That prick. I can't think about him right now."

"Kate … are you drinking?"

"Not since I left the house. Why, you can tell?"

"Yeah. Your voice."

"It's medicinal, Sel. Believe me, it helps. I was so nervous I couldn't think."

"Look, are you coming home now? It's getting dark and you won't be able to accomplish much anymore. Come home and get some rest."

"I think this storm is done. It's getting lighter out."

"Yeah, I see it, but it won't last long. The sun sets in, what, maybe five minutes or so? What else can you do at this point?"

"I've got an idea," Kate said. "It's not somewhere I wanted to go, but I have to do it. I can't come home until I know."

"Are you talking about—"

"I'm real close to Friar Tuck's now."

"Kate, don't you go in there. Not by yourself."

"I have to, Sel. I think this may be all my fault."

"Your fault? How could it be *your* fault? Kate, I don't know what you're talking about. But let me get somebody to come with you. Kirk's home with the kids, but I could call Greg or somebody. Don't go in there alone."

"God, don't call Greg. He's so judgmental. The last thing I need is a judgmental Bible thumper right now. Try Darryl or Brian. No! Not Brian either!"

"Why not Brian?"

"I don't know. I'm ... a little uncomfortable with him."

"Uncomfortable? Why?"

"I don't know. It's just a feeling, I guess."

"Do you have Darryl's number?"

"On the computer, in our address book. But tell him to meet me. I'm here now. I'm parking."

"Kate, wait! Just give me five minutes."

"Sel, get over it. I can take care of myself. I'm here now, and I can't wait. I'll meet up with him at the next stop if he wants to."

"Next stop?"

"Bye, Sel. I'll call you later." She hung up as she pulled into the gravel parking lot of Friar Tuck's Tavern. Pickup trucks with oversized tires and battered old muscle cars from the seventies filled it almost to capacity. Kate squeezed her small Honda into a space next to a Dodge Ram pickup, cleverly painted in several shades of primer so that it might blend in with the surroundings. On its back window was a sticker depicting Calvin pissing on the number 24.

From the outside, Tuck's was a small, square, dingy-looking building constructed of cinder blocks and corrugated metal. Its two windows had been knocked out and filled in with glass blocks. Old-fashioned neon-tube letters affixed to the front of the building screamed "PACKAGE GOODS" in a color somewhere between Halloween orange and arterial blood.

Kate took a deep breath; let it out in a gust. In the dying light, she eyed the entrance to Friar Tuck's. As she watched, two bearded men in shitstompers came out, laughing and shoving each other on their way to an old Chevy Camaro. As she watched them take off, and listened to their raucous voices carrying out the car window as they receded, she reflected on her reasoning for being here, and assured herself that it was sound.

Earlier in the day, she'd been angry with herself for not getting out of bed and ensuring that Tim took his cellphone with him. And she still was. But when Alan Curtis had come to call, with his less-than-subtle hints that Tim may have been seeking some form of escape from tensions at home, another, darker explanation for Tim's having left his cellphone behind had occurred to her.

Suppose he'd left it there intentionally? Suppose he didn't want to be contacted?

It was a theory that, initially, she had rejected outright. They had compromised. Everything was okay. Certainly their lovemaking had been sincere. It stood to reason that the rest of it had been as well.

Eleven hours ago, she'd thought that beyond question. But today's events forced her to view everything that had happened yesterday in a different light. What had begun as a niggling idea in the back of her mind demanded acknowledgement, and with a fervor that grew with each passing hour in which Tim was not found.

Could Alan have been onto something? She hated to admit it, but yes, he could have. For the last six months, she'd been wrapped up in her own little world, and all that time she'd been pushing Tim away. And last night, perhaps, he'd reached his breaking point. Perhaps he'd staged the entire make-up scene, the sex, the pillow talk, all of it, for her benefit. Or just to avoid conflict. He hated conflict. His default solution was to run away from it.

Yes, it all fits.

Kate could only think of two explanations for Tim's continued absence at this hour. And as abhorrent as this one was to her, it was infinitely more attractive than the alternative.

She never thought she'd see the day when she'd hope to catch Tim drinking, but that day had arrived.

Just give me a chance, she thought. *Give me a chance to make it right, please!*

She opened the ashtray and pulled out a crumpled five-dollar bill. She stuck it in the waistband of her pajamas. She hadn't yet found the time to get dressed today, but she was beyond caring about that.

Her cellphone rang. She let it. She'd not be talked out of this. She got out of the car and strode purposefully across the parking lot and into the bar.

"Kate? Kate? Shit!" Selena said, and hung up the phone.

She tried dialing Kate's number back, got four rings and a voicemail message. *She's not going to answer it. I know how she is when she gets like this.*

"Is Kate okay?" Lindsey asked.

"She's still looking. She's not coming home for a while yet. You guys may as well go to bed if you want. Did you get your teeth brushed?"

"Yeah, we're ready. G'night, Selena."

"Good night, girls. Try to get some rest."

When the girls had trooped off to Lindsey's room, Selena went to the computer and opened the address book. Realizing, too late, that she didn't even know Darryl's last name, she scrolled through the list of Tim's and Kate's friends, relatives, and business contacts anyway, hoping to stumble across Darryl by accident. No dice.

Now what?

She found numbers for Greg and Brian, but Kate had declared them both off limits. Kirk was home with the kids. How about Charles? No. Not after the way she'd reacted to his name earlier.

She wondered where Kate's comment about being uncomfortable with Brian had come from. Was it his flirtatiousness? It was true that Brian was an ogler. Selena had caught him at it several times, and he was a bit more frank about it than most men. Most men, when caught staring at her, would glance away. Not Brian. He would give her a crooked little smirk, or sometimes a wink or a thumbs-up.

But that didn't make him dangerous. Selena didn't think Kate had anything to worry about with Brian. He was all bluster. He was the proverbial big teddy bear.

Oh, what the hell.

She made the call.

9

"Time to get to work," Lindsey said.

"Finally!"

"I think we should forget about the jigsaw puzzle until we get some more pieces."

"Yeah. Let's work on the other clues." Amanda got out the first one they'd skipped earlier in the day. It was printed in their father's hand:

SECRET NUMBER
1) A type of horse that is also a fraction = A
2) State between California and Washington = B
3) Find the special A that is from B.
4) Add together the four digits of the year this A was made

This is your SECRET NUMBER. You might need it later.

"This is easy," Amanda said. "'A type of horse that is also a fraction:' that's a quarter. Jenny and Jill are quarterhorses. But 'equals A,' what does that mean?"

"It means whenever we see the letter A, we substitute the word 'quarter,'" Lindsey said.

"Oh, okay. What's the state between California and Washington?"

"I think it's Oregon. We should check and make sure, though."

"I have Game of the States in my room," Amanda said. She crept out to get it, and they verified Lindsey's guess.

"So B equals Oregon from now on," Lindsey said. "Number three says find the special A from B. That means find the special quarter from Oregon."

"The state quarters!" Amanda said. "The ones Daddy has on that big poster board in the basement."

"How are we gonna get down there? We'll have to go right past Selena."

"Maybe you have one in your bank."

Lindsey smiled. "Good idea!"

They emptied Lindsey's piggy bank, separated out all the quarters, and went through them one at a time.

"I found one!" Lindsey said, holding up her prize. "It says 'Oregon' on the tails side. There's a picture of Crater Lake. Whatever that is."

"'Add together the four digits of the year this quarter was made,'" read Amanda. "What year was it made?"

"Two thousand five," Lindsey said. "So that means ... the secret number must be seven."

"Seven. Okay. So what do we do with it?" Amanda asked.

"Nothing yet. It says to save it for later."

"So let's get to work on the other clue," Amanda said.

Lindsey picked up the half sheet of paper with the series of phrases and numbers on it.

CLUE #3 (Part 1 of 2)
What a squirrel hides = 1 2 3
A fruit = 4 5 6 7 8 9
Something that bounces = 10 11 12 13
A flower = 14 15 16 17
A color = 18 19 20 21 22
A part of your body = 23 24 25
Something you drink = 26 27 28 4 29
A bird's home = 30 31 16 3
The opposite of night = 32 33 9
Sometimes found in pillows = 34 35 11 21 19 29 36 16
Meat from a cow = 10 29 17 37
Poppy's middle name = 38 7 11 39 40
Something that opens = 41 42 43 44
What you find in a pen = 45 1 46
This month = 26 2 47 9
Something you find in a garden = 48 49 8 3

You need to find the rest of this page to solve this puzzle.
I think you will find it, but you may have to sleep on it first!

"What the heck is this?" Amanda said, looking over her sister's shoulder. "It totally goes over my head."

"A squirrel hides nuts," Lindsey said. She grabbed a pencil from her desk and wrote NUT next to that line. "Maybe that means that one is an N, two is a U, and three is a T."

"Okay," said Amanda. "So what's the next one? Something is a fruit and it has … six letters. Apple? No, that has five letters."

"Orange," Lindsey said, and wrote ORANGE next to that line.

"Write the letters over top of the numbers, so we can see which is which," Amanda said.

"Great idea." She did that. "The next one is easy. 'Something that bounces.' Ball."

"A flower with four letters," Amanda said. "Rose."

Lindsey dutifully copied the letters over the numbers while thunder rumbled outside.

"A color with five letters," Amanda said. "How about black? Oh, snap, or white?"

"Or brown, or green," Lindsey added. "I guess we can't answer this one yet."

"The next one either," Amanda said. "A part of your body with three letters. There must be a hundred of 'em."

"Let's move on. 'Something you drink.' Five letters."

"Milk? Soda? No."

"Water," said Lindsey.

"Or juice," said Amanda.

"Oh, man, why did you have to think of that? Now we can't answer this one either."

Amanda shrugged. "It's not *my* fault."

"I know, I didn't mean it, Manda. If we get one wrong, it might mess us up and then it'll be hard to fix it later. Better to be careful now. What's next? Oh, it's easy: 'a bird's home,' four letters." She wrote NEST over the numbers.

"Now we're getting somewhere," Lindsey said. "'The opposite of night.' Easy-peasy." She wrote DAY over the numbers. "'Sometimes found in pillows.'"

"Does 'feathers' work?" Amanda asked.

Lindsey counted the letters. "Yup." After writing that one down, she said, "'Meat from a cow' is beef, that's easy. But what's Poppy's middle name?"

"Frank."

"Okay. 'Something that opens.'"

"Door?"

"We'll try it," said Lindsey.

"Ink is what you find in a pen."

"And the next one is 'This month,' July."

"The last one is 'Something you find in a garden.' That totally could be anything."

"All right, we'll skip it for now," said Lindsey.

They both stared at what they'd done.

"Now what do we do?" Amanda said.

"Maybe we're supposed to put 'em in order. Oh, no, that won't work." Amanda laughed. "Your secret message is: 'Nut orange ball rose, something or other."

Lindsey laughed with her. "Nest day feathers beef frank. Now I understand!"

They giggled until they cried.

"All right, let's get serious," Lindsey said. "This has to mean something."

"Yeah, it means we need the rest of the page, like Daddy said."

"Snap! I forgot that part. Hey, I just noticed something. These numbers aren't all in order. See, something you drink is 26, 27, 28, 4, 29. There's a four in there. Then maybe ..."

"Four is an O. We already got that one."

"So 'Something you drink,' five letters, and the fourth letter is O?" I can't think of anything. Can you?

"Not really," said Amanda.

"Let's see if there's any more like that. Here's one: nest is 30, 31, 16, 3. We already have sixteen and three. They're ... let's see ... S from rose, and T from nut. Those are right!"

"'The opposite of night' is 32, 33, 9. We had nine from orange, it's an E. But day ends in Y. Day has to be right ..."

"So orange must be wrong. What's a fruit that ends in Y?"

For a moment they both drew a blank.

"Cherry," Lindsey said. She made the corrections. "Okay, that makes the first letter a C, and it's also the fourth letter in 'Something you drink.'"

"Now juice works."

"Right. It sure does. Now, feathers has an eleven in it, which is ... A, that's right. And a twenty-one, which is also in 'A color.'"

"Nineteen's in both words, too."

"Yeah. Twenty-one is a T and nineteen is an H, we know that from feathers. So if we put 'em in for the color ... it must be 'white.'"

"Wow, good work, Lin. We're almost done. What else don't we have?"

"'A part of your body' and 'Something you find in a garden.' Part of the body is 23, 24, 25. Do we have those anywhere else?"

They both looked.

"I don't think so," Amanda said.

"I don't see 'em either. How about 'Something you find in a garden?'"

"Eight and three."

"Good job. Eight is an R. Three is a T."

"Dirt!"

"That's it. Everything's done except that part of the body thing. Should we just guess?"

"What if we're wrong?"

"Then we'll fix it later. I'm gonna write 'leg.'"

"No, let's say 'arm.'"

Lindsey rolled her eyes. "It doesn't matter, Manda. Fine, we'll write 'arm.'"

"So now how do we find the rest of the page? It says we may have to sleep on it. I hope that doesn't mean he wants us to go to bed and he'll give us Part 2 in the morning."

"I don't think so, Manda. There must be some clue he gave us somewhere that will help us find Part 2. What about the secret number?"

"Seven? How does that help? Seven what?"

"I don't know. There has to be *something*. Think!"

They thought, and they thought, and they thought. They wracked their brains to the point where they became numb and distracted. Amanda's eyes were the first to begin to blink slowly, and Lindsey's weren't far behind.

It's April, my freshman year of high school, and the first really warm day of spring. Greg's car is broken down again, so we're riding the bus home from school. Number 562. I can't remember the driver's name, which is weird 'cause I see him every day. But so what? The only thing I really care about is getting home so I can go outside and play some ball. I'm hoping like hell I can convince Mom to let me do my homework after dark. Maybe while I'm listening to the O's. They're moving that new guy, Cal Ripken, from third base to shortstop. I wonder how that's gonna work out.

I'm sitting next to Paula Weingarten, and I've got a killer crush on her, but she just stares out the window, ignoring me. Randy's in the back of the bus, where he always sits. He's a junior. Two seats in front of me is my other brother Greg, a senior now, and next to him in the same seat is his buddy Alan Curtis (who really ain't that bad a guy when he's not around Greg). Across the aisle from them, in a seat by himself, is Lynch, all hunched over like usual. He grew so much this year, he'd probably be over six feet if he stood up straight, but he's always hunched. And he's the first guy I know to have a beard. I mean a full beard. It's wispy, but it's there, all right. Even Greg only has a little milk mustache. Greg shaves his chin just because some of the other guys on the football team do. There's no other reason for it. But Lynch, now, he could use a shave. And some astringent or something. He's got the worse case of acne I've ever seen. Maybe that's why he don't shave.

My buddy, the old Lynch that was my best friend all my life, is gone now. This guy sittin' here … I can't reach him. No one can. It makes me sad.

I think the drugs done it, but who knows? Maybe it woulda happened anyways. He always was a little off-kilter, as far back as I can remember. I guess I've known it ever since he told that lie to Francine somethin'-or-other about how his dad died.

"Hey, watch this," Greg says, loud enough for everyone to hear. The driver (what the hell is his name?) glances in his oversize rearview to see what Greg's up to now, then forgets about it and looks back at the road. My brother leans across the center aisle into Lynch's seat, gets right next to Lynch's ear, and says, "Hot dog!"

"Stop it," Lynch says, putting his hands over his ears. He doesn't look at Greg. He just stares straight ahead.

"Hot dog, hot dog, hot dog," Greg says. Alan Curtis is laughing, so hard his face is turning almost as red as his hair.

"Stop it, stop it, stop it!" Lynch yells, pounding the heels of his hands into his temples. "They don't like it when you say that!" There's dirt in the creases of his neck and under his nails (which are too long), and a blizzard of dandruff falls onto his shoulders when he pounds his head like that.

"Boys," the driver says. "Leave Lynch alone."

"I didn't touch him!" Greg says, offended.

My brother gets straight A's and he's the star running back on the football team and he gets all the girls and he thinks his shit don't stink. He's goin' to College Park next year and a lot of people can't wait. Me included.

The driver's ignoring them, so Greg says, "Who doesn't like it when I say hot dog, Lynch?"

Alan says, "The wonks, stupid. Right, Lynch?"

"Yes, the wonks. They hate that word."

The "wonks," whatever the hell they are, are part of Lynch's world now. He talks about 'em every day. First time I heard of 'em was back around October. It was a Saturday, and it was cool but the sun felt good when it hit you, and I decided to take a walk down the tracks by myself. When I passed Lynch's house, he came out and started walkin' with me. For a while we just walked without sayin' nothin'. Then we got close to the trestle, and Lynch said we oughta go skip some stones like we did that day we met. So we did, and we talked about a few things, but I noticed that Lynch couldn't keep his mind on anything very long. Then we walked back to the farm, and all the way he kept gigglin' and snickerin' to himself for no reason I could figure out. Every time I asked him what the fuck he was gigglin' at, he'd act like I was interruptin' him at talkin' to somebody else, and he'd just say "nothin'."

I was waitin' for the right time to ask him about my arrowheads, but it never came. He never asked me about his Tennyson, either.

Before long we ended up at the barn, and we climbed up into the hayloft, and made some lounge chairs out of bales, and I started lookin' at some dirty magazines that my brothers left up there. Lynch, he didn't seem to have no interest, but he looked up into the rafters and said, "You see 'em?"

I looked up there. "See what?" I said.

"The wonks."

I asked him what a wonk was.

"Little orange guys about this high," he said, holding his hands about a foot apart. "They're watchin' us. They're laughin' at us."

I remember I looked at him and I got an idea and I said, "Lynch, have you been smokin' that shit again?"

"What shit? Oh, the flakes? No, not lately. Why?" And then he busted out laughin' like I said the funniest thing he'd ever heard. Or somebody else did.

"'Cause you ain't actin' right," I said. "Are you sure you ain't high?"

"No, I swear. I haven't had any smoke for a couple months now." And he giggled some more.

And I thought, *He's lyin' his ass off, or his brain is fried, one or the other.* Then I made up some kinda lie about why I had to go home, and he wandered off across the field and I went in the house. And that was the last time I really hung out with him.

Since then, he's just got worse and worse. Sometimes I wonder what woulda happened if I'd've stuck with him last year, when he turned into a loner. I wonder if he'd still be like this now, or if I coulda done somethin' about it.

"Hey, Lynch," Greg says, "why don't you take a shower tonight? Are you waitin' for the wonks to tell you it's okay?"

"Yeah, and maybe ya should ask 'em 'bout a little trip to the dentist, too," Alan added. "Ya look like ya could use a little help there."

"Stop it! Don't talk about dentists!"

"Why not?" Greg asks. "We're just tryin' to help you out."

"No, you're not. You're *picking* on me. You're not my friends."

Greg turns around and shoots me a wink, expecting me to join in the merriment. "Whatsamatter, Timmy?" he says. "Don'tcha think it's funny?"

I'm thinking, *No, it's not funny, it's sad,* but I join in anyways and I say "Hot dog!" and Lynch screams, "Stop it!" and we all laugh.

But I have to fake mine, and I don't like the feeling it gives me.

The jukebox played Garth Brooks' "Friends in Low Places." A few lusty male voices in the crowd joined in.

Kate stood just inside the door, surveying the scene.

The bar was the size of your average three-car garage. The lighting was dim. A stagnant haze of cigarette smoke made everything appear slightly out of focus. The bar occupied the opposite wall, backed with a twenty-foot-long mirror, a neon Bud Lite sign, and dozens of bottles of liquor in three tiers, each with its red plastic pouring spout. A large television on the wall showed two sportscasters sitting at a desk, and behind them the diamond at Camden Yards, rain puddling on the tarp and sparkling in the stadium lights. Four booths lined the right wall of the room. A resounding *crack!* signaled the breaking of a fresh rack from the pool table to her left, followed by the clunking and rumbling of a couple of balls finding pockets. Tables and chairs occupied the floor space between the pool table and the booths.

Kate heard a few female voices, but the vast majority of the patrons were men.

The conversation in the room immediately dropped in volume as she saw several pairs of eyes swivel to look at her. She heard a whistle or two, and she heard someone say, "Surf naked!" and snicker.

She *felt* naked, and the realization came to her that she very nearly was. In the frigid air conditioning and her soaking wet pajamas, she was showing off her wares to a room full of men. She folded her arms across her breasts.

It was too late to turn back.

She took a step toward the bar.

A patron in a Red Man hat rose from the nearest table and interposed himself. His grease-stained t-shirt stretched over an ample belly.

"Hey, beautiful. You look a little worse for wear and tear. Like you been rode hard 'n' put away wet, so to speak."

His tablemates greeted this comment with a chorus of ribald laughter.

May as well get right to it, Kate thought. "I'm looking for someone," she said to the man.

Red Man revealed every one of his yellow and somewhat haphazardly arranged teeth. "Here I am," he declared, spreading his palms. His breath wafted into her face. It smelled of beer and sausage and ashtrays and tooth decay.

"I'm looking for a *particular* someone," she said. "My husband. His name is—"

"We got an extra seat here," he said, "if you're lookin' for some comp'ny. Well, not really, I guess, but you could sit on my lap. I'll give ya somethin' to surf on."

More laughter.

Now she'd had enough of this clown. How dare he? A red tide of indignant anger rose up from somewhere within her, carrying away any lingering shreds of apprehension and self-doubt like so much sea-wrack. "If you're not going to help me," she said, "then please get out of my way."

Red Man's smile disappeared. "Or what?"

In a voice only he could hear, she said, "Or I'll make you sorry you were born a male."

The man stared at her for a long second, and then broke into raucous laughter. "She's a sassy one, she is!" he said.

But he sat down.

There, Kate thought. *That wasn't so hard, was it?* Emboldened by her success, she moved on toward the bar. As she passed, she could feel the men's eyes on her backside, and she hoped her wet pajamas weren't as stuck to her skin as they felt.

A single empty barstool beckoned to her. She took it. Men in jeans and t-shirts occupied all the other seats. Some wore baseball caps. Most had facial hair in one form or another, and most smoked. Some were busy talking among themselves, but the ones who could see her stopped what they were doing to check her out.

The bartender turned to face her, smiled, and approached. His face was long and drawn, the eyes dark under a heavy brow ridge and a high forehead.

"How can I help yuz?" he asked.

"I'm looking for somebody. I was wondering if you'd seen him."

The bartender shrugged. "'Pends who it is," he replied.

"My husband. Tim Raither. He's tall, dark hair—"

The bartender's eyes grew wide. "You're Timmy's wife?" he said, grinning. "Damn, he did all right, didn't he?"

"You know him?"

"Know him? Fuckin' A, I know him, he owes me two hundred bucks. He left an open tab here."

She heard laughter behind her. A glissando of alarm rolled up her spine. Craning her neck around to look, she found a group of men now standing between her and the door, staring and grinning like hungry hyenas. Other men, and one woman, hastily exited the building, casting worried glances behind them. The pool players abandoned their game and leaned on their cues to watch.

She turned back to the bartender. "Look, uh … are those guys gonna give me any trouble?"

The bartender snorted, seemed to consider the question. "Trouble?" He took a drag from his cigarette and balanced it carefully on the edge of an ashtray. "It depends on what yuz mean by 'trouble.' I won't let nothin' happen to yuz in this here bar, but I can't say what might happen when yuz leave. In the parkin' lot, I mean. Yuz unnerstand what I'm sayin'? Is yer car parked close?"

"Not especially," she said.

"Then yuz better haul ass when you walk out that door."

Garth Brooks stopped singing, and the inevitable Lynryd Skynyrd song came on. "Gimme Three Steps." *Apropos.*

"Look, lady, the cops have already been here," the bartender continued. "I'll tell yuz the same thing I tol' them. I ain't seen Timmy in a coupla years now. But I'll be keepin' an eye out for him, and so will ever'body in this here bar. If we see him, we'll let the cops know. Y'hear?"

Kate nodded.

"Here," the bartender said, placing a shot glass on the bar before her. "On the house. Captain Morgan. Timmy's favorite."

"Thanks," she said. She downed the shot without a second thought. Liquid courage. "And thanks for your help. I'd best be moving on."

Red Man spoke from inches behind her right ear. "Hey, sugarplum," he said. "I gotta better idea. Howzabout I make you glad you were born a female?" As he spoke, his hand caressed her back, and moved down toward her butt. His fingers found the waistband of her pajamas, and slipped under it.

Shocked, she spun on her barstool to face him, pushing his hand away in the process.

"Whassamatter?" he asked. "Don'tcha like me?"

"Look," she said. "I'm sorry I threatened you earlier. I'm just going to leave now, and I'll not bother you anymore. Deal?"

"Oh, she'll not bother me anymore," the man said, and let out a loud guffaw. "Didja hear that, Sam?" he asked, turning to his compatriot. "She'll not bother me anymore."

He turned back to Kate. "Woman," he said. "It's too late. Y'already got me bothered."

"I can think of a coupla things she could do to take care of that, Buck," Sam said.

"Me and Sam, we think you oughta come out to the truck with us. We'll make it worth your while. Are ya hearin' me?"

"I hear you, but I'm not interested."

"Oh, you're not interested. Well *you* say that, but *they* say different," he said, indicating her breasts with one thick, dirty finger.

She looked all around her, and she saw too many men. Some wanted to hurt her, and others wanted to watch. None would stand up for her. She was trained in self-defense, but all the martial arts training in the world wouldn't get her out of this. Could this really be happening?

She was paralyzed with dread.

A pair of iron hands grabbed her upper arms and pinned them to her sides. Somehow, Sam had slipped behind her. Her legs were free, but the stool she was sitting on was between her and her attacker. She was helpless. Buck, with a big yellow-toothed grin, reached out and seized her breasts in two meaty fists. He squeezed hard, eliciting a squeak of pain from her. That brought more intensity to her struggling, but Sam only clamped down on her all the harder. She lashed out at Buck with a foot, but from her position on the barstool, the kick was awkward and feeble. It glanced off Buck's shin. He laughed at her and moved to her side, where she couldn't try for another. Then one hand slid down her belly to her pants.

It was happening. Unbidden, a scream ripped through her throat.

"Hey, Buck!" the bartender yelled. "Getcher hands offa her. I don't want no trouble in here. Besides, that's Timmy Raither's wife."

"So?" Buck responded. "Timmy Raither's an asshole. He owes me fifty bucks. I figure I might settle up with him right here."

"Buck, get outta here. You, too, Sam. Take your shit outside. I mean it."

Buck grinned. "You heard the man, woman. We're takin' our shit outside. And you're our shit. Bring 'er, Sam."

"Sorry I'm late, Kate," came a familiar voice from the door. She saw his gleaming shaven head first, over the crowd.

Brian. All six feet, seven inches of him. His tank top bared the tattoo of Bluto on his massive right bicep, and that of Wile E. Coyote on his left. The men standing in his path parted to let him through and he emerged from the crowd like a two hundred seventy pound Moses. She knew his fierce appearance and current demeanor belied his essentially peaceful spirit, but that was okay. Right now she needed fierceness. Despite her misgivings about the man, she'd never been so glad to see him.

He stopped in front of them, his gaze taking in the scene from beneath lowered eyebrows, his entire body radiating menace. "You wanna back off a bit, dudes," he said to Buck and Sam.

Sam released her arms and she slid down off the barstool. With one hand, Buck shoved her back into Sam's chest as he turned to face Brian. "Why? Is she yours?" he asked.

Quick as a rattlesnake, Brian's fist lashed out, and Buck fell to the floor, bleeding from the nose. At the same time, Kate planted her heel in Sam's groin, doubling him over in pain.

"Anybody else got any stupid questions?" Brian asked.

"Here, now!" the bartender called out. "No fightin'! This is a civilized place, goddammit!"

Sam backed up with one hand clutching his crotch, the other extended, palm out, toward Brian. "We don't want no trouble, man," he wheezed. All those watching became strangely still.

"Come on, Kate, we're leaving," Brian said, and he took her hand and led her out the door. No one stood in their way.

Outside the building, Brian said, "Get in my SUV, quick. I sucker-punched that guy, but in a few seconds they'll figure out which three or four of 'em is gonna come after us. Hurry up."

They got into Brian's black Escalade. He started it up and got them out of there in a spray of gravel, just as the posse came boiling out the door looking for blood.

Amanda's eyes snapped open. It was almost fully dark in Lindsey's room.

"Oh, no! We fell asleep! Lindsey, wake up!" she said, shaking her sister's shoulder.

Lindsey moaned something about being left alone.

"Lin, we have to get up."

"I'm tired, Manda. We'll work on it in the morning. I can't think straight when I'm this tired."

Amanda looked at Lindsey's alarm clock. It wasn't even nine yet, but she supposed her sister was probably right. Maybe they should take their father's advice. It had been a long and stressful day, and they were both exhausted. They'd do better in the morning, fresh and rested. "Let's get up at seven, okay?"

"Okay," Lindsey said.

Amanda set the alarm, then climbed into the top bunk and lay down, clutching her stuffed unicorn to her side. The rain had started again. She lay there on her back and stared at the ceiling three feet above her and listened to the storm while her mind raced.

"Whew! My hand hurts," Brian said.

"Why'd you hit him in the face?" Kate asked. "Faces are hard."

"I know. I'm not a fighter. It was instinct. I wanted to break his face."

"Well, you did."

"Yeah. I did. I just hope I didn't break my hand, too."

"Thanks for rescuing me," Kate said, without a trace of sarcasm.

"No charge," Brian replied as he drove. "You kinda held your own, I noticed."

"Anybody can kick a guy in the nuts. Did Selena call you?"

"Yeah."

I'll kill her, she thought.

"And it's a good thing, too," Brian continued. "Not to put too fine a point on it, but what the fuck were you doin' in there, alone, dressed like that?"

"Looking for Tim," she replied, as if speaking to a child. "I've checked all the roads. There's nowhere else to look but the bars."

"So you decided it would be a good idea to go into the seediest backwoods joint in the county—*by yourself*—and stage your own personal wet t-shirt contest."

"I wasn't thinking about what I had on. And it seemed like as good a place to start as any."

"Jesus Christ. That was a bonehead move, Kate. You shoulda called me. I'm only five minutes away, you know."

"I thought I could handle it."

"Handle it? What I saw when I came in, was that you 'handling' it, Bunny Buns?"

"Brian," she said, "I know crassness is hardwired into you, but could you possibly refrain from calling me 'Bunny Buns?' I don't like it."

"Sure. If you can refrain from bein' stupid."

They were quiet for moment.

"All right, you have a point," Kate said. "I was pretty scared there toward the end. I'll be more careful from now on."

"Damn right, you will. And you shoulda told me sooner how serious things were gettin'. Me and Darryl coulda been helpin' you."

A few raindrops spattered on Brian's windshield as they traveled. Then, ahead, they saw the wavefront of the coming downpour, marching across the landscape to meet them head-on. It was sharply delineated and clearly visible, kicking up spray on the road surface. It hit them like the fall of a guillotine, and visibility plummeted to near zero. Brian flicked his wipers up to high.

"So where are we going?" Kate asked.

"I'm takin' you home."

"No. I don't want to go home. I have to keep looking."

"Not your house, Bun—uh, Kate. My house. We're meeting Darryl there. Me and Darryl'll take over the barhoppin' from here. You can get a shower and put on some dry clothes. I have some extra stuff there that'll probably fit you. Don't worry, I washed it. Once you're cleaned up, you can come out with us, or stay at my house, or we can take you home. Your choice. Look, here we are now." He pulled into his driveway and put the car in park.

"I don't want to be here, Brian. Take me back to my car, please."

"No way."

"Why not?"

"In the first place, there's about a dozen guys there that want to kill us. Second, I don't trust you. I don't think you're thinkin' clear. How do I know you won't make another mistake like the last one? Tim would never forgive me if I let you get hurt. No fuckin' way. Darryl and I will take it from here. I'm in control now. Relax and enjoy it."

Brian had a long history of choosing exactly the wrong thing to say to women. That one was his crowning achievement.

Kate gripped her keys tightly in her right fist.

Amanda thought about her Daddy, trapped somewhere, helpless, or maybe even dead. She teared up at the idea that she might never see him again.

Daddy, she thought. *Daddy, Daddy, Daddy, where are you? Don't leave me, I love you!*

She'd seen TV shows and movies in which people said that they could somehow feel that their loved ones were still alive, and wondered if there was anything to it. She decided to try it herself. She closed her eyes and she concentrated as hard as she could on feeling her Daddy's ... life force ... or soul ... or something. She wasn't sure what to call it.

Nothing. She couldn't find him. She fought the beginnings of panic and settled herself, making an effort to remain calm and keep her mind open, and concentrated some more. She tried to think about everything that was "Daddy" to her at the same time and smash it all together in a big ball of the essence of Daddy-ness. The look of his face, the sound of his voice, his laughter, the way his hand felt when it held hers, the roughness of his cheek when he kissed her, the dirt under his nails, the smell of his cologne, even the smell of his breath when he belched *(nasty!)*. She felt that if she thought about all these things really really hard, she would be able to feel her Daddy, and maybe even hear his thoughts, and maybe he could hear hers, too.

She wasn't in Lindsey's room anymore. She was in some secret place behind her eyelids. She had no eyes, no ears, no body. She was just a point floating in nothingness, a bright speck in the darkness. At times she seemed to be moving so fast that it scared her, at other times she was perfectly still. Sometimes her secret place seemed like a tiny closet, and sometimes it seemed as huge as space itself.

Another speck winked into existence, the only other thing in her world that wasn't black. The point of light grew no larger, yet she felt rather than saw that it was coming nearer, drawn to her.

A sound came from it, but it wasn't really a sound. A thought, she guessed. Her secret place had no sound.

"*To strive, to seek*," it said.

Daddy?

"*To find, and not to yield*," it continued.

Now I know you're Daddy. Are you telling me not to give up?

Don't assume that everything I say is symbolic, it said. *Sometimes I mean exactly what I say!*

Brian moved as fast as he could make his bear-like frame go, and still Kate kept a good lead on him as she fled along the shoulder of Orenzo Mill Road, hellbent for Friar Tuck's. His lungs labored and his legs burned and the rain stung his face, forcing him to squint. He could barely see where he was going.

If he was gaining ground on her, it was so little as to be unnoticeable. But he wasn't about to give up. Though she was quick, he knew that sooner or later her footwear would betray her. Flip-flops were not good for running, even in dry weather.

She'd bolted from the car as soon as it had come to a stop in his driveway. He didn't know if she'd been planning her escape from the git-go, or if something he'd said had set her off. Either way, she was gone and it was not a good situation.

He watched as she stumbled and lost one flip-flop. She stopped to retrieve it and went on running with it in her hand. Then she thought better of it, probably after having come down on the sharp pea-gravel of the shoulder, and put it back on. She continued her flight, but at a slower pace. Brian closed to within twenty feet of her.

"Kate!" he called. "Slow down, will ya? I just wanna talk to you!"

She ignored him.

"Kate, please stop! Why're you runnin' like this?"

They pounded on.

Ten feet.

She stopped and whirled on him. He skidded to a halt to avoid bowling her over.

"Back off, Brian!" she said. "I don't want to hurt you."

Brian extended his hand to her and said, "Come on, Kate. Come back to the house with me. Whatever I said, I'm sorry. Just come back with me. It's rainin' like a bitch. Let's go back and dry off, then we can talk. Okay?"

For a second, he thought she was going to acquiesce. Then she spun and took off away from him again.

"Shit!" he said, and resumed pursuit. This time she had less of a head start on him, and the end result was a foregone conclusion. The distance closed to eight feet … six … another few steps and he'd …

He reached out and put his hand on her bouncing shoulder.

She did a quick ninety to the right and jumped into the grass on the side of the road. As he flew past her, she dropped her keys in the grass and assumed a stance that could only mean one thing: she was a practitioner of some martial art or other.

That could be a problem. He was more than double her weight, had a foot and a half of height on her, and a much longer reach. All that notwithstanding, he had never been much of a fighter. Even in the days when he'd been a bouncer, his imposing physical presence alone had usually been enough to deter violence. When forced to fight, he could, but if he didn't score an incapacitating blow in the first few punches, he was out of his depth.

If Kate was trained, it worried him.

Besides that, he didn't think he could bring himself to raise a hand against Kate in any case, even to defend himself.

A car whizzed by behind him, launching a sheet of water onto his back.

He kept his attention on Kate.

"I told you once, Brian, I don't want to hurt you. But if you make me, I will. Now please leave me alone. You did what you had to do. Let me do what I have to do."

"But what you think you have to do is gonna get you hurt. Be reasonable, Kate. There's a better way to go about this." He took a step toward her and extended his hand again. "Just come back with me." He took another step. "I promise—"

In a blur of motion, she punched him once in the ribs, once in the solar plexus, knocking the breath out of him. Then she delivered a spin kick that split his lower lip before he could react to the punches.

"Ow!" he cried. "Jesus ..." He staggered backward, belatedly raising his hands before his face in self-defense, and reopened his eyes, which had slammed shut with the blow to his face. He expected to see her coming at him with another attack out of a Jackie Chan movie, but instead, he saw she was face down in the grass, struggling to get up from the slippery surface. Her legs were toward him. She must have lost her footing when she launched that kick at him.

Brian reacted without conscious thought, using his best attribute to its greatest advantage; he dropped his entire weight on top of her, pinning her legs to the ground.

She tried without success to pick herself up with her arms. She screamed and began hailing him with a flurry of slaps to his head, but because she was face down and dealing the slaps behind her back, they were no more than annoying. She screamed again in frustration.

Brian got one of Kate's wrists in each of his hands and stopped her from slapping. He then clamped them together in his left hand.

She was immobilized. He waited as she struggled fruitlessly for a moment, growling like an animal. When she gave up, he said, "I don't wanna hurt you either. If I let you go, are you gonna be nice?"

"Yes!"

Brian let go and she commenced flailing at him again.

"Damn it!" he said, and reclamped her wrists. "Now I know I can't trust you. Now we play my way."

He got his right arm between Kate and the ground, and squeezed her thighs tight together, keeping his left hand clamped on her wrists. Then he got his legs under him and heaved her up like a bag of cement. He let go of her hands as he threw her over his shoulder, head and arms behind him and legs hanging down in front of him. She snarled wordlessly and tried to kick him, feebly slapping his midsection with the tops of her feet. She punched at his kidneys with her fists as he set off for home. But for an occasional wince, he disregarded the blows and hoped he wouldn't piss blood in the morning.

She stopped pummeling him and reached up with both hands to snatch the waistband of her pajama pants. Turning his head to the right, he saw nothing but bare skin. Her own weight hanging over his shoulder was pulling her out of her pants.

"Brian, stop!" she yelled. "My pants are coming off!"

"Hold onto them. I'm not stoppin' until I get inside." He was enjoying the respite from the rabbit punches, and he had no intention of giving her another chance at him. He was lucky to have escaped their first encounter with nothing more than a bloody lip.

On top of that, he had to admit that it was kind of fun to be carrying a half-naked woman buns-up over his shoulder. He couldn't help himself: he took another peek. A long one.

As Brian trudged on through the rain, Kate kept a death-grip on her pants and screamed at him, "Bastard! Prick! Let me go, you son of a bitch! Big stupid asshole!" Then she repeated herself for a while, until at last she either got bored with it or just ran out of names (Brian didn't care which), and held herself to occasional inarticulate growls the rest of the way.

Another car passed them as they neared the house. It slowed, and Brian saw its two occupants staring at them through the windows, as if wondering whether they should interfere, or maybe call the police. Kate managed a weak "Help me," but the car picked up speed again and was gone. Brian walked on, his drenched shoes scattering runoff water all around.

Minutes later, home at last, Brian muscled his human bundle through the sliding glass door, which he had, thankfully, left unlocked. He sidled past the dining room table, into the living room, and bent over, dropping Kate onto his leather couch with a loud *slap!* and a spray of water. Then he backed away from her a few steps, keeping himself between her and the still-open sliding glass door.

Kate immediately yanked her pants up, and was off the couch and coming at him, like a feral cat. He held his ground, palms forward, intent on keeping her from getting past him, even as a part of him couldn't help but notice the quivering motions under the wet t-shirt. Captivated, he failed to notice that she'd raised her arm until the slap came across his face, hard. His head whipped to the right under the blow, and the sting was like a sudden drop into icy cold water.

"I hate you," Kate said. "You bastard."

"Kate—"

"Fucking no-neck Neanderthal! Get out of my way."

"No."

"Let me go, I said!"

"No."

"So, what, am I kidnapped now? This is the twenty-first century, mister! Didn't you get the memo? You can't carry women off to your cave and have your way with them anymore."

Brian felt a twinge of remorse. But, aside from the slap, at least her attack was only verbal, at this point. He could deal with the guilt, as long as she didn't start wailing on him again.

"Kate, listen to me. I'm just trying—"

"And you're supposed to be Tim's best friend. You disgust me. You're no better than those barbarians you rescued me from."

Brian noticed that her left eye didn't look at him. Tim had once told him that he could always tell when Kate had been drinking by that lazy eye, before slurred speech or any other symptom had a chance to set in. The eye was always the first thing to go.

"What kind of friend would I be if I let you go back into a bar lookin' like that?" he said. "Look at yourself! If I let you do that, and you ended up gettin' hurt, which you would, Tim would never forgive me. I'm doin' you a favor!"

Kate froze, stared at him with her good eye as if she'd forgotten who he was. "All right," she said in a barely audible voice.

"What?"

"I said, all right! I get it, okay?"

"So ... you're not mad at me?"

"Oh, I'm still mad. But I believe you that you were just trying to help."

"I was."

Kate nodded. Brian watched, amazed, as she seemed to wilt like a day-old hibiscus bloom; the feral cat became a terrified little girl. "I'm scared," she said. She sniffed and wiped her nose with the back of her hand. "God, I'm so scared. Where is he? Brian, *where is he?* What if he's ... what if something bad happened?"

"Let's just take it one step at a time, Kate. He can't be far. We'll find him."

"We?"

"Me and Darryl," he said, "and you, if you want. But we need to get cleaned up, and you need to put some real clothes on. By that time, Darryl should be here and the three of us can go back out."

Kate wrapped her arms around herself, shivering. Her eyes darted all over the room, as if searching for escape.

"You cold?" Brian asked. "Sorry. I keep the A/C up high in here." He handed her a throw blanket from the basket beside the couch. "Here."

Kate drew the throw around her shoulders. Brian watched her sniffle for a bit, wondering what to do. He noted with alarm that she wiped her nose on his throw.

"I'm sorry about the way I acted," she said. "It's just that I want him so bad, I feel like I have to do something, anything ... and I guess maybe I haven't been thinking straight."

Brian expelled a lungful of air. "That's the most sensible thing I've heard you say all day."

"Yeah. Sensible. That's me."

Brian gently probed his swollen lip with his finger. "Jesus, Kate. What was that hai-yah stuff you pulled on me back there on the road?"

"Taekwondo."

"I've never had that done to me before."

"I'm way out of practice."

"You coulda fooled me. You ain't gonna use it on me any more, are you?"

Kate regarded him for a moment, then said, "I'm not planning to."

Brian nodded and said, "I guess that'll have to do."

"I'm all right now," Kate said. "Really. I'll do it your way. I promise to behave." Her eyes still refused to settle on him, or anything else.

Brian lowered his eyebrows. What was behind this sudden change of heart? She'd already given him reason to mistrust her. Why should this time be any different?

"So where're these clothes you talked about?" she asked. "I'll change, so we can get going."

"Settle down," he said. "We can't go yet."

"Why not?"

"I told you, we have to wait for Darryl. And we both need to clean up. We're covered with mud and grass and God knows what else. I smell like an elephant. And you look like hell."

She sighed. "You said something about a shower earlier?"

"Yeah. You want one?"

"Since we're stuck here for the time being. Like you said, I'm a mess. I feel like I haven't bathed in days."

"There's no window in there, in case you were—"

"No window? You think I'm trying to escape?"

"Crossed my mind."

"Well, it crossed *my* mind that you might try to leave without me while I'm in there. I'm warning you, I *will* walk back to my car if you're not here when I get out."

Brian doubted that she'd ever be able to find her keys out there in the grass, but kept that to himself. "Looks like we got each other over a barrel," he said. "I promise I'll be here."

"All right," she said. She got up from the couch, taking the throw with her, and headed back into the hallway. "Where do you keep towels?"

"In the closet right across the hall from the bathroom. The bathroom's on the left. There's some girly shampoo in there, and some body wash, too."

"What about the clothes?"

"Right back here," he said.

As Brian guided her back the hallway to the spare bedroom, she said, "Are you telling me that you actually held onto one girl long enough for her to leave clothes behind?"

"Yeah, Cassie. She lived here more or less permanently for a while," he said as he opened the last door on the left for her. "There's some clothes in the closet here, and some more in the top two drawers of that dresser."

"Thanks. And by 'permanently,' you mean …"

"A couple weeks."

"Hm. That a record for you?"

"Pretty much. Cassie was somethin' else."

Kate sighed, shaking her head. "Okay," she said, "let's have a look at your souvenir collection." She opened the top dresser drawer and began rummaging.

Brian leaned against the doorjamb and watched as she went through the drawer, discarding items as fast as she could pick them up.

"No … no … no … *definitely* no," Kate said, as she shifted unwanted items to the left side of the drawer.

Seeing Kate from the rear made him think of Cassie, the hot little number who had last worn those clothes. Cassie'd been small, like Kate. So small, he had once picked her up by the armpits, settled her onto himself as she wrapped her arms and legs around him, and walked around the house with her while doin' the nasty. Now *that* was something he wouldn't mind doing again …

Stop it!

"These would probably fit," Kate said, eyeing a couple of tops, "but they're not much improvement over what I have on now. Didn't your girlfriend ever wear anything that covered her midriff?"

"She had a flat tummy. They looked good on her. They'd look good on you, too." *Maybe* too *good,* he thought.

Kate shot him an evil glare over her shoulder—was she a mind reader?—but she turned back to the dresser and continued without comment.

At last she said, "All right. I guess these jeans'll do. And this top, though it's a bit short for my taste. And low cut," she added, looking at the garment dubiously. "Never mind, it'll do."

"Underwear and bras in the next drawer down," Brian said.

"I'll not wear anybody else's underwear," she said. "I don't care if you washed it or not. I'll do without, if you don't mind." She turned to face him, and the throw parted in the middle like a cape.

If he didn't mind? Brian swallowed. He'd already seen more of his best friend's sexy wife this night than he'd ever hoped to, and the thought of her in those low-cut jeans without underwear gave him the squirmies.

Finding a spot on the ceiling to study, he forced himself to think about dead skunks, maggots, the day he severed the tip of his left middle finger on a table saw …

"But what about … you know, your boobs?" Brian said. "You need to put something else on 'em besides that top, or you're gonna drive me and Darryl and everybody else crazy."

"You could look somewhere else."

"Well … I mean … ," he said, as his eyes dropped back to her chest, where the still-wet shirt clung to her, as transparent as gauze.

Something about Kate's posture, or the set of her jaw, or some other subtle cue, tipped him off: the feral Kate was back. She was drawn as tight as a winch cable, and he had enough experience with those things to know you didn't want to be around one when it snapped. "You know what?" she said, drawing the blanket closed in front of her, "I'm leaving. Right now. I'm not in the mood for this game. I could beat you senseless right now and walk out of here smiling. Is that what you want?"

"No, not really. Chill out, Kate. I'm tryin' to help, honest. I just want you to cover up some, is all."

"For my sake or yours?"

"Both. Does it matter?"

Their eyes met for a long instant; then Kate said, "What do you suggest, then? And this better not be sexual in nature."

Brian let out the breath he'd been holding. "How 'bout a big sweatshirt? It's not that hot out since the storm, and it'll cover you up so you don't look so damn fuck-me gorgeous."

Kate gave him a lazy-eyed stare and for a moment he thought he was in for a thrashing. Then, "Brian," she said, "you just can't help yourself, can you? Even at a time like this, can't you for one minute stop thinking about sex?"

"Believe me, if you knew how hard I'm tryin'. I'm not used to this, but I'm doin' the best I can."

She considered that. "Fine. Get me a sweatshirt. That should help you keep your mind off my body."

"And everybody else's mind, too. I mean, we're goin' clubbin', sort of."

"Whatever. I'm going to the shower. Can I trust you not to barge in on me?"

"Yeah. Yeah, believe me, I don't wanna mess with you."

"Good. And I'm parched," she said. "Do you have a soda I could have?"

"I got Diet Coke."

"Perfect. I'll get it when I come out. Ten minutes."

She advanced toward him, ostensibly on her way to the bathroom. He held his position.

Kate lifted her eyebrows. "Excuse me?" she said.

Warily, Brian moved aside to allow her to pass, and watched as she went back up the hallway. She stopped at the bathroom door, and he was afraid she was about to make for one of the house's two exit points, but she turned her gaze back to him.

"Ten minutes," she said again, then slipped into the bathroom and closed the door behind her. Brian heard the lock being engaged and sighed, draining the tension from his body.

No bra ... no underwear. God help me.

He heard the shower start up as he went back to the kitchen, trying to think about blood, pain, coffins, vomit, nails on the chalkboard. He got two Cokes out of the pantry. They were warm, so he got two glasses and filled them with ice.

Thinking about pain was easiest, as his hand throbbed with it. Open gashes adorned the second knuckles of two swollen fingers. Teeth had done that. He flexed his fist experimentally, and grimaced.

He took an ice pack from the freezer and held it against his wounded hand as he walked to the master bath. Rooting in the medicine cabinet for some painkillers, he noticed a small cardboard box, and an idea occurred to him.

He opened the box and withdrew a little white pill in a blister pack. "Hello, little roofie," he said to it, smiling as if addressing an old friend.

Roofies. Give a woman one pill and she'd pass out in a half hour. She'd sleep like a stone for six to eight hours, and during that time you could do whatever you wanted to her. When she woke up, she'd have no memory of what happened while she was out. It dissolved easily and had no taste and no odor.

It was illegal in the states, but Brian had picked up ten of them when he was in Europe the previous year. He had nine left.

Oh, yeah. This'll definitely do the trick.

He took the pill into the kitchen, ground it up with a spoon, and dumped it over the ice in one of the glasses. He poured Diet Coke over it, swirled it with the spoon. Then he poured the other glass, this one sans powder. He made sure he knew which one was which. It wouldn't do to knock *himself* out.

10

The rain has stopped. Total darkness reigns in the well, but outside his tiny round window, the flashing of lightning has been replaced by lightning bugs blinking in synchronized precision. Tim doesn't mind the lightning bugs, but he can't concentrate with the katydids battering his eardrums.

He can remember many late-summer camping trips, and how the katydid and cricket songs would lull him to sleep each night, and how he treasured that racket. But now this aural assault is driving him to the brink of madness. Their stridulating cries are magnified in his enclosure, and they seem to him as loud as a passing freight train. *Katy did, Katy didn't. Katy did, Katy didn't. Katy did, Katy didn't.*

Hundreds of individual insect songs work in concert. Insects in phase resonate, amplify one another; those out of phase interfere with each other. The net volume oscillates in a shifting, sinuous rhythm, exhibiting aspects of both order and chaos. Under the right mental conditions, the modulations can bear an eerie similarity to human speech.

Tim begins to think he can hear words disguised in the rhythm of the night, anonymous voices murmuring just below the threshold of hearing, whispering secrets.

He imagines he can recognize occasional phrases. He feels the voices are speaking either to him or about him, or both. His interest piqued, he concentrates on trying to determine the speakers' identities, and individual voices emerge from the muddle. He hears Lindsey and Amanda laughing. He hears Kate whispering "I love you." He hears Amanda calling "Daddy, where are you?" Once he is certain that he hears his mother and father, talking about him like he's not there, saying, "He'll never be the same, never be the same, never be the same, never be the same." And then Kate saying, "No no, yes yes, no no, yes yes, I love you, I love you, I love you." Then Amanda, "Daddy? Daddy? Daddy?" He hears a strange voice (could that be his own?) saying, "'To strive, to seek, to find, and not to yield.'" He hears his brother Greg with mocking laughter in his voice, saying, "Lassie, come quick! Timmy fell in a well, fell in a well, fell in a well!"

He is so very tired, but each time he begins to drift off, another voice comes to him and jerks him awake.

Amanda opened her eyes and sat bolt upright in her bed. "Huh? Daddy?" She spun her head around, searching for the source of the voice, for now it seemed that she'd heard an actual sound. She was back in Lindsey's room. The rain had stopped, and in the resulting quiet, she could hear the ceiling fan's hum as it whirled without end. Below her, Lindsey slept on. The room was dimly lit by the red glow from Lindsey's clock numerals: 9:21 PM.

No one else was in the room.

Thirty minutes had passed. Amanda was confused. Had she heard a voice or not? Had Daddy come to her in her secret place, or had she fallen asleep and dreamed the entire thing?

He said he meant exactly what he said. What was he talking about?

She lowered her head into her hands, thinking. They were supposed to sleep on it ... that was the last thing he said in the last clue. Is that what he was talking about that wasn't symbolic? Sleeping on it?

Ah! I'm so stupid! She lifted her pillow to see what her father had left under it ...

Nothing. *Darn it, I was so sure I was right.*

Then she remembered where she was.

She thought about waking Lindsey up, but decided she'd make sure she was right first. She climbed down from the bunk, tiptoed across the floor, and went back to her own bedroom.

Katy did, Katy didn't, Katy did, Katy didn't, Katy did, Katy didn't.

As disturbing as sleep has become to him, he finds it is still preferable to constant pain. It is his only refuge. So he keeps trying to go there. He closes his eyes.

I'm not sure how this keeps happening, but here I am again, back on bus 562, on the way home from Slate Ridge High.

It's raining today, again. They say it's been one of the rainiest Mays on record, but who cares about all those other Mays? I only care about this one, and this one sucks, that's all I know.

I'm the first one on the bus, 'cause my sixth period classroom is real close to the school's front door. I sit in my usual seat, five rows back on the right. A few kids come in and head for the back, an area forbidden to freshmen like me. One of 'em is my brother Randy, who walks right by like he doesn't know me, nose buried in a book. Then Paula comes in, and I get up so she can take her regular window seat next to me, where she can ignore me all the way home.

Who understands girls?

Lynch boards the bus next. He sits in the second seat behind the driver, Mr. What's-his-name.

Ten minutes later, and all the seats have students in them except the second seat on the right, because that seat belongs to the only seniors, Alan Curtis and my brother Greg, and everybody knows it. Alan and Greg could sit in the back if they wanted, but from there it would be so much harder to torment Lynch.

Greg and Alan come swaggering onto the bus, and they both bitch-slap Lynch on the back of the head before sitting down. My brother's always had a mean streak, but I'm surprised every time Alan does something like that. He's not near as cruel as Greg.

Lynch doesn't do a thing about the bitch-slaps. He just stares out the window. Kind of like Paula.

I frown. Why don't they leave him alone? It's not his fault he's that way. He can't help it.

Once the bus starts moving, that's when the real fun starts.

"You know what I heard?" Greg asks Alan, loud enough for Lynch to hear. "I heard Lincoln was an alien."

That gets a response from Lynch. "Abraham Lincoln was the sixteenth president of the United States. He was born on February 12, 1809 and he assumed office on March 4, 1861. He freed the slaves. He died on April 15, 1865 after being shot in the head by John Wilkes Booth. He was a great man."

"He was an alien," Greg insists.

"No he was not."

"Yes, he was. He came from the planet Wonk."

"There's no such planet, Greg Raither."

"There ain't?" Alan says. "Then where do them wonks come from?"

"They don't come from anywhere. They're just here."

"Where?" Greg asks, snickering.

"Here. All around us."

Greg looks around with his eyes all goggled out like he's shocked or something. "You mean they're on this bus with us?" he asks.

"Yes."

"Where?"

"I told you. All around us."

"Oh, yeah?" Greg says. "Well, *hot dog*, you fuckin' wonks! Go away!"

"Stop it!" Lynch screams. I mean, he *screams*.

"Why?" Greg says. "Don't you want 'em to go away? Hot dog, hot dog, hot dog!"

Now Alan joins in with Greg, hollering, "Hot dog, hot dog, hot dog!"

"Stop it!" Lynch says. "You don't understand. They don't go away. You'll just make them angry. They're very dangerous. They set fires, you idiots!"

Uh-oh. Now he's done it.

"Who're you callin' idiots, you fuckin' looney tune?" Greg says.

"You two! You're idiots if you mess around with wonks. You don't understand. They're bad. They'll burn your house down!"

"You don't get to call anybody an idiot," Greg says. "Especially me and my buddy. Take it back, or I'll shove your teeth down your throat." Greg stands up, and looks for all the world like he's ready to make good on it.

Somethin' snaps in Lynch. My old pal jumps up out of his seat and hollers, "Leave me the heck alone!" into Greg's face, and like magic I see the deer-antler knife in Lynch's right hand, and it's pointed right at my brother's throat.

Greg, for the first time in his life, is scared shitless. I can tell 'cause he's white as school paste and his eyes are big and round.

I should probably be scared too, but I'm not, at least not for myself. I'm scared for my brother, and I know exactly what I have to do.

So I start to stand up, and Paula puts a hand on my leg like she's tryin' to stop me, but I ignore her and I walk the two steps up the aisle to where Greg and Lynch are frozen in place, and I say, "Lynch, what are you *doin'*?"

"I'm gonna kill this fartsmeller," he says.

Lynch used to be able to cuss with the best of us, but since he lost his marbles, I ain't heard a single swear word come out of him. It's weird.

"No, you ain't," I say with perfect calm, if I do say so myself. "It'll make a big mess. You know how much you hate messes."

Lynch blinks and backs up a step, and I take advantage of it and wiggle right between him and Greg. "That's a nice pig-sticker," I say. "Where'd you get it?" Even though I know the answer, 'cause he told me last summer, but I just want to give him somethin' to think about besides slittin' my brother's throat.

"My father gave it to me," he says.

"Can I see it?"

"No. It's mine."

"Just for a minute, Lynch. I'll give it back to you. I just wanna check it out. You trusted me with Tennyson, remember? It's me. Timmy. Your friend."

Lynch hesitates, and for a second, I think he's gonna give it to me, but I guess right then the driver musta looked in the mirror and seen what was goin' on, 'cause all of a sudden he slams on the brakes. Me and Lynch, we both lose our balance. The knife gets knocked outta his hand and falls on the floor and I see it sittin' there with its hilt made out of bone, no it's a deer antler, and its deadly-lookin' blade and I think I gotta get to it before Lynch does, and right then, Alan, he reaches down and grabs it and—

—chucks it out the window.

Then Lynch goes totally fuckin' crackers, I mean pure batshit out of his mind. He screams, "You ... you ... snotsucker!" so loud I think his throat must start bleedin', and then he sits in his seat and puts his head in his hands and starts bawlin' like a baby.

I sit down next to him and put my arm around him and say, "It's okay, Lynch. It's just a knife." Nobody even brings up the idea of stepping off the bus to get it. Not right now.

The driver looks at me in the rearview mirror, and I wave at him to get us rollin' again. "He's okay now," I say. "Take him on home. He won't hurt nobody."

I guess even the driver knows I'm in charge now, 'cause he does what I told him, and once the bus starts movin', I look at my brother and I say, "When the fuck are you gonna grow up?" and he don't have nothin' to say back to me.

Nobody says a damn word all the way to Myrtle Drive, and once we get there, Lynch looks at me once before he stands up, and says, "'Yet all experience is an arch / Wherethrough gleams that untravell'd world, whose margin fades / For ever and ever when I move.' Thanks for being my friend, Timmy." Then he gets off the bus and drops his backpack on the ground and sticks his hands in the pockets of his old CPO jacket and starts walkin', with his head bowed down in the rain. But he don't walk toward the house at the end of Myrtle Drive where he lives with his mama. He goes back toward his knife.

And somehow I know I'm never gonna see him again.

Once he's off the bus, people start talkin', and now my brother's back to his normal self. He glares at me and I know he's gonna get even with me later for makin' him look like a pussy. But I turn around and Paula, holy shit, she smiles at me, and that makes everything worth it.

Katy did, Katy didn't. Katy did, Katy didn't. Katy did, Katy didn't.

Selena paced.

Where the hell are they? she thought. *First Tim goes missing, now Kate and Brian both.*

She knew it was a waste of time, but she dialed Kate's cellphone again, and got no answer. Then she dialed Brian's phone again. No answer.

Shit! Something must have gone wrong.

At least it had finally stopped raining. For good this time, she hoped.

The house phone rang. She checked the caller ID: Brian's house. She snatched it up. "Where the hell have you been?"

"Sorry, I've been kinda busy."

"I've been worried sick. I tried to call you. Is everything okay?"

"Yeah, it's okay now."

"Where's Kate?"

"She's here with me, in the shower. I mean, she's in the shower, not me. Sorry I took so long, but I've had my hands full. Selena, she's an emotional train wreck. I'm lucky I got her back here. She went ballistic and tried to beat the shit outta me, and she almost did."

"*What?* Why?"

"That's the thing, I dunno. I got her out of the bar and everything, which, by the way, it was just in friggin' time, but on the way to my house, somethin' I said musta pissed her off—"

"Why is she in the shower? And why are you at your house, anyway? You were supposed to bring her here."

"Yeah, but I called Darryl and he's meeting me here. I'll get her home as soon as I can. She's a real handful." He related the entire story to her and finished with, "She ain't herself, Selena. She's stressed out to the max and she's better than half ripped on rum, and she's not thinkin' straight."

"Bring her home."

"She won't let me. Aren't you listenin' to me? It's like she's possessed. I told her she could come with us, but that was just to shut her up. There's no way I'm takin' her with us. She'd be a total distraction. And I don't want responsibility for her, to be honest. I need to be able to concentrate on finding Tim. And she needs to be home, with you."

"I already said that."

"I know, and I told you she won't let me. But I got an idea. That's why I'm callin' you, because I want you to know how I'm doin' it."

"Why? How are you doing it?"

"I'm gonna give her a Rohypnol. For her own good."

"Rohypnol?"

"Yeah. It's a sedative. It'll make her sleep. It's what she needs. Also, it's what *we* need, 'cause it's the only way I can think of that I'm gonna be able to get her home. And then we won't have to worry about her for eight hours or so."

"Wait a minute. Rohypnol ... are we talking about roofies?" Every nerve in her body was on alert.

"Well ... yeah. That's the street name."

Brian had at least had the grace to come off as a bit embarrassed, and that may have bought him a few seconds' reprieve, but he had no notion of the danger he was in. He could not have known that Selena herself had once been on the wrong end of a roofie; of all the people in the world, only Kate knew this.

Brian was on very thin ice indeed.

Selena felt her pulse pounding in her temples. She had to make a concentrated effort not to scream her next words at him. "Brian ... explain to me right now, and this better be good: why do you have that shit in your house?"

"Well ... it's like ... I mean—"

"Just say it, Brian! Do you have sex with unconscious women, or not?"

"No! I never did that. I mean, I only used it once, and I didn't—I mean, I couldn't."

"So what did you do? Undress her? Don't answer that, I don't wanna know. Lowlife creep! To think I was starting to like you."

"Selena, listen to me. I never touched that other girl. I felt so bad about it that I just—"

"And now you have Kate over there—"

"—let her sleep."

"—and you think you're gonna do that to her? You don't wanna go there with me, Brian. If I could reach through this phone and choke you, I would."

"I'm not gonna hurt Kate. What do you think I am?"

"That's what worries me. She tried to warn me about you, and now I know why."

"If I was gonna rape her or something, do you think I'd be callin' you up and tellin' you about it first? Think about it!"

Selena took a moment to get her emotions in check.

"Selena? You still there?"

"All right. I'm gonna give you the benefit of doubt and assume that you meant well. But do you understand—"

"Look, you ain't here. I am, and I have to do somethin'. She's irrational and I don't want her goin' out again, and the only way I could think of to stop her was to knock her out. I figured a roofie would do the same job as a Louisville Slugger and wouldn't hurt her near as much. In fact, she could use the rest. You don't want me to do it, all right, I won't. It was a stupid idea. But I hope you have a better one, 'cause I don't."

"Just get her over here. I'll handle her. Oh my God, you're a walking disaster. I had no idea you were so morally bankrupt. It's no wonder you're still single."

"But—"

"All Kate needs is to talk to somebody who's not burdened with a ychromosome."

"Yeah, but how am I supposed to get her over there? Tie her up?"

"Put her on the phone with me when she gets out of the shower. *And don't talk to her.* For once in your life, just keep your mouth shut."

"I'll try. But Selena, I'll be honest with you, I'm scared of her. This ain't Kate over here, it's somebody else, and she scares me. I got lucky the first time. If she decides to take me out, I'm not sure I could stop her."

He paused for a moment. Selena could hear the muffled voice of her best friend on the other end. It sounded like she said, "What happened to that sweatshirt?"

"Is that Kate?" Selena said. "Let me talk to her."

"Hold on," Brian said. "I'll put you on speaker."

Selena heard a click, and then she heard Kate say, more clearly this time, "You were right about these clothes. I feel more naked than when I'm naked. Where's that sweatshirt you promised me? Come on, hurry up, I've gotta get out of here."

"There's one hangin' on the back of my bedroom door," he answered.

"Brian, shut up," Selena said. "I told you not to talk."

"Selena?" Kate said.

"Yeah, it's me. Listen, Brian's told me what's been going on, and I think you need to come home for a while. You and I need to talk. Let the boys handle the road-running for a bit while you get some rest."

"What, you too?" Kate said. "I can't come home now, Sel. There's too much work to be done. By the way, thanks for the drink, Lothario."

"Hey, where did you get that?" came Brian's voice.

"Right there on the counter. Why, wasn't it for me?"

"Not *that* one. Did you—? Oh, no."

"What is the matter with you?" Kate said. "You got any more Coke? I finished this one. I'm parched."

Selena, able to hear but not see, grew worried. "Brian," she said. "What's going on over there?"

She heard another click as Brian turned off the speakerphone. Then his voice came back on the line: "I fucked up," he said.

"Lindsey!" Amanda whispered fiercely. "Wake up!"

"Huh?"

"I found Part 2!" She stuck a half sheet of paper in Lindsey's face.

Lindsey studied it muzzily, blinked, and sat up. "Shut! Up!" Lindsey said, now fully awake. "Where was it? How did you find it?"

"Daddy told me."

"Huh?"

"I fell asleep, and I heard Daddy's voice. I dreamed it, I guess, or something ... first he just said those poetry lines that he always uses when he wants us not to give up. You know what I'm talkin' about?"

"Um ... 'To strive, to seek,'" Lindsey started.

"'To find, and not to yield,'" they finished together.

"Yeah, that," Amanda said.

"Sir Pennyworth, or somebody like that."

"Whoever. Then he said he meant exactly what he said."

"In your head."

"Yeah."

"Amanda, are you losing it on me, too?"

"I'm not! Okay, so it was a dream. Whatever, it doesn't matter, Lin. The point is, I started thinking about what he meant, and I thought maybe he meant exactly what he said when he talked about sleeping on it. He said, in the clue, that we might have to sleep on it before we found it. So I thought, how could we, you know, actually sleep *on* something? And I thought maybe—"

"Under the pillow!"

"No. Close, though." She held up Part 2. "I found this under my mattress."

Lindsey smiled. "Good job, Manda. I don't know about the dream part, but never mind that. Let's just get on it."

On the bottom half of the paper was written:

Clue # 3 (Part 2 of 2)
1 6 11 14 18 5 23 7 29 26 22 3 19 8 15 24 30 32 34
12 2 37 38 9 13 20 31 28 16 33 44 17 48 10 25 49 4
46 47 42 43 40 27 39 41 35 36 45 21

Lindsey smiled. "We so got this. All we have to do is put the letters that we already figured out in place of the numbers. I'll read you the numbers, and you read me back the right letters."

"Okay."

"One."

"N."

"Six."

"E."

After the first four letters, they knew they were right. "'Near,'" Lindsey said. "The first word is 'near.'"

After nine letters they had:

N E A R W H A R E.

"Never mind," Lindsey said. "Let's just keep going."

N E A R W H A R E J E T H R O

"Hey, look," Amanda said. "This says 'Jethro.' That was Mom-mom's cat's name. But he's dead."

"I think this A here is supposed to be E. That would make the second word 'where.'"

"'Near where Jethro.' That makes sense. But 'Near where Jethro' what?"

"Don't know yet. But where did this A come from? Hah! It's from 'arm.' Told you 'arm' was wrong."

"No you didn't. You said it didn't matter."

"Whatever. So the part of the body could be 'ear' or 'eye.' We don't have to decide yet. I'm just gonna put the E here."

"Okay, let's finish it now."

"Oh, great. The next one is twenty-four. That's from 'part of the body,' too, right?"

"Yup."

"We'll have to guess again. How about 'eye?'"

"That would make twenty-four a Y."

"Y it is, for now. Next?"

After they'd transcribed the rest of the letters, they had

N E A R W H E R E J E T H R O Y N D F L U F F Y L I E
I S A R E D B E I C K L O O K U N D E R I T

"That doesn't work," said Amanda. "Try 'ear.'"
Lindsey made the changes.

N E A R W H E R E J E T H R O A N D F L U F F Y L I E
I S A R E D B R I C K L O O K U N D E R I T

"Finally!" Lindsey said. "'Near where Jethro and Fluffy lie is a red brick. Look under it.'"

"Fluffy was Mom-mom's other cat that died."

"I know."

"What does he mean, where they lie?"

"I think it means where they're buried. Do you know where that is?"

"Yeah. I was with Poppy when he buried Fluffy. They're both behind his garage."

They locked eyes with each other.

"All we have to do—"

"—is go to Mom-mom and Poppy's house and find a red brick somewhere behind the garage!"

They high-fived each other.

"It's too late now," Lindsey said. "It's almost ten o'clock. Kate would kill us."

"Kate's not here, though."

"Well, Selena would kill us *for* Kate. I say we go back to sleep, get some rest, and get up first thing in the morning and go."

"Sleep! There's like no way I can go to sleep tonight. Let's just stay up all night."

"You're right. I don't think I can sleep, either. Wanna watch TV?"

Amanda nodded, and Lindsey turned on her television, with the volume down to a low murmur. She leaned back on the futon side by side with her sister and put on Nickelodeon. A few minutes later, she saw that Amanda was asleep. Lindsey was having a hard time staying awake herself. She fought it for a while, but soon gave up and closed her eyes.

Selena opened the back door and Brian came through, carrying Kate's inert shape. Selena did her best to wither him with her stare as she held the door. His bleeding, misshapen lip took her aback. Kate must have dealt him quite a blow. She hoped she hadn't inadvertently shown sympathy by her expression.

"Where do you want her?" he asked.

"Put her on the couch," she said.

Brian lowered Kate with an elaborate show of gentleness, probably for Selena's benefit more than Kate's, Selena thought. Darryl followed Brian through the door, having driven Kate's car behind Brian's Escalade. Small and wiry, Darryl was the opposite of Brian in more respects than one. Selena often wondered how such diverse people could remain friends for so many years.

"Hey," he said, waving. He tossed her the keys to Kate's car. "Had a bitch of a time finding these."

"Thanks," she said, snatching the keys out of the air. She liked Darryl, in spite of his many Deadhead affectations (the scraggly goatee with the single wooden bead dangling from it being the only one that really bothered her). But he was a quiet, polite man, who would do anything for anybody. He called himself a "kind" person, and Selena believed that he truly was that, if a trifle disconnected at times.

"That's some lip," she said to Brian. She let the trace of a smile play across her face.

"If you're saying that he deserved it for what he did to Kate," Darryl said in a tone sterner than any she'd ever heard from him, "maybe you should try to remember which came first."

"Well, I guess we better get movin'," Brian said. "Do you need anything else?"

"I can handle it from here," Selena said. "I think you've done enough damage for one night. Go do something positive."

At the look on Brian's face, Darryl said, "Come on, Brian. Forget about it."

"Yeah, okay. Just so you know, we're goin' to Cappie's first, then Basilone's and the Fireside. We'll let you know what we find."

"Do that," Selena said. "Now get out."

I'm on my way from English to Geometry class, and all of a sudden I see my brother Greg comin' from the other direction. "Hey, Timmy," he says, a big ol' shit-eatin' grin on his face. I know that shit-eatin' grin, and it means he's about to lay somethin' on me that he thinks'll hurt. "Didja hear?"

"Hear, what, Greg?" I say, with just a bit of I-don't-care-but-I-can't-stop-you-from-telling-me in it. I keep walkin', and he reverses himself so he can walk with me.

"I got sent to the office today."

"Whoop-ee. For what? Pickin' your nose in class?"

"I seen Freddie Karstow starin' at Colleen's ass—"

Colleen is Greg's current squeeze. They been goin' steady now for almost a month.

"—so I punched him in the mouth. Mr. Markline saw it, and he sent me straight to the office."

"So? Whaddya want, a medal?"

"I ain't done. While I was waitin' outside Mr. Kinard's office, I heard the secretaries talkin'. Guess who quit school."

That snaps me around. "Who?" I say, even though I'm pretty sure I know the answer.

"You know who," he says. "Your old buddy. Ol' Looney Tunes."

Can't say I'm surprised. It explains why I ain't seen Lynch since last week, when the whole thing with the knife went down.

A day or two after that happened, I rode my bike over to where the knife went out the bus window. No sign of it. I guess Lynch got it, or somebody else did. On the way back, I thought about stoppin' over his house, just to see how he was doin'. But I chickened out.

Anyways, I figured he was playin' hookey or pretendin' to be sick or somethin', and I was wonderin' how long he could stretch it out. Figured he had to be comin' back to school pretty soon.

Guess I was wrong.

The smartest guy I ever knew, and he can't even finish school. Lynch would come up with the right word for that, but I can't think of it.

When the men were gone, Selena settled herself on the sofa with Kate. She spent the night there, although she wasn't really needed. Kate never moved a muscle. She breathed evenly, and every once in a while let out a single snore, then lapsed back into peaceful breathing.

For a while, Selena channel-surfed and dozed. The air conditioning was blowing right on her, so she covered herself and Kate with a soft blanket from the coat closet.

Around three-thirty, Darryl called. They'd asked at all the local bars, and no one had seen Tim. They'd even met a guy at Cappie's, by the name of C.C., who claimed to have been an old drinking buddy of Tim's. He said they'd once beaten the living b'jesus out of each other over a bottle of Jack. That sounded authentic, the boys thought, so they believed him. C.C. knew all the places where the binge drinkers went to keep the party going after the bars were closed. He took Brian and Darryl out to the old abandoned slate quarries, where they asked around the local winos about Tim. No one had seen him.

Selena had a growing feeling of dread within her. No one had yet voiced the possibility that Tim might be dead, and she wasn't going to be the first, but she was beginning to think her best friend was going to be needing an awful lot of TLC in the coming weeks and months.

Brian and Darryl said they were going home to get some rest, and they'd come back out at first light.

Kate mumbled in her sleep around four or five, but said nothing intelligible.

At five-thirty, Selena rose and pulled herself together to go home. Kate opened her eyes and Selena said, "It's okay, Kate. You're home."

"Home?"

"Yeah."

"How ... Is Tim here?"

"Not yet. Go back to sleep, girlfriend. I've gotta go home for a bit. I'll call you in a couple of hours to make sure you're up, okay?"

"'Kay."

Kate closed her eyes.

Selena checked to make sure Lindsey and Amanda were all right, then quietly left the three sleeping ladies to their dreams. She hoped they were nice dreams, because reality was starting to suck.

11

SUNDAY
5:42 AM

With soft gray light seeping into the well from the opening far above him, Tim twitches in a fitful doze.

He has spent most of the night hovering at the very brink of consciousness, a human rope in the tug-of-war between the opposing forces of agony and fatigue, tormented during his short periods of feverish sleep by phantoms from a forgotten childhood. He is immersed now in a different dream, one in which he is convinced that he has been swallowed alive by Satan, and now lies at the bottom of that great infernal gullet in a vile stew of half-digested body parts.

As he emerges from the dream, he can find no evidence to dispel the notion. Except for the cold. Satan's innards should be hot, shouldn't they? At least warm.

He lifts his weary gaze toward the light, tracing the great black throat to the top, where Satan's mouth is open in a silent scream, allowing Tim tantalizing visual access to the world of light and freedom. But even were he in any shape to attempt an ascent, it would be to no avail. Before he could reach the top, the Devil would simply slam his teeth together and swallow.

Just ask Rocky Raccoon.

As Tim looks at Rocky, reality comes crashing back, banishing Satan's throat to the dreamworld from which it came.

Reality is not much of an improvement.

There is some good news: he has not drowned. Even at the height of the storm last night, the water level in the well rose no more than a couple of inches, and has now settled back down around the level of his navel.

But there is a lot of bad news.

His head is pounding. His right shoulder and arm blaze like they are on fire. His ribs send stabbing pain into him with each breath.

He can no longer feel anything in his legs. This too is bad news.

In place of the katydids, birds now provide the racket, singing with insane persistence like it's just another day.

His attention is again drawn upward, toward that unattainable freedom. As the light grows, he can now tell that what he thought last night to be trees blowing in the wind were, in fact, fern fronds hanging over the mouth of the well. This must be part of the colony of bracken that stretches between the trail and the wall.

That's how I ended up down here, he thinks. *It was hidden under the bracken. Stupid of me …*

The light from above grows as Tim contemplates his fate. The minutes pass so slowly. …

During lucid moments, he has spent a lot of time thinking about—what else?—the possibility of rescue, which seemed not quite so hopeless once he realized that his daughters might find him by following the clues. But even that shred of hope is fraught with peril, for the girls as well as for him. The second clue, for instance, would send the girls down the railroad trail, to the bridge over the swamp. By now, that would already have happened, without him there to make sure they were okay. What if the water was high after the storms? He hopes Kate had enough sense to go with them.

And that's only the first of so many things that could go wrong. He has to depend on his daughters' ingenuity, and probably the assistance of his wife, to get past them. He must have faith.

Come on, girls! Please find me today. Don't let me spend another night down here.

He hears a snapping sound from above, like sheets on a clothesline on a windy day, and the light dwindles, eclipsed.

He looks up and sees a silhouette at the well's mouth, a person's head and shoulders, and he is dizzy with relief, knowing that he's been found, that he will live after all.

"Hey!" he says. "I'm here! Help me!"

Then another silhouette joins the first one, with an identical sound of sheets snapping and rustling, and as it settles its wings, Tim understands that it is not a man, but a huge bird.

His heart thuds in his chest once, twice, three times.

Turkey vultures. Two of them, with their unerring sense of smell, have located him and his friend Rocky. Perched on the lip of the well, they are, at least temporarily, stymied by the dimensions of the vertical shaft. Though

Tim and Rocky are beyond their reach, it is not in their nature to leave good offal behind. So they sit.

And wait.

As horrific as Tim's predicament is, at least he's safe from being scavenged alive by carrion birds. They're probably more interested in Rocky than in him anyway, but he wonders if, in his present condition, they would even be able to distinguish him from a corpse.

Lindsey rolled over and stretched. She opened her eyes a slit, just enough to be able to tell that the room was full of light.

She told herself she'd get up in two minutes. It was summer. There was no rush.

Then her eyes snapped open. *Daddy!*

She leaped from her bed, and looked up at the top bunk. Amanda slept on her side, cuddling her stuffed unicorn tight against her body.

"Manda!" she said. "Wake up! It's morning."

"Huh?"

"Come on, get up. I'm gonna go see if Daddy's home yet. If he's not, I'm leaving. Are you coming or not?"

"Yeah, okay. I'm getting up."

Lindsey went first to Tim and Kate's bedroom. The bed was still made.

She went to the living room. No one. Kitchen: empty. The house was silent but for the sound of voices coming from the family room. She went there, and as she got closer, she could tell the voices came from the TV. It must have been on all night. Kate was asleep on the couch. She was half sitting up with her head leaning on the sofa back, mouth open. A blanket covered her legs, with Widget nestled in the crook of her knees. Lindsey felt a glimmer of affection for her stepmother, and immediately repressed it.

Selena was gone. Kate was home, but no Dad.

She crept back to her bedroom, being as quiet as she could to avoid waking Kate.

"Daddy didn't come home," she told Amanda. "Selena's gone, and Kate's asleep on the couch."

"Should we wake her up?" Amanda asked.

"No. Let her sleep. We'll leave her a note."

They dressed and brushed their teeth. Lindsey put her cellphone in the pocket of her jeans shorts.

"I'm gonna wear these Hippie Girl sunglasses," Amanda said.

"As long as you bring 'em, I don't care if you wear 'em or not. In fact, we should bring the rest of the stuff, too."

"All of it?"

"Everything. I don't wanna have to come back here to get something we need."

"Good idea." Amanda packed pencils and paper, along with all the clues and objects they'd collected so far, into a small backpack and slung it over her shoulder, while Lindsey wrote a note for Kate and left it on the kitchen table. They each grabbed a Pop Tart from the pantry and a Sunny D from the fridge, then tiptoed past Kate's sleeping form and out the back door, closing it softly behind them.

Outside it was like an instant replay of the day before: bright and sunny, and starting to get warm already. The sky was an unblemished blue from horizon to horizon, with no trace of the clouds that had enshrouded it last night.

"Lin, the sky's so pretty!" Amanda said. "It's purple."

"It's your glasses."

"Oh. Well, it's still pretty."

The easiest way to get to their grandparents' house was to hop on their bikes, ride through Belle Forest to Griffith Road, and back Griffith Road to the house

"Let's ride," Lindsey said. She opened the door of the shed where their bikes were kept.

"Mom-mom might see us if we go that way," Amanda said.

Lindsey paused in mid-motion, imagining the two of them riding up Mom-mom's driveway like a little parade. "That's true," she admitted. "She'll want to know what we're up to. And she might not like us digging behind the garage. Or worse yet, she might tell Kate."

"If we walk," Amanda said, "we can sneak up on the garage from behind, where she won't see us."

A tract of forested land connected their house to their grandparents', following the course of Sadler's Run. Poppy hadn't sold it when he sold the rest of the farm, and couldn't have even if he wanted to, because it was too steep and wooded. The girls had crossed it a few times with their father, using a trail trodden by several generations of Raithers.

Lindsey shrugged. "You're right, I guess. Let's go."

Leaving the shed door open with the bikes inside, they set off toward the privet hedge that divided their back yard from the wild country beyond it.

"Alan, I'm sorry to have to tell you this," George Booker said, "but the news people want a liaison. I've been putting them off for a long time."

Alan had been up all night, too wired to even take a coffee break or a short nap. But the strain was starting to show now. He'd been awake for more than twenty-four hours, and he was beginning to feel himself run down, and he knew he looked it.

He also knew that if he kept going, he would find his second wind and be good until this evening. He just had to stay busy and alert.

He hadn't yet figured out a way to approach Kate Raither about his and Booker's suspicions regarding her husband. He knew that it had to be done, and he was the only one that could do it right. He still wasn't sure what to say, but he knew he had to say *something*, and soon, unless one or both of his missing people turned up.

"Fine," he said. "I guess it's time I was talkin' to 'em. Thanks, Book." He knuckled his eyes and made his way over to the TV crews.

Lindsey and Amanda cut through a gap in the privet hedge, into a meadow that had once been one of their grandfather's fields, but was now overgrown with brush and saplings. They set off down the well-worn path that cut through the sloping meadow to the edge of the woods.

"*Eek!*" Lindsey screamed. "A bug! Amanda, get it off me! Hurry!" She held her left arm out toward her sister.

"It's just a ladybug," Amanda said, gently taking the beetle onto the pad of her forefinger. "They're good luck."

"I don't care. A bug is a bug."

The ladybug took wing and flew straight toward Lindsey's face. She flinched away, and then the bug veered off and disappeared.

Amanda clapped a hand over her mouth to stifle a giggle. Her eyes sparkled with merriment. "You're so silly, Lin. It can't hurt you."

"Stop laughing at me. Do I make fun of you for being scared of snakes?"

"No," Amanda replied. "But you're scared of snakes, too. Besides, it makes sense to be scared of snakes. Snakes scare the crap out of horses, even if they're not poisonous. And then you can get thrown and get hurt real bad. Poppy taught me that. He's scared of 'em, too."

"Well, Mom taught me to be scared of bugs. That makes sense, too."

"No, it doesn't. I can understand bees and spiders and stuff, but you're even scared of ladybugs."

Exasperated, Lindsey said, "Amanda, I just don't like 'em, okay? Do we have to make a big deal about it? You're not gonna change my mind."

"I give up," Amanda said. "Let's keep going."

Past the meadow, the trail entered the old-growth forest that had been there since pre-colonial times, and ran all the way through it to emerge in the pasture behind Poppy's house.

From the edge of the woods, the path followed a runoff gully down toward the streambed. The girls slipped and slid down this part of the trail, as the recent rainfall had made it slick and treacherous. They reached Sadler's Run, then turned right and followed it for a while. They were deep in the valley now, enclosed in a sylvan paradise with wooded hills rising on either side of them, shutting out the rest of the world, and it always made them feel as if they were the only people on earth. Even Lindsey enjoyed it, bugs and all.

Daddy had shown them all the landmarks, each one christened by some ancestral Raither. They passed the swimmin' hole, and continued on until they reached Greg's Ford, where they stepped from rock to rock across the creek, and continued downstream. Here, the trail was level and straight and free from obstructions, and they ran for awhile until they reached the place where the trail turned left, uphill, to get around a deep and jumbled ravine that cut across its course. They had a choice of following the trail up the gully, around the top of it, and back down the other side, or taking the shorter but sloppier route across the mouth of the gully where it dumped into the stream itself. They chose to stay on the path.

Once they'd gone over the upper end of the gully and come back down to the streambed, they ran until they reached Thinking Rock, where Sadler's Run met Bottleneck Branch. Past Thinking Rock, they crossed the stream again at the Crossing Log, then ran the last hundred yards of trail as it passed through a stand of pines and finally into the pasture behind their grandparents' house. They could see the barn directly before them, and beyond it, the garage and the house. At the top of a slight hill to their right was the run-in shed for Poppy's two quarterhorse mares. Jenny, the bay, and chestnut Jill munched placidly in their grandfather's sole remaining pasture.

The girls climbed the fence and ran flat out across the pasture. The horses picked up their heads in curiosity as they passed, and Jill gave a piercing whinny that echoed off the rear wall of the barn so that the girls heard it twice.

"She's saying hi. She recognizes me," Amanda said as they ran.

Lindsey looked at her. "Yeah, right."

"She does! Poppy lets me ride her sometimes. She knows me. Horses are smarter than you think. If you'd come with me sometimes, you'd know."

"Poppy doesn't really like me that much. He's got more time for you."

"That's 'cause he doesn't know you like he knows me. Whose fault is that?"

"Exactly. That's what I'm saying."

"Exactly. At least we agree."

Meanwhile, the horses had gone back to what they'd been doing. The girls dashed through the rear door of the barn. They flitted past the tack room and the stalls to the narrow stairs that led to the upper level. The front door was upstairs, for the ground level was higher on that side of the barn. This opening was big enough to drive a tractor into, but it was currently closed off by the sliding barn door. As Lindsey prepared to lean into the heavy door, an orange cat came cantering out to them from somewhere in the hayloft, where it had apparently been sleeping off the morning.

"Hi, Thomas," Amanda said, smiling and stroking the cat's head. Thomas, clearly delighted with the attention, purred and meowed at the same time, making a growling noise.

"I hate that cat," Lindsey said.

"You hate Thomas? Why?"

"Because he's ugly. He's all scruffy and he's got scars. And look at his ear."

"*Her* ear," Amanda said. "Thomas is a girl. And her ear is like that because she got in a fight. She's a barn cat, Lin. But she's real nice. Look how she loves people."

"Hmph," Lindsey said. "And what a stupid name for a girl cat, anyway. Whose idea was that?"

"Daddy's."

"Oh." Dismissing the subject, Lindsey gave the barn door a good shove, and it clattered open, rolling to the right in the overhead track from which it was suspended. The house and garage were right before them now, and the girls realized that they were in plain view if their grandmother should chance to look out her kitchen window. Mom-mom would have a thousand questions if she saw them. Amanda bid Thomas a hasty adieu, then slipped out the door. Lindsey shoved it closed behind them, and they both scrambled to the back of the garage, where they could not be seen from the house.

One of the first things their grandfather had done with the money from selling the farm was to build this garage and fill it up with toys. Constructed of cinder blocks, the five-car garage stood thirty feet from the house. The girls knew that, inside, it resembled the showroom of an auto dealership. In it were their grandmother's sensible Volvo, their grandfather's red Dodge Ram pickup, the '77 Corvette he kept for Sunday afternoons, the '04 Cadillac Seville he drove most of the rest of the time, and his bass boat on its trailer. The vehicles gleamed as if wet, especially the 'Vette and the bass boat. The floor had a coat of glossy gray paint and was swept clean every day. The brilliant white walls were adorned with framed photos of their grandfather, holding huge fish or shaking the hands of local celebrities and politicians. Glass curio cabinets displayed trophies, and tools hung on the wall in precise ranks over a workbench that you could eat off of. Poppy kept his playground spotless inside.

Out back, however, among tall weeds, an old oil drum stood against the wall, along with a pair of tires, a pile of broken cinder blocks, a compost heap, and a rust-locked disc harrow.

Amanda pointed to the rear corner of the garage on their right. "Right there's where the cats are buried. So there must be a brick somewhere around ..."

"Here," Lindsey said.

Lindsey knelt to the ground between the disc harrow and the compost heap, where a single red brick, buried so that only its top surface was visible, drew her like a magnet. Amanda joined her.

Lindsey grabbed the brick and wiggled. It broke loose from the earth easily, and she pulled it free. Underneath was a note sealed in a ziplock bag. Amanda picked it up. An earthworm exposed by the brick's removal retracted itself into the ground.

"Gross! Did you see that?" Lindsey asked.

"It's just a worm," Amanda replied. She opened the bag. The note was moist from being under the brick for God-knew-how-long, but it was still legible.

Did you bring the orange string? I hope so, because you need it now. Stretch it out from this hole to the left as far as it will go. Under the other end of it, against the garage wall, you will find the next clue.

"Oh, Dad, why do you do these things to us?" Amanda asked.

"Did you bring it?"

"Yes, right in here." Amanda fished in her backpack and got out the orange string they'd found in the Mason jar under the bridge. They untangled the knots and stretched it out as they were instructed. Both groaned when they realized where the other end of the string ended up: directly over the middle of the compost heap.

"Ugh!" Lindsey said. "I am *not* digging in that with my hands."

"There's shovels and rakes in the barn."

They returned to the barn and brought tools back to the garage.

The compost heap consisted of last fall's leaves, grass clippings, rotten tomatoes, watermelon rinds, and other things the girls couldn't identify, and the smell grew ever more interesting as they pulled clumps of it aside and got closer to the bottom. About halfway down, they disturbed a large blacksnake, and they both jumped away and screamed. Roused from its nap, the serpent slithered out of the compost heap and along the base of the garage to their right.

Reacting without conscious thought, Lindsey immediately put distance between herself and the snake, screaming the whole way. She ran a good fifty feet before she stopped, turned, and noticed that Amanda had matched her step for step. They stood heaving for a second or two, and staring at each other with wide eyes.

Lindsey broke into a grin. "Makes sense, right?"

"Totally," Amanda agreed.

"Do you think it's safe to go back?"

"It better be, because we're standing right where Mom-mom can see us. It's a miracle if she didn't hear you screaming."

"Me? You were the loudest."

Cautiously, the girls advanced on the compost heap. When at last they'd convinced themselves that the coast was clear, they resumed their digging and scraping. No more snakes appeared in the five minutes it took them to expose the bare earth beneath the compost.

Lindsey held one end of the string while Amanda stretched it out again, and pushed the point of her shovel into the soft mud where the string ended. The shovel went in a couple of inches, then stopped. They heard a metallic scraping sound.

"Something's in there!" Amanda said. She pulled up a shovelful of dirt, then knelt and dug with her hands. She exposed a small part of something black. A bit more digging, and they could see the top of a cashbox. It was sealed inside a clear ziplock freezer bag. Amanda freed it from the dirt, opened the bag, and took out the box.

Their eyes met, excited smiles on their faces.

Amanda tried to open the box, but it was locked.

"The key, the key!" Lindsey said.

Amanda rummaged in her backpack and brought forth the key from the Mason jar. She tried it in the lock. The lock turned, and the lid came open. Inside was another freezer bag.

The second bag contained five more puzzle pieces, a compass, and a piece of paper. On the paper, their father had written:

> The child must merge
> With mother's urge,
> And flow in one direction.
> There stands alone
> Unyielding throne,
> A setting for reflection.
> In shadows dark,
> A tiny spark
> Illuminates the test
> That stands between
> You and your dream:
> Fulfillment of your quest!

"Oh, God, I hate poetry," Lindsey said.

———

In six days we graduate from high school. Me and Darryl and Brian and Paula.

I have to keep saying that to myself. Even when I say it out loud, it doesn't seem quite real.

It's Saturday night. Paula and I are on our way back from the last Awards Banquet of our high school careers. I got Senior Athlete of the Year and the Outstanding Sportsmanship Award, *and* a free ride at Loyola on a lacrosse scholarship, and I'm feeling pretty full of myself right now.

With Greg in College Park and Randy in Alaska or Eugene, Oregon, or wherever he is now, it's finally my turn to shine in this town.

Paula ain't so happy, though. She's mad at me for some reason. I can tell she's mad 'cause she's just starin' out the window and she won't answer me when I talk, but I can't tell what she's mad *about*.

Maybe it's 'cause I'm going to Loyola next fall, and she wants to know what's gonna happen to "us." She's started in on that a couple of times in the last few weeks, but I don't have an answer, so I keep trying to change the subject.

I got a feeling it might be a bad idea to tell her I'm looking forward to Loyola, 'cause I hear the girls there throw themselves all over the lacrosse players.

I think I'm gonna ignore her for now, and pretend like I don't know she's pissed. It's too beautiful of a day to get all wrapped up in all that girl drama. Just look at that sky—

Just look at that big black smear in the sky, over on the horizon to the right.

"Holy shit," I say. "Somethin's burnin' over there."

It breaks Paula out of her mood, 'cause she looks over and says, "Ooh, I wonder where it is? Let's find it."

"Okay," I say. "Sounds like fun."

For a minute or two, as we're heading down Route 5 toward Sycamore, I start to wonder if it might be *my* house on fire, and there's a sinking feeling in my gut. But as we get closer to the intersection, the smoke slips farther and farther behind us. Once we make the right onto Route 128, I can tell it's off to the right a little too much.

I can see that black column of smoke without turning my head now, and it reminds me of the last time I saw one like that, the day the old cannin' factory burnt down, about eight years ago.

We cross in front of the elementary school, eyes glued to the smoke, trying to figure out where it connects with the ground. "Turn right here," Paula advises me, even though I can see plain as day that the fire is somewhere down White Horse Road. We make the turn, and from this range, we can see the smoke boilin' and rollin' as it rises, like somethin' alive.

Now I'm gettin' that sinking feeling again. It ain't my house that's on fire, but I got a feeling I know whose is. As we get closer to Myrtle Drive, we can both tell that's where the fire is.

I start thinkin' about all the times I thought about comin' over here to visit my old buddy over the last two years, and never did it. I should have, I know, but it's just, I been so busy! I mean, with lacrosse, track, the farm, keepin' my grades up, the debate team. And Paula, of course. It was always somethin', and I kept tellin' myself I'd make it over there someday. Is it my fault that I have a life?

Please, don't let it be too late.

I make the left turn onto Myrtle Drive like I'm on autopilot, a huge knot in my stomach. My mouth is dry as sand. The smoke is blotting out the whole sky ahead, and now the smell hits us, too.

Oh shit. Shit, shit, shit. He did it, that crazy fuck, he really did it.

Fire engines and police cruisers got the road blocked up ahead. There are tons of people, standin' and watchin' the fire on the other side of the blockade. I park the car in the middle of the street, and me and Paula get out without a word and start walkin'.

When we get up to where the crowd is, I can see Lynch's house. Or what's left of it. The walls are as black as the inside of a chimney, and there's huge orange flames shootin' out of every last window. From here, it looks like the house don't have any insides at all, just a gigantic fireball in there eatin' its way out. Even at this distance, I can feel the heat of it on my face, and the sound is like ... well, I've never heard a tornado, but I've seen some on TV, and I imagine this might be what one sounds like.

Then I see my dad in the crowd, talkin' to a deputy, Jarvis I think his name is, and I grab Paula's hand and make my way over there. When Dad sees me, he comes over and shakes my hand—which is about as affectionate as he ever gets—and says, "I'm sorry, son."

"So ... he was in there?" I ask him.

"Don't know for sure yet," Dad says. "But no one around here has seen him since this morning. His momma neither. I think they're prob'ly in there."

"Oh, Jesus," I say, and I start to feel like I weigh a ton, and I can't hardly even stand up. "Oh, Jesus Christ. Jesus Christ on a pogo stick, Lynch. What'd you do this time?"

"This is really gonna mess up our graduation," Paula says.

I look at her like she hasn't said anything at all, and I say, "I wasn't there to save him this time. And I coulda been. I shoulda talked to him."

"What?" she says. "Are you nuts? There's nothing you could've done about this, Timmy."

"Yeah," I say. "Maybe not. But maybe there was. I'm sorry, Lynch. I'm sorry, old buddy." All of a sudden I can't stop the tears from rollin'. Paula sees it, and she starts to cry, too. Her hand slips back into mine and we squeeze each other real tight.

Grudgingly, in stages, Kate regained consciousness. It was like being born. She didn't know where she was or what day it was. Her mouth tasted like mud.

Morning news was on the TV. On *her* TV. In *her* family room. She was on her own sofa.

I'm at home, she thought. *How——?*

Oh my God!

Elation filled her heart. To Widget, curled up in the crook of her bent knees, she said, "That was the absolute freakiest dream I have ever had in my life." Then, as she tossed off the blanket and sat up, she called out, "Tim! You'll never believe—"

The room whirled around her, and she stopped cold, gripping the sofa arm.

"Woo!" she said. "Sat up too fast." When the spinning subsided, she stood and moved into the kitchen. "Tim?"

She went on through the house, keeping one hand on something stable at all times, as the vertigo was still with her. The closer she got to her bedroom, the more insistent grew the alarm that crept up on her.

When she opened the bedroom door and saw that the bed was still made, she knew. The room tilted, and Kate stared at the bed in numb realization.

It had been no dream.

Something didn't add up. She struggled to pull scattered thoughts and memories together, wondering if she was losing her mind. She was afraid to trust her own recollection for fear that it might be tainted by what she *wanted* to be true.

Or by what she dreaded *might* be true.

She remembered being at Brian's house for some reason, but after that … nothing.

She shuffled numbly into the bathroom, then back to the kitchen, and started a pot of coffee. She needed it badly. She tried to be quiet, so as to avoid waking the girls for a bit. She could use a few minutes to get her bearings, recover her equilibrium.

She peered out the window into the driveway. Both vehicles were there. The shed door was open, and she could see the girls' bikes in there. Had she driven herself home? Or … had she never left?

She looked down at herself for the first time. She saw clothes she didn't recognize. Clothes she *never* would have chosen for herself, in any case.

The hell?

She picked up the handset and took it with her back to the family room, thinking that Selena would be able to shed some light on this mystery. Kate still felt a bit lightheaded, so she sat down on the sofa to make the call, and was about to turn the TV off when something on the screen caught her attention.

"—was last seen at this playground," came the voice-over on Channel 11. "As of this morning, she is still missing, and presumably has been abducted. We spoke with Captain Walter Curtis of the Sheriff's Department this morning." The scene shifted, and Alan appeared on screen, big as life, with a microphone in his face and playground equipment behind him. His eyes were red, like he'd been up all night. He probably had.

"We got no suspects at this point in time," Alan said. "We have evidence that the child was kidnapped, but like I said, right now we can't say who the perpetrator mighta been or where they mighta got to."

Back to the voice-over as the scene shifted to a brick Cape Cod home with a "K" in the middle of the storm door: "Madison's family declined to be interviewed on camera, but a man who came to this door told us that they were together and clinging to each other for support, and they were all praying for Madison's safe return."

The scene disappeared, to be replaced by the talking heads in the Channel 11 studio.

"Terrible story," one commented.

"Indeed it is," the other answered. "Once again, the Amber Alert on six-year-old Madison Kingsmore is still active. Apparently, she has been abducted from a playground at Maple Hills Elementary and is still missing." A picture of little Madison came on the screen. "If anyone sees her, please call the number at the bottom of your screen immediately, or dial 911."

So now it's a kidnapping, is it? she thought. The last she'd heard, they hadn't known for sure. Some new evidence must have come to light.

Kate switched off the TV. She wasn't in the mood for that.

She dialed Selena's number, and her friend answered on the first ring.

"You're up," Selena said.

"Yeah. What happened to me?"

"It's a long story. I'll tell you later. But listen, Brian and Darryl went out last night after you came home and they hit all the bars. No one had seen Tim all day."

"Oh. So he really is gone, right?"

"Gone? No, he's not gone! Don't lose hope, Kate."

"No, I'm not. It's just ... I wasn't sure. I'm a little confused, I guess."

"Oh, God, I'm sorry, Kate. Listen, I'm on my way. I'm leaving the kids with their grandparents, and I'm coming over to get you. I think we should start canvassing the streets, asking people if they know anything. Do you feel up to it?"

"Yes. I suppose. I'm a little woozy, but it'll pass."

"Good. I'll be over in an hour and a half."

"Okay. I'll be ready. Sel ... was I drunk?"

"Kind of. Like I said, it's a long story. Later, okay? I've really got my hands full here."

They hung up.

Kate went back into the kitchen. As she poured herself a cup of coffee, she went over in her mind what she knew to be true.

Her husband had disappeared and no one had been able to find him. She'd searched the roads herself. Brian and Darryl had covered the bars. The cops were everywhere, and no one had seen Tim. It was as if he'd fallen off the face of the earth.

She should call Dottie. As much as she dreaded the idea, she knew it was her obligation. Dottie would want to know.

Of course Dottie would want to know. It would give her something to talk about for months. Dottie would assume, naturally, like Alan did, that Tim was "out on a bender." In fact, Kate knew exactly what Dottie's first word would be, once she heard.

"Oof." That was what Dottie always said when Tim embarrassed her. That included everything from "going out on a bender" to buttoning his shirt wrong. "Oof," as if someone had kicked her in the gut. Poor Dottie. Feel her pain.

I'm not ready for that.

She had an unbearable urge to talk to someone. Her sister Donna, preferably, but anyone would do. Donna was in Ocean City with her boyfriend for the weekend, and Kate felt a small twinge of remorse for bothering her, especially at this hour. But she rationalized that, with all this going on, Donna'd probably be pissed if she *didn't* call her.

She picked up the phone and dialed Donna's cell. It rang until the voice mail message came on.

She hung the phone up on its cradle.

Then she noticed a loose piece of paper on the kitchen table. She picked it up and read Lindsey's handwriting.

> Kate,
> Don't worry, we're going to find Dad. We know what to do.
>   L & A
> P.S. I have my cell.

She almost swooned. Nerveless fingers dropped the paper to the floor. She ran to Lindsey's room and opened the door. Empty. She turned next to Amanda's room. Also empty.

"Oh my God." She wanted to do so many things at once that she stood in one place, eyes darting around, feet moving first in one direction, then another. At last, she sat in the kitchen chair and repeated herself: "Oh my God."

They're out there somewhere. They're out there with that predator. "Oh my God oh my God oh my God."

She grabbed her cellphone and speed-dialed her stepdaughter. It went straight to voicemail.

"Oh, no," she said. "She doesn't have it turned on. I'm gonna *kill* you, Lindsey!" The girl was forever forgetting to turn her cellphone on. Kate dialed her again, and this time she left a message that could not possibly be misunderstood.

She looked out the back door, as if she might find them in the yard. She paced, thinking furiously. She needed to get the girls home, and she needed to find her husband. Where to start? Call Alan again?

No, she couldn't waste his time. He was busy finding a little girl who really had been kidnapped. *A little blonde girl, just like …*

"Stop it," she said aloud. By force of will, she stopped pacing, took a sip of coffee, sat down. She set the coffee cup aside with a trembling hand. *They're fine. They've only been gone a little while. They'll be back soon, and then we'll go look for Tim together.*

She retrieved the note from the floor and read it again, and this time it hit her. "The treasure hunt," she said. "So that's what they're up to. And it might even work." She just wished they'd woken her before they left, trusted her with their plans. Then she could have—

Of course. I would have stopped them. They knew that.

She felt a curious blend of frustration with and admiration for her stepdaughters.

Under normal circumstances, Kate was not prone to prayer, but these were far from normal circumstances. She closed her eyes. *Please let them all be safe,* she prayed. *If I can only get them all home, I swear I'll be a better wife, and a better mother, from now on. Just give me that chance.*

She got up and paced some more, floundering. The phone rang. Without bothering to look at the Caller ID, she picked up the handset and said, "Thank God you called back!"

"I don't know who you thought I was, dear, but I'm sure it wasn't me."

Kate gasped. "Hello, Dottie. I'm sorry, I was expecting someone else."

"That's quite obvious, dear. Is everything all right? You sound a bit nervous."

"Oh, yes, everything's …" Kate's throat grew constricted and she was unable to get the rest of her sentence out.

"Kate? Are you there?"

"Could I—," she croaked. She started again. "Could I call you back in a few minutes? I've got a bit of a situation here."

"Yes, of course, but first tell me this: are my granddaughters at home? Because I've been watching the news this morning and—"

"I know. I saw it. I'm sure the girls are fine. They—"

"What do you mean, you're sure they're fine? Are they there or not?"

Kate sighed in exasperation. It seemed she'd not get away with sugarcoating this. "No."

"Well, where are they? Are they with Timothy?"

"Maybe. I hope so."

"What? Kate, you're being cryptic, and it's wearing thin. Can you please tell me what is going on?"

"I wish I knew. The girls are outside somewhere I don't know where and there's this predator running around kidnapping little blonde girls and Tim's been gone since yesterday morning and I don't know where *he* is and Alan's too busy looking for that Madison girl to care about Tim and I can't even figure out how I got here. You think it's wearing thin on *you?* You have no idea."

A long pause at the other end of the line made Kate wonder if she'd lost the connection. Then Dottie dropped the bomb. "Oof."

"Oh, don't you do that to me," Kate said. "Don't you dare say 'oof' to me right now, because I am in no mood to play head games with you this morning, Dottie. I have an honest-to-Christ emergency on my hands right now, and I don't have time for your drama queen act. I'm serious."

"I'm—"

"I know what you're going to say. You think Tim's out drinking. He's done something to disappoint you, I know that's what you believe because it's what you *want* to believe! You get some sick, twisted pleasure out of it. But I'm telling you right now, Dottie, Tim is not 'out on a bender.' He left on his bike yesterday morning to hide the treasure for the girls and he said he'd be right back and he's still not back, and I'm telling you something's gone wrong and *he needs help!* And those two girls of ours, they have minds of their own and God knows I love them, but now *they've* gone off to find their father and I'm here all by myself and all I can do is sit here and wait for Selena, and she won't be here for another hour, at least. Meantime, I have no idea what I should be doing. I don't know whether to get out there and search, or sit here and wait for the girls to come back. If I have to sit here, I'll go completely nuts, but someone has to do it and I can't be two places at once. What am I supposed to do?"

"Kate, I want you to get hold of yourself. I'm coming over. Do you hear me? I'm coming over right now and we'll figure out something to do, between the two of us. I'll see you in five minutes, dear. Hold tight. I'm coming. Did you hear me? I'm coming."

Click. Without so much as a goodbye, Dottie had disconnected. Kate looked at the handset like it was a strange bug, and hung it in the cradle. She looked down at the rumpled mess she had become as a result of sleeping in her clothes.

Or somebody's *clothes*, she thought. *I'd better change.*

Turns out Dad was right. Lynch *was* in that house when it burned, and so was his mom. The funeral is tonight. Closed casket, of course. I'm not goin'. People are startin' to say some whacked-out shit about what happened, and I'm not ready to deal with it. I know if I go, somebody's gonna say the wrong thing to me, and there's gonna be some ugliness. Lynch would hate that.

Besides, it wouldn't be right for me to go to his funeral. Seein' as I haven't seen him in like two years, it would be, what's it, hypocritical to go to his funeral and pretend like I cared.

Tomorrow is graduation. Paula was right, too. It's wrecked. I don't really wanna go to that either.

I do plan to get drunk afterward, though. *Really* drunk.

"This is hard," Amanda said. "Give me codes anytime. This poetry could mean anything."

They concentrated on the poem. For the time being, they'd stashed the compass and the new jigsaw pieces in Amanda's pack.

"Told you I hate poetry," Lindsey said. "And that's why. Teachers are always trying to get us to say what we think the poet means, and most of the time it's just a bunch of words. It could mean anything. I think that's like, the definition of poetry. A bunch of words that don't mean anything."

"If that's true, then Daddy's pretty good at it."

After restoring their grandfather's compost heap to something that resembled its original appearance, the girls had retired to the barn to sit on a bale of straw and think about the new clue. They'd spent nearly half an hour on it and gotten nowhere, other than hungry, thirsty, and frustrated. In addition, they both had to use the bathroom.

"I guess Kate hasn't woke up yet, or she would've called us by now," Lindsey said, and she pulled out her cellphone. "Uh-oh. It's not on. Maybe she *has* been trying to call us." She tried to turn on the cellphone, but it kept dying. "Snap! It's dead."

"Oh, Lindsey, you gotta be kidding me. It's not a good time to have a dead phone."

"Shut up! You don't even have one."

"That's because Daddy says I'm too young, but if I did have one, I wouldn't let it go dead on a day like this."

161

"It's just as well," Lindsey said. "I don't wanna hear from Kate anyway. We have too much to do today. And she'd prob'ly just yell at us and tell us to come home."

Sudden movement at the house distracted them from their conversation. They watched through the open hayloft hatch as their grandmother came out of the house like she'd been shot from a gun. The screen door slamming behind her sent a sharp report across the yard. She moved about as fast as a woman her age can move, oblivious to the watching eyes in the barn, and disappeared into the garage. Then they heard the garage door rolling up, and saw Dottie's boxy-looking Volvo pull out and turn left onto Griffith Road.

"Wow, she was totally in a hurry," said Amanda.

"Wonder where she went?"

"I don't know, but I know where *I'm* going now. I'm going inside and go to the bathroom. You comin'? While we're in there, we can use the phone and call Kate."

"Okay, but isn't the door locked?"

"Nahhh. Mom-mom and Poppy never lock their door. They say when the time comes they have to start locking their doors, it'll be time to move out."

"Let's go then."

The girls ran to the house and entered through the door Dottie had just used. Amanda made a beeline for the bathroom. Lindsey waited for her, walking in circles to distract herself from the fullness of her bladder. At last, Amanda came out, and Lindsey took her place.

When they'd both relieved themselves, Amanda said, "Let's see what Mom-mom's got in the fridge. I'm starved."

"Amanda! That's not right."

"Are you kidding? It's our *grandmother's* house. It's like being at home."

"When someone's here, it is. Not when nobody's home."

"Lindsey, she so wouldn't mind, trust me. She loves to feed us."

They found a jar of strawberry preserves in the refrigerator, and some peanut butter in the pantry, and made themselves sandwiches. They poured glasses of sweetened iced tea and sat down at the table to eat.

"Hey," Lindsey said, spotting an old book lying on the table. "I didn't know Mom-mom read this stuff, too." The book had but one word on the cover: "Tennyson." She picked it up and held it for Amanda to see. "Isn't this the guy—?"

"Yeah, that's him. 'To strive, to seek,' and all that."

"That's so weird," Lindsey said. "We were just talking about him last night."

Amanda's eyebrows shot up. "That *is* weird, Lin! Do you think it means somethin'?"

"Yeah," she said, putting the volume back on the table where she'd found it, "it means we need to keep looking at Dad's dumb poetry for whatever it is we're missing. Let me see that stupid thing." She reached across the table toward her sister with an open hand.

Amanda produced the paper. Lindsey took it from her and studied it as she took a bite of her sandwich. "Hey," she said through a mouthful of food, "this might be something."

"What?"

Lindsey held up a finger as she finished chewing, swallowed, and said, "Look, it says, 'The child must merge / With mother's urge / And flow in one direction.'"

Amanda shrugged. "So?"

"Well, the word 'flow' is kinda funny here. I mean, why didn't he say 'walk' or 'run' or 'travel' or even 'go?' The word 'flow' makes me think of water, like maybe he's not talking about mothers and children at all. You haven't learned about similes and metaphors yet, have you?"

"Learned about what?"

"Similes and—forget about it. It's something we learned about in Language Arts. They do it a lot in poetry. It's a way of talking about something by talking about something else."

Amanda stared at her.

Lindsey frowned. "You're not getting this, I know, but I think I might be right. When he says, 'A child must merge / With mother's urge,' he's not talking about you and me. I think he's talking about rivers or streams. You know how when a small river *flows* into a big river, and then they both *flow in the same direction?* See how that works? He's trying to trick us into thinking that he's talking about kids and moms, when he's really talking about water."

Amanda's eyes lit up. "Ohhhh! Like where Bottleneck Branch goes into Sadler's Run."

Lindsey took a swallow of tea. "Exactly. That might even be the place he means. Let's read on: 'There stands alone / Unyielding throne, / A setting for reflection.'"

"Well, we know what 'unyielding' means."

"Yeah, it means somebody that doesn't give up. Dad loves that word. But it can also mean something hard, like a sidewalk."

"What about 'A setting for reflection?' Does he mean a mirror? Or maybe he's talking about the way the sun reflects off of water, you know, like the way it did under the bridge yesterday."

"Hey, you're getting the hang of this," Lindsey said with a smile for her sister. "'There stands alone.' By 'there' he must mean where the two rivers come together. So something 'stands alone' near where two rivers join, and it's a hard 'throne.' Hmm. 'A setting for reflection.' A *place* of reflection.

Something hard that you sit on, and there's reflections there." She finished the last bit of her sandwich.

Amanda slapped herself in the forehead. "Duh! He's talking about Thinking Rock!"

Thinking Rock was one of the landmarks in the forest, and had been called that by their father and their uncles, and by their father before them. Poppy claimed it had been called that when he was a boy, so no one knew who really named it, but it seemed like a good name. Situated at the confluence of Bottleneck Branch and Sadler's Run, Thinking Rock perched high up on the angle of land between them. It was a large gray sandstone boulder, round as a basketball except for the top, where it was flat enough that one could sit up there and have a nice view of the wooded valley below. A small tree with three trunks grew from a large crack in the middle of it, and Tim always told the girls that someday that tree's roots would split the rock and the forward part of it would fall into the creek.

Lindsey swallowed. "That's it! 'A place of reflection' means a place where you think, it's got nothing to do with mirrors. He thinks he's so clever, our Dad."

"Not clever enough for us! Boy, for somebody that says they hate poetry, you did a pretty good job of figuring that out."

"I couldn't have done it without you, Manda. We're a team."

"Okay, now that we figured that part out, what does the rest of it mean?"

Lindsey read, "'In shadows dark / A tiny spark / Illuminates the test / That stands between / You and your dream: / Fulfillment of your quest!' He means we're going to find the next clue somewhere near Thinking Rock. That's what he means by 'the test.' I don't know about the shadows and the spark, but I think we'll hafta go there and find out. Are you ready?"

Amanda's face went ashen. "Lin," she said. "Poppy says not to go there. He says it's dangerous."

"He does? Poppy said that? Are you sure you don't mean Mom-mom? Mom-mom would worry about us getting hurt, but not Poppy."

"Poppy's not worried about us getting hurt."

"Then what is he worried about?"

"He says it's a special place."

"So? What kind of special?"

"Well, you know how Poppy believes in ghosts and stuff ..."

"He doesn't really believe, Manda. He's just tellin' stories, is all."

"No he's not. He believes. And he says Thinkin' Rock was special to the Indians—"

"Native Americans."

"Whatev. It was a special place to them, and because we're part In— Native American, we can feel it too, just a little bit. He says ... something like, you can always find truth there, but not to go unless you're ready for it."

"What does he mean by 'truth?' Why was he bein' all spooky about it like that? Was he tryin' to scare you?"

"Yeah, he was. That's what I'm tellin' you. He was tryin' to scare me because he doesn't want us to go there."

Lindsey stared at her for a long moment before saying, "I betcha he made that up because Mom-mom told him to make us stay away."

"Maybe. But he seemed awful serious when he said it."

"Poppy never has that much to say about anything, unless Mom-mom tells him to say it."

"You never really listen to Poppy. If you did, you'd know that what you just said—"

"Daddy lets us go up there, and he never said anything about all that."

Amanda hesitated. "That's true ..."

"We have to go to Thinking Rock if we want to find Daddy. But we'll be careful, okay? We'll keep an eye out for truth, and if we see any, we'll run like crazy."

Amanda finished the last of her sandwich, drank her tea, and said, "You promise?"

Lindsey rolled her eyes. "Yes, I promise! Let's go. I so don't wanna be here when Mom-mom comes back."

They rinsed out their glasses and put them in the dishwasher, put the preserves back in the refrigerator, brushed crumbs off the table, gathered up their belongings, and scrambled out the door. It slammed behind them.

Lindsey thought about mentioning that they hadn't yet called Kate, but decided against it.

12

Kate heard a sharp rapping at the front door.

"Perfect," she said. "A right-wing control-freak battle-axe is just what I need." She'd changed her clothes, brushed her teeth, and run a brush through her hair a few times, but she still felt disheveled and a bit lightheaded. She didn't feel ready for company, least of all with someone who constantly held her up to the light to inspect for flaws.

She opened the door to admit her mother-in-law (who, at sixty-seven, still bottled her hair black). Without hesitation, Dottie came to her and wrapped her in a strong embrace. After a moment, Kate brought her arms up from her sides and gave her mother-in-law a few gentle pats on the back, thinking, *This is so phony.*

"Are you all right, dear?" Dottie asked. "I've never heard you so out of sorts."

Kate nodded her head as they separated. "As all right as can be expected."

"I want you to tell me everything that's happened. Start from the beginning. Sit with me," she said, and sat down on the living room sofa. Given a choice, Dottie always preferred the living room to the family room, perhaps, Kate thought, because the comfortable clutter of the family room somehow offended her.

Kate was unsure of how to begin. It was a matter of habit for Kate to filter all information going to Dottie, and that automatic algorithm was going on in her head even as she sat in the armchair facing her. But her natural wariness of Dottie clashed with her near-insatiable need to talk to

166

someone. Here was a willing ear, and there wasn't another one immediately available.

Oh, what the hell, she thought.

"Tim left yesterday morning, a little after six o'clock," she began. "I was still in bed." That was the tiny snowball that started it, and once she got started, it was like trying to stop an avalanche. She held a few things back, like her suspicions that Tim may have been drinking, her adventures in Friar Tuck's, her mysterious return home that she couldn't remember; but other than those details, she unburdened herself of all the events of the last twenty-four hours, ending with the note Lindsey had left this morning. Through it all, Dottie sat, attentive, impassive, and as still as Mt. Rushmore.

When Kate stopped talking, Dottie made no sound or motion for a long five seconds, and Kate wondered if she'd fallen asleep with her blue eyes wide open.

"All right," Dottie finally said. She handed Lindsey's note back to Kate.

"Selena is coming over, and we're going to go out and cruise the neighborhoods, ask around. It's the only thing I can think of to do at this point."

"That might have been a nice plan, had my granddaughters not turned up missing. Now everything has changed."

"Yes, that does kind of throw a spanner in the works."

"Here's what we're going to do," Dottie said. "First of all, we're going to wait right here for those girls to come back, which I'm sure will be soon, and when they come back we're putting them under lock and key. If your friend shows up before the children do, then you may go with her while I stay here and wait for the children. Do you have any idea at all where they might have gone?"

"None."

"Then we must wait.

"Secondly, we're going to call that young Curtis boy and get him over here. I don't care what he's doing; he can make time for me, because I have a word or two for him. We'll tell him the girls are now missing as well. I think that might get his attention."

"I doubt we can even get through to Alan. I know he's still out in the field, because I saw him on the tube a few minutes ago, and he looked like he'd been up all night. We may as well try to get hold of the President."

Dottie smiled. "I *can* get hold of Alan Curtis, and I shall."

"How?" Kate asked.

"Simple," she replied. "I'll call his father."

Another knock at the door startled them both. "It can't be Selena," Kate said. "She always uses the back door, and she doesn't knock. Besides, it's too soon."

"Well, are you going to see who it is?"

Kate went to answer it, and was stunned to see Alan Curtis standing on her front porch in his white shirt, snappy Stetson, and gray pants piped with black. The sudden conviction that this could only represent bad news knocked the breath out of her. Struggling to find her voice, she croaked out, "You've found him? Is he okay?" Dread left her feeling hollowed out, an empty vessel, ready to receive whatever toxic brew Alan might decant.

"Ma'am?" Alan said. "Is who … no, we ain't found him. No, ma'am, I'm sorry to've scared you like that. We ain't found Timmy yet, and we did look. I put my best man on it."

"Then … it's not the girls, is it? Please don't let it be the girls."

"You mean your daughters? No, why? Ain't they here?"

"No, they're not. They went to look for Tim," Kate said.

"By themselves? Them girls oughtn't to be out there alone, Kate. I thought you understood me when I said—"

"They left before I woke up," Kate said. "Come on in, will you?"

Alan stepped into the living room. "Mornin' to ya, Miss Dottie," he said. He glanced back and forth between the two women.

Kate sat down in the armchair and put her head in her hands. She'd been so afraid Alan was going to tell her they'd found Tim's body that she had trouble pulling herself together. She tried to get control of her involuntary trembling, but was only half successful.

Dottie took over. "You say you put your best man on finding my son?" she asked.

"Yes, ma'am," Alan said, nodding.

"And who would that be?"

"That'd be Sergeant Booker, Miss Dottie. There's no one I trust more than him."

Dottie nodded. "All right, then," she said. "If you haven't found Tim and you haven't found the girls, then why are you here, Alan?"

"Well, let's just talk about them girls first. How long they been gone?"

"As I said, they left this morning before I got up," Kate said, "and they're not back yet. They left me this note." She handed the note to Alan.

Alan read it, then said, "Well, at least we know they left on their own. But it don't say where they went. Do you know?"

"No, I'm afraid I don't. You see, they were on a treasure hunt. Tim was hiding the treasure when he disappeared. Lindsey and Amanda think if they can follow the clues all the way to the end, they'll find Tim. At least, I assume that's what they're thinking. They didn't discuss it with me."

"I see. Now, who made up the treasure hunt?"

"Tim."

"You didn't work on it together?"

"No, it was Tim's idea. He kept it all to himself."

"I see. So you ain't got any idea where he went yesterday mornin'?"

"That's right."

"And you ain't got any idea where the girls mighta gone *this* mornin', neither."

"No, I don't. I told you that."

"Well, then, did they leave anything else behind that might help us figure out where they're at? The clue, or whatever, that told 'em where to go next?"

"No, I've already looked. They didn't leave anything but the note."

Alan was silent for a moment. He checked his watch. "Well, it's gettin' nigh on lunchtime now, an' I expect them girls'll be rollin' in here any minute to fill their bellies. The way kids are, they get all distracted an' such an' they take longer about their business than we think they're gonna. So I'm not gonna worry about 'em unless they don't show up for lunch, you foller me? I figure like as not they're ridin' their bikes over in Belle Forest, or at some friend's house. I can remember many a summer's day me and the Raither boys spent the whole day playin' in the fields and woods, and we never came back unless we got hungry. But I will keep an eye out for 'em when I get back out on the road, an' if I see 'em, I'll bring 'em on home myself. That sound good?"

"I guess," Kate replied. "Yes, that would help. Thank you."

"An' when they do come back," he continued, "don't you let 'em outta your sight again. Foller me? Until we catch this guy, it's not safe out there."

"You know it's a man?"

"By the shoe size, yes, ma'am. It usually is a man anyways, unless it's a custody case, which this ain't."

"So let me get this straight," Kate said. "You don't know where my husband is, and you don't know where my daughters are, in fact you didn't even know they were missing until you got here. So why are you here?"

"Well, when it comes to it, y'see me an' Sergeant Booker, we been talkin' about things. Now your husband is off the books right now, you understand, I mean we ain't officially reported him missin' yet. Only me an' Book know about it. I put Book on it yesterday, and he looked everywhere he could think of, you foller me? And he didn't find any sign of him. So we got to thinkin' maybe he ain't off on a bender at all, foller me? So that leaves a coupla things it could be. One of 'em is that maybe he got kidnapped himself."

Both Dottie's and Kate's hands flew to their mouths as they gasped.

"Now, don't get yourselves all worked up about that, because it ain't likely. First off, adults don't usually kidnap other adults unless there's money or ... well, you know, sex involved. Now I can see you an' Timmy are comfortable here, but I don't think ya got the kinda money that people would kidnap for, you foller me? No offense, now."

"None taken."

"Does he have any bank cards with him, or credit cards?"

"No," Kate said. "He left his wallet here. And his cellphone."

"All right then. I don't think it's likely that Timmy's been kidnapped, but we had to consider it, you foller me? Especially since we already had one kidnappin', and there was a chance maybe they were by the same guy. So anyways, we tossed that out. It just don't foller. Now Kate, what size shoe does Timmy wear?"

"What size shoe? Eleven, I think, why?"

"Dang, I was hopin' you'd say somethin' else. But in that case, does he have any New Balance cross-trainers?"

"I don't know. He has maybe twenty different pairs of sneakers back there. I don't know what he has. Alan, what are you getting at?"

"Well, see now …" Again he glanced over at Dottie, who was taking everything in without comment—so far. "Y'see, when two strange things happen in the same town on the same day, chances are they're connected, you foller me? The simplest way to explain two crazy things is if they both have the same explanation, and most of the time, that's the way it works out. For instance, if Timmy and Madison Kingsmore'd been kidnapped by the same guy, that would be one way to explain both things with one explanation. Foller me?"

"For heaven's sake," Dottie said, "stop hemming and hawing, and say what you mean."

"Well, y'see, me and Book, we started wonderin' if …" Still Alan seemed to be unable to say what he needed to say. "Mrs. Raither …" A pause as he glanced at the two Mrs. Raithers, then he added, "Kate, I mean. I'm sorry to have to ask ya this, but how is Timmy when he's around your daughters? I mean, is he … appropriate?"

Kate took a moment to absorb Alan's intent. "Oh. My. God. You have got to be kidding me," Kate said. "You … I mean, have you lost your mind? You think *Tim's* the kidnapper? That's the most ridiculous—"

"Now, I didn't say that," Alan said, backing up a step.

"You *know* Tim, you've known him for years! He would never—I mean, he was on a bicycle, for God's sake! You think he carried that little girl off on his bike?"

"Yeah, me and Book, we talked about that too, an' the kidnapper did use a car, and it's good that Timmy's wallet is here. But we hafta cover all the bases, you foller me? Look, I've known Timmy forever, an' I don't wanna believe this any more than you do. What I was hopin' for was somethin', *anything*, that could rule him out as a suspect. I mean positively, absolutely rule him out. Because if I don't get that, then I gotta *consider* him a suspect. I wouldn't be doin' my job if I didn't. Now I've let this go on way longer than I should've. I haven't mentioned his name to anyone, and it's been all night. I've done that outta respect and friendship. But if you can't help me out here, then I ain't got a choice. I got to put his name out there."

"*Walter Alan Curtis the Third!*" Dottie thundered, rising to her feet.

"Yes, Miss Dottie?"

"I was with your mother on the day you came into this world. And I'll not stand here and allow you to speak of my son that way in my presence! My son has had problems, we all know that, but he is *not* a child abuser. I don't need any *evidence* to rule him out. And you have the nerve to come into his own house and make this absurd accusation in front of his wife and mother? Shame on you! You are not welcome here! Get out! Get out now and go do your job. Find Madison Kingsmore, find my son, and find my granddaughters."

"Yes, ma'am, I will. I'll be goin' now. I'm sorry to've offended you ladies. If there's anything—"

"Get out!" the two women shouted.

A chastised Alan Curtis hustled out the door, got into his car, and drove off.

"Cretin! Imbecile!" Dottie said. "Pay no attention to that stupid little man," she said to Kate. "Don't you entertain for one second the idea that he might be right."

"I don't. But that's not what worries me. He's going to name Tim as a suspect. It'll make the news. It'll ruin Tim's life, and it won't matter that he's innocent, because from now on, people will always wonder. They'll stare at him and whisper about him, and watch every move he makes if he's around children. Reporters will watch over our house, follow him around. He won't be able to take it. *I* won't be able to take it."

"Then, Kate dear, it's up to you and me to make sure that doesn't happen."

"How?"

"We've got to find your husband *before* Alan makes it happen."

"How?"

"I don't know for sure. But I know we can do it. Unfortunately, we're hampered now by the fact that Lindsey and Amanda are missing. But it's almost eleven-thirty. Alan was right about one thing: those girls should be coming in soon for lunch."

"If they don't get here before Selena does, I'm gonna lose my mind."

"This might seem obvious, but have you tried Lindsey's cell?"

"Yes, of course. But I'll try again right now." She did, and she got the voicemail again. "No answer," she said. "But I think I'll text her. Sometimes she ignores the phone if it rings, but she'll read a text message."

CRB VBD NOT KIDDING

171

"That should do it," she said.

The phone rang. "See?" she said. She checked the caller ID. "Damn, it's Brian." She answered it.

"Kate. It's me, Brian. Don't hang up. I just wanted to make sure you were okay."

"You mean physically? I'm fine. I had a rough night, I guess, but I'm okay now."

"Good. That's good. Kate ... I'm really, really sorry. I don't know how else to say it."

"You're sorry. Well, you ought to be. Do you have any idea how you humiliated me, carrying me like a sack of grain? You have no—"

"I'm not talkin' about that."

"Then, what *are* you talking about? Is there something else you need to apologize for? Oh, my God. Is it Tim? Is he—?"

"No, not at all ... oh, hell. Selena didn't tell you?"

"Tell me *what*, Brian? Spit it out."

"I didn't mean to do it, Kate. I mean, I did at first, but then Selena made me see it was wrong, and she was right about that, and I was gonna pour it out, but you snuck up behind me and then it was too late and—"

"Brian! *What did you do?*"

"I, uh ... I slipped you a roofie."

Kate's mouth fell open as understanding came. The memory gap, the dizziness, the soundness of her sleep ... it all jibed with Selena's account of what it was like to be roofied.

Her heart thumped as the full implication set in. The way Brian looked at her, behaved with her, had always made her wary. But was he capable of the level of betrayal she now imagined?

"Brian," she said. "Did you—"

"No, Kate! It was just to put you to sleep. And it was an accident, anyway. I'm so sorry it happened."

"What do you mean, 'happened?' Something like that doesn't just 'happen.' You drugged me. And you have the balls to call it *an accident?*"

"Look, I was worried about you. I thought you were gonna get yourself killed. I wanted you safe and getting some rest. So it seemed like a good idea at first. But then ... anyway, I'm not sorry about the way it turned out, because me and Darryl did the job, and you lived through the night. Which was all I was hoping for."

"How do I know you didn't ... take advantage of me?"

"I'd think there'd be a way you could tell, Kate. But ain't my word enough? I swear to you, nothing happened. Look, Kate, we could argue about this all day. But time's wastin'. Could we set it aside until after we find Tim?"

Kate felt reality slipping from her grasp. Everything was falling apart. Even her supposed friends seemed to be working against her. Her world was fragmenting, breaking into a bewildering array of facts, ideas, assumptions, and suspicions. For an eternal second, she stood with the phone to her ear, mutely confused.

Then she began to put it back together.

She *had* been out of control yesterday, working herself through her stages of grief. It had taken a figurative slap in the face from Brian to help her realize that. She had spent the last twenty-four hours being baffled and controlled by events, thwarted by circumstances. She was sick of it. It was time for her to stop being driven, and start doing the driving. She knew her husband was out there somewhere. She knew she had a job to do, and she would do it. She'd do it alone if she had to, but at this stage she would be foolish to turn down any help that was offered.

"Kate? Are you still there?"

She took another moment to compose herself. Brian was right. She would bury the hatchet, at least for the time being.

"Fine," she said. "We'll set it aside for now."

"Thanks."

"You're right about one thing, Brian. I panicked yesterday. I made some mistakes."

"Huge mistakes."

"Yes. Huge ones. I still have an issue with you for the way you did it, but I suppose I should thank you for bringing me back to earth."

"Don't mention it. Listen, Darryl wants to talk to you."

Dottie came into the room, wearing a quizzical expression. Kate held a hand up to her, palm out. *Wait.*

"Put him on," Kate said.

Darryl's voice came on the phone next. "Listen, Kate, he feels really bad. I mean, he's like all broken up about it and shit. Maybe you should … I mean, I know it was wrong and all, but you were totally out of control, and—"

"Darryl—"

"—remember, he did save your ass."

"I know all that. Forget about it. I don't have time for any more drama. I need all the help I can get today. Can I count on you?"

"We're here for you," he said. "I was supposed to take Jerome to a birthday party today, but I got Beth to handle it, so we got all day."

Kate blew out a noisy breath. "That's a relief. Thank you."

"All good, man."

"Did you guys get any sleep?"

"Crashed for a couple hours at Brian's house. We're good. What do you want us to do?"

"Where've you been looking today so far?"

"All we've done so far is recheck everything you did last night, but we figured it was worth the effort, with the sun out now and everything."

"And?"

"Nothing. There's no way Tim's roadmeat, or we would've found him by now."

Kate winced. "Nice way to put it."

"Sorry. We also cruised all the parking lots, and looked behind buildings, everywhere we could think of that he could've gone. It's like he just disappeared, poof! So we ruled out the roads and last night we ruled out the bars. For the last fifteen minutes we been trying to get into Tim's head, you know, think like him. Where would we go to hide a treasure if we were Tim?"

"Come up with anything?"

"Nope. We figured you might know. You know the kinds of things he likes to do, places he hangs out with the girls and all. We're not in that part of his life, you know?"

"The bike trail. I didn't get a chance to check it out yesterday, with the storm and all. He and the girls love that trail. Could you guys do that for me? You'll have to do some walking. Start, say, at Griffith Road and go all the way to Orenzo Mill. Maybe even a little past it."

"Okay. Sure."

"He hid one clue on it that we know about, and maybe he'd not use it twice. Or maybe he would. I just don't know. There are trails splitting off of it everywhere, and old buildings and stuff. That's the one place where he could have ridden that we didn't look yet."

"No sweat. We'll handle that. What're you gonna do?"

"I've got another whole problem now. I have to stay here for a while. When I can get out, I'm going to go door to door. But it would be great if you could help me out with the trail."

"We're leaving now. We'll call you."

"Thanks."

Kate hung up, and Dottie said, "Sounds like you've got some help."

"Yes. Thankfully—"

The phone rang again.

"My God," Kate said.

It was Selena this time. "Kate, I'm almost there. Are you ready to go?"

"Oh, shit, Sel. I can't go." She explained the new situation, then asked, "Can you do the neighborhoods without me? And keep an eye out for those girls while you're out there, too, if you don't mind. If you see them, tell them I want them home right away."

"Absolutely. What about the bike trail?"

"Darryl and Brian are covering that. By the way, why didn't you tell me what Brian did?"

"I was going to, later. You have enough to worry about."

"I'm so ready to kick his ass."

"I'll help. I was so mad at him last night, I couldn't even look at him."

"I bet."

"I'm pulling into Belle Forest. I'll call you."

"Thanks."

They hung up.

"You have quite a network," Dottie said.

"How 'bout that?" Kate said with mock surprise. "We have friends that care about us. I know that must be hard for you to believe."

Dottie raised her palms to Kate. "I meant no offense. I was complimenting you."

Kate considered, decided to take it at face value. "Sorry. I thought you were being sarcastic."

"Apology accepted."

Kate nodded. "You know, I think Lindsey and Amanda may have the right idea."

"How so?" Dottie asked.

"Tim's been missing since yesterday morning. Since then, I've been all over the countryside searching for him. So have the cops, and Brian and Darryl, and now Selena, too. Nobody's found anything. And it took two kids to pick up on the one crucial fact that we all missed: *Tim left a set of written instructions where he could be found.* All we have to do is follow them."

Dottie put her finger on her lower lip. "I suppose so ..."

"I mean, how stupid could we get?" Kate continued. "Looking for him in ditches and in ba—well, all over the place, and the whole time the answer was right here in the house. And remember, the clues were written for children. Smart children, I'll grant you, but children. If *we* could see them, I'm thinking we should be able to solve them fairly easily."

Dottie nodded. "But the girls took them."

"Yes. Like I said, smart children."

It's been a year since I blew out my ACL, and this damn knee still hurts sometimes. Injuries suck. So do surgery and physical therapy. I've never been much for pain.

If there's a silver lining, I guess you could say that, since the knee kind of derailed my lacrosse career, I've been working harder on keeping my grades up. I wanna get that Business Administration degree in two more years, and I've got a little bit of catching up to do.

Funny thing happened today. I was home for the weekend to do a little laundry for free, and I ran across Lynch's Tennyson book in my old room. I completely forgot I had that thing. But there it was, sitting on my old rolltop desk all by itself, like it was just waiting for me to come in there and find it. And I got this crazy idea that I should give it back to him. For "closure." That's what they call it nowadays. "Closure." Not sure what, if anything, gets closed by having a little ceremony, but I understand the concept, and it's worth a try.

And that's what brings me here, not to his gravesite, which I've never even seen. To the old house. I'm trespassing, but hell, everybody does it nowadays. There's even a path through the weeds that leads down to the ruins. I've got Tennyson with me, and I'm gonna find me a suitable place—maybe I can figure out where his bedroom used to be—and leave it there.

I can see the house ahead of me. There's even less left of it than the last time I was here. The front face of it has fallen down, leaving three sides and the interior. It looks like the back side of a dollhouse. You can see there's barely enough left of the first floor rooms to support the second floor. That second floor is sagging big-time, and the fact that the roof fell onto it probably ain't helping matters. And of course it's all black as coal.

It's so quiet here. This is springtime. There should be birds, right? But this place is as silent as—

Never mind.

The wind is rattling the tree limbs a little, and my feet crunch as they come down. Little gray puffs come up every time I take a step, and the smell … it still smells like smoke here.

The amazing thing is that nobody has bulldozed this place yet. It's a prime location, at the end of a quiet dead-end road. There should've been a house built here by now.

I guess it's 'cause of what happened. Or what people *say* happened. I'm still not sure I believe it. I mean, Lynch was crazy, but the Lynch I knew never would've done anything like what they say he did.

It came out a few days after the fire, once they got the two bodies out of there and identified 'em. First they just told us it was Lynch and his mom, and that was bad enough, but then they had to say that Lynch's mom was stabbed twenty-eight times before she burned.

I'll admit it, the first thing I thought about was that deer-antler-handled knife. But I felt bad about it right away. He couldn't've.

They never found the knife, or any other murder weapon that I ever heard of, but still they blamed the whole thing on Lynch. It was easy for 'em, 'cause he *was* crazy and everybody knew it. They say he stabbed his mom to death, then set the house on fire, maybe to cover up what he did, or maybe 'cause he was sorry for what he did, and then somehow got himself burned up with it, either accidentally or on purpose.

There were some other theories, too. They said something about maybe an "intruder" might've done it, or maybe one of Mrs. Lynch's boyfriends.

(She had plenty of 'em, and some of 'em weren't exactly the cream of the crop, if you know what I mean.) I even heard some people talkin' about the ghost of Lynch's dad comin' back for his revenge. I don't know where that came from. Revenge for what? But anyway, folks kept bringin' up how Lynch used to talk about "the wonks," and how he always said the wonks liked to set fires. They said that the wonks were really just a part of Lynch, a part that got a charge out of setting fires. Lynch did have a thing about fires, if anybody knows that it should be me, and I think it went back to that time me and him—

Anyway, in the end, they pinned it all on him.

I can believe the fire part, I guess, but the stabbing? I just don't know. Nobody really knows what happened in this house that day, and nobody ever will. The only thing I know for sure is that Lynch is dead. My buddy is dead.

I do sort of an air shake, like we used to do back then, going through the motions to see if I still remember it. Yep, I do.

Lynch, I miss ya, old buddy.

I don't know why, but I just started thinkin' about that day when I got stung by a wasp, and how hard we laughed, and how we did our secret handshake and swore we'd come back and explore the basement of that old building. That was one oath we maybe shouldn't have made, considering the way it turned out.

In fact, I guess I *do* know what made me start thinkin' about that, after all.

Nowadays they call this house "haunted." Kids come down here at nighttime and try to spend the night and, I don't know, have séances and stuff, I guess, then they all tell each other about what they saw and heard while they were here. And it keeps gettin' bigger and bigger and creepier and creepier. I think that's why they can't sell the place, and why they've never bothered to come in here with a bulldozer and knock the rest of this house down. It's been a couple of years now, and if they don't do it soon, it's gonna turn into one of those, what do they say, urban legends? Can you have an urban legend way out here in the sticks? Rural legend, maybe.

Goddamn it, why did I have to think about the final scene in *Carrie* just now?

Maybe 'cause the last time I was here, I was with my ex-girlfriend, Paula. Bein' here made me think about Paula, and that made me think about the day we both went to Corner Video and rented the videotape of *Carrie* and watched it together. Creeped us both out, like it's creepin' me out right now. I'm half expectin' to see Lynch's bloody arm come reachin' for me out of the ashes.

Gotta get a grip on myself. Came this far. Do something!

What do I do? Looking up at the second floor, I can see my original

177

plan isn't gonna work. No way I can get up there to where Lynch's bedroom was, and even if I could, it's buried under what's left of the roof.

The silence here is really startin' to get to me. Any sound'll do. A car. A dog barking. A passing plane, or a lawn mower somewhere. Anything.

Nothing. It's like I went five hundred years back in time, to when there were only Indians here.

No. Even then, there were birds.

I make my way around the house to the back side, passing between the house and the old detached garage where Lynch's dad used to work on his cars. The garage is still standing. There's an old car in there, covered with about a quarter-inch of dust. The windshield is all busted out. Somebody named Scott spray-painted on the wall that he was gonna be with Jennifer forever. Or maybe Jennifer did it.

I walk all the way around the house and come back to the front. I made the whole trip and didn't find any good place to set this book down. Where would Lynch have liked it to be?

Now I'm thinkin' about this Tennyson book of poetry sittin' here all alone in this deadly quiet, amongst all this rubble, these ashes, gettin' rained on, and probably tore up by some dumb-ass teenager who thinks it's funny to tear up books. And I realize, this is a mistake. Lynch wouldn't've wanted that. Lynch would've wanted me to take care of the book until the day I die. That's what he would've wanted.

Stupid. This is just stupid. What the hell am I doing here?

I sit down on a stump and hold the book in front of me. Pretty. Nice work on the cover. It's old and it's beaten, but it's a nice book. What was the name of that poem, the one Lynch said was his favorite? Something to do with Greek mythology. "Odysseus?"

I've never really looked at this book. It's been in my room for five years, and I've never even opened it.

"Ulysses." That's what it was. Hmm.

I open the book.

Lindsey and Amanda flew out Mom-mom's back door, past the garage, down the dirt road, through the barn, and across the pasture. Jenny and Jill had moved to the far side of the field. They looked up, and went back to their munching.

"I'll bring you some apples next time!" Amanda yelled.

The girls climbed the fence and entered the woods. They ran through the pine grove, crossed over the Crossing Log, and soon reached the confluence of the two streams.

Thinking Rock loomed above them like a granite god. A natural system of roots and rocks formed a sort of steep stairway from the opposite bank up to the top of the Rock. It was negotiable, if one was careful. But Sadler's

Run coursed between them and the foot of the stairs, running a foot deep and twelve feet wide, with no stepping-stones or logs on which to cross. They didn't want to go wading on the slippery rocks of the streambed when they knew of a perfectly good crossing place a hundred yards upstream.

They passed Thinking Rock and continued up the path and cut left onto the game trail that led to the crossing. On the way back to the stream, Amanda tore her shirt on the encroaching brambles, but once there, the way was clear. They stepped onto a large rock that jutted out into the water from their bank. From the end of this rock, only four feet separated them from another one on the opposite side. A third, smaller rock was situated midway between the two large ones. The water, constricted at this point by the three stones, ran swift and deep, and fell two feet in elevation on the downstream side of the spill. A misstep here would mean a good soaking at the least, but two short hops brought the girls safely to the other side.

They turned and went back downstream along a seldom-used trail that ran treacherously close to the bank, at some intervals actually hanging over the undercut stream bank. The girls picked their way along with care.

About halfway back to Thinking Rock, they passed into a large, clear, flat area. A neat circle of stones in the center of it was filled with ashes and partially burnt logs. Nearby was a jumbled stack of sticks and large fallen branches.

Amanda knelt and held her hands over the ashes. "It's still warm," she said.

Lindsey's gaze swept the immediate area. "Look over there." She pointed into a natural dell formed by two knobs of the hill that projected toward the stream. A lean-to, constructed of wrist-thick sticks and pine boughs, occupied the crotch of these two knobs. Someone had spread a ratty old tarp across the boughs, and left some moldy-looking blankets bunched up under them. A plastic Shenandoah's Pride milk crate rested beside it, filled with bric-a-brac the girls didn't care to try to identify. They saw a small pile of empty bottles and cans near the lean-to, and more next to the fire circle. Coke, Spam, pork and beans, and a few bottles of the type the girls knew usually contained alcohol.

"Somebody's been camping out here," Amanda said.

"Maybe it's kids from Belle Forest," Lindsey said.

"Maybe."

"Whatev. It's creepy. Let's get out of here before they come back."

"Yeah, let's."

They continued on to Thinking Rock and stopped at its foot. "Are you sure this is a good idea?" Amanda asked. "We've never been here without Daddy."

"If Daddy didn't think it was safe, would he have hidden a clue here?"

They climbed the natural stairs to the top of Thinking Rock, passing the dark cave it sheltered on the way up. On the rock's vertical face were deep etchings that may have been natural striations in the stone, but that the elder Raithers claimed were Native American pictographs. If so, they were so softened by time and weather that no meaning could be discerned from them.

The girls reached the top, and as they stepped carefully around the circular depressions ground into the stone by Native American pestles, a peculiar sensation came over them, as if the air were somehow richer, more pure. The woods around them seemed to shift into sharper focus. Every tree seemed to shimmer with a barely perceptible vibration of life. The sensation was much stronger than they'd ever felt before, and recalling their earlier conversation, they both wondered.

"It does feel weird up here," Lindsey said.

"Yeah. My skin's all creepy-crawly."

"Do the trees look different to you?"

"Totally," Amanda said.

"Is that the 'truth' Poppy was talkin' about?"

"Who knows? I'm scared, Lin."

"Let's just find the next clue and get out of here. It has to be around somewhere. Let's see that poem again."

Amanda dug in her backpack and brought out the poem. She and Lindsey sat side by side and read it together. "'In shadows dark, a tiny spark illuminates the test,'" Amanda muttered. "What's he talking about?"

"Oh, snap," Lindsey said. "I hope it's not what I'm thinking."

"What?"

"Remember on the way up, we pass that little cave back under the rock? The one where we always wonder if something lives in there?"

"Oh, no."

"Oh, yes. There's some pretty dark shadows under there."

"But what about the spark?"

"I don't know. Let's go down and check it out."

Descending the stairway was trickier than climbing up, so they went slowly. About a third of the way down, they stopped at the point where they could see into the little cave. Its ceiling was the bottom surface of Thinking Rock; its floor was earth. Tim and the girls had often speculated whether it might be home to a fox or a raccoon or a nest of snakes.

Peering into it, they could see nothing but blackness—*except for the blinking red light*. Like a tiny heartbeat, it pulsed on and off in the dark recess of the cave.

The girls met each other's gazes. "What is it?" Lindsey asked.

"I don't know. Something Daddy put in there, I guess."

"Well, at least it's not an animal. It's a blinking light. Like a little Christmas bulb."

"But what if there's snakes in there? They could be all around it. I'm *so* not stickin' my hand in there."

"Me neither. But we have to get that thing out if we're gonna save Dad." Lindsey looked around her and grabbed a yard-long stick from the hillside. She leaned toward the cave, extending the stick before her. She shifted her weight to her left foot, and lost her footing. She gave a small yelp of surprise and pain as she slid down to the next step, but caught herself there. She examined her left arm where she'd scraped it on a rock. It oozed blood.

"Ouch. That hurt," she said. "Manda, hold on to my waist while I try again."

Lindsey stepped back up and leaned to her left, this time with Amanda standing behind to help support her. She jabbed the stick into the hole and waved it around. She struck something that made a metallic sound, and some dried leaves, but nothing that sounded or felt (or reacted) like an animal. No snakes came boiling forth from the hole. No swarm of bees, plague of locusts, or avalanche of frogs. "I think it's safe," she said. "But I still don't wanna reach my hand in there."

"Me neither."

"Well, one of us has gotta do it."

They watched each other for a moment, each waiting for the other to give in.

"Rock, scissors, paper?" Amanda suggested.

Lindsey shrugged. "Why not?"

"But we both have to pinky-promise that we'll do it if we lose."

"Pinky-promise? Come on, Amanda. That's kid stuff. I'll do it if I lose, all right?"

Amanda stared at her.

"Oh, all right. Pinky-promise." She extended her little finger and hooked it with Amanda's. "Ready now?"

"Yes."

"On three, right? One, two, three!"

Both girls threw Rock.

"One, two, three!"

Both Scissors. They laughed at themselves.

"One, two, three!" Lindsey showed Scissors, Amanda Paper.

"Darn it!" Amanda said. "Okay, Lin, help me get up there."

Lindsey helped Amanda climb up onto the little shelf of ground in front of the cave opening. Amanda paused and faced Lindsey, visibly gathering courage. She took a deep breath and held it. Then, with her face turned away from the hole and her eyes squeezed shut, Amanda grimaced as she reached into the hole with her right arm. It went in up to the shoulder. "I feel something," she said. "It's another box like the last one, I think."

"Is that all?"

"No, there's lots of leaves and stuff. I got the box. Wait, I dropped it. Okay, I got it again. Here." She handed the black lockbox to Lindsey and shuddered. "Ugh! That was so nasty."

"But you did it, Manda. Good job."

The box was identical to the one they'd found behind the garage. Secured to the top of it by a strip of duct tape was a tiny pulsing red LED. "Where do you think Daddy found a little light like this?" Amanda asked.

"Prob'ly at Radio Shack," Lindsey said.

"Or out of one of those blinking lollipops. Like, maybe he ate the lollipop and then taped the inside of it on here!" They both laughed at the image of their father eating a blinking lollipop. "Well, let's open it up. I left the key up on top."

They climbed back to the top of Thinking Rock and sat down with their new prize. The key had worked its way to the bottom of Amanda's pack and she had to remove a few things before she found it. Lindsey took it and inserted it into the keyhole.

"Uh-oh," Lindsey said. "This key doesn't work."

"What do you mean, it doesn't work? It has to."

"I'm telling you, it doesn't fit. We need a different key."

"But we don't have any more keys. And we don't have any more clues to *find* another key. The only clue we have is inside that box."

"It must still be in the cave, then."

"Jeez, I hope not. I don't wanna go back in there."

"It has to be, Manda. Where else would it be? Are you sure you didn't feel anything else in there? A plastic bag, or anything?"

"No, nothing."

"I'll do it this time," Lindsey said.

Amanda rolled her eyes. "It's okay," she said. "I'm smaller, it's easier for me to get up there on that little ledge. I'll look again."

They retraced their steps to the cave. Amanda reached in and pulled out leaves and sticks from the hole so she could more easily feel the bottom. Then she stuck her arm in once again. "Hey, I found something. But it's not a key."

"What is it?"

Amanda pulled out a CD in a pink jewel box, sealed in a freezer bag, and showed it to Lindsey.

"Huh?" Lindsey said. "A CD? It says something on it. What's it say?"

"Oh, no. It's another poem." She read:

"It seems you still need one more thing
To get into this box.
So you must listen with four ears
When Mr. Buffett talks.
Its hiding place is known to him,
In this I can't be wrong;
For fifteen times he mentions it
Within a single song!"

"Great," said Lindsey. "Well, at least that one's not too hard to understand. We have to listen to that CD to find out where the key is. I don't suppose you brought a CD player in that bag of yours, did you?"

"'Fraid not."

"Then I guess we'll have to go back home and listen to it."

Amanda's eyes snapped wide open. "Oh no!"

"What?"

"We forgot to call home while we were at Mom-mom's house. OMG, we are so going to get it."

"Maybe Kate hasn't woke up yet."

"She's gotta be awake by now. It's, like, really late. We had lunch already. We better hurry up and get home."

"Manda. I so don't want to deal with Kate right now. She'll prob'ly be so mad, she'll make us stay inside."

"What'll we do then? We have to get to a CD player."

Lindsey paused and considered. "What about Deanna? We could take the trail up to her house." Amanda's friend lived on Horne Drive, the end of which was a short hike up a side trail from Thinking Rock.

"She's got swimming lessons on Sundays. Grayson might be there, I guess ..."

"Never mind," Lindsey said. "He wouldn't even let us in the house unless we ate worms or somethin'." She started on her way back to the top of Thinking Rock as she continued: "We could go to Lexie's house, but we'd have to go right past home to get there. Mom-mom doesn't have a CD player. It looks like we gotta go home. But I'm not letting Kate tell us what to do. She's not our mother. This is important, and I don't care what she says."

Amanda looked stricken. "Lin, she's our stepmother."

"So? She's just somebody Daddy fell in love with. It doesn't mean we have to love her. Or that she loves us. Don't step on this root here, it's broken."

"Thanks. Yeah, but, Lin," Amanda said, "I think she does love us. She's stricter than Mom, but I really think she likes us. And sometimes I like her, too. At least, when she's not making me clean my room."

Lindsey was incredulous. "Listen to you, defending her! You're the one she picks on all the time. What's up with you?"

"It's just that … I think …"

"Listen. Daddy got to choose who he married, right? I mean, he picked her out himself. Right?"

"Yeah, but—"

"But did we get a choice? No. We just have to love her, because Daddy picked her. It's not fair."

"But I'm sure Daddy did a good job of picking. I bet he thought about that whoever he picked out had to be good for us, too."

"Oh, I'm not so sure about that. Have you ever heard what Mom says about her? And about the way Dad picked her out?"

"Sure. How could I not?"

"Well, what does that tell you?"

"That Kate is nicer than Mommy."

"*What?*"

"It's true," Amanda said. "Mommy always says not to say mean things about people, but she says mean things all the time about Kate. But Kate *never* says anything mean about Mommy. Even though I bet she prob'ly wants to."

As they reached the top, they heard the distant peal of the church bells from Sycamore Methodist. "Hear that?" Lindsey said. "It's noon already."

"Jeez," Amanda said. "This day is flyin' by." She hurriedly repacked her backpack, which, with the addition of the two metal boxes, was considerably more full than it had been when they'd left that morning.

"I can't believe you said that about Mom," Lindsey said.

Amanda stopped packing and looked up at her sister. "You won't tell her, will you?"

"You don't understand 'cause you're just a kid. You don't even remember when we all lived together."

"Do, too! I was four when we moved out of Daddy's house, you gooseberry. I remember it real good."

They began the descent of the Thinking Rock stairs yet again, backing down carefully with Lindsey in the lead.

"Manda," Lindsey said. "I'm not gonna tell on you for what you said about Mom."

"Thanks. I still love Mom."

"I know you do."

"I'm just sayin'."

"I understand. Have you ever talked to Dad about it?"

"No. I never talked to anybody about it. Just you."

"Okay," Lindsey said. "Let's keep it that way."

"Okay."

"And I still can't think of anything else to do but go home and take our chances with Kate. Have you got a better idea?"

"No, not really."

They reached the bottom of the stairs and started back up the trail. In their haste, they didn't hear the man's movement until they were upon him.

As they pushed aside a low-hanging branch and burst into the little campfire glade they'd passed through earlier, they came face-to-face with a large bearded man, scowling at them from ten feet away. Lindsey recognized the unkempt beard and hair, the tattered pants, the black Kiss t-shirt faded nearly to gray.

Paralyzed, they stared back at him.

"Lin," Amanda whispered, tugging on her sleeve. "It's that guy we saw at the bridge. The one that talks to himself."

"I know."

"I gotta tell ya, Book, I've been workin' this job for nigh on twenty-two years now, an' I ain't never felt so low as I did walkin' outta Timmy Raither's house today. Them two ladies humbled me good. Especially Miss Dottie."

Alan Curtis and George Booker had met at the local Wawa market for a short break. They sat in Booker's car, next to the free air pump, drinking coffee. Alan, between bites of a Boston crème donut, had just finished giving Booker the gist of his conversation with Kate and Dottie.

"Hmph," said Booker. "Miss Dottie could humble just about anybody when she's got a good mad on."

"Not me, though. You may have noticed that normally I ain't a man who's easily humbled."

Booker snorted. "That's why you're a captain and I'm still a sergeant, boss."

"Book, you'll be a sergeant when you retire, an' that's because it's the way you like it. We both know that." He took the last bite of his donut, chewed, and swallowed. "Now, I been ponderin' this situation ever since I left the house, an' I just think we been makin' a mistake, lookin' for Timmy at the bars. He ain't at the bars."

Booker nodded. "And the fact that he disappeared on the same day as Madison Kingsmore really is just a coincidence."

"Exactly. We got us a kidnapper that's taken a little girl, and we got Timmy Raither who's rode off and got himself hurt or killed somewhere, and neither one of 'em got anything to do with the other."

"And then we got Timmy's two girls out lookin' for *him*," Booker added. "And nobody knows where *they* are, on a day when there's a pervert on the loose. Whew! What a mess."

They sat in silence for a few moments, sipping coffee. Booker broke out a fresh toothpick.

"All right, the way I see it is this," Alan said. "We got to prioritize here. I still see Madison Kingsmore as priority number one. She's a child and she's in the most danger. Number two is Timmy Raither, because it looks like he might be in danger, too, although I'm startin' to think we might be lookin' for a body with that one. And number three is Timmy's girls. But if they don't show up within the next hour, then they get bumped up to number two. You foller?"

"I'm with you."

"Anyways, I want everybody keepin' an eye out for all four of 'em. Add Timmy and his girls to the list. Thirty-nine year-old white male, dark curly hair and brown eyes. About six foot, maybe two, two-ten. Two white females, ages thirteen and nine, I think, both blonde and blue-eyed. Don't know what any of 'em's wearin'. You got it?"

Booker had been scribbling in his notepad as Alan spoke. "Yeah, I got it."

"Good. Put the word out as soon as we're done here."

"Will do, Cap."

"Now, do we have anybody who ain't workin' at the present time?"

"Sheriff sent Morales, McGee, Upshaw, and Greineke down to get some sleep."

"How long ago?"

Booker checked his watch. "Been about four hours now."

"Wake 'em up. I want every unit out on these roads, lookin' for these people. Do it now. But call in the bulletin first."

"Got it."

Alan drained the last of his coffee. "You know, we made the national news. People are eatin' this stuff up."

"I heard."

Alan shook his head ruefully. "I'm tellin' ya, Book, this is the craziest shit to go down in this county since …"

When it became apparent that Alan wouldn't or couldn't finish his sentence, Booker filled in: "The Lynch house?"

"Yep," Alan said.

That black day had been a pivotal moment in the history of Sycamore, and lived on in the mass memory of the community. It still came up in conversation occasionally, especially in the Sheriff's Department, where it was the barometer against which all other events shocking and nefarious were measured. Yet, Alan, for as long as Booker had known him, had always shied away from the subject. Alan had known the Lynch boy personally; maybe that's why it seemed like it affected him more deeply than it did most people. Alan never talked about it, and Booker never asked.

That Alan had brought it up at all was surprising. Booker waited patiently to see if Alan would continue, or change the subject.

"Y'know," Alan said, "we never knew when we were kids what Lynch's mom said about him."

"You mean that he killed his father?"

"Yep. We always heard it was an accident. I didn't find out about it until I joined the force."

"Scary, ain't it? That a kid would kill both his parents like that. Years apart."

"I guess. Still bugs me about his daddy, though. That boy loved his daddy like you wouldn't believe. Used to brag on him all the time, almost like he was still alive."

"Wouldn't be the first time a child killed his parents."

"Or the last."

"Or made up memories about a dead parent."

Alan exhaled noisily.

Booker kept still.

Alan opened the car door and began levering himself out of Booker's cruiser. "We're cleanin' this mess up today, Book," he said as he stood. "All this attention is startin' to wear on my nerves."

"I hear you, Cap."

13

The man stood in the center of the clearing, right in the girls' path. His black eyes, deep-set in a heavily lined and pitted face, pinned them to the spot. They could not go forward, and they had nowhere to go behind them except back to Thinking Rock, a dead end. It wouldn't have mattered, anyway. They were both too frightened to move.

"You're the ones, aren't you?" he asked. "You're the ones."

"What do you mean?" Lindsey asked in a quavering voice. "What ones?"

He lowered his eyebrows. "Never mind," he said. "What are you kids doin' here? You don't belong here."

"We're going home," Lindsey answered. "And we're kind of in a hurry. What are *you* doin' here?"

The man took a step back, as if surprised to have been asked a question. "That's none of your beeswax. Where's home?"

"It's close," Lindsey said.

"Where's your parents?"

Lindsey flashed a *Don't-tell-him-anything* glance at Amanda. His asking where their parents were set off all her alarms. All she wanted to do was figure out a way to get him to move so they could streak past him and get home.

Amanda seemed willing to let her do all the talking. She stood staring at Lindsey in mute entreaty, as if to say, *Take care of this!* Her summer tan had disappeared, with all the blood having drained from her face.

188

"My Dad's back there," Lindsey said, pointing back toward Thinking Rock. "He'll be along in a minute."

The man glanced over their shoulders and smiled, showing more gaps than teeth. "Back there? There's nothing back there but Thinking Rock."

The girls' eyes met. "How'd you know it was called Thinking Rock?" Lindsey asked.

"Everybody knows that," he replied. "I'm not a child. I'm not stupid."

"I never said you were stupid," Lindsey said. "It's just … I didn't know everybody knew that." Lindsey kept Amanda behind her with an extended hand as she took a couple of steps backwards. This guy gave her the willies.

"Didn't anybody ever tell you girls that it isn't safe up there? It's dangerous, very dangerous, to those of the blood. I'm not of the blood, but I think you might be. They said somebody of the blood would be coming."

"*What* blood? *Who* said?"

"Never you mind that. What's your Dad doing up there, if he really is there, like you say? Looking for something?"

"He *is* up there," Lindsey said, "and he's thinking. Thinking about how he's gonna kick your ass into next Thursday if you touch us!"

Amanda's mouth fell agape.

The man scowled at her for a few heartbeats. His eyebrows seemed to get bushier as his frown deepened. His dark eyes stared them into the ground, his hands clenched and unclenched and clenched again.

Then he leered. "You're lying," he said. "There's no one with you. You're alone. You shouldn't be out here alone like this. There's some nasty people in this world. Don't you know that?"

Lindsey felt her lip begin to tremble.

"You shouldn't lie," he continued. "Bad things happen to liars. And you shouldn't curse, either."

"Please, mister," Lindsey said. "Could you please just let us go? We're really busy."

"You shouldn't be in this place," he said. "You should mind your own beeswax. That's all I do. I mind my own beeswax, mind my own beeswax. I don't hurt anybody. You're gonna get me in trouble. I've been good. I have an important job to do. And you're gonna get me in trouble."

"If you want to stay out of trouble so much, then you should let us go past."

"You're rude," the man declared. "I don't like rude people. My Dad always said to ignore rude people. So that's what I'm gonna do. I'm gonna ignore you."

"I'm sorry if I was rude," Lindsey said. "We just wanna go home. We promise we won't get you in trouble."

"Lotsa people promise," he said. "But most people don't *keep* their promises. You should always keep your promises. It's very important."

Lindsey, exasperated, said, "I'll keep my promise."

The man stopped and appeared to consider. "Okay," the man replied. "You can go." But he didn't move. "By the way, where'dja say you were going?"

Warning bells again. But it seemed to Lindsey that there'd be no harm in telling the truth this time. It might even help if he knew how close to home they were. "We live right up the hill there," she said, pointing to her left. "Where do you live?"

The man smiled broadly. "By this still hearth," he replied, "among these barren crags."

"You mean you live here?" Amanda said. "But where's your family?"

The scowl returned. The man's face flushed and it seemed he might explode. The girls' hands sought each other in fear.

"I don't have any family," he said. "I don't need anybody. I got ... never mind. I don't need anybody." Now a curtain of gloom dropped across his face.

"Sorry," Lindsey said in a small voice.

The man looked at the ground, his anger having passed that quickly. "The truth is, my head doesn't always work right." He pointed at his head and made a scrambling motion with his finger. "I have good days and bad days. And now I, well, you can tell, I guess ..." he gestured vaguely at the scattered bottles around the campsite. His gaze dropped back to his feet.

Lindsey felt pity for him.

"Mister, we're sorry about what happened to you, but you shouldn't be living here in these woods. This place belongs to our grandfather. He wouldn't like it if he knew you were here."

"Awwwwww, Jeezy Pete! Please, please don't make me move again. You don't know how hard it is to find a place where you can stay and be left alone. All I want is to be left alone." As he spoke, he seemed to sink further and further down into himself, his facial expression drooping like hot wax, his arms wrapping themselves about his midsection, his back hunching over as if he were in pain.

The man's mood swings were disturbing, but there was a part of Lindsey that could not help but feel protective of him. At the moment, he seemed more pathetic than threatening, and Lindsey decided to take advantage of it while it lasted.

"Mister, I already told you we wouldn't tell on you. If you let us go home, we'll promise not to tell anyone that you live here. You can keep on staying right here for as long as you like. Deal?"

The man seemed to draw deeper and deeper into gloom as Lindsey spoke. When he answered her, his demeanor was one of total submission. He seemed unable to look them in the face, instead gazing at the ground somewhere off to his left as he spoke. His shoulders slumped, and his cheek took on a nervous tic. "What've you got in the pack there, girlies? Any food?"

The girls looked at each other, perplexed.

"No," Amanda replied. "But maybe we could bring you some back?"

"Sure," Lindsey said. "We could do that. But, please, mister, can we go now? We're really in a hurry."

"How about books? Got any books, or magazines even?"

Lindsey quietly whistled the Twilight Zone theme music, a habit she'd picked up from her father.

"Our Dad could help you," Amanda said. "He's had problems, too. He understands."

"That's a good idea," Lindsey said. "We won't tell our grandfather you're here, because he might get mad. But if we tell our Dad, he'll prob'ly want to help you."

"People always say that," the man said, pouting. "But they don't mean it."

"You don't know our Dad," Amanda said. "I promise he'll help."

"What makes you think that?"

"Because he's my Dad. I know he will."

"No, I meant … never mind." The man lifted his gaze to meet Amanda's. "Pinky-promise?"

Amanda swallowed, looked at Lindsey.

Lindsey widened her eyes, and gave the tiniest shake of her head, *No!*

"All right," Amanda said. "Pinky-promise." And she approached the man, right little finger extended.

"Amanda!" Lindsey said in a fierce whisper. But it was too late.

The tension was thick in the house. It had been nearly an hour since Alan Curtis left, and the girls had not returned. Kate's anxiety had intensified to a fever pitch. She sat at the kitchen table, holding a cup of coffee in two trembling hands, while Dottie stood, staring out the back door. The two women had barely spoken, each lost in her own thoughts.

Dottie broke the spell. "The barn door was open."

Kate looked up from her coffee. "Excuse me?"

"I've been replaying the morning's events over and over in my head. I may be misremembering this, but I could swear that when I left the house this morning, the barn door was open."

"Is that unusual?"

"Yes. With Edward in Wyoming, only the farmhand would be going in and out of there. And he comes in the evening, generally speaking."

Kate's face lit up. "Are you sure it was open?"

"No. Not absolutely. I'm so accustomed to Edward taking care of the barn, most days it hardly registers on me whether it's open or closed. I could be confusing today with another day. But I have a clear mental image of the door being open. Could it be just a case of wishful thinking?"

"It's Tim!" Kate said, excited. "It's got to be. It makes perfect sense. He spent his entire childhood around the farm. He knows all the nooks and crannies, all the hiding places. It would be only natural."

"Yes. The more I think about it, I'm convinced he must have been there. I'm going now. You should wait here for the girls. I'll call you and let you know when I find him."

"Like hell," Kate said. "That's my husband. I'll go, and you can wait here."

"It's my home. I know where to look."

Kate stared. "Fine. We'll both go. I'll leave the girls a note."

Kate wrote the girls a hasty note on a napkin:

> Lindsey & Amanda,
> I've gone with Mom-mom to her house. We'll be back in 15 min. *Do not* leave this house until we get back! It's not safe. I'll explain later.
> Love, Kate

She left the note on the kitchen table, where the girls would be sure to find it, since she expected them to come in and scrounge for something to eat before they did anything else. Then she and Dottie got in Dottie's car and backed out of the driveway.

As soon as the back door closed behind the two women, Widget saw her chance. An unattended cup on the kitchen table called to her. It must be investigated. If it contained something good, she would nudge at it until it tipped over, then lap up the spillage. It was great fun.

Getting on the table when her people were home usually worked out badly for her, but when she was alone, it was allowed. She hopped up on one of the chairs, then slithered between the chair back and the table edge up onto the tabletop. She strolled across it as if she owned it, which, of course, she did, and sniffed at the forgotten cup. Once was enough. Whatever was in the cup was bad. It was not for her. She knocked it over anyway, just for fun.

A napkin on the table spoiled her fun. It was most inconveniently located to absorb most of the brown fluid. None of the spillage made it to the floor, where she could watch it splatter, and perhaps bat at the falling stream with her paw. This was no fun at all.

Bored, Widget jumped to the floor and wandered off in search of a nice sunny spot in which to lie.

Still refusing to meet their eyes, the man extended his pinky in Amanda's direction and Amanda took a step toward him, extending her finger as well. Just as they were about to link, Amanda stumbled. Her hand dropped a couple of inches as she caught her balance, and the two pinkies missed each other cleanly.

"Whoops," Amanda said, stifling a giggle with her hand. "Missed. Here, try again." She extended her pinky once more.

"No ... it's prob'ly best if we don't," the man said. "That was a sign. We shouldn't ignore it."

"You sure?"

"Yeah, I'm sure. I don't wanna make 'em mad. But we still have a deal, right? Pinky or no pinky, a deal's a deal, right?"

"Yeah, sure," Amanda said. "A deal's a deal, Mr. ... Hey, what's your name, anyway?"

The man's jaw fell open, closed again, opened and closed once more. His eyes darted all around the forest. "You want to know my name?"

"Well ... yeah. That's what people do when they meet."

"Nobody ever asks me my name."

"Well, I'm asking."

"Amanda, leave him alone," Lindsey said. "If he doesn't want to tell us his name, he doesn't have to."

"Lee. My name's Lee."

"Is that your first name or your last name?" Amanda asked.

"First. It's short for Leland."

"Okay, Mr. Lee. I'm Amanda. And this is my sister, Lindsey."

"Amanda!" Lindsey said. Then, after turning back to Lee, "May we please go now?"

Mr. Lee stepped out of the trail and gestured for them to continue on their way. "We made a deal. I'm not a cheater or a liar, like my mom."

Lindsey hurtled past him without ceremony, grabbing Amanda on the way by and dragging her along. At the far side of the clearing, they turned and looked back.

He was gone. Vanished. From the ashes in the firepit, a lazy tendril of smoke curled into the sky.

"Where'd he go?" Amanda said.

Not deigning to answer, Lindsey whirled and lit out for home, with Amanda right behind her. They moved as fast as the trail would allow, slowing down when forced to for safety's sake, but running flat out whenever possible, and casting frequent glances over their shoulders for signs of pursuit. They ran until they burst forth from the gap in the privet hedge and arrived in their own back yard. They stopped there, gasping for breath, leaning over with hands on knees. They were jazzed up with adrenaline, their lungs laboring. Lindsey still had a feeling like she had a target painted on her back, and she shuddered.

"Made it," she said.

"Do you think he followed us?"

"No, I don't think so. Not this far, at least."

"My legs hurt," Amanda said.

"Mine, too."

"I was so scared, Lin."

"Me, too. That guy scared the crap out of me."

"I'm glad you were with me. I don't know what I would've done if I was by myself. Even though he turned out to be all right."

"I still don't trust him," Lindsey said. "He was weird. Talkin' about blood and all that."

"But I don't think he would've hurt us."

"He might not have. But we don't know for sure. You can't tell how he's gonna be from one second to the next. What if he got mad again? What if he started thinking we were alien spies or something? I don't wanna be around him anymore. And we're so telling on him as soon as we get a chance."

"But, Lin, we made a deal."

"We made a deal not to tell *Poppy*. That's all. We didn't say we wouldn't tell anybody else. We even *told* him we were going to tell Dad. So that's what we'll do."

"Okay."

"Now, let's go listen to this CD. We have to get this box open."

"You mean, if Kate doesn't kill us first. Or ground us."

Lindsey groaned. "I think I'd rather be killed than grounded right now."

Amanda only nodded.

"Ready?" Lindsey asked.

"Yup."

They walked up through the yard, around the pool, and to the back door. "Here goes nothin'," Lindsey said. She opened the door, stuck her head in, and said, "Hello? Kate?"

No answer came. They both entered the house and closed the door behind them. "We're home!" Lindsey said.

Still no answer.

"Where is she?" Amanda asked, reaching down to stroke Widget's head. "Her car's here."

"Maybe she's sleeping. I'll check the bedroom."

A quick inspection of the house revealed that they were alone, but for the cat.

"She must be outside somewhere, then," Amanda said.

"Maybe she's out lookin' for Dad," Lindsey said. "Let's listen to this CD before she gets back. Want to use the one in your room?"

"Sure."

As they passed the kitchen table, Amanda said, "Looks like Widget's been at it again."

"I know, right?" Lindsey said. "Not our fault this time. And I'm not cleaning it up."

In Amanda's room, they took the CD out of its case and put it in the boom box. The display showed twenty tracks. They played the first one.

"What are we listening for?" Amanda asked.

"A secret message, I guess," Lindsey asked. "The poem says 'When Mr. Buffett talks,' whatever that means. I guess we'll know when we hear it. Or I hope we will."

"It must mean Jimmy Buffett," Amanda said. "Daddy listens to him sometimes."

"That's prob'ly it," Lindsey agreed. "Do you know what he sounds like?"

"Not really. I might know him when I hear him. But I know this song is Avril Lavigne. I don't think there's a secret message in here."

They listened to tracks two through six and heard Black Eyed Peas, Rihanna, and Carrie Underwood, in addition to two performers they couldn't identify. They had just decided to skip straight to track twenty and get it over with, when they both stopped talking, listening to the man's voice on track seven. "That's him!" Amanda said. "I know this song!" They listened for a bit. It was a song about creosote plants and antebellum houses, something they couldn't connect with at all, and they were making annoyed faces at each other when Mr. Buffett sang the song's title. "Life Is Just a Tire Swing."

"Tire swing!" they said in unison.

"The key's in the tire swing," Lindsey said.

"Should we listen and count how many times he says it?" Amanda asked.

"Why?"

"Because the poem said he would mention it fifteen times."

"Manda, I don't know about you, but I don't think I can stand to listen to this whole song just to count the 'tire swings.' I've heard enough. Let's go."

They shot out the back door and ran across the yard to the big maple tree, under which Tim had used a sturdy nylon rope to hang a tire from his old Buick. Lindsey got there first, looked inside the tire, and there it was: a small silver key, identical in appearance to the first one they'd found.

"Box, box!" Lindsey said.

"It's in my pack, on top," Amanda said. "Here, get it out." She turned around so Lindsey could open her pack.

"On second thought," Lindsey said, "let's get out of the yard before Kate comes back from wherever she is. Come on, we'll go behind the hedge."

"We can sit in my fort," Amanda said. "I have some lawn chairs down there."

"Your fort?"

"Yeah. Just follow me."

They ran down to the bottom of the yard and through the privet hedge. Amanda led them to a small clear area the size of her bedroom, where the grass was short and sweet-smelling, and the young trees enclosed them like a mother's arms. Amanda and her friend Deanna had found the place a couple of summers ago, and still used it occasionally, to sit and talk, or listen to the birds or watch the clouds.

"Wow. Cool," Lindsey said. "So this is where you and Deanna always disappear to."

"Yep. And one time I brought Jerome here, too."

"Jerome?"

"Yeah." At her sister's bug-eyed face, she added, "So?"

"Jerome's a boy!"

"Duh."

"But—"

"He's our cousin, Lin. It doesn't count."

"He's not really our cousin. Uncle Darryl's not really our uncle, so you could marry Jerome if you wanted to."

"Who said anything about getting married? Could we just work on this clue?"

Amanda stripped off her pack and unzipped it. She got out the box and handed it to Lindsey.

Lindsey inserted the key.

"It works!" she said. The lid opened, and inside were more plastic bags. The one on top contained five or six more jigsaw pieces.

"Put that one back in my pack," Amanda said. Lindsey tucked the puzzle pieces in with the other stuff.

The second bag contained only a single piece of paper, on which was printed in large block letters:

SVVRB UKLYF VBYMH CVYPA LAHIS LHAFV BYMHC
VYIAL YLZAH BYHUA

And beneath that was written:

This code is easy to solve. But you must have the key. The key
is a number. Do you know what the number is? To solve the
code, you must go that many letters down the alphabet for
each letter. For instance, if the key was the number 2, then you
go backwards 2 letters. So the first word would be QTTPZ.
Good luck!

"Well, at least he told us how to do it," Amanda said. "But what's the
key?"

"That's easy, *kunumunu*," Lindsey said. "It must be our secret number,
remember? It was seven. All we have to do is count back seven letters for
each—Hey, what's wrong? Are you crying?"

Amanda's lip trembled, and her lower eyelids held back unshed tears.

"I didn't mean to make you cry." Lindsey said. "Is it 'cause I called you
kunumunu? You know I'm only kidding."

"No ... it's just seeing Daddy's handwriting, I guess. I'm so *scared*, Lin!
What if we can't do it? What if we can't find him? I miss him so bad!"

"I miss him, too, Manda. And I'm scared, too. But we *will* do it. We're
going to find him. Look how far we've got already! Don't worry. Look, let's
solve this code right now. You packed paper and pencil, right?"

Amanda nodded.

"Well, come on, we're wastin' time."

Amanda sniffed as she got out the paper and pencil and handed them to
Lindsey.

"I'm gonna start by writing the alphabet across the top here," she said.
"Then we'll write what each letter means right underneath of it. That'll
make it easy for us." When she'd finished writing the alphabet, she said,
"The key was seven, right? So what's seven letters before A?"

"There *aren't* any letters before A."

"Yes, there are. We go back to the end of the alphabet for that. See how,
in the example he gave us, the B became a Z? See, one letter before B is A,
and two letters before is Z. Get it?"

"That makes sense, I guess."

"So seven letters before A would be ... let's see, Z, Y, X, W, V, U, T.
It's T. Now we write the rest of the letters across the bottom row like this:"

A B C D E F G H I J K L M N O P Q R S T U V W X Y Z
T U V W X Y Z A B C D E F G H I J K L M N O P Q R S

"Now all we have to do is replace the letters. You read the
letters to me, Manda, and I'll decode 'em."

Amanda read off the message to Lindsey, and Lindsey wrote:

LOOKU NDERY OURFA VORIT ETABL EATYO
URFAV ORITE RESTA URANT

"I think we have to regroup the letters now," Amanda said.

"Look ... under ... your ... favorite ... table ... atyo ... *at your* ... favorite restaurant! Mickey D's! He's gotta mean Mickey D's!"

"Let's go!"

"Quick, pack everything up."

Amanda began shoving things back into her backpack. "I'm leaving this box here. My backpack is too full," she said. "There's nothing in the box, anyway."

"Okay. Let's go get our bikes. We're almost there, Manda. I can feel it!"

They went back to the hedge and peered through it, alert for any indication that Kate may have returned. They didn't see anything. She might be in the house where they couldn't see her, but at least she wasn't in the back yard. They decided to chance it. They broke from cover and ran to the shed.

They got their bikes out, closed the shed door behind them, and rode Garland Drive down to the bottom. There they stopped, checked for traffic, and turned right onto White Horse Road. Kate would have disapproved of them riding on that road, especially without helmets, but it was only for a short distance. A hundred yards along White Horse, they turned left onto Summit Circle. From there they would take Virginia Street over to Orenzo Mill, cross that road onto the grounds of Amanda's school, Sycamore Elementary, and ride through the playgrounds and teacher's lots until they could cross Route 128 to McDonald's. They rode as if the devil himself was on their tails, with both hope and fear in their hearts.

Neither of them thought about the fact that they'd once again forgotten to notify Kate of their whereabouts.

Jerry woke up with the grandmother of all headaches. He reached over and tipped the alarm clock toward his face so he could read it. After noon. He laid his head back down on the pillow and closed his eyes.

He wanted to die. He couldn't remember the last time he'd been this hung over.

Last night, he'd taken a much-needed break from the daily grind of childnapping. He'd gone to the hotel bar, gotten politely sloshed, and happened upon an underage girl with a fake ID whom he'd had no trouble seducing. He'd brought her to his room, and used her for his enjoyment. He was reasonably certain she hadn't enjoyed it as much as he, but her pleading and whimpering only made it sweeter for him. Then he'd popped a bottle of Maker's Mark and gotten smashed while she watched, struggling against her bonds and wondering what he'd do next. She must have been relieved when he finally passed out.

He'd sent her packing at dawn, after the first time he'd thrown up. He'd removed her gag and released the tiny clamps from her body. Had he not felt so sick, he would have licked the blood that beaded up, but in his condition he simply released her from bondage. She wasted no time in scurrying to get her things.

She wouldn't tell. Her daddy would kill her if he had any idea she hadn't been over Maryanne's house. Even if she did spill to somebody, Jerry would have disappeared long before anyone could get there.

He still had a job to do. He had to get over this hangover and get to work. He needed to check on Darling Madison first, then get back to the playground. He levered himself out of bed, feeling unclean, contaminated. A shower would take care of that, and perhaps bring him back to life as well.

Tim now spends more time in delirium than out of it. His dreams, feverish and frightening though they are, are a blessing and a refuge.

In one of his wakeful moments, he studies his right arm in horror and disgust. He's made a crude splint for it out of a piece of wood that was presumably once part of the well cover, and a strip of the towel he's ripped with his teeth. This keeps the arm from bending between the wrist and elbow and alleviates some of the pain, but it's still not a pretty sight. It is black, blue, and purple from shoulder to fingertips; the arm swollen and the skin waxy, tight as a drumhead; and there are two festering puncture wounds where the bones of his forearm ruptured the skin.

The task of getting the useless limb in front of him was slow and torturous. He had to take several breaks during the process, and he nearly passed out a couple of times, but he refused to give up. He wanted to find out, *needed* to find out, what had happened to his body, and now knows with certainty that the shoulder is separated and his collarbone broken, as well as the two bones in his forearm.

He looks at the puncture wounds. Although they are no longer bleeding, they are red, swollen, and filled with pus. He thinks about how long the wounds and the exposed bone ends were immersed in the foul water, and wonders how long it takes for sepsis to set in. He examines his arm for the telltale red streaks, and doesn't think he can see any, but it's too dark to tell for sure.

He wonders about the condition of his legs, as well, but that's out of the question.

Thirst still burns his throat. His lips and tongue feel dry and pebbly, like an old washcloth hanging in the shower.

He has a sinking feeling that he won't survive another twenty-four hours in this pit. He needs medical attention, and soon, if he is to survive.

Above him, the buzzards, whom he has named Heckle and Jeckle, have returned. All throughout the day, they have come and gone. Each time they disappear, he prays for them not to come back.

But they always do.

14

To Kate and Dottie's disappointment, the barn door was closed. Just the same, they walked out to the barn and checked it inside and out. They also looked around the pasture, and Kate walked up the hill to the run-in shed, passing Jill and Jenny on the way and giving one of them (she thought it was Jill) a pat on the muzzle.

When she came back from the pasture to rejoin Dottie (who had remained at the barn, idly stroking Thomas' back as she waited for Kate), they went together back to the house. They walked all the way around it, checking under the front porch, behind the big oak, and behind the shrubs surrounding the house, all favorite hiding places of Dottie's boys in their younger years. They found no sign of Tim or his bike.

"He's not been here," Kate said.

"No. It seems not."

"Damn. I was so ready to believe ..."

Dottie made no reply.

"I guess we'd better get back to the house."

"A moment. I need to powder my nose. Want to come in with me? I'll just be a minute."

"All right."

They came back around the house to the mudroom entrance. Dottie opened the screen door and held it for Kate, who entered at her mother-in-law's invitation.

They came through the mudroom into the kitchen. Dottie laid her keys on the counter and left Kate standing in the kitchen while she went to the bathroom. Kate sat at the breakfast bar, listening to the hum of the air conditioning and the ticking of the kitchen clock. The clock had a picture of a Rhode Island Red on it, matching the kitchen's rooster décor, and she knew that at the top of the hour, it would crow, just like a real rooster. She swept her gaze around the always-immaculate kitchen, thinking, *Does she ever cook in here?* The room looked better than the kitchens in many of the homes she showed to clients. Only two objects might distinguish it from a model home: a hardback book on the breakfast bar, and a jar of peanut butter on the counter next to the sink, sticking out like the proverbial sore thumb.

The book she could live with, but the peanut butter was just too much. Kate couldn't control herself; she picked up the jar and put it in the pantry, thinking how unusual it was for Dottie to leave something out like that. Thinking, indeed, how odd it was for Dottie to be eating peanut butter at all.

She went back to the breakfast bar and examined the book. It was an old and much-worn volume of Tennyson's poetry, with only the author's name on the front, and again on the cracked spine. Its age was apparent not only from the amount of wear, but from the sheer quality of the workmanship: the leather cover embossed with a floral design, the gilt inlays. Opening the book, she found that the yellowing pages felt, in comparison to those of your average Jackie Collins paperback, as smooth as rose petals. *They don't make books like* this *anymore*, she thought.

She flipped through the pages to the front endpaper, where she saw, written in pen, two nested Ls. Someone's initials, probably. She made a mental note to ask Dottie about it.

Moments later, Dottie came back into the kitchen. "I'm sorry," she said. "I just needed to collect myself. I allowed myself to entertain hope back there, however briefly, and … well, I was weak."

Oh, no, Kate thought. *Here it comes.* "What do you mean?"

Dottie stared at her for a moment. "Kate, dear, I hate to be so blunt, but you do realize that there's a very real possibility that we're wasting our time? That Timothy is exactly where he wants to be, and he will turn up exactly when he wants to turn up? Have you considered that?"

There you are, Dottie. The real you. I wondered what had become of you. Kate weighed her options. Should she come clean? Tim's alcoholism had been a point of contention between Kate and Dottie for years, and she would not have Dottie believe, even for a second, that they were on the same side.

But she was not in the mood, and had not the time, for a long drawn-out discussion with Dottie, particularly when she had first-hand knowledge that could bring it to a screeching halt before it started.

A burst of static came over the police scanner, sitting in its spot in the window over the sink. Then they heard a man's voice, saying something about ... stopping at McDonald's? Could that be?

"That was George Booker," Dottie said. "I'd recognize his voice anywhere. His mother worked at Ringgold's for many years, right up until it closed. And his great aunt was Mary Meeks, who was my Latin teacher in high school. A spinster her entire life, you know."

"Hm." Kate said, with a touch of impatience. *Gossip, Dottie? Really? Now?*

Dottie looked out the window toward the barn and the pasture, and sighed. "Edward never wanted to sell the farm. The housing boom was raging, and the pressure to sell was relentless, but he loathed other farmers who caved, and the houses springing up all around us sickened him. He held out for the longest time. But he was getting old and tired, and in the end, the money was too much to turn down. If any of our sons had shown an interest in taking over for him, he'd not have sold for any amount of money, but with all of them going to college ..."

Kate kept quiet. She was eager to get back to the house, but something told her she should give Dottie time to work her way around to whatever it was she wanted to say.

"You might find this hard to believe," Dottie said, "but of the three of them, Timothy was always my favorite."

Kate barked a short laugh. "Oh, come on," she said.

Dottie took a deep breath before continuing. "You must understand, I never allowed myself to *show* favoritism when my boys were growing up. In fact, I was quite proud of all of them. Gregory was successful in everything he did. He was athletic, intelligent, as handsome as his father. He could do anything he put his mind to. But he was arrogant. He was better than everyone else, and he knew it. And he felt no compunction about saying it.

"Randall was, well, he's always been Randall. He was similar to Gregory in many ways, but so different. He was just as talented, but had no interest in proving it. He was happy with himself and that was enough for him. He never thought about the future, Randall, he lived only for the moment. He's still that way. He goes aimlessly in one direction, gets bored and chooses another. He never makes plans, yet he always seems to find a way to come out on top. It was easy to love him, but frustrating to watch him waste his potential, hard to be proud of him.

"Then came Timothy. He seemed to strike the perfect balance. He took on the best characteristics of his two older brothers, and none of their faults. He was bright, athletic, and full of drive, yet so compassionate. He was everything to me. He could do no wrong. His one fault, if it could be said to be a fault, was his sensitivity. He had a tendency to take things so personally, to assume responsibility for things that were beyond his control. I tried to show him how to take a step back from things once in a while, but it was too ingrained in him. He tried to fix everything that was wrong with anything. It tore him apart."

Kate nodded. She had seen this inclination in her husband.

"Then, of course, there was the drinking," Dottie continued. "It began in high school, and I blame myself for it, partially, because at first I viewed it as normal teenage experimentation, camaraderie with friends, that sort of thing. Not dangerous, you see. And I did nothing to stop it. I decided to let him find his own limits.

"But I failed to see how his fix-everything mentality, combined with the drinking, could turn into such a powder keg. When he was a senior, he lost a dear friend. Naturally he felt partially responsible, and that, I believe, was when he discovered the application of alcohol as an escape from a world he could not control. Shortly thereafter, he was off to college, and I had missed my opportunity to straighten him out."

Dottie paused, gazing at the floor.

"He has a disease," Kate said. "It's not your fault."

"Perhaps," Dottie said. "But I ... well, we'll never know now, will we?" Her eyes came back to Kate's. "At any rate, when he married Paula, that's when the drinking got completely out of control. I believe, in coming back to his roots, in marrying his one-time high school sweetheart, in a way he was trying to make reparations, to ... to do penance. It was not something he would have understood in so many words, it was just part of him. It was yet another manifestation of his ... *insatiable* need to fix people. He saw something in her that needed to be fixed, and he felt the need to be the one to do the fixing."

"Yeah, he's like that," Kate said.

"Yes. And unfortunately, it defeated him. In Paula, he had set himself a truly unattainable goal, and that is what finally pushed him into his downward spiral." She gave a heavy sigh, signaling the end of her narrative.

"The reason I'm telling you all of this, Kate, is because I want you to understand why it is that I'm so negative about Timothy sometimes. He was so golden to me ... it was very difficult for me to face his ... failures. It still is."

"And this is the way you protect yourself. By always assuming the worst about him."

"Yes. After a certain number of unpleasant surprises, one learns to be prepared for them."

"Well, it doesn't apply anymore. You're hiding behind it. You're using it to rationalize your own behavior."

Dottie paused. "Perhaps."

Kate considered. Should she take all this at face value? This whole elaborate confession could have been a deliberate deceit, a trap to trick Kate into making her own admission.

But somehow, this one had the ring of truth to Kate. Could even Dottie have, on the fly, faked such a ridiculous, yet authentic, combination of vulnerability and hubris? True, she'd been quiet for the last hour or so, seeming lost in thought at times. She could have been using that time to rehearse her deception until she had it down to a T.

No. Kate was sure she had just caught a genuine glimpse into the soul of her mother-in-law, and about the most intimate one that she was ever likely to get. If true, it would mean that Kate's and Dottie's attitudes toward Tim, as different as they were, both grew out of love for him.

Maybe they *were* on the same side.

"Let me ask you something," she said. "Do I seem to you like another one of Tim's 'fix-it' projects?"

Dottie gazed at her for a second. Then she said, "At first, I thought you were. I assumed it. You have needs, Kate, of course you do. We all do. And I think Tim enjoys fulfilling yours.

"But over time, I have begun to see that you enjoy fulfilling his, as well. And I don't in any way believe that you are the black hole of neediness that Paula was. When you and Tim fulfill each other's needs, I don't see ... pathology."

"You don't see pathology. How wonderful! What *do* you see?"

She paused. "Teamwork, I suppose."

Kate lifted an eyebrow. "Love, maybe?"

Dottie nodded, her mouth a thin line. "Perhaps. I'm afraid to get too optimistic about it, but ... he seems to have changed since he's been with you, I'll admit that. Changed for the better."

"Then why, for God's sake, would you stand there and try to tell me he's out there somewhere, drunk as a skunk?"

Dottie fidgeted with a tissue she'd withdrawn from somewhere on her person, like magic. "I don't know. Habit, I suppose. This is very difficult for me, Kate. I'm trying. I pray to Heaven I won't come to regret it."

Kate softened. "You'll not," she said. "Listen, I have something to tell you that might help. It's about last night."

George Booker was northbound on Route 5, watching for signs of the four missing people, *anything* strange. He was doing his best to keep his eyes peeled, but truth be told, he found it hard enough just to stay awake. He'd been working for more than twenty-eight hours straight. Fatigue was setting in. *Wasn't that long ago,* he thought, *I used to pull shifts like this and not even blink. Guess old age is taking its toll.*

Worse, he was becoming desensitized to little blonde girls. Every time he saw one (and on a sunny Sunday in July, girls abounded), his heart lurched. But each time, it was just another little blonde girl. Not Madison Kingsmore. Not one of Timmy Raither's girls.

As he approached Sycamore corner, the area surrounding the traffic light where Route 5 crossed Route 128, his stomach growled. He hadn't eaten since yesterday. *Or was that this morning?*

As a lifelong resident, George remembered the old Sycamore, the prototypical country town of twenty years ago. On the four corners of the crossroads had been the post office, the bank, Walsh's Feed & Farm Supply, and Smitty's Hardware. Nearby were Sycamore Elementary, the local Methodist church, Ringgold's Market, and a few other small businesses. This nucleus had been in place for more than a generation, largely self-sufficient and completely static.

Walsh's was the first casualty of the area's suburbanization. That location was now a used car lot. The bank moved to a new and larger building next door to the post office, with a video rental store moving in to occupy the old building.

Next to go was Smitty's Hardware, a victim of the big-box hardware superstore that sprang up five miles to the south. George would never forget Smitty's creaky hardwood floors, on which regulars had gathered every morning, sharing coffee and gossip with neighbors. Where that venerable old building once stood was now the site of Sycamore's first true harbinger of civilization: McDonald's.

The last of the Sycamore icons to fall was Ringgold's Market.

For fifty years, the people of Sycamore bought their groceries at Ringgold's, right across 128 from the elementary school. George's mother worked there for years, and so did George himself for a short time, stocking shelves as a teen. The Ringgold family members who'd owned it and worked in it had been on a first-name basis with most of their customers, but the coming of the housing developments changed all that. Seemingly overnight, the population exploded, and the Ringgolds weren't able keep up with the demand, fiscally, logistically, or socially. The newcomers demanded full-scale chain-style supermarkets, and they got them. One cropped up right next to Hechinger, and then two more appeared across the street from each other, three miles to the west on 128. Their arrival put the writing on the wall for Ringgold's, but it wasn't until the coming of the Wawa convenience store, right next door to McDonald's, that the Ringgolds surrendered to the inevitable. It was the final stroke in the murderous makeover of Sycamore, Maryland.

The building still stood, vacant, crumbling, and graffiti-covered. Eight-foot-high letters, emblazoned on the building's black slate roof in fading white paint, still proclaimed RINGGOLD'S to the world.

Longtime residents, George included, greeted McDonald's and Wawa with a blend of curiosity and disgust. It was like a good car wreck; they couldn't help but come have a look. And the businesses thrived, supported mainly by newcomers, but also by many old-time Sycamorese, who decried the march of progress even as they drove home with their heart attack in a sack.

George checked his watch. Time to grab a bite to eat.

Rounding a corner, he saw the Wawa just up the road. Past that, he saw the Golden Arches. As he buzzed past the Wawa, where he and Alan had met that morning, he tossed his splintered toothpick out the window, and then pulled into the McDonald's parking lot. He'd already called dispatch. Time for a short break, to do something about the vacuum in his midsection and give his mind a rest.

Jerry studied himself in the mirror. He licked the fingers of his right hand and used them to smooth down an errant lock of hair. He straightened his tie. *Passable*, he thought.

Four Advils and a can of Coke had knocked his headache down to a tolerable level, but the nausea was still with him. He knew it would probably plague him until evening. Crawling back in bed, attractive as the idea was, wasn't an option. He had to evacuate this motel room, go feed Darling Madison, then get back to the hunt.

He picked up the keys to his rental and strode out of the room, taking down the Do Not Disturb sign as he left. Let the maid make what she would of the stains. What did he care what she thought? He was a ghost.

"So what do you think now?" Kate asked.

"Well," Dottie said. "That's quite a story, dear. I know a little more about Brian now than I ever wanted to know; but then I've never trusted that young man from the first time I met him. Even at seventeen, there was something about him that made me uneasy. And I still don't trust him."

"I know what you're saying."

"How do we know what really happened last night? Just because Brian says he did a thorough search of all the local watering holes, must we believe that it happened? Without question? Knowing him, and knowing Darryl, they probably got drunk themselves last night. They probably hit a bar or two, got distracted by a nice set of legs or something of the sort, and forgot about the rest."

"Dottie. Brian's a jerk, but I don't think they did any partying last night. In this case, I trust them."

"You're free to. But I don't. If I could talk to George Booker ..."

"I don't understand you, Dottie. It's like you *want* Tim to be drunk."

Kate's cellphone rang. She dug it out of her pocket and checked the Caller ID. "It's Darryl," she said as she pressed the answer button. "Did you find anything?" she asked him.

"No. We've been all up and down this trail, man, from Griffith all the way to where the cannery used to be. We looked on all the side trails and around all the buildings. Especially the station."

"I already checked that. Twice."

"I know, but it was dark then. And we asked around, too. We got nothin'. We saw some people hangin' around the old Lynch house, but we didn't bother to check 'em out. He wouldn't have gone down there, would he?"

"I don't think so. He'd never encourage the girls to trespass. It was probably just kids with a Ouija board."

"Yeah, that's what we figured. Anyway, I don't think Tim was on the trail. If he was, we would've found his bike, if nothing else."

"Damn," Kate said. "I'm running out of ideas. Well, Selena's going through the neighborhoods asking around. I suppose you could join her, or do some of your own. If it's not asking too much. You guys have done so much already."

"Kate, shut up. We talked about this. We're droppin' everything until we know something. Tim's like our brother."

"That's good to know, Darryl. I appreciate it, I really do. Do you have Selena's cellphone number?"

"No."

Kate gave him the number. "Listen, Dottie and I've been wondering. What bars did you hit last night?"

Darryl gave her the list of establishments, and he also recounted to her the story of meeting C.C. and going to the abandoned quarries that they'd told Selena the previous night.

"All right," Kate said. "Thanks. It sounds like you guys were pretty thorough. Thanks so much."

"It was nothin'."

"Tell Brian I forgive him, but he's still an asshole."

Darryl chuckled. "You got it."

Kate hung up and repeated the conversation to Dottie.

"It does sound like they were rather thorough ..." Dottie said. "And this came from Darryl, not from Brian?"

"Yes."

"Still. There are places alcoholics drink that the rest of us don't know about. Like the quarries, but there are many such. I still don't consider it ruled out. I think ..."

"Whatever," Kate said. "Look, Dottie, can we get out of here? The girls may be back by now."

"They'd have called. But I agree; it's time to go. I'd like to make one short detour on the way," Dottie said. "It'll just take a minute or two."

George Booker sat in his cruiser in the McDonald's parking lot. He'd just finished his Big Mac and was sipping contentedly on a Sprite while he broke out a fresh toothpick. He felt good. In fact, it was the best he'd felt since … *yesterday? No, it was the day before.* He stuck the toothpick in his mouth and leaned back in his seat, resting his head. That felt good, too. What he needed was a five- or ten-minute power nap. That would recharge him as nothing else could.

A glorious, dreamy lassitude stole over him, like the turkey and football kind. His fatigue, combined with the burger resting in his stomach, brought it on like a nine-pound hammer. In seconds, he was out.

He awoke to the sound of rapid gunfire, every nerve in his body firing at the same time. French fries went everywhere. In confusion, he looked all around him for the source of the noise, and jumped again at the sight of a person standing next to his car, face only inches from the glass next to his head.

Then he realized it hadn't been gunfire, it had been this person rapping on his window that had awakened him. He recognized her. Regaining his composure, he rolled down his window.

"Afternoon, Miss Dottie," he said. "What brings you to this fine establishment?"

"George Booker, is this what we taxpayers are paying you to do? Sleep on the job? Shouldn't you be out searching for my son and my granddaughters? Not to mention that little girl that was abducted yesterday?"

"That's what I've been doing all day, Miss Dottie," he replied. "And all night last night, and all day yesterday, I might add. We're doing the best we can, Miss Dottie."

"Well, while you were doing the best you could, did you happen to notice my granddaughters going in or out of 'this fine establishment?' Because it happens to be a favorite of theirs. Oh, of course you didn't!" she said, slapping her forehead. "You were doing the best you could, with your eyes closed. How could I have forgotten?"

"It was only for a minute. I'm sure they didn't—"

"I want to ask you a question, George."

"Okay, shoot."

"You were the one charged with finding my son yesterday, were you not?"

George nodded hesitantly. "Alan asked me to check around, sure. Off the books."

"Where did you look?"

"Well, I …"

"Just answer me honestly. I won't be offended."

"Okay, I looked at the Fireside Inn, Cappie's, Friar Tuck's, and Basilone's. And I checked 'em all again, earlier today. Nobody's seen him. If they do, they know to call me. And they will. Most of 'em owe me for one thing or another. Or they owe Alan. You know how it works."

"Unfortunately, yes, I do. What about other places? After-hours places? Did you think about that?"

"Believe it or not, Miss Dottie, I did think of that all by myself. And I know where they all are in this county, and I checked 'em all out this morning. I know what I'm doing. Believe me, Timmy's not out drinking. I'd stake my reputation on it."

Dottie blinked at him with watery blue eyes. She managed a half-hearted, "Hmph. Such as it is."

"Yes, ma'am. Such as it is."

Dottie seemed to recover herself. "Get back to work, George. You don't have the luxury of closing your eyes until those four people are found. Do I make myself clear?"

"Yes, Miss Dottie."

"Good. Kate and I are going back to her home to await news. Perhaps the girls are there now. If they are, we'll notify you. If not, I expect you to notify us should you learn anything. Anything at all. Do you understand?"

"Of course, Miss Dottie. I'll keep you posted, personally."

"Thank you."

Dottie stalked off and got into a car driven by a younger, blonde woman, who must be Kate Raither. George watched as they pulled out of the lot, drove to the red light, and turned left onto 128. He rolled his window up and straightened his seat. *Guess I just got a small taste of what Alan must have gone through this morning with that woman,* he thought. *She does humble a man.*

He called into dispatch again to tell them he was leaving McDonald's. He also informed them that he'd just spoken to the grandmother, and that the two sisters had not yet returned to their home. Then he put his car in drive and pulled out onto Route 5, heading north.

This time we're ready. I got my BB gun and a flashlight, and we're gonna explore the basement of that old building we found yesterday.

When I got home yesterday, Mom asked me where I been all day. I didn't wanna tell her, so I made up some kinda lie, but Mom, she can sniff lies out like a beagle on a rabbit. Either that, or I'm just a crummy liar. Either way, she got the truth out of me, and boy, was she pissed. She wailed on me with a Hot Wheels track, and sent me to my room right after supper. She said if I ever went that far from home again, it'd be even worse for me.

So here we are, me and Lynch, already breakin' the rules. Lynch swore he'd go downstairs with me today, and no way he'd go back on his promise, and no way I could let him out of it. I told Mom I was goin' to Lynch's house, which wasn't a lie. She don't have to know where we go the rest of the day, and after today, we don't have to go back there no more. Unless we want to.

I love walkin' on these tracks in the summertime. Most of the way, it's only woods on both sides, and everything's green and shady and cool. All along the way to the old building, there's honeysuckle growin'. It smells so good, I could just sniff it all day, and we stop every once in a while to suck the little drops of juice out of some of the flowers. It's quiet back here, except for the birds and the squirrels, and it makes me and Lynch feel like there's nobody else on the whole planet except for us.

"Finish that book yet?" Lynch asks me. He's been naggin' me to read *The Phantom Tollbooth* for months, so I finally started readin' it just to shut him up. I didn't expect to like it, but actually it ain't bad. I'll never let on to Lynch that I like it, though.

"About half."

"So whatcha think?"

"It's okay, I guess. Kinda weird. Magic tollbooths and talkin' dogs and castles in the sky and all that. I like stories about the real world better."

"But it *is* about the real world, Timmy. It's about learning. You just have to see through the puns."

"See through the *what?*" I say, and right then my bee sting starts itchin' again, so I reach up to scratch the back of my neck.

Lynch sees me do it and laughs. "Still itchin', huh?"

"Shut up."

We keep walkin', and pretty soon we see the old building, lookin' pretty much the same as it did yesterday.

"I asked my mom last night if she knew what this place was," Lynch says.

I just gotta shake my head. I tried like hell to keep my mom from findin' out where we were, and he just up and told his. His mom don't give a shit what he does. Sometimes I wish I could trade places with him. And then I think about it, and I figure I'm better off with the mom I got.

"Did she know?" I ask him.

"Yeah," he said. "She told me it was an old cannin' factory. She said my grandmother used to work there back around World War Two. But it closed up when the railroad shut down back in the fifties."

"Hm," I say. I ain't really interested. I just wanna shoot some bats and find out what's in the cellar.

We leave the railroad tracks and cut through the brush to where the closest doorway into the building is.

"What's a cannin' factory?" I say.

"You kiddin' me? It's where they can stuff, you moron."

"Can what?" I say, as we go through the doorway. Inside, it's like one big room. There's a couple of little rooms off to one side that look like they mighta been offices, but most of the place is like the biggest gym you ever saw. Except a lot junkier. There's a huge hole in the roof that lets some light in, and like I said, there's lots of windows, but still it looks dark in here compared to outside.

"Tomatoes, I think," Lynch says. "Mostly." We stand still for a minute while our eyes adjust and listen to the cooin' of the pigeons in the rafters. I look up there to where those big foot-thick wooden rafters are, and I'm pretty sure I can pick out a bat or two clingin' to 'em. I start pumpin' my BB gun up.

"What are you doin'?" Lynch says.

"Whatcha think I'm doin'? I'm gettin' ready to plunk me some bats."

"Don't shoot the bats," he says, puttin' a hand on the barrel of my gun and pushin' it down toward the floor. "Bats eat mosquitoes."

"Lynch," I say, "do you have to take the fun out of everything?"

"Sorry. I thought we came here to explore the basement."

I sigh and aim my gun at a little triangle of smoky glass that's still hangin' from the frame of one of the windows, and pull the trigger. The glass explodes with a tinklin' sound, and some of the bats answer by squeakin' at each other real high-pitched-like.

"Okay," I say. "Let's see what's down there." The stairs are at the whole opposite end of the building, so we start makin' our way across the old wooden floor, goin' in between all the junk. There's big long tables, some of 'em on their sides. Layin' all over the floor is lots of pipes and big pulleys and old dusty belts and piles of chains, and some machines we can't figure out. There's a bunch of old rusty buckets shaped like laundry baskets, a couple of big metal tubs with doors on the sides, and all kinds of other shit that don't look like anything useful, like the stack of square metal plates on that one table. Then there's all this stuff hangin' from the rafters: wires and hoses and pipes and chains with big hooks on 'em, the most perfect Tarzan swings you ever saw.

For boys like me and Lynch, this place is like a dream come true.

Right in the middle of the big room, the floor sags like a gigantic trampoline, and we jump up and down on it a little. We're afraid to get too crazy on it, though, 'cause it might give way and dump us into the cellar the hard way.

We're gettin' close to the stairs now, and I can't resist pumpin' a few BBs into that damn wasp nest that got me yesterday. "Little bastards," I say. "Show *you* who's boss."

Lynch just laughs at me.

We stop at the top of the stairs that lead into the basement and stare down into that hole. Holy shit, is it dark down there. I get my flashlight and shine it into the hole. Can't see anything but old wooden steps covered in dust, and at the bottom, a stone wall on the left and a stone wall straight ahead. To the right, it's just a dark hole.

"Well?" Lynch says, and down we go.

The first couple of steps are fine, but when I get to the third or fourth one, it makes a sort of dry dusty crackin' sound that I don't like at all. "Skip this step," I say, and I keep goin'.

I guess the whole staircase must be about a dozen or fifteen steps, and when I get about halfway down, and Lynch is a coupla steps behind me, the whole staircase starts to groan and creak. Then, as I'm watchin' it, the bottom step breaks off, and the whole staircase swings like a windshield wiper until the next step hits the floor.

Me and Lynch freeze, waitin' to see if anything else is gonna happen. Nothin' does. I could swear I heard nails squealin', the ones that hold the top end of the stairs in place, like they was about to pull out, and I look up there to see if it's gonna hold.

"It's okay," Lynch says. "Go on down."

We keep goin', and I don't feel quite right until my feet touch the packed dirt at the bottom, and then right away I start laughin'. "Shit," I say. "That was max cool."

"Point the flashlight over here," Lynch says, and I shine it on the bottom of the steps where he wants it. He looks real close and says, "They'll be okay. The stringers were rotten, where they touched the ground, and they broke when we put our weight on it, is all. The rest of it'll hold just fine."

"Whatever you say, Lynch." I point the flashlight into the basement, and jeez, look at all that junk. I thought the top floor was a mess! This ... I mean, this is just—

"Looks like a bomb went off in here," Lynch says.

Yeah, that's about it. It's just as big as the room upstairs, and no matter where I point the flashlight there's a hunk of somethin' that musta been useful to somebody a long time ago, but it all looks like pure junk now. I look up at the ceiling, and I can see how big ol' rafters like telephone poles support the floor above us. Right in the middle, two of 'em are snapped. That must be where the floor sags when you walk on it.

"This place must be full of termites," Lynch says when he sees them rafters.

I look at him. "They don't sting, do they?"

Lynch laughs and says, "No, they just eat wood. Are we goin' in there, or not?"

I'm lookin' across this acre of shit, and thinkin' that I can only see where the flashlight is pointin', and meanwhile there's all this pitch blackness on both sides of the flashlight beam, and what's in *there*? I think I hear scuttlin' sounds, and I'm thinkin', to hell with the termites, this place must be full of *rats*. Which would be okay if I could see 'em, but walkin' across there with rats hidin' in the darkness all around us, man, I don't know if I'm up for that.

Right then, I spot one, a rat that is, and he's sittin' on a big box of some kind, right in front of a big metal thing looks like a boiler or a water tank. I hand the flashlight to Lynch, and I say, "Hold this on that goddamn rat over there, Lynch," and he does, and I start pumpin' up my BB gun. "It's okay if I shoot rats, right?"

"Oh, yeah, man. Rats are fair game. I don't know if you can kill it with a BB gun, though. It looks like a pretty big one."

"We'll see," I say, and I bring the gun up and look down the barrel, and I put that goddamn rat right in the notch and I pull the trigger.

Thunk! A puff of dust or rust or somethin' pops up off the tank behind the rat, and the rat disappears.

"Shit!" I say. "I missed him."

"Hey, look at that," Lynch says. He's still got the flashlight pointed where the rat was, and I look over there as he says, "You punched right through that old water tank. See, it's leakin'. Musta been awful rusty."

"Ha!" I say. "I sure did! Lemme take another shot at it." And I pump another BB into that old tank.

"Let me take one," Lynch says, and we trade the flashlight for the gun, and Lynch pokes another hole in that old tank. Now it's really leakin', and we can see a stream of water comin' out of it about as big around as a pencil. This gets us both to laughin' so hard that we have to lean on each other to keep standin' up.

"Hey, Timmy," Lynch says then. "Turn the flashlight off once."

"Huh? Are you kiddin'? No way."

"Oh, come on. It'll be cool. Just for a second."

"Uh-uh. This place gives me the creeps."

"Chicken."

"Am not."

"Are, too."

"Am not."

"Why don't you do it, then?"

"Don't feel like it."

"Oh, come on, you wuss. Just for a second. Just to see what it looks like."

"I know what it looks like. It's dark."

"All right, listen. I got a surprise for ya. But you have to turn off the flashlight. Just for a second."

"What kinda surprise?"

Lynch rolls his eyes. "Jesus Christ, Timmy," he says. "Just do it, will ya?"

I don't really wanna do it, but I really do wanna know what Lynch's surprise is, so I say, "All right. Just for a second."

I turn the flashlight off. A little light is comin' down from upstairs, but other than that it's darker than Tom Sawyer's cave.

"Okay, that's a second," I say, with my finger on the flashlight switch ready to flick it.

"Wait," Lynch says. "I ain't ready yet."

"Well, hurry up, will ya? You said a second."

"Hold on. Almost ready." And I hear Lynch messin' with his pockets, and then I hear a sound anybody would know: a cigarette lighter openin' up.

"Hey," I say, but that's all I got time for before Lynch strikes the lighter and then I see sparks shootin' out from somethin'. He flips the lighter closed and holds his arm out like the Babe did when he was callin' his homer, and in that hand he's holdin' somethin' that's spittin' sparks all down his arm, and he acts like it don't hurt, but he turns his face away from it.

"What is that?" I ask.

"Bottle rocket," he says, and right then it takes off, hissin' and spittin' fire as it flies right across that dark cellar, and then, far away, it hits somethin' and blows up with a little pop and a flash.

Lynch, he whoops, and I whoop right along with him, 'cause that was about the coolest thing I ever saw. I can still see the trail it left in the dark in front of my eyes, and the flash at the end.

"Holy shit!" I say. "That was max cool. You got any more?"

"Yeah," he says. "Three. I found 'em upstairs in that old bedroom we don't use. Musta been my dad's."

"Can I do one?"

"Sure," he says. "Look, I'll show ya."

I flip the light back on and Lynch shows me where the fuse is, and how to hold it by the long red stick, real loose in my fingertips, so when the rocket goes off, it pulls out of your grip. "You're supposed to put it in a bottle," he says. "But we ain't got any bottles, so this works just as good. The sparks sting a little bit, but they don't really burn ya."

So he hands me the lighter and I flip it open and roll the little wheel a coupla times, but nothin' happens. "How do ya work this thing?" I ask him.

"Here," he says, and takes the lighter from me. "Hold your arm up."

I hold my arm like Lynch did, and he strikes the lighter and lights my fuse for me. Then I stand there a few seconds while the sparks sting my arm, and then *shhhoooof!* off it goes.

It flies right over to where that rat was and pops, and before we have a chance to start laughin', there's this hellacious *WHOOMPH!* and a huge ball of fire explodes over there, and this wave of heat slams us right in the faces.

We look away from the heat, then we both look back, and holy shit, the whole floor at the other end of the cellar is burnin', and I mean ragin', and the whole place is lit up like daylight now.

"Jesus Mary and Joseph," I say. "This ain't good."

"Hell, no," Lynch says. "I guess it wasn't water in that tank."

And that's when it dawns on me. "Lynch," I say. "We gotta put this out. If that tank explodes—"

"Put it out with what?" Lynch says. "We gotta get the fuck outta here, that's what we gotta do."

"Yeah," I say, "you're right," and I sprint up the stairs, Lynch right behind me. I remember that rotten step and I jump over it. Somethin' cracks real loud, and I think, *Aw hell no, please no.* I skip the last two steps with one last jump and I'm off the stairs. Then I turn around and watch the whole fuckin' staircase come loose from the top and fall into the basement.

With Lynch still on it.

I'm like frozen. I stand there starin' down through this hole in the floor, watchin' like a dumbfuck while Lynch scrambles off what's left of the stairs, cussin' a blue streak. When everything stops movin', I say, "Are you okay?"

"Yeah," he says. "Scraped my shin pretty good here, but nothin's broken." Then he turns and looks at the fire, and I can see his whole face lit up like the Fourth of July. "Oh, hell," he says. "I'm fuckin' trapped down here." And he looks up at me, and I can see by the look on his face that he's about to piss his pants. Come to think of it, so am I.

"Lynch!" I say. "Jesus, what are we gonna do?"

"Get me outta here!" he yells. "Don't let me die, Timmy!"

"Okay," I say, even though I don't have any fuckin' idea what to do. "Okay, let's see. We need ... we need a rope or somethin'."

"Chains!" Lynch hollers. "Get some of that chain up there. And hurry up, Timmy! The fire's gettin' real hot. I think this tank may blow soon."

"Okay!" In a flash I'm sprintin' across the floor, and I hop up on one of the tables that's got a hook and chain hangin' over it and I grab that chain and pull. It don't move. I look up into the rafters and I can see the chain is looped over a big sprocket or somethin', and when I yank on it, it don't budge at all. This won't do.

"Timmy!" screams Lynch. "Hurry up! I'm roastin'!"

Now I remember that pile of old rusty chains we seen on the floor and I hurry up and get over there. I grab a length of chain from the top and start pullin'. It keeps comin' and comin' like it must be a hundred feet long, so I hold onto the end of it and start runnin' back toward the hole in the floor where the stairway used to be, draggin' that chain behind me. When I pass over the soft spot in the floor, I can see smoke comin' up through the cracks in it. Holy shit, this place is gonna come all the way down, and it won't be long, neither.

There's a part of me that's scared to death it's gonna blow up any second, and that part wants to get outta this building *right now*, with or without Lynch, but I shove that part down deep inside. Lynch wouldn't leave me here, no way, and I won't leave him neither.

I get back to the hole, and I'm draggin' this heavy length of chain behind me that still goes all the way back to the pile I got it from. I drop the free end down to Lynch and right away he grabs it and tries to climb it, but it just pulls more chain across the floor.

"Hold on!" I say. I gotta wrap it around somethin'."

"Hurry!" he screams, and I can tell he's cryin' now, but criminy, I ain't gonna say nothin' about it. I'm cryin', too. So I run back into the middle of the room, and I grab some of that chain and I wrap it a few times around a big square pillar in the middle of the floor, and I holler, "Okay, try it now!" and right away I see the chain go tight. I stand by the pillar for a second or two to make sure it's not gonna slip, and then when I'm sure, I run back to the hole. I see Lynch shimmyin' up that chain like a goddamn monkey, and when his hand gets near the top, I grab it and yank him up onto the floor like he don't weigh nothin'.

We don't even say anything, we just get up and start runnin' across that old wooden floor, and Lynch runs smack into one of them iron hooks hangin' from the ceiling, but he don't even slow down enough to cuss at it. We just get the hell out of that building as fast as we can, and when we get back to the railroad tracks, we stop and turn back and look.

Black, oily-lookin' smoke is just pourin' out of the hole in the roof, and goin' straight up into the sky. Folks must be able to see it for miles around.

"Oh, man," Lynch says. "That was close. I thought I was a goner."

Right then there's this huge groanin' and crackin' sound, then a big boom and some clatterin' noises, and a shower of sparks comes out the roof, and I know the floor just fell in. Then lookin' through the windows, we can see big flames comin' up from the cellar, and all of a sudden there's the godawfulest *BOOM* I ever heard, and big sheets of flame come launchin' out of every hole in that building at the same time, and bits of burnin' wood and shit go flyin' every which way. We both cover our heads up and keep 'em that way until all the stuff that was flung up into the sky stops comin' down around us, scared to death the whole time that somethin' might fall right on us.

"Jesus Christ on a pogo stick," Lynch says. "That was close."

I'm so shook up that I can't even say nothin' back to him. I'm starin' straight ahead with my mouth open, and I'm shakin' all over like a cold Chihuahua. I ain't never been so scared in my life.

"You saved my life, Timmy," Lynch says. "Jesus, you risked your own life and you saved mine." And he grabs me up in both arms and gives me a big bear hug.

"I owe you my life," he says. "And I'm gonna pay you back someday. I swear it."

"Okay, Lynch," I say, thinkin' this is kinda awkward and wishin' he'd let me go. "Whatever you say."

Then he does let me go and he takes a step away from me and he says, "I swear it," and he holds up his hand for our secret shake. I do it with him, mostly so we can move on to another subject.

We hear more crackin' and grumblin' noises comin' from the cannin' factory, and we turn to watch as the walls start cavin' in.

"Fuck me with a big stick," Lynch says. "We're gonna be in so much trouble."

"No, we're not," I say. "Did you tell your mom you were comin' here?"

"No. I never tell her nothin' about where I'm goin', you know that."

"I didn't tell mine neither. So as far as anybody knows, we were at Thinkin' Rock all day. Ain't that right?"

Lynch looks at me and smiles and nods. "Yeah. We were at Thinkin' Rock all day. And we made boats out of milk cartons and floated 'em in the stream."

"Yeah, yeah, that sounds good. Later on we'll mosey back to my house and pretend we were there all day and we don't know nothin' about no fire."

"Let's get the hell outta here before somebody sees us," he says, and without another glance back, we break and run like our asses are on fire. Which they are, in a way.

Before we get to Orenzo Mill Road, though, Lynch stops and says to me, "Listen, maybe we oughtn't to cross that road."

"Why? We have to, if we wanna get home."

"Yeah, but what if somebody sees us? We gotta get back to Thinkin' Rock without bein' seen. Let's cut through the woods here until we get to that stream that runs behind the school. It's not that far. Then we can follow the stream and go under the road."

"And then that stream runs into Sadler's Run, don't it?"

"Yeah. We can follow the streambed all the way to Thinkin' Rock."

"Great plan. Let's do it."

So we strike off through the woods. It takes longer, and we get pretty tired, and all the time we're running from that fire like it's following us. We hear lots of sirens go screamin' past us off to our right, where the road is.

We have to cross Cooper Road on the way, but it's just an old dirt road through the woods and there's no cars on it. Nobody sees us but the birds.

Just before we get to the stream behind the school, we run across somethin' we ain't never seen before. It's an old wall, broke off in the middle, and we can see where there used to be two windows in the wall, but now it just looks like three square teeth stickin' up.

Lynch, he comes screechin' to a stop. "Holy shit, Timmy! Check this out."

"It's an old house, so what?" I say.

"Maybe. Maybe it's a mill or somethin'. Look, you can see where the other three walls used to be. Let's go down in there."

"Lynch, hell no," I say. "We gotta get out of this area. There might be police crawlin' all over, lookin' for whoever set that fire. Or what if somebody's lookin' for us at home? We gotta get back. We'll come back another day and explore this thing."

Lynch, he looks kind of glum, but he says, "Yeah, I guess you're right. Let's keep movin'."

So we hit the stream and we go right underneath Orenzo Mill Road, and not too long after that, we see Thinkin' Rock ahead of us, and finally we start to relax a little. We rest a while on top of the Rock, and we go home later and do just like we planned, and from now 'til the end of time nobody will ever know that me and Lynch burnt down the old cannin' factory.

But we know. Me and Lynch both know, and I don't think we'll ever forget it.

15

Dottie was silent as they left McDonald's and headed toward home.

"Are you satisfied now?" Kate asked.

Dottie sighed. "You mean that Timothy's not drinking again? Yes, I suppose so."

"Good. Can we move on, then?"

"Move on to what? You must realize that this is scarcely good news. If he's not drinking, then …"

"I know where you're at," Kate said. "I sort of went through the same thing yesterday. If he's not drunk, then he must be dead, right? But we can't just assume that, Dottie. He could be hurt. He could've fallen and hit his head and gotten knocked out. He could have broken his leg. Been bitten by a snake, or a spider, and be sick. Maybe he's caught in a bear trap. Who knows? But I do know one thing. Until someone comes up with a body, I'm going to assume he's alive. And I'll not stop looking for him until he's found, or I fall over dead myself. Now, are you with me or not?"

Dottie took her eyes off the road to look at her daughter-in-law for a moment, and Kate saw those ice blue eyes reflect something she'd not seen before. Could it have been respect?

As they pulled into Garland Drive, Dottie said, "You're right, of course. What can I do to help?"

"Thank you," Kate said. "First, let's find out if the girls got home. Everything else depends on that."

As soon as the car stopped in the driveway, Kate flung the passenger door open and ran for the back door. She burst into the house and yelled, "Girls! Are you here?"

No answer.

"Damn," she said. In short order, she checked the entire house. It was empty. As she came back to the family room, Dottie was just entering the house. "Are they here?" she asked.

"No."

"So we must find them first. Then find their father. Kate? Are you all right?"

"Yes. I just realized something. I think I know where they are. Would you mind staying here for about fifteen or twenty minutes while I check something out?"

"Of course not. But where are you going?"

"I didn't make the connection this morning, but I remember noticing their bikes in the shed. There's only one place they'd have gone without riding their bikes, and that's into the woods. Since they've not been here yet, I assume they're still down there. I'm going after them. And when I find them, which shouldn't take long, the four of us are going to find Tim."

"I hope you're right," Dottie said with an uneasy quaver in her voice.

"Me, too. I'll be back as soon as I can. Hopefully with two girls in tow."

"I shall keep my fingers crossed. And Kate?"

"Yes?"

"Please be careful. We don't want to lose anyone else today."

Lindsey and Amanda crossed the grassy school grounds to the bus loop in front of Sycamore Elementary, then rode the main entrance out to the shoulder of Route 128, Sycamore's primary east-west thoroughfare. There, they waited for traffic to pass so they could cross safely, and once on the opposite side, they entered the parking lot of the defunct Ringgold's Market.

As was their habit, they rode around to the right side of Ringgold's, then turned left to go behind the market. Coming from behind Ringgold's on the left side, they passed into the cemetery of the tiny Sycamore Methodist Church. They crossed the cemetery on a gravel path, shivering, as they always did, when they passed the grave marker bearing the inscription "We Shall Meet Again," then went around the back of the church itself and passed into the McDonald's parking lot.

They leaned their bikes against the building and went in.

"Snap!" Amanda said. "There's somebody sitting at our table. Now what?"

"We'll just have to wait 'til they leave," Lindsey said. "Mmmm, I smell French fries. I know we just ate, but I want some. Since we're stuck here, we may as well get in line."

"Good idea," Amanda said.

"I have some money," Lindsey said. "You want anything?"

"I guess I'll take some fries, too."

With the lunch hour rush in full swing, it took several minutes to get their fries, and by that time, their table was free. They dropped their food onto it and slid into the seats.

"Let's find this clue," Amanda said, sticking her head under the table. "There's nothin' down here. Unless you count smashed French fries."

"Are you sure? There *has* to be something down there. Oh, no! What if somebody else already found it?"

"Can't be," Amanda said. "Daddy would've hid it really good, so nobody would find it unless they were lookin' for it. Like us. Don't you think?"

Lindsey paused to consider. "You're right. He wouldn't just leave something on the floor, 'cause somebody would've found it for sure. Even if nobody else did, the people who work here would've found it when they mopped up."

"It's gotta be hidden somewhere," Amanda said, and she slid her entire body under the table. "Aha! I found it!"

"You did?"

"Yeah. It's taped to the bottom of the table. It's an envelope." Lindsey heard a ripping sound as Amanda peeled the envelope loose. "Here it is."

Amanda climbed back up to her seat and dropped the sealed white envelope on the table. Lindsey grabbed it and tore it open. More jigsaw puzzle pieces tumbled out.

"Is that it?" Amanda asked. "No more clues?"

Lindsey checked inside the envelope. It was empty. "Nope. Just puzzle pieces. I guess we're supposed to finish it now. How many pieces do we have, total? There's nine here."

Amanda opened her pack and fished around. She brought forth the last bag of pieces they'd found, from the second lockbox. It contained seven pieces.

"Okay, this makes sixteen," Lindsey said. "Let's have the rest. We're going to figure this stupid puzzle out right here at this table."

Lindsey began arranging the pieces on the table. After a few moments, she looked up to see that Amanda, still digging, hadn't yet brought out the rest of the pieces. She started removing items from the pack and placing them on the seat beside her. She had her lips pursed and her eyebrows lowered.

"They're all together, in a plastic bag. We put 'em all in one bag, remember?" Lindsey said.

"I know that, *kunumunu*," Amanda snapped. "But it's not in here."

"What do you mean, it's not in there?"

"I mean *it's not in here*. Look for yourself." Amanda handed the pack over to her sister, and Lindsey double-checked Amanda's search.

"Oh, no you ditn't," Lindsey said. "You did not lose the puzzle pieces! You're right, they're definitely not in here. Now we'll *never* find Dad!"

Amanda went sheet white. "Don't say that, Lin. Please don't say that."

"Well, there's no way we can find him if we don't have all the puzzle pieces. We're done."

"I didn't mean to lose 'em," Amanda said, her eyes brimming with tears.

"All right, stop sniveling," Lindsey said. "They have to be somewhere. We'll find 'em."

"I'm not sniffling," Amanda said.

"I said, 'stop sniveling,' not 'stop sniffling.' It means stop crying."

"Well, why don't you just say crying if you mean crying!" Amanda flared. "Jeez. You act like you know *everything*. What makes you think you're so much better than me?"

Lindsey sighed. "Amanda, do we have to go through this again? I just wanted you to not be sad, that's all. Let's quit arguing and think about where the pieces could be and we'll just go back and get 'em, okay?"

Amanda nodded, her bottom lip protruding. "Okay."

"They didn't fall out on the bike ride over here, did they?"

"No, they couldn't have. My bag was zipped up tight. You saw it."

"All right. How about in the meadow? They could be there," Lindsey said.

"No, I only took out the last box there, the one we found at Thinking Rock. And it was empty, remember? We took everything out of it first." She paused. Then an expression of horror came over her face. "Oh, no, Lin! Oh no, oh no, oh no!"

"What?"

"I think I know where it is. Come on, we have to go!"

"Where?"

"Remember the last time I emptied my bag? Because I was looking for the key to open the box?"

"Oh, yeah. That was ..." Lindsey's eyes grew wide. "Oh, no ... don't tell me ..."

"Yup. On top of Thinking Rock. We have to go back there and get it!"

Jerry finished his breakfast and dabbed at the corner of his mouth with a napkin. He picked up his check and carried it to the register, paid his tab with an Andy Jackson, and took two dollars from the change to leave it on the table as a tip. The waitress, or server, whatever they liked to be called these days, had been good to him. She'd signed his check "Jodi" and dotted the "i" with a tiny heart. That always grabbed him by the gonads. It was so child-like.

On the way to Madison's hiding place, he'd found a greasy-spoon on Route 5 that served breakfast all day, and stopped in to order his customary hangover cure: two scrambled eggs, toast lightly buttered, a cup of coffee, and a glass of ice water. It hadn't been easy getting it down, but he was starting to feel a bit better now.

Next, he was off to Wawa to pick up a hot dog and a Yoo-Hoo for Darling Madison. From there, he'd take his car to its secluded parking spot off of Cooper Road, and the hunt would begin.

"Dammit to hell!" Alan Curtis said aloud to the windshield. "Now I gotta worry about them, too."

Those girls of Timmy's weren't home yet. Alan had just taken a call from George Booker to that effect, and moments later it had come over from dispatch. As if he didn't have enough to do.

He'd been hoping that they'd show up for lunch, but now that they hadn't, he had to admit it was starting to look peculiar. He wracked his brain for an explanation, but could come up with nothing that made sense. This day was getting more and more twisted as it went on.

"I hope there ain't no *more* surprises waitin' for me."

Absently, he stroked the fur of the sleeping kitten in his lap. She'd demolished the tin of Sheba he'd bought her, then curled up on him and settled into a deep and satisfied slumber.

"Manda, I *so* don't wanna go back there. We might run into that guy again."

"His name is Mr. Lee. And maybe we won't run into him. But in case we do, maybe we should take him some food. We said we would, remember?"

"I remember. But I never meant to go back there. I just agreed to that so we could get the heck out."

"But we have to go back. So we have to take food."

Lindsey sighed. "Fine. How 'bout a cheeseburger and fries?"

"It looked like he likes Spam and baked beans. Maybe we should go over to Wawa and get some of that for him."

"Okay. I could go for a Snapple, anyway. Those fries made me thirsty."

"Sweet! Me, too. Let's go."

"But this time, let's go down to Thinking Rock by the other trail. The one that starts at the bottom of the sleddin' hill. I don't wanna go past the house again."

"Good idea. And if we cross the stream at Thinking Rock, and we're real quiet, Mr. Lee might not even know we're there. Then we can go out the same way."

"Good plan," Lindsey said, holding her hand up for a high five.

Amanda smacked it and said, "Ow! That was a good one."

As they left the cool comfort of McDonald's, the heat slammed into them like a fist. They rode their bikes next door to Wawa, dashed back into the A/C, and picked up a can of baked beans for Mr. Lee. Wawa didn't have any Spam, so they grabbed a pack of hot dogs and some Doritos instead. They also picked up two Snapples for themselves.

As they waited for one of the checkout registers, Lindsey noticed a man dressed in suit and tie at the opposite register. He stared at her. Or at *them*, rather. When he noticed her returning the stare, he didn't avert his gaze. Lindsey was the one to drop her eyes in embarrassment.

"Amanda," she whispered. "See that guy over there? The one that looks like he just got out from church?"

"Where? Oh. The one with the Yoo-Hoo? Yeah," Amanda said, then looked away from him. "Lindsey, he's so looking at me."

"Yeah, he's been staring at both of us."

"What should we do?"

"Don't pay any attention to him. He's checking out now, maybe he'll leave."

The girls watched as the man paid his money, got his change, and with a final challenging stare at them, turned his back and walked out the door. Outside, they saw him round the corner of the building and disappear.

"Oh, he was icky," Amanda said. "You think he left? For real?"

"I hope so. It's a good thing our bikes are on the other side of the building."

The girls paid for their loot and slipped out the door into the oppressive heat. They half-expected to run into the well-dressed man, perhaps waiting on the side of the building, right next to their bikes.

They both stopped, afraid to go around the corner.

"You go first," Lindsey said.

"No way. You're the oldest," Amanda said.

"Well, one of us has gotta go first."

Amanda sighed. "Rock, scissors, paper?" she asked.

Lindsey rolled her eyes. "Never mind. I'll do it. But I'm going that way." She pointed away from the building. She walked at an oblique angle away from the building, out toward the gas pumps, until she could see around the corner.

The bikes leaned against the wall. No one was there.

"It's okay," she called to Amanda, and she ran back to the building. Amanda met her there, and they got on their bikes. As they pedaled,

Lindsey said, "That's two creepy guys in one day. One that looked nasty, and one that looked pretty."

"I like the nasty one better," Amanda said.

"I didn't like either one. But at least—"

"Hey, there he goes," Amanda said. She pointed to the rear of the building. The nicely dressed man double-timed it across the parking lot, and stepped off the blacktop into the woods behind Wawa. He carried a distinctive pink shopping bag.

"He's taking that little path, the one that goes over to Ringgold's," Lindsey said. "What's he up to? Did he park his car at Ringgold's?"

"Why would he do that?"

"I don't know. Why would he walk into the woods at all? Especially dressed like that? And with a bag from Justice?"

Neither had an answer.

"Well, whatever, let's get out of here," Lindsey said. "We gotta get back to Thinking Rock."

All along the path to Ringgold's, Jerry couldn't stop thinking about the two girls he'd seen in Wawa. *What a scrumptious package!*

He got up onto the loading dock and brushed imaginary dirt from his pants. Then he went through the broken door and down the short passage to Madison's corner.

"Hello, Madison, darling! How have you been? I've brought you another hot dog and some more Yoo-Hoo. Your favorites!"

"I want my mommy and daddy."

"Of course you do, darling, and they'll be here soon. Today, I hope, but by tomorrow at the latest."

"My real mommy and daddy?"

"Why, no dear, your new ones. I've explained that to you."

Madison began to cry.

"Oh, Madison, darling, what a mess! You've wet the bed, my sweet. I'll have to turn your mattress over now. Fortunately, I've brought the new clothing I promised you."

"I want my mommy and daddy, I want my mommy and daddy, I want my mommy and daddy," she said, droning the mantra continuously as Jerry spoke to her. He no longer noticed it.

"I'm going to release you so you can go into the bathroom right over there and get out of your clothes. Here are some clean towels, and I'll bring you some water for washing. I have some right outside."

He unlocked her cuff and shooed her toward the bathroom. As she shuffled off, she said her mantra over and over.

"You might want to use the toilet while you're in there, darling, so this doesn't happen again. There might even be some water in it. Now don't think about trying to get away! There's only one door, and I'm right here next to it." He stepped outside for a moment and grabbed the five gallon bucket full of rainwater he'd left there, brought it inside, and took it to Madison in the bathroom. She was disrobing, so he looked away. It wouldn't do to get all worked up right now. He went back to her mattress and flipped it upside-down. The urine hadn't soaked through to the far side. It would have to do.

The little TV set droned on about an accident on I-95. He finished preparing the mattress, listening to the news with one ear and for Madison's return with the other, but then something the newscaster said penetrated his consciousness. He looked up at the snowy screen.

The face of his darling Madison was on TV. That was to be expected, but what followed was decidedly worrisome. The next face on the screen was that of the man whom he'd pushed into the well yesterday. Authorities speculated as to whether the same person or persons may have been behind both disappearances. A bit too close to the truth for Jerry's liking.

Madison shuffled back from the bathroom, in fresh clothes, little bare feet slapping softly on the concrete floor.

"I want my mommy and daddy," she said.

He held up his hand to her as he stared at the television in shock. Two more familiar faces were on the screen. The faces of the man's two daughters, who evidently, according to the newscasters, had some knowledge of their father's whereabouts and were out searching for him. The faces he had seen with his own eyes, not ten minutes ago.

This was bad news indeed. If they truly knew where he was, then things were about to get very hot around here.

However ...

If he planned this carefully, and if his luck held, he could make this entire situation work out to his advantage. A slow smile slithered across his face.

Oh, this is too perfect.

Kate pinched the briar stem gingerly with her thumb and forefinger, between two thorns, and pushed it down, then stepped on it. She was no Iroquois tracker, but she could tell by the bent crease in the stem that someone else had done the same thing earlier today. *The girls were here*, she thought.

Now she knew she was right.

She continued past the briars, ducked beneath a hanging vine, shouldered her way through the branches of a couple of bushes, and then she was inside. The undergrowth was sparse, and a clear path lay before her, leading down the hill toward the stream.

She had been on the trail a few times with Tim, and was familiar with the landmarks. She figured they were down there somewhere, at the swimming hole, maybe, or Thinking Rock. She called out, "Lindsey? Amanda? Are you here?" But she received no reply other than a sudden cessation of birdcalls around her.

As she started moving down the trail, her cellphone rang. She dug it out of her pants pocket and checked the ID: Selena. She pressed the answer button.

"Please tell me you have good news," she said.

"No. Not yet. Are the girls back yet?"

"No."

"Shit. Listen, Kate. I've finished with Belle Forest. No one has seen Tim or the girls, but they all know we're looking for them now."

"Okay."

"I heard a lot about this kidnapping. Did you know about it?"

"Not the last time I talked to you. I saw it on the news since then."

"They think there's a sexual predator out there, Kate. I'm worried about the girls."

"Don't worry. I think I know where they are and I'm on my way to get them."

"Good. That's a relief."

"Sel, did Darryl call you?"

"Yeah, just a few minutes ago."

"Good. I don't know how to thank you for all your help. *All* of you."

"We couldn't do any less. We all love you guys. Even Brian, I suppose. We stick together."

"It's a good feeling, and I need that right now. But look, I'm going down into the woods behind our house. I'm pretty sure that's where the girls are. I'm gonna lose my signal soon, so call the house if you find anything out, okay? Dottie's there. I'll call you when I get back."

Kate hung up and continued down the trail. Every so often, she picked up Lindsey's or Amanda's footprints in the soft loam. It was obvious even to a city girl that she was on the right track, and her excitement grew with each step she took. She called out to them from time to time, but then she decided to listen instead, reasoning that she'd hear the girls before they heard her, and then would be the time to yell.

She reached the bottom of the slope and passed the swimming hole. The girls were not there. She kept on.

She crossed the stream and continued. Occasional clear evidence of the girls' earlier passage presented itself and heartened her.

She passed Thinking Rock. She had thought this might be a good hiding place for a clue, especially in that little cave underneath it. But if that had been their destination, they were gone now. She was almost through to the other side, and for the first time she worried that she might not find them. What would she do if that happened?

She went all the way to the pine grove, and there she turned back and retraced her steps. She hadn't seen any tracks in a while, and to her inexperienced eye, the continuous carpet of pine needles before her seemed undisturbed. Besides, if they'd come this way, she and Dottie would have seen them at the farm. She must have missed them. Perhaps they'd left the trail, or taken that side trail near Thinking Rock, the one that led up to the sledding hill at the end of Horne Drive. She'd have to branch out a bit on the way back.

She reversed direction and started walking toward home, her brow knit with real concern now. She looked to either side of the trail as she walked, scanning for anything that resembled a hiding place or any hint of the girls' location. She started up the side trail leading to the sledding hill, but she found no footprints, so she gave up and returned to the main trail.

Then, as she moved back toward the swimming hole, she heard rustling across the stream from her. She thought she saw movement over there, but the undergrowth was too thick to make out who or what it was.

"Lindsey? Amanda? Is that you?" she said. When she received no answer, she said, "Come on, you two, I need you to come home. I'm not mad. Are you hiding from me? Come on out, I really need you. I promise I'm not mad."

More rustling in the bushes, and this time she was sure she saw movement of the branches as whoever (or whatever) it was moved away from her.

She bit her lip. *Maybe it wasn't them*, she thought. *The girls would have answered. I think.*

She had to find out, one way or the other. If it turned out to be nothing, *then* she'd go home.

She realized the stream would not be easily crossed here, so she moved up the trail in search of a crossing. She hoped she'd not have to go as far as Greg's Ford.

Then she found a small game trail, one she hadn't seen on the way down. It had been used recently, by the look of it, and right there on the side of it, attached to a briar about three feet above the ground, was a scrap of pink and green fabric that Kate recognized. It was a piece of a top she'd bought for Amanda just last month.

Her breath quickening, she hurried down the path to the stream. She saw the three rocks forming a natural crossing, and she took advantage of it.

On the far bank she stepped onto the trail that led to Thinking Rock. The place where Kate had heard something moving lay somewhere along this trail. She tried to move quietly, listening intently for any other sounds.

As she traveled, the undergrowth encroached on the trail more and more. It seemed to be grasping at her. The air grew hotter; her breath came in ragged gasps. Insects swarmed around her eyes, and a cloud must have passed in front of the sun, for she could swear it was darker. It was as if the forest tried to prevent her from making any more progress.

She pushed on.

She was beginning to think that it wasn't worth this, that she was killing herself to follow a deer or a raccoon, when she heard a metallic clink, like someone dropping a can.

"Girls?" she said, and picked up her pace. Undergrowth obscured her view of what lay ahead. She rounded a corner and stepped into a scene she could never have expected.

16

Squinting in the midday glare, Lindsey envied Amanda her Hippie Girl sunglasses. She felt a headache coming on.

As they passed behind Ringgold's, Amanda said, "Hey, that door's open."

Lindsey looked up at the loading dock of the old market, where the back door stood ajar. She hadn't noticed it on the way past earlier.

"Who cares? Keep your eyes on the ground, Manda." They rode on, retracing their route back to Orenzo Mill Road. Along the way, they kept their eyes peeled for the missing puzzle pieces, but without success.

At Orenzo Mill, they turned left and rode back to Route 128, where they turned right and rode along the shoulder all the way to White Horse Road. They'd never done this on bicycles before (and Kate would have blown a gasket, had she known), but they knew the route well from traveling in the car. They turned right onto White Horse, then left on Horne Drive.

Horne Drive was a secluded dead-end street, very much like Garland Drive, to which it ran parallel, with the valley of Sadler's Run between them. It was an older street with a dozen or so homes built during the fifties and early sixties. Amanda's friend Deanna Watters lived on that street. Lindsey and Amanda flew past her house without slowing down. At the end of Horne Drive, they rode right off the blacktop and onto the narrow dirt path that led across the field to the top of the new sledding hill.

The land sloped downward into the wooded valley of Sadler's Run, starting off at a gentle grade, but increasing in steepness as they went on. It was not as steep as the old Sleddin' Hill, but what made for prime sledding

231

on this one was the way it tailed off at the bottom into a wide, flat apron, where sledders could glide until their momentum was spent.

When the dirt path dwindled to nothing and the hill got too steep for them to continue riding, they dismounted and walked their bikes to the bottom, aiming for the opening of the path that led to Thinking Rock. With undergrowth crowding both sides of it, and hanging vines framing it like an arch, the entrance resembled an open mouth.

Lindsey and Amanda left their bikes on the verge and entered the woods for the third time that day, Amanda carrying the brown plastic bag from Wawa.

Kate burst into the house through the back door, startling Dottie, who jumped as if she'd been caught at something. "Sorry," Kate said. "Did I scare you?"

"You caught me deep in thought," Dottie answered. "Did you find them?"

"No. But they were definitely there. I found this." She held up the black lockbox she'd found in Amanda's "fort" in the meadow.

"What is it?"

"It's a lockbox. Tim had two or three of them he was using to hide clues in. I didn't find this one until I was on my way home. I'd have saved myself a lot of trouble if I'd thought of it sooner. I went most of the way to your house looking for them, but if I'd seen this first, I'd have known that they'd already left the woods. They found this clue, they solved it, probably sitting right there in the meadow, and they're gone again, wherever the next clue led them."

"Oh, my," Dottie said. "Then they may very well have been here while we were out."

"No," Kate replied. "They'd not leave, once they read my note."

"Well ... I'm afraid I have some bad news."

Kate's heart sank. "What now?"

"You probably didn't notice when you came into the house earlier, but the note we left seems to have been ... destroyed."

"Destroyed! How?"

"Coffee."

Kate stared blankly at her for a moment before comprehension dawned. "Widget!" she said, grating her teeth. "That's her thing. She knocks glasses over all the time, just to watch them spill."

"Well, this was a particularly inopportune time for her to do it."

"Great. I'll bet they were here, and if not for that cat ... How could I have been so stupid? I yell at the girls all the time for leaving glasses out, and then I did it myself. And then to leave the note on a napkin, when I know how that cat is!"

"It isn't your fault, Kate. Or the cat's. No one could have foreseen—"

Kate silenced Dottie with a glare. "It *is* my fault," she said. "I know my cat. I was in such a hurry to get out of here, I didn't use my head. And now we have to figure out where they went next," she said. "This is marvelous. Just marvelous." She turned and stalked into the kitchen, then stopped in her tracks and said, "What's this? Did you make sandwiches?"

"Yes," Dottie said. "I took the liberty ... you haven't eaten all day, as far as I'm aware. I made tomato sandwiches. Would you like one?"

"Oh, my God, yes," Kate replied. She hadn't had time to think about eating, but the food on the counter in front of her made the gnawing emptiness in her stomach hard to ignore. She took a sandwich from the plate and bit into it. Tomato juice dribbled down her chin, and she wiped it with her fingers. "Oh, this is heavenly," she said. "Thank you." To Kate, there was nothing quite like the first tomato sandwich of the year, made from fresh warm tomatoes out of the garden or from a roadside produce stand, not from a supermarket. A bit of mayonnaise, some salt and pepper ... The tension drained out of her as she savored the taste.

She swallowed and said, "By the way, I found something else down there, something you're not going to be happy about. There are winos living in your woods. I found their camp."

"Winos!"

"Yeah. Hobos."

"Not hobos. There haven't been hobos since the trains stopped running."

"Bums, then. Indigents. Homeless. Whatever you want to call them. They've got a little campsite down there next to the stream, with a shelter and a fire ring and bottles all over the place."

"Sweet Jesus. Edward will be livid. How many are there?"

"I didn't see any at all, just their camp. But it was a small camp. I'd say no more than two or three. Maybe only one. At any rate, once we find the girls, I don't want them going back down there until it's taken care of."

She popped the last corner of the sandwich into her mouth and talked around it. "I just thought of something. Could you excuse me a second? I have to check the shed."

She went out the door again. As soon as she saw the bike shed, she knew she was right. When she and Dottie had left for Dottie's house, it had been open, with the bikes inside. Now it was closed.

She walked over to the door and nudged it open it with one finger. The bikes were no longer there.

She returned to the house, where Dottie was waiting. "Damn it!" she said. "They've left on their bikes now. Come on. We're going back on the road. Or do you want to stay here?"

"No, I'll come. But let's leave another note. And make sure there are no coffee cups near it."

Kate wrote three notes, all the same:

> If you're reading this, CALL ME IMMEDIATELY, and STAY PUT!

She left one on the fridge, one in the bathroom, and one taped to the back door, and made sure each one was secure.

"That should do it," she said. "I'll drive this time. Let's go."

Although the air was cooler inside the forest, it felt somehow thicker and heavier than it had in the open, and was absolutely motionless. The girls moved as quietly as they could, speaking only in whispers. As they negotiated the tricky switchback trail down into the valley, a nimbus of tiny gnats followed them, persistently alighting near the corners of the girl's eyes in search of moisture.

They stopped when they reached the main trail at the bottom of the hill. Sweaty and miserable, they stood once more at the confluence of Bottleneck Branch and Sadler's Run, with Thinking Rock towering over them on the opposite side.

They studied the stream.

"It looks awful deep," Amanda said.

"And slippery, too," Lindsey said. "Lots of big rocks. But we have to try, Manda."

"We could go cross where we crossed last time."

Lindsey shook her head. "No way. I'm not goin' past that campsite again. That's the whole reason we came down this way, remember?"

"I thought we came this way so we wouldn't have to go past our house."

Lindsey rolled her eyes. "*And* so we could sneak past your creepy friend. Will you quit arguing with me? We're crossing here. We'll just have to go really slow and careful. Hold my hand."

They stepped into Sadler's Run and began wading for the opposite bank, each one being careful to make sure she planted her lead foot securely before lifting the one behind. The water rushing past their calves and the breeze that accompanied the water's flow cooled them down and chased the gnats away. They completed the crossing without complications and stepped onto the opposite bank, water streaming from their shoes.

"We made it!" Amanda said.

"It's not as hard as it looks, as long as you're careful."

They were now back on the path that led up to the top of Thinking Rock, where they'd stood just an hour or so earlier.

It seemed to them like days ago.

"Well, what are we waiting for?" Lindsey asked.

At the top, they found that the sensation of heightened awareness from earlier had increased in potency, to the point where it was uncomfortable. A peculiar rhythmic pressure in the air made the fine hairs on their arms stand up, and the forest around them seemed to throb with a subsonic humming that they felt in their abdomens rather than hearing. Attuned as they were, they knew that the forest breathed, like a living thing. Their eyes ached from trying to take in the intensity of color and vibration of life around them.

"Lin," Amanda said. "Do you feel it?"

"Yeah. I'm startin' to think Poppy was right about this place."

"You don't think it's the height?"

"No. We're still in a valley. The heat and humidity, maybe, doin' stuff to our brains. I don't know. But I know it's weird and I don't wanna stay here any longer than we have to. I'm totally not interested in finding the truth or whatever, I just wanna find that bag. Where is it?"

They ascertained within seconds that the bag of puzzle pieces was not on top of the rock. They knew precisely where they'd been sitting earlier when Amanda had emptied her pack, and they saw no sign of the bag.

"Oh, this is great," Amanda said. "Now what'll we do?"

"We have to think," Lindsey said. "Think hard, Manda. When was the last time you saw that bag?"

"Right here."

"Are you sure?"

"Yeah, I'm positive."

"So somewhere between here and Mickey's, we lost it."

"The only other thing I can think of is that we left it at the fort."

"We did leave a box there. But you said there was nothing in it."

"It was empty. But maybe the bag fell out while we were looking for stuff in my pack."

"Hmm," Lindsey said. "It's possible, I guess."

"Do you have a better idea?"

"Not right now. Let's go check. It's not far."

A loud snap came from the woods, somewhere down at stream level. They froze.

"What was that?" Amanda whispered.

"Shhh. I don't know. It sounded like somebody stepping on a stick."

They kept quiet and listened for a good half-minute. No more sounds came from below. Then Lindsey walked in a half crouch over toward the edge of Thinking Rock, trying to keep her profile low. She peered over the edge.

"I don't see anything," she said in a normal tone of voice. She stood up and turned to face Amanda. "Maybe a branch fell out of a tree. We have to find that bag. Let's head up to the meadow."

"If we're going to the meadow, we'll have to go past Mr. Lee after all, so it's a good thing we brought food."

"No, we don't have to go past him. We know we can cross the stream here now, so we're gonna do it again. That way we can go around his campsite on the other side of the stream. Even if he's over there, he won't know we're going past. We should be able to make it to the meadow with no trouble."

"But what about our bikes? They're on the wrong side of the woods."

Lindsey smacked herself in the forehead. "Shoot! I forgot that. Well, for now, let's not worry about the bikes. We'll get 'em later if we have to. Let's get out of here; this place is givin' me a headache."

They made their way back down the stairs beside Thinking Rock. As they turned and prepared to recross the stream, a deep voice came from behind them, startling them both out of their skins.

"Lookin' for this?"

They turned, and there stood Mr. Lee, holding the plastic bag full of jigsaw puzzle pieces.

As he drove, Jerry took four more Advils for his headache. He chewed two Tums for the queasiness in his stomach. Then, as an afterthought, he chewed one more Tum, to counteract the effects of the Advil on his stomach lining. He finished off his bottle of water.

He made a left onto Cooper Road, driving slowly along the winding dirt surface until he saw the tiny spur off to the left, an old driveway choked with weeds. He brought the car almost to a complete stop before pulling into the side road, where the oil pan scraped as the wheels settled into ancient ruts. Branches squealed along the side of the car, similar to the sound of fingernails on a chalkboard. Jerry smiled. He'd always loved that sound. He drove the car until it was out of sight from Cooper Road, then put it in park.

He was on his way back to his original playground hiding place, where he'd encountered Tim Raither the day before. He assumed that only he knew where to find this Raither guy. Except, perhaps, for Raither's daughters, who, according to the news, were thought to be following him. So, he reasoned, that trail would eventually lead them ... here. If he was very, very lucky.

He changed into his working clothes. Blue jeans, a dark t-shirt, baseball cap pulled down close over his face, and running shoes. He'd lost his kitten yesterday, so he'd have to improvise. He started walking down the trail through the woods that led to the school playground. The air was stifling and he wore a sheen of sweat within the first minute.

A pair of buzzards took wing from directly in front of him. They climbed up above the treetops and disappeared.

As Jerry neared the old foundation, he realized the carrion birds had been near the well, at the bottom of which lay the late lamented Mr. Raither. He leaned over the well's dilapidated wooden cover, which, having been burst through from the top, now hung in tatters.

Then he caught the stench of rotting flesh wafting its way up out of the shaft, and he drew back. This answered, without a shred of doubt, any question about whether Mr. Raither still clung to life.

Resuming his course, he reached the small wooden bridge across the stream, crossed it, and then took the smaller trail to the right rather than staying on the main trail, which went straight up the hill via the rotting stairs. He wound through the woods until he reached the edge near the playground, and crouched down behind the undergrowth. When the two blonde girls showed up looking for Daddy, he would be there to greet them.

"I saved it for you," Mr. Lee said. "You left it on top of Thinking Rock. I figured you'd be back for it."

Lindsey stood stock-still.

"I *thought* that's what happened," Amanda said. "Thanks for saving it for us. It's kind of important." She advanced to take it from him. Mr. Lee made no move to extend it to her, so she stopped a few steps short of him.

"They're pieces from a jigsaw puzzle," Mr. Lee said.

"That's right," Amanda said.

"It's part of a game we're playing," Lindsey added, before Amanda could blurt out something she didn't want Mr. Lee to know. "We have the rest of the pieces, but we have to finish the puzzle to win the game."

"Oh," Mr. Lee said. "Okay. Here you go." He held the bag out toward Amanda.

Amanda took two more steps, reached, and took the bag from him. "Thanks, Mr. Lee. We brought you some food, like we promised."

Mr. Lee's face lit up. "You did? What is it?"

"We brought baked beans and Cool Ranch Doritos. They didn't have any Spam, so we got a pack of hot dogs. You can cook 'em on a stick."

Mr. Lee recoiled momentarily. "I'll take the Doritos. And the beans, I guess."

"You don't want the hot dogs?" Amanda said.

"No. Don't care for 'em," he said.

The girls glanced at each other.

"We're sorry," Amanda said. "We didn't know. We'll keep the hot dogs."

"It's okay. It was nice of you to bring me food."

"We didn't think to bring a can opener," Amanda said as she handed over the Doritos and the can of beans. "Do you have one?"

Mr. Lee put the food down on a rock behind him, reached into his deep pants pocket and pulled out a long, sharp hunting knife in a leather sheath. He grasped it by the deer-antler hilt, unsheathed it, and brandished it in a ray of sunlight for them. It gleamed like it was brand new. It was probably the shiniest thing the man owned. The girls took a step backward, eyes wide. "Here's my can opener. It's my *everything* tool. I use it for *everything*," he said with a wink. "It's very sharp. Want to see it cut something?"

"No!" Lindsey said. "That's all right."

He resheathed the knife and put it back into his pocket.

The girls released their pent-up lungfuls of air.

"Well," Lindsey said. "We really have to be going now, Mr. Lee. We've got to finish our game. So we'll see you later, okay?"

"There was a lady down here a little while ago, looking for you," he said, stopping them in their tracks.

Lindsey and Amanda gaped at each other. "Who?" Lindsey said, although she thought she knew the answer.

"It was a lady calling your names, that's all I know. I hid from her. But she looked like you two, a lot. Was she your mother? She was pretty, like you. Not like my mother. My mother was ugly."

"It had to be Kate," Amanda said.

"Yeah," Lindsey said.

"She's gonna be really mad when she finds us."

"Not if we find Daddy first."

"You mean you didn't tell your Dad about me yet?" Mr. Lee asked.

"No, we haven't had a chance yet," Lindsey replied. "Maybe later today."

"You didn't tell your grandfather, did you?"

"No," Amanda said. "We promised we wouldn't. Besides, he's in Wyoming."

"Wyoming!" Mr. Lee said. "Wyoming is the forty-fourth state. It became a state on July 10, 1890. Its capital is Cheyenne."

"He'll be back tomorrow, though," Lindsey said, with a warning look at Amanda.

"Hey, could I help you with the puzzle?" Mr. Lee said. "I like puzzles. I'm good at them. That one looks easy. I bet I could finish it in about thirty seconds. Or less. Wanna see me?"

"Thanks, but I think we can handle it," Lindsey said.

"I don't know, Lin," Amanda said. "We can use all the help we can get." And she took off her pack and sat down on a rock, then began getting out the rest of the pieces.

Lindsey rolled her eyes, exasperated. "Amanda!" she said. "We really have to go!"

"But Mr. Lee said he'd help us."

"Amanda, could I talk to you alone for a second?"

"Excuse me, Mr. Lee," Amanda said. "My sister wants to yell at me." She got up and walked over to where Lindsey still stood.

"Are you *insane?*" Lindsey whispered. "We have to get away from him!"

"But, Lin, he's a nice man. And I feel sorry for him. He doesn't have any friends."

"He's not a nice man, Manda. He's messed up. He's nuggin futs."

"Daddy says not to say nuggin futs. It's a cuss."

"Well, you just said it."

"That doesn't count!"

"Manda, will you listen to me? He might be nice now, but how long before he flips again? You can't tell with crazy people." Then she looked over Amanda's shoulder and saw Mr. Lee rooting in Amanda's pack. "Hey!" she said. "What are you doin'? That's our stuff!"

It was too late. He'd already extracted most of the puzzle pieces. They were on a flat spot on the ground nearby ... assembled. "For always roaming with a hungry heart," he said, as if to himself, "much have I seen and known. But I've never seen anything like this puzzle. It looks like it says something, but I can't really read it. I need a few more pieces, then it'll be done." He seemed to be taking genuine delight in solving the puzzle.

The girls looked at each other, shrugged, and walked over to watch as Mr. Lee fit pieces into it.

"Here, I'll get them," Amanda said. She gave Mr. Lee the rest of the pieces. He opened the bag, and together the three of them completed the puzzle.

They all backed off and studied it in bewilderment.

"I don't think it's even English," Lindsey said.

The pattern on the finished puzzle *did* seem to be arranged like words on a page. Discrete shapes like letters were grouped into sets of two, three, four, or five, like words. The "words" were set in lines, one after another. But if they *were* letters and words, they were either from a different alphabet or so stylized as to be unrecognizable.

"Maybe we're looking at it upside-down," Amanda said, and she moved to the opposite side to study it from that angle. "Nope. Doesn't look any better from this side."

"Maybe it's just a design," Mr. Lee said. "It doesn't say anything at all. It's just a picture."

"No," Lindsey said. "Our dad made it. It says something."

"Your dad *made* this?"

"Yes. I told you, it's part of a game. We have to figure out what it says. If we do, then we win."

"Your dad must really love you."

"He does," both girls said.

"My dad used to make toys for me."

Amanda gazed at Mr. Lee's face. "We saw you yesterday, you know."

"At the swamp, yes."

"You knew?"

"Yes, of course. I knew you were the ones almost as soon as I saw you."

"The ones? What ones?" Lindsey asked. It was the second time he'd called them that.

"Never mind," Mr. Lee said. "Mind your own beeswax."

"What were you doing all the way up there?" Amanda asked.

"I go there a lot. It's easier for me to focus there. What were *you* doing up there?"

"Playin' our game, just like we are now. But we rode our bikes. That's a long walk."

"Not for me. I walk everywhere."

"How come we've never seen you on the roads before, then?"

"I don't use the roads. I follow the creek. You can get almost anywhere by following the water. And nobody sees you."

"These are definitely letters," Lindsey said. "See, here's an A and this looks like it says ZAW. Maybe it's another code. Oh. Oh, wait. Oh! It's a mirror image! It's not ZAW, it's WAS backwards. See, it starts out 'I AM A …' something or other. We need a mirror to read this."

"You girls wait right here," Mr. Lee said, and he disappeared back up the trail, toward his campsite.

"Quick, Amanda," Lindsey said. "Get the pieces. We're gonna scoot while he's gone."

"No, I don't want to," Amanda said. "He's gonna help us."

"How's he gonna help us, Manda? You think he has a shaving mirror back there? He hasn't combed his hair in two months. He's probably going back to get a bigger knife so he can kill us easier. Plus, what is this stuff about us being 'the ones?' It gives me the creeps."

"Lin, if he was going to hurt us, he'd've done it already. I trust him."

"Well, I don't. Come on, we have to move now."

The sound of Mr. Lee crashing through the undergrowth came to them then, his footsteps pounding closer. He burst back into view, out of breath and holding his prize out for them to see. It was an old rearview mirror from a car. "I found it one day," he said. "I thought I could use it for shaving and stuff. But I never ..." he trailed off, gesturing aimlessly with his hands. "Anyway, here it is. You can use it."

He held it out to Lindsey, who reached out and took it from him. She caught Amanda's eye, mouthed "Sorry," and held the mirror above the puzzle. She looked in it and read:

I AM A WHITE ROCK IN A FIELD AT THE END OF A
DEAD END ROAD. THE LAST TIME YOU PASSED ME
ALL WAS COVERED IN WHITE AND YOU DID NOT
SEE ME. BUT YOU WILL FIND ME IF YOU GO THERE
NOW. THERE IS A KEY UNDER ME.

"The last time you passed me all was covered in white," Lindsey said. "Sounds like snow, maybe."

"A field at the end of a dead end road," Amanda said. "I wonder if that could mean ..."

"The sledding hill!" Lindsey said. "That must be it. The last time we were there, everything was covered in snow. It had to be, because we were sledding. So we didn't see this, this white rock or whatever."

"The last time we were there was like a half hour ago," Amanda said. "And I definitely didn't see any snow."

"Yeah, but Dad couldn't have known that. As far as he knew, the last time we were there was last February, when it snowed like a foot and we missed three days of school. Remember?"

"Oh, yeah. I remember that day. You had two snot-cicles hanging from your nose." She covered her mouth to contain a giggle.

"Did not!"

"Did, too. It was so gross!"

Lindsey rolled her eyes. "So what if I did? Somewhere in that field is a white rock. We prob'ly went right past it. Let's go find it!" she said, and got up to gather their belongings.

She turned to see if Amanda was going to help, and caught her sister with her tongue thrust out in Lindsey's direction, and using her thumb to make a piggy nose. "Nice," she said, as Amanda put on a straight face. "Are you coming or not?"

"I'm coming," Amanda said. Then turning to Mr. Lee, "Thanks so much, Mr. Lee. You were a big help. We'll bring you some more food."

"No more weiners, please," he said.

"Okay, no more weiners. Bye!"

Mr. Lee watched as the girls turned from him and crossed the stream. He watched them scrambling back up the hill that he had earlier seen them descend. He watched until they disappeared from view.

"Come, my friends," he muttered, "'tis not too late to seek a newer world." Then he roused himself, crossed the stream, and followed them up the trail.

17

Lindsey and Amanda emerged from the forest sweaty, itchy, and exhausted.

"I am so done with that guy," Lindsey said. "I hope we never see him again."

"He's a nice man," Amanda said.

"You just think he's nice 'cause he helped us with the puzzle. But that doesn't make him nice. It just makes him weird. I'm tellin' you, there's somethin' not right about him."

"Lin, don't you think if he wanted to hurt us—"

"He keeps callin' us 'the ones.' What does that mean? The ones he wants to cook over his fire tomorrow?"

"I know he's not all there, Lin, but that doesn't make him a cannibal."

"I know he's not a cannibal. But he still could be a sick pervert that murders little girls. He's not right in his head, Manda."

"If he was a sick pervert," Amanda said, "he'd be following us, wouldn't he? Do you see anybody following us?"

Lindsey glanced back at the gap in the undergrowth through which they'd exited the woods, a sinister portal on which she wished she could slam the door and throw the deadbolt. But no door existed, nothing to protect them from whatever might appear there.

"Let's just find this rock," she said, "and get as far away from here as we can."

"Fine," Amanda said.

They left their bikes where they lay, and began zigzagging around the field, eyes to the ground. After a few minutes of fruitless searching, Lindsey said, "I wonder how big this rock is supposed to be? Because if it's a big rock, it should stand out like a sore thumb in this field. Don't you think?"

Amanda stood staring off into the distance.

"Hello, Earth to Amanda."

"Is that it over there?" Amanda said. She pointed to a white gleam about two thirds of the way up the hill toward Horne Drive.

Lindsey followed Amanda's gaze, smiled, and said, "Gotta be! Let's go." A sudden burst of energy brought them to the rock in a matter of seconds. It was as big as a five-dollar watermelon, half-buried in the ground. High grass nearly obscured it from view. On a less sunny day, they might have searched for hours before running across it by chance.

"What kind of rock is this?" Amanda asked. "It doesn't look like it belongs here at all."

"No, it doesn't. It looks like the big white rocks they use around bridges and stuff, like the ones up on the bike trail."

"Yeah, only bigger."

"Let's see if we can move it." Lindsey got down on her knees, put both hands on the rock, and shoved. It moved a little, but then fell back down. "It's too heavy, Manda. Help me."

Amanda knelt beside her, and together they pushed on the rock. It rolled away from its spot, exposing a socket of moist brown dirt. And under a thin layer of the dirt was a plastic bag.

"Oh, please let this be the last clue!" Amanda said. "Please, please, please!"

Lindsey reached in, swept the dirt away, and lifted the bag. It contained a single sheet of paper, folded in thirds like a letter. She opened the bag and pulled the paper out. As she did, a small object dropped out of it and fell to the ground.

Amanda stooped and picked up the object: another piece of paper, greenish in color and intricately folded into the shape of a skeleton key.

"It's a dollar bill," Amanda observed. "I didn't know you could do oral gummy with dollars."

"It's origami, not oral gummy," said Lindsey. "And it's not a dollar. I see a zero there," she said, pointing. "And the guy on it has dark hair. George Washington has white hair, so it must be a ten-dollar bill."

"Whatev," Amanda said. "Either way, it's a key. But how is this supposed to unlock anything? What does the paper say?"

"Nothing," Lindsey said, unfolding the paper. "It's blank. I guess it was just sort of an envelope for the key."

"So this is it?" Amanda said. "It's over? Our prize is ten dollars? No, it can't be. There must be something else in this hole."

Lindsey set the paper aside, Amanda dropped the key, and the two used their hands to scoop great handfuls of earth from under the rock. They excavated to a depth of six inches, without success, then began to lose hope.

Amanda stopped digging to flex her aching fingers. Lindsey paused and examined the dirt packed under her nails. They looked at each other, and a silent communication passed between them.

"There's nothing else," Lindsey said. "This must really be the end. This is the treasure."

"It can't be," Amanda said. "If it's the end, then where's Daddy?"

A shadow passed over them. Soaring on the thermals above, two buzzards circled.

Deanna's brother Grayson Watters had watched the girls enter the forest while standing astride his bicycle at the end of Horne Drive. What were they up to? Bored, he stood and watched the place where they'd disappeared for a while. He couldn't stand those two goodie-two-shoes sisters. He wondered if he ought to go do something to their bikes. Play some kind of trick on them. Maybe jam some sticks into their sprockets.

Nahhh, he thought. *Too far to walk.* It'd be easier to play a trick on them right here, when they came back. They had to come back past him, and he'd get 'em then. He'd show 'em who was boss.

He rode his bike back and forth for a bit as he plotted his revenge on them for daring to ride on his street. He especially hated that Amanda girl, mostly because she was Deanna's friend, and any friend of his sister was an enemy of his.

As he reached the end of Horne Drive on one of his trips, and was preparing to turn around and do it again, he saw the girls reappear from the woods. He stopped pedaling and watched.

They walked right past their bikes like they'd forgotten them. Were they going to walk all the way home? That would put them even more at his mercy! How sweet would *that* be?

He could tell they were talking, but at that distance he couldn't hear their voices. They acted like they were searching for something, turning their heads this way and that, walking in a zigzag pattern. Then he saw Amanda point at him, and they both began running up the hill in his direction. Had they seen him? No. They made it a little more than halfway to him, then they stopped and knelt on the ground.

As he watched the girls, a stray movement at the edge of the woods caught his eye. He sucked in his breath. It was the largest, ugliest, scariest looking man he'd ever seen in his life. The man had just come out of the woods and was walking straight toward Amanda and her sister. They couldn't see him because they had their backs to him, and they were focused on whatever they'd found on the ground there.

Grayson watched, rapt, as the man drew closer and closer to the girls. He wondered if they'd ever notice.

Then, as the man got within twenty feet of the girls, he did something that chilled Grayson's blood. He reached into his pocket and pulled out an object. The sun flashed off the object, giving Grayson a nice fat green spot in the center of his vision. Whatever the thing was, it was long and it was shiny and, OMG, it was the biggest, hugest, sharpest knife in the whole world and he was going to sneak up behind them two girls and slash their throats and there would be blood all over the place and he was watching it happen and he turned away and he heard the screaming begin behind him and then he heard it stop and he pedaled his bike as fast as his legs could pump, back to his house, and he ran inside and ran down into his basement and shut the door behind him and stood with his back against it, panting and weeping. He wiped his eyes and nose with the back of his hand, and sat down on the sofa. Finally feeling safe, he started up a game of Grand Theft Auto and tried to relax.

It would be more than a half hour before Grayson would work up the nerve to stick his head out of his own front door, and by that time, it would all be over.

Kate and Dottie had spent the last half hour driving around Summit Circle, peering between and behind houses, and stopping to ask kids if they'd seen Lindsey or Amanda. When they saw adults, they asked the same questions. A few of the adults already knew the girls were missing, from having seen them on television.

Everyone they spoke to wished them luck, said they'd pray for them, or promised to keep an eye out. Some expressed sympathy. Kate wasn't sure how to take that last, but decided to accept it in the spirit in which it was intended.

"I think we've about covered this neighborhood," Kate said.

"Yes, I agree," Dottie said. "If anyone sees them, we'll find out about it immediately. There's nothing more we can do here. But we have been productive, don't you think?"

"Yes, I do. We got the whole neighborhood on alert. What do you say we work our way down Virginia Street toward the school?"

"You're calling the shots."

"Yes," Kate said dryly. "Of course I am. Hey, Dottie, by the way, I meant to ask you something earlier. I noticed that book on your kitchen table—"

"The Tennyson."

"Yes."

"It was your husband's. I found it in his room. I picked it up a few weeks ago when I was dusting, and thought I'd read a few poems with my coffee in the mornings."

"Really? It was Tim's?"

"It surprised me, too. He was never much for poetry, that boy. But there it was, plain as day."

"It has the initials 'L.L.' written inside it."

"Does it? That might shed some light on the mystery."

"You know who 'L.L.' is?"

"Yes, I think I do. The book must have belonged to Leonard Lynch. Timothy's closest boyhood friend."

"His closest friend? That's odd. Tim's never even mentioned him to me."

"That doesn't surprise me. He's been dead for many years."

"Wait. Not the one who died when they were seniors."

"Yes, that one. Timothy was a senior, but Leonard had left school by that time. Timothy felt responsible for his death, for whatever reason, and as far as I know he has not talked about it to this day. I think he may have willfully forgotten about Leonard. With the bottle's help, of course.

"But the boy practically lived with us. His home life was ... difficult. His father passed away when he was eight, and his mother never seemed to care much where he was. So he stayed with us, more often than not. He was like a fourth son to me, right up until ..."

"Until ..."

"I'm afraid ... you see, he never really properly expressed his grief over his father's death. Everyone has a theory about what happened to him, but mine is that his grief eventually caught up with him. And he lost touch with reality."

Lindsey saw a spot of light dancing around in the grass uphill from them, and she realized it was the sun, reflecting off some moving object.

As she tried to puzzle that out, she heard legs swishing through the grass behind them. Amanda must have heard it at the same time, because both of them whipped their heads around and screamed when they saw how close he'd gotten before they noticed it.

"Hi, girls," Mr. Lee said. "Whad'ja find?"

He held the shiny object in his right hand.

If he was a sick pervert, he'd be following us, wouldn't he?

"Nothin', Mr. Lee," Lindsey said, with a bit of quaver in her voice. "Just a blank piece of paper. Why do you keep sneakin' up on us like that?"

"I wanted to give you this." He extended the rearview mirror to them.

The girls looked at it but made no move.

"It's okay, you can take it," he said. "I think you might be needing it again." He crossed the distance between them and reached out. Amanda reached out too, and took the mirror from his hand.

"Thank you, Mr. Lee," she said. "That was nice of you." She put the mirror in her pack with her other things.

Lindsey's heart still thudded in her chest. "Is that all you came for?" she asked.

"Well ... not really," Mr. Lee replied. "I was hoping you might let me watch while you finish your game. If you wouldn't mind." He stared at the ground.

The girls exchanged a glance. "It's okay with me," Amanda said.

Lindsey nodded. "All right, Mr. Lee. But could you just stay over there? I'll feel better."

"I'll stay right here," he said with a grin. He dropped down in the grass and folded his legs, criss-cross applesauce.

Lindsey stared. She'd never seen a grown man sit like that. She looked at Amanda again and Amanda shrugged.

"Okay," Lindsey said. "We didn't find what we expected. We just found this piece of paper."

"And here's the key we were lookin' for," Amanda said. She displayed the origami key for him. "It's a ten-dollar bill."

Lindsey gave her a stern look.

"Oops. Sorry," Amanda said in a low voice.

This seemed to disappoint Mr. Lee. "Aw, Jeezy Pete! I missed it? The game's over?"

"Well ... we hope not," Lindsey said. "But we're kind of at a dead end." She held up the sheet of paper, turning it so Mr. Lee could see the inside surface. The entire sheet was covered with a security pattern like the inside of an envelope, but in pink rather than blue. "See, there's nothing on this but pink squigglies."

"There is too something on it," Amanda said. "It's got words on it. I can see 'em from here, Lin."

Lindsey looked at her sister as if she had sprouted antlers. "Manda, there's nothing on this page. See?" And she held it up for Amanda to see.

"Very funny, Lin," Amanda said. "You think I'm a *kunumunu?* If you won't read the note, then give it to me and I will." She snatched the paper from Lindsey and read:

> "Congratulations! You have found the key,
> Although you may not comprehend its worth.
> Two doors this key unlocks. Now you must choose—"

"Amanda!" Lindsey interrupted. "It's your glasses!"

"Huh?"

"Your Hippie Girl glasses! They're red! Lift 'em up and see what you see."

Amanda raised the sunglasses up over her brow ridge, and her mouth dropped open. "It's nothing but pink squigglies."

"Just like I said."

She put the glasses back on her nose. "Now it's a note."

"So what does it say?" Lindsey said. "Are you gonna finish it or not?"

Mr. Lee sat rocking back and forth with excitement, watching the proceedings with a childlike grin.

"Where was I?" Amanda said. "Oh yeah:

> "Two doors this key unlocks. Now you must choose
> Which door appeals to you the most. This key,
> Unfolded, might it simply recommend
> Pecu ... Pee ...

"I can't read this, Lin. You take over." Amanda passed the sheet and glasses to Lindsey, who continued:

> "Unfolded, might it simply recommend
> Pecuniary pleasures at the mall?"

"What's that mean?" Amanda asked.

"I think it's Dad's way of saying 'go shopping.' Be quiet and let me finish this.

> "Of course! And that is one door that this key
> Unlocks. But if you're in the mood to tap
> Into your deepest reservoirs of strength—"

"Hey, wait a minute," Lindsey said, suspicion dawning. "Is this poetry again?"

"No, silly," Amanda said. "It doesn't even rhyme."

"Yeah, but ..."

"It's called blank verse," Mr. Lee said. "Iambic pentameter. A lot of English poets used to use it, like—"

"What are you saying?" Lindsey interrupted. "Is it poetry, or not?"

"Oh, yes," Mr. Lee said, the direction of his gaze and the loopy smile suggesting that his attention was somewhere other than on the girls, perhaps somewhere in the Sea of Tranquility on the moon. "It's definitely poetry."

Lindsey and Amanda exchanged looks.

"Keep going," Amanda said.
Lindsey picked up where she'd left off:

> "Into your deepest reservoirs of strength,
> A greater prize may lie at journey's end.
>
> "Relax! Sit down, and listen while I tell
> About where lies the boon of which I speak.
>
> "A short bike ride away from here, a path
> Delves into forest green. Onto this trail
> You must set foot, the hidden glen to find.

"OMG, does all poetry have to sound like Yoda?"
"Lindsey!"
"All right, all right!

> "Across a bridge of oaken planks, just past
> The hollow stump, turn left and forge into
> The bracken field. An olden wall will soon
> Appear, in aspect as three broken teeth.
> You'll find, betwixt the left and middle teeth,
> One stone is loose, and once removed, your prize
> Will be at last revealed. A simple task!
>
> "You disagree? Then give an ear as I
> Divulge, dear sleuths, the other door your key
> Unlocks. Still folded must it be when you
> Return it whence it came, for only then
> Unfetters it your father's mind. Then lost
> Will be the key to you, but gain'd will be
> The secret path. From there, it's up to you.

"That's it," Lindsey said.
"That's it?" Amanda said.
"Yeah."
"But what does it mean?"
"It means we have to find this wall. That's where Daddy went."
"But where is it?" Amanda asked.
"I told you, we have to find it," Lindsey said. "He gave us all the clues. There's a bridge, and a hollow stump, and a, a ..." she paused and looked at the paper. "A bracken field. Whatever that is."
"Big ferns," Mr. Lee said.

250

"So all we have to do is find this wall and we find the treasure."

"And Daddy!"

"Yeah. And Daddy."

Mr. Lee, still smiling, looked from one girl to the next as they spoke.

"Let's go, then," Amanda said.

"Wait," Lindsey said, studying the paper. "Where does it say … Oh, no. It doesn't say where to begin. It just says, 'A short bike ride away from here.' That could be anywhere."

"Well, we know it has to be close to home. So we could find it, maybe, if we kept lookin' everywhere we could think of … and if we had a whole lot of time."

"But we don't have a whole lot of time. Daddy's in trouble. We have to find him fast."

"There has to be another clue in there. We missed something, Lin. Read it again."

Amanda watched as Lindsey bent to the paper and read silently, her eyes flicking back and forth across the page.

"Hey, wait a minute," Lindsey said. "What's this 'other door?' It says we have to return the key 'whence it came.'" She looked at Amanda.

"It came from under the rock," Amanda said. "We have to put it back under the rock? What good would that do?"

"Not the rock. We have to take it back where it was before the rock."

Amanda's mouth dropped open. "Back to Daddy? But why?"

"It says, 'for only then unfetters it your father's mind.' What does 'unfetter' mean?"

"It means unlock," Mr. Lee said. "Take the chains off."

Lindsey stared at Mr. Lee for a moment, then back at the page. "So we have to … Yeah, that makes sense. He wants us to bring the key back to him, still folded, and then he'll tell us where this secret path is."

"But, Lin, we can't …"

Both girls stood dumbfounded as the realization settled in: the trail ended here.

After a long day of emotional pinnacles and plunges, the facade of resolute toughness at last crumbled in both of them, and they became what they could no longer pretend not to be: little girls who had lost their Daddy.

"This isn't fair," Lindsey said. "We've come this far, and now he uses *himself* as one of the clues? We have to *find him* to *find him*. Ugh, I'm so *mad* at him!" she said, stomping her foot for emphasis. "What are we supposed to do now? What good is this stupid clue? What good is this stupid key? What good are these stupid glasses?" She ripped the glasses from her head and flung them away in disgust.

They landed in front of Mr. Lee. He picked them up, bent the temples out to fit around his face, and pushed the glasses onto his nose.

"We'll *never* find Daddy," Amanda said.

Lindsey struggled to hold back tears, then gave up, wiping her eye with the back of her hand.

"What do we do?" Amanda asked.

"We go home," Lindsey said. "We did the best we could, but it didn't work. So now we'd better go home and show this to Kate. Maybe she knows where this old wall is."

"She won't know," Amanda said. "Daddy wouldn't tell her anything."

"You're prob'ly right about that ..."

"Please, Lin. Daddy needs us. We have to at least try."

"But, Manda, we don't know where to start looking. We can't even guess. It could take all summer long to find this 'secret path' without Dad's help. We'll just have to hope he comes back, or maybe the police will find him."

"The police aren't even looking for him. They're stupid."

Mr. Lee spoke up: "I wish you would've been truthful with me."

The girls stared at him.

"I thought we were friends," he continued. "If you were my friends, you would have been truthful with me. But you haven't been, have you? You told me you were just playing a game, but there's much more to it than that, isn't there?"

The girls nodded.

"You could have saved us all a lot of trouble if you'd told the truth. I told you it's very important to tell the truth. Very important. I have a job to do; they told me so. My job is to help you do your job, but I can't do it if you keep lying to me. Are you ready to tell me the whole story now?"

The girls looked at each other for a moment, shrugged their shoulders. "See, Mr. Lee," Lindsey said, "our Dad made up this treasure hunt. He wrote all the clues, and he hid the treasure. But when he went out to hide the treasure, he never came back. It's him we're looking for. Not any stupid old treasure."

Mr. Lee stared at her for a moment. It was impossible to tell what he was thinking, and for that frozen moment, Lindsey thought maybe she'd made a mistake.

After a long pause, he asked, "When did your father disappear?"

"Yesterday morning."

Mr. Lee was silent for a moment or two more. His mouth sagged open as his eyes focused on infinity. "'That which we are, we are;'" he said. "'One equal temper of heroic hearts,' ..."

Amanda and Lindsey turned to each other with incredulous eyes, then back to Mr. Lee.

"'Made weak by time and fate,'" he continued, "'but strong in will' ..."

The girls finished it for him: "'To strive, to seek, to find, and not to yield.'"

Mr. Lee's unfocused eyes settled on them. "How did you know that?" he said.

"Our dad," Lindsey said. "He uses that on us all the time. Usually when he wants us to push ourselves and not give up."

Mr. Lee's face lit up with a brilliant, gap-toothed smile. "He does? No bullhockey?"

"No bullhockey. How did *you* know it?"

"It's Lord Tennyson," he said, spreading his hands as if that explained everything. "It's blank verse; I tried to tell you about it. It's just like the poem your dad wrote." Then, as if to himself, "He read it," he said. "He really read it."

"Mr. Lee?" Amanda said. "Are you okay?"

"I'm fine," he said. "And don't worry about your Dad, either. He's in a dark place, but it's not too late. We're gonna bring him back. It's time to close the loop. I've waited so long, so long. I've been so patient. 'How dull it is to pause, to make an end, To rust unburnish'd, not to shine in use.'" He stood, and did a little caper in the grass. The girls watched in stunned silence.

"It's time!" he said. "It's time, it's time! I have a part to play, like I did with my Dad. My Dad needed me to help him before he could find the light, and I did it. I would've done anything for him. I loved my Daddy, like I'm sure you love yours. You're very nice girls, both of you. You're so much like him, so much like him. Now it's time for me to repay my debt. I have a job to do. It's very important. 'Some work of noble note may yet be done, Not unbecoming men that strove with Gods.'"

Mr. Lee fell silent now, and the girls waited patiently.

"Could you read that part about the bracken field again?" he asked. "I kinda spaced out before, but I think I heard something. I think I know why I'm here."

Lindsey and Amanda exchanged another look. Amanda widened her eyes slightly, questioning. Lindsey shrugged, walked over to Mr. Lee, and held the sheet out to him. "Here," she said. "You're already wearing the glasses."

"Oh yeah," he said. "I forgot."

The girls watched as Mr. Lee held the page before his eyes, eyes that then lost all focus.

As he takes the sheet of paper, all sound stops, leaving behind the kind of dead, thunderous stillness only the profoundly deaf can truly comprehend. The wind stops. Lindsey and Amanda cease moving. A honeybee, passing between him and the girls at roughly chest height, now hangs motionless in the air before him.

Somewhere in the back of his mind, Lee is aware that this kind of experience is not new to him.

He straightens the paper with a snap of his wrists and bends his gaze to it. It's a copy of the local newspaper, not the front page, but one of the inside sections. The community news. It appears to be covered with print, but when he looks closely at the letters, he finds that they are only smudges. Only the dateline and one caption stand out in sharp focus. A Wednesday in November, over thirty years ago. *"Sycamore man chokes on hot dog, dies."*

With the unmistakable feeling of being trapped in a recurring nightmare, a curious sense that he knows what's about to happen next and yet doesn't know, and is powerless to change it in any case, Lee begins to read the article. The words coalesce on the page as his eyes scan the lines: "A local man perished at his home Saturday when a hot dog became lodged in his windpipe as his wife and son watched. Leland Lynch, of the 800 block of Myrtle Drive, was having lunch with his family when ... leaves behind his wife, Patricia Lynch, 36, and a son, Leonard Lynch, 8 ... will be missed ... services to be held at ..."

He looks away from the page, blinking back tears. His father, wiping his hands on a greasy rag, watches him, and says with a smile, "You want to slow down with that hot dog, son. You don't want to choke to death on it."

Eight-year-old Leo Lynch jams the rest of the frank into his mouth, chews a few times, and takes a mighty swallow. "Hungry, Dad!" he says around his food. "Let's get back to work."

As his father sinks to his knees, lays down on his back on the dolly, and rolls himself back under the Chevy, Leo understands what's going on. He's back home again, in his own driveway, helping his Dad change the oil pan gasket on his '69 Chevelle. A part of him realizes that he's also in a field next to a white rock, but he's grown accustomed to the plasticity of time and space and is no longer surprised by it. He's unstuck in time, like Billy Pilgrim.

"Keep an eye on that jack, son," his father says from beneath the car.

"I will, Dad." He knows not to let anything bump into the jack while his father's under the vehicle. His main purpose in being here is to ensure that doesn't happen.

"Hand me the nine-sixteenths socket, will ya?" his father says.

He loves working with his father like this. It makes him feel important and proud that his father trusts him. His Dad knows a lot about cars, and Leo enjoys learning from him. Aside from hunting and fishing, this is the best quality time they get as a father and son.

Leo listens to the clinking sounds from under the car, then the sound of the ratchet as his Dad begins loosening the nuts. Leo loves that sound. As he listens to the ratchet's song, another sound, a loud metallic creaking, drowns it out, and a jolt of terror rocks Leo. To his horror, he sees that the car is moving, rocking back and forth.

No, no, no, not this part! grown-up Leo thinks. Not again! I don't wanna know this part! He tries to stop it, to wake up, to get off the rollercoaster, but he can't. He's strapped in for the duration of the ride.

"Son?" his father asks, voice rising in panic. It's the last thing he'll ever say. Little Leo watches as the jack leans forward with the movement of the car. Petrified, he watches the jack slip to the ground and the car come crashing down onto the upper half of his father's body with a sickening muffled clank. Lee Lynch's legs spasm once, then go still. A river of blood flows from beneath the car toward little Leo's feet.

"Dad!" he screams, in both times.

Then he hears the voice of his mother say, "Uh-oh," as if she just dropped a piece of toast. He drags his eyes away from the sight of his father's legs amid all that blood, and sees his mother standing next to the car's trunk with the oddest expression on her face. "What did you see?" she asks him.

He should move, he should do something, but he's rooted to the spot. As a rivulet of blood reaches his left sneaker and bends around it, he says, "The car fell on Dad! There's blood all over the place! Help him!"

"That's right," she says, nodding. "The car fell. If you tell anybody I was here, people will ask questions. And then they might think I *pushed* the car, and they'll put me in jail and you won't have anybody. So you just mind your own beeswax, Leo. Understand?"

"Yes, ma'am, but Mom, you have to—"

"Tell me again, what happened?"

Leo stops. "The car fell on Dad."

His mother nods. "I'll call an ambulance," she says with perfect serenity, and walks leisurely into the house, leaving Leo with the mutilated corpse of his father. As the tears stream down his face, he glances back at the paper in his hand, the one with the headline that now reads, "*Sycamore man crushed by car in driveway, dies.*"

Like a kick in the stomach, he knows the horrible, gruesome truth again, the truth that he can never make himself forget for very long, the truth he has to experience each time as if it were the first time.

He screams and screams and screams.

Again, the paper changes. It's now a sheet of white paper with red squigglies all over it.

Time starts up again.

"Mr. Lee?" Amanda said.

"It's … uh … it's Leo. My name is Leo. Lee was my father's name."

"Oh. Okay, Mr. Lee-Oh. Are you okay?"

"Yes. I mean no. I don't know."

"You screamed," Amanda said. "You said—"

"'Dad.' I know," Leo said. "Sorry. I was just ... thinking about something." Then he looked back at the sheet of paper with the pink squigglies all over it. "Where was I? Ah. Here we go." A smile spread across his face as he read.

"That's what I thought," he said at last. He looked into the sky and said, "I understand. I'm ready."

Catching Amanda's eye, Lindsey whispered, "Told you. Nuggin futs."

"It's like he wrote this clue for me," Leo said as he lowered his gaze to the girls.

They looked up at him, puzzled.

"I know where this place is," he said.

"You do?" they both asked.

"Sure I do. Sure I do. 'An olden wall, in aspect as three broken teeth?' There's only one place that could be. Been there lots of times myself. And I know where the bridge is, and I even think I remember this hollow stump."

"Are you sure?" Lindsey said.

"Yes. I'm sure," he said. "Been there many times, like I said. Minding my own beeswax."

The girls shared a look, afraid to believe.

"Where is it?" Amanda asked.

"It's over behind the school. There's a nature trail back there. The entrance is right next to the playground."

Amanda's jaw dropped. "I know where that is!" she said.

"Well, if you go in the woods right there, you'll go down the hill for a while. Then you'll come to a stairway, but don't use it, because it's very dangerous. Walk down beside it. Right after that, you'll see the bridge. And it says here the hollow stump is on the other side of the bridge. You turn left there and walk through the bracken, and pretty soon you'll see the wall. You can't miss it."

"Mr. Lee ... I mean, Mr. Leo, are you sure?" Lindsey asked.

"Was Abraham Lincoln the sixteenth president of the United States?" he said.

"Huh?"

"It means yes. I'm very sure. Positive, I'm positive. Don't you understand? This is my job. I've been waiting for so long. So very long."

"Whatev," Lindsey said. "I don't have any better ideas, do you, Manda?"

"Nope."

"Let's get our bikes, then. It's time to blow this popsicle stand." Lindsey took off back down the hill, but before she'd gotten very far she sensed that Amanda wasn't with her.

"Lin, wait!" Amanda said.

Lindsey stopped and turned around.

"Thank you very much, Mr. Leo," Amanda said. "You helped us twice now. If we find our Dad, I'm gonna tell him that we couldn't've saved him without you. Because it's true."

Leo grinned his gap-toothed smile. "You're welcome," he said. "When you see Timmy, tell him we're even now. He'll know what I meant."

Amanda backed away from him. "You really *do* know my Dad?"

"Of course I do. You think I was born yesterday? A long time ago, he was my best friend. And he was always nice to me, even when everybody else was being mean."

"But how do you know who my Dad *is?*"

"I've been expecting to meet you for a long time. They told me you were coming, and here you are. Besides, you look like him and you act like him. It doesn't take Sherlock Holmes to figure out you're his daughters."

"Well, why didn't you tell us that in the first place?" Lindsey demanded. "You were the one bein' all preachy about not lyin' and all."

Looking abashed, Leo said, "Sorry about that. I wasn't sure, at first, and I was scared. Then when I *was* sure, I was ashamed, I guess. I didn't want Timmy to find out what happened to me. Sometimes when you're *between* like I am, it's hard to tell who you really are, or what you're supposed to do. In fact, I didn't completely figure it out until just now. I'm sorry if I caused any problems."

"It's okay," Amanda said. "You're a nice man, Mr. Leo, and I'm gonna tell my Dad that he should help you."

"You don't have to do that," Leo said.

"But I want to."

"I just hope you find him. Good luck, girls."

"Thanks. Good luck to you too, Mr. Leo. Could we have our clue back?"

"Oh, sure," he said, and extended the page toward Amanda.

She took the paper, and glanced down at the key in her other hand. Then she checked the expression on her sister's face to see if they were on the same page.

Lindsey nodded. "Go ahead."

Amanda nodded, and offered the key to Mr. Leo. "Take this, Mr. Leo. We don't need it as much as you do, and you helped us so much. I bet you could really use it."

Mr. Leo gave a quick shake of his head as if he might refuse, but then he paused, and said, "Yeah, it might come in handy, come to think of it." He took the key and tucked it into his pocket. "Thank you, my friends."

"Goodbye, Mr. Lee, I mean Leo," Amanda said. "We'll come back to see you as soon as we make sure Daddy's okay."

"Goodbye, friends. Oh, and one more thing: tell your Dad he can keep the book. I don't need it. It's in my heart."

Leo stood, watching as the girls ran to the bottom of the hill, retrieved their bikes, and began walking back up the hill. Both girls thanked him once more as they passed him again. Then they went back to Horne Drive and got on their bikes and pedaled out of Leo's sight, leaving him smiling after them.

He still had one more task to complete before he could rest.

Leo Lynch gazed across Route 128, at Cappie's Bar, where he could get a fifth of Thunderbird or Wild Irish Rose for a couple of bucks. He started walking.

18

Alan Curtis sat at his desk, fuming. He'd come to headquarters to do some paperwork and spend some time in the solitude of his office, recharge his batteries. He'd lost count of the number of neighborhoods and back streets he'd cruised that day, with nothing to show for it. He'd taken an untold number of calls and leads, all of which had turned out to be false alarms. He was tired, grumpy, and discouraged.

He couldn't ever remember having been this frustrated by a case. Throughout his career, he'd been known in the department for being able to solve seemingly unsolvable riddles like this. It was second nature to him. All he had to do was to keep his mind and senses open, to notice details without getting bogged down in them, and sooner or later he would enter a sort of fugue state of mind in which everything would become clear. It usually happened when he least expected it, when the linchpin came along, the keystone, the piece of the puzzle that made it all fit together. He could almost hear the *click!* when it happened. If he made an active attempt to enter that state, it seemed to impede him rather than help, so he tried not to force it, but rather to just go with the flow. It always worked.

Problem was, it wasn't working *this* time. He knew deep down that everything that had happened the last two days was connected. Coincidences bothered him. Somewhere, somehow, something connected it all, but he couldn't figure it out. And his patience was wearing thin.

On top of that, he'd decided he had to come clean about Timmy Raither being a suspect in Madison Kingsmore's abduction. Although he didn't personally believe that Timmy was involved, he knew that if he didn't do this by the book, and it came out anyway, it would smack of a cover-up.

It had been one of the most difficult decisions he'd ever had to make, and it was going to play hell with his relationship with the Raither family, but he didn't see a way around it.

Hopefully, they'd soon find the real perpetrator, and Timmy would be exonerated without too much damage to his rep.

He heaved a sigh, and reached for the phone.

Just as his hand was about to touch it, it rang, and he snatched his hand back as if to avoid being bitten. Then he picked up the handset, and said, "Captain Curtis."

As he listened to the voice on the other end, his mouth fell open and nerveless fingers dropped the handset. It bounced off his right leg and clattered to the floor.

Jerry worked under any conditions, some pleasant, some not so pleasant. But he particularly loathed hot, humid weather like this. The sweat ran down his ribs, trickled into his eyes from beneath the brim of his cap. It was difficult to breathe. The gnats drove him to distraction.

During summer months, he preferred to work in the early mornings. Today was one of those days when one just had to make sacrifices, and his sacrifice had been rewarded. He held his breath as his disbelieving eyes beheld what he had hoped for, but dared not depend on: the two little blonde girls he'd seen at Wawa, coasting into the school parking lot.

Unbelievable, he thought. He'd come here on the longshot chance this might happen, but it stunned him to see his plan come to fruition so easily.

"That's right," he said under his breath. "Come to Papa."

He watched as the two girls, chattering and pointing with excitement, pedaled up onto the grass, around the playground fence, and into the forest … following in the footsteps of their unfortunate father, whether they knew it or not.

He gave them time to penetrate into the woods far enough that he could fall in behind them without arousing their suspicion. Then he rose from his crouch. It was time to make his move.

He licked his lips.

Lindsey and Amanda rode their bikes like they'd never ridden before, pushing themselves to exhaustion. As they coasted down the hill to the entrance of the rear parking lot of Amanda's school, they knew they were close, and they couldn't get there soon enough.

They pedaled across the parking lot to the edge of the kiddie playground. They got up onto the grass, and rode between the trees and the waist-high fence until they reached the sign that said NATURE TRAIL –

NO VEHICLES. They didn't know whether bicycles counted as vehicles or not, and at the moment they didn't care. They rode right down the trail until they were several yards within the forest.

As the gravel gave way to squishy earth, they dismounted and dropped their bikes beside the trail. They would continue the rest of the way on foot.

"Hey, what's that?" Lindsey said. She stopped, pointing back into the trees they'd just passed. Ten feet off the trail, leaning up against a tree, was . . .

"Daddy's bike!" Amanda cried. "He's here! *Daddy! Daddyyyyyyyyyyyy!*" she yelled.

"*Dad! Are you here?*" said Lindsey, raising her voice to match Amanda's.

Then they both fell silent and listened. The whispering of the trees was the only reply.

"Maybe he can't answer us," Lindsey said. "Let's keep looking."

Tim's dreams and his reality are interchangeable now. One segues into the other, and back again, frequently and without warning. He can no longer tell the difference. Sometimes he's in a well, and sometimes he's at the bottom of Satan's black throat. Sometimes he's aware of the year, and sometimes he's reliving an episode from his past.

Sometimes Heckle and Jeckle and Rocky talk to him, and sometimes they don't.

He wonders if, perhaps, he has already died.

In his lucid moments, Tim understands, and accepts, that no rescue is coming. Remembering, as he now does, that last clue, the one under the white rock, that requires the girls to come to him, he knows how truly hopeless his situation is. Given a whole summer to search, they'd never find this patch of woods, let alone this hole in the ground. And he doesn't have a whole summer. At times, it feels to him as if he has only hours, perhaps mere minutes, to live. And that's all right with him.

He longs now for quick release, for freedom from this suffering. There is no hope of survival. He is ready. He only wishes he could somehow pass on a last message to his wife and his daughters. To tell them how much he loves them, how proud he is of them, how sure he is that they'll be okay after he's gone. To tell them how sorry he is that he has to go.

But there can be no final message. To leave them without their knowing these things is worse for him than any physical pain.

He slips back into unconsciousness.

Lynch, he spent the night at my house last night and we minded our own business and kept our mouths shut while the whole county went plain crackers over that fire. I guess our Thinkin' Rock lie musta worked, 'cause nobody ever asked us where we was yesterday or nothin'. Everybody was too busy talkin' about the fire to care about us.

By the time we got home from Thinkin' Rock, you could still see the smoke from my house, and all evening until dark, you could hear the sirens goin' by.

This mornin' we got up, and Mom and Dad was still talkin' about it, so we quick up and disappeared before anybody could ask us any questions. We walked back to Thinkin' Rock again, and now here we sit, talkin' about the same thing everybody else is talkin' about: the fire.

"One of the firemen that got hurt was a friend of my dad's," I say to Lynch.

"I know," he says. "I heard 'em talkin' about him last night. Paul Martin?"

"Marshall," I say, "Paul Marshall."

"Is he gonna be okay?"

"Yeah, I think so. I heard Mom tell Dad this mornin' all he had was a broken collarbone. I feel real stinkin' bad about it, though."

"Me, too. About him and the other two guys, too."

We don't have no more about that subject to say, I guess, 'cause for a while we both get real quiet.

Then Lynch says somethin' to break the silence. "Listen, let's go back and make a fort behind the Teeth." That's what we call the wall we found yesterday, 'the Teeth.' We already have a nickname for it.

"Not today, Lynch. I'm stayin' out of that whole area for a while. Maybe next week."

"Yeah, I guess you're right."

More silence. Then Lynch says, "I meant what I said yesterday."

"About what?"

"About owin' you my life."

"So, what, you gonna be my slave from now on?"

"No. I'm gonna repay you."

I just gotta laugh at that. "Yeah, right. With what? Baseball cards? It's gonna take an awful lot of baseball cards to be worth your whole entire life. Unless you got a Babe Ruth card. You got one of those? 'Cause if you do, we'll call it even."

"Shut up, you dipshit. I'm gonna pay you back by savin' *your* life one day, that's how."

"Shit, I hope I don't ever *need* savin'."

"You will. And I'll be there."

"You don't know nothin'."

"Yes I do."

"How?"

"I got my ways."

"What ways?"

"I can't tell you."

"Why not?"

"'Cause you wouldn't believe me, that's why. And you'd prob'ly laugh at me."

"Lynch, no I wouldn't. You can tell me, I'm your best friend."

Lynch gets real quiet for a few seconds, then he says, "You swear you won't laugh?"

"Yeah, I swear."

"Okay. You can't tell anybody this, Timmy. I never told anybody else in the whole world about this. Nobody can know except me and you. Deal?"

"Deal." We do the shake thing.

Nobody says nothin'.

I only got so much patience. "Well?" I say.

"I'm gettin' to it!" he says. "All right. I gotta tell you this while I still can. Listen. You're gonna think this is crazy, but ... I still talk to my dad sometimes."

I wind up and give him a froggie in the arm and I holler, "You shithead, I thought you was gonna tell me somethin' real!"

"Timmy, I'm serious," he says, rubbin' his arm. "Damn, that hurt."

I just stare at him. "What d'ya mean, you're serious? Your dad—"

"He's dead. Yeah, I know. But I still talk to him sometimes, when I'm just about to fall asleep, or about to wake up. And sometimes I feel like he's still around even when I'm awake, like he's inside of me, seein' things through my eyes, you know?"

Now I start to feel sorry I punched him in the arm, 'cause he's got his head all screwed up about his dad, and who could blame him? I reckon if my dad died right in front of me like Lynch's did in front of him, I wouldn't be wrapped too tight either. "Yeah, but Lynch, that ain't real," I say. "You must be dreamin' or somethin'."

"That's what I thought, too, at first," he says. "But he tells me things that there's no way I could know if he didn't tell me, and they turn out to be true. Like the knife. Remember when I told you he gave me the knife, and you didn't believe me 'cause I was only eight when he died? Well, he really did give me the knife. I was thirteen. He told me where I could find it in the attic one day, five years after he was dead, and I went right there and found it."

"Lynch," I say, "I ain't got any idea what you're goin' on about. What knife? And case you forgot, you're only ten. You ain't never been thirteen."

"Oh ... oh, shit," he says. "I forgot, that hasn't happened yet, has it? No, that comes later."

"Lynch. What the fuck. Are you losin' it?"

"Yeah. Maybe. Timmy, listen, quick, while I can still tell you. Time ain't a straight line for me. It's more like a ball of yarn. Am I makin' sense?"

"I'll tell ya what makes sense. I think you been readin' too much of that Roger Zelinski guy, that's what I think. Now, that makes sense."

"It's Zelazny, and it's funny you should mention him, Timmy. He had some ideas about reality that weren't that far from the truth. Makes me wonder if he knew ..."

I stare at him. All of a sudden he don't sound nothin' like the Lynch I know. In fact, he don't sound like any ten-year old I ever met.

"Listen," he says. "Here's one thing I've learned: Every deed, good or bad, is like a pebble tossed into still water. And the ripples follow you. All your life. There's ripples catchin' up to you right now, after all these years."

And now I'm gettin' really scared, 'cause while he's talkin', he seems like he's gettin' older. His hair grows, and Jesus, he gets a beard, and his jaw gets squarer, his hands get big and gnarly, and he gets these pits all over his face, and his teeth get yellow and crooked, and some of 'em disappear.

"Lynch," I say. "What's happenin' to you?"

"Never mind," he says. "You do realize that we're not really here, right, Timmy?"

"Not really here? On Thinkin' Rock?"

"Well, we are, but we're not. You know what your dad says about Thinking Rock, right? That you can always find the truth here? Well, the truth has layers, like an onion. You and me, being here, that's one layer. But there's another layer underneath, and that one is a real dark place for you, and for me it's ... well, let's just say this is gonna be the last time we talk in this life."

"Last time! Why?"

"Because it's gonna take you a while to catch up with me. You will, eventually, but we're gonna have to take some time off, you and me." He sighed. "I told you the time would come when you'd need me, Timmy. And now the time is here, the time for me to fulfill my oath."

"Lynch, you ain't makin' any—"

"It's time for you to wake up, Timmy," he says. "You need to stay awake. Help is on the way. Hang on, and don't go to sleep again."

"Goddammit, Lynch, I'm just as awake as you are! What the fuck's gotten into you?"

Then Lynch waves a hand in front of my face and says, "Bye, Timmy. Thanks for everything. Wake up, now."

"Wait, no! I wanna stay here. Oh no, *no*, *NOOOO!*"

Lindsey came to an abrupt halt. Amanda nearly crashed into her from behind. Turning, Lindsey faced her sister and asked, "Did you hear something?"

"I'm not sure," Amanda replied. "It seemed like ... Why? Did you?"

Lindsey nodded. "Something's wrong. Daddy's here somewhere. But we're running out of time."

"Yeah, that's it. How did we ... We both heard it, right?"

"I didn't exactly hear it. Just felt it. Like a voice inside my head. I know this sounds whack. But you felt it, too, didn't you?"

"Yeah. Totally weird. So what should we do?"

"Stop wasting time, that's what. We gotta find this hollow stump." As they continued down the trail, passing to the right of an ancient spreading oak tree, Lindsey again took point, and an invisible length of spider silk caught her in the face.

Jerry watched from thirty feet away as the older girl (*Lindsay? Something like that*) wiped at her face and spat in disgust.

As a precaution, he stayed low and tried to avoid showing too much pale skin, but the girls were intent on their mission, and not alert for hidden observers. That was good for him.

What was bad for him was that they were not alone. They had each other. He'd never taken more than one at a time, and he didn't fancy starting today. Too much risk was involved, too many variables. Two girls, desperate to defend themselves, and each other, could make things complicated.

No, he would have to find a way to get them apart from each other, then take them one at a time. Or wait for them to separate themselves.

He followed them, and bided his time.

Ahead lay the ramshackle staircase of which Leo had warned them. "I see what he means," Amanda said.

They examined the ground on either side.

"It looks safer on the left," Lindsey said.

"Neither side looks safe to me."

"The left side looks safer than the stairs. And we have to get down there. Let's go."

Lindsey led the way. The slope was steep and slick with mud, but stones protruded from the ground that she could use as steps. She made it to the bottom safely. "Throw me the backpack," she said.

Amanda tossed the backpack to her sister, who then stood waiting for her.

"Come on, Manda. It's easy."

"I'm scared," Amanda said.

Lindsey rolled her eyes. "I'll come back up and help you." She put the pack on the ground, climbed halfway up the slope, and stood, holding her arms out to Amanda. "Come on now. I'll grab you. You won't fall."

Amanda took a single step down, slipped a bit, and hastily climbed back up. "I can't do it," she said.

"Manda, you haven't even tried. Come on, we don't have time to waste on this. Come on!"

This time, Amanda turned her back to the slope, put her hands on the ground, and moved one foot backward and down the slope. She groped with it for a foothold, found one, and brought the next foot down. Lindsey put her hands on Amanda's butt to steady her.

Amanda took another two steps in the same manner. It was slow and painstaking, but it was working. She took a fourth step backward. And her foot slipped. It came out from under her, and she landed on both knees in the mud. Lindsey, trying to catch her, lost her balance, and fell backward. She tried to hold on to Amanda to keep herself from falling, but succeeded only in pulling Amanda with her.

Both girls ended up at the bottom of the slope, bruised and covered with mud.

"Way to go, *kunumunu*," Lindsey said, flinging mud from her fingertips.

"You pulled me down," Amanda said. "I would've been okay if you hadn't grabbed me."

"Well, *you* knocked *me* down, that's why I had to grab onto you. Besides, none of this would have happened if you'd come down by yourself like I did."

Amanda pouted. "Sorry."

Lindsey stood, brushed herself off. "It's okay. Are you hurt?"

"Not really."

"Good. Let's keep going. I'll take the pack for a while."

They ran down the trail to the next bend, where they stopped and gaped in stunned paralysis.

"Lindsey, look!" Amanda said, pointing at the airy green cathedral that Tim had admired the day before.

"Isn't it beautiful?" Amanda asked. "It's just the kind of place Daddy would've picked to hide the treasure."

"Yeah," Lindsey said. "It is. And right there's the bridge. That's our next landmark."

They raced to the bridge and thundered across across it.

Lindsey stopped on the other side, where, squatting right next to the trail amongst a clump of ferns, as if trying not to be noticed, was the hollow stump.

"We're supposed to turn left here," Lindsey said. "Let's go."

They left the trail on the side opposite the stump, and began walking through the bracken field. Lindsey caressed the tops of the fronds with her fingers as she passed, watching as they responded with slight dips and bows.

From the top of a slight ridge, they saw it.

"The three teeth! There they are!" The girls broke into a run as their goal at last presented itself. They came to the wall, stopped, looked at each other.

"Where?" said Amanda, gasping.

They looked through one of the window holes into the building's former interior. They had completely forgotten about the loose stone, only inches away from them now. It was no longer the object of their search.

"He's gotta be here somewhere," Lindsey said. "His bike's still here. You go around that side, I'll go this way." They split up and circumnavigated the entire foundation, meeting at the opposite side. Then they came back to the Teeth.

"Daaaaaaaad!" Lindsey shouted. "Are you here?"

"Hey, Lin," Amanda said. "Do you think Daddy might be hiding, just to mess with us?"

Lindsey considered that for a second, then said, "No, he'd not do that. It's been too long."

Amanda covered her mouth with her hand and giggled.

"What's so funny?"

"You sounded so much like Kate when you said that: 'he'd not do that.' That's just the way Kate says things."

"So? Your point is …?"

"Nothing. No point at all. I'm just sayin', is all."

"Well, don't say it."

"I didn't say it, until you made me. Jeez! You don't have to get all huffy about it."

Lindsey froze. "Did you hear that?"

"Hear what? All I hear is—"

"Shh!" Lindsey said, holding up her palm. "Listen."

Amanda fell silent.

Lindsey stood still as stone, head cocked at a slight angle. Amanda did the same.

Like magic, the music of the forest sprang into being. The buzzing of insects. The lyrical chattering of a small cascade in the stream. The wind in the trees. The lovely piercing trill of a hermit thrush in the treetops.

"You mean that bird?" Amanda asked.

"Shhh!" Lindsey said, emphatically shaking her head no.

A breeze arose, drowning out the other sounds with its soughing. It tugged at their hair, and made of the bracken a rippling sea of green. The waving fronds seemed to beckon them to come around the building again, to the right side, and a bit farther up the hill.

The rogue zephyr passed on, and the air grew motionless once more.

Still, Lindsey stood silent, waiting. Amanda did the same.

Lindsey began to believe she had imagined the sound, and had opened her mouth to say so, when it came again: a sharp whistle, clearly not that of a bird or any other forest animal. Coming, it seemed, from the other side of the building.

"I heard it that time," Amanda said. "It sounded like ... it sounded like Daddy."

"Yeah. Whistling from inside a barrel," Lindsey said.

Jerry watched the girls cross the stream, then leave the trail to cut through the ferns. As they passed over the opposite ridge, he crept up behind them and peered around a tree trunk. The girls stood motionless next to the old wall, not too far from his car. They explored around it, came back to the near side. Then he heard a whistle, as of a cowboy whistling at horses or cattle. He looked around. Was there someone else in the woods with them?

Then the girls started heading around the foundation again, to the right side.

Excellent! They were marching almost right up to his car. Now if only he could get them separated ...

I'm in a dark place, a tunnel. There's beautiful light at the end of the tunnel, if only I can get there. I need to get there. But my legs aren't cutting it. I run and I run, but I may as well be on a treadmill.

I hear my girls' voices. They're out there, beyond the end of the tunnel, in the light. If I can get to the light, I can be with them again.

There's Lindsey's voice again, calling my name. Now Amanda's, too. They're looking for me!

Slowly, reality dawns on him, like the sun burning through dense fog.
This is really happening, he thinks. *This isn't a dream. They're out there, looking for me, outside the tunnel.*

Lynch said help was coming. He said it. But that was years ago, wasn't it? Or was it just now?

He struggles to claw his way through the multiple gauzy layers of fantasy and truth that enshroud him like a caul.

Truth. It's like an onion, he said.

It's a well, not a tunnel. I'm at the bottom of a well. And somehow, my daughters are up there. They've come all this way, looking for me. Lynch was right. Help is on the way!

Heckle and Jeckle have flown off, he notices.

"Hey," he tries to yell, but his voice comes out as a thin whisper. "I'm down here." Again, no sound comes out of his tortured throat.

How did my girls get to Heaven? They're so young. They shouldn't have reached the light before me.

He's drifting again, but he snaps back.

No. None of us are in Heaven yet, Tim. Stay awake, now. Like Lynch said. Stay alive. Get their attention. Somehow.

His vocal chords aren't going to do the job. Luckily, he has one trick left up his sleeve.

This has to work, or I'm a goner. He forms a circle with the thumb and forefinger of his left hand, puts them between his lips, and lays the tip of his tongue against them. Then he draws in the biggest breath he can, ignoring the grating agony in his ribs, and blows it back out with as much force as he can muster. He nearly passes out from the pain, but the piercing whistle lets fly from his lips and reverberates in the well until he has to hold his good hand against his left ear.

They had to hear that.

A wave of vertigo strikes him. The whirling is so intense that it threatens to drive him back into unconsciousness, but he rides it out, clasping the wall and gritting his teeth. Once it passes, he rests and listens and readies himself for another whistle in case the first one brings no response. He waits for perhaps thirty seconds (but then, his time sense is badly distorted, it could as well be thirty minutes), and lets loose another whistle, this one louder than the first.

Come on, girls. Come on!

He hears the voice of his youngest daughter yelling, "Daddy? Is that you?" After that, he hears the sounds of rustling and sticks breaking (a sound strangely akin to the blowing of sheets in the wind) and then—*oh, can it be true?*—the silhouette of a head appears in the circle of light at the top of the well.

Or is it one of the buzzards?

Is this all just another dream?

"Daddy? Are you down there?" comes a voice.

Was that Amanda?

Wait. What if it's a trick?

Unsure whether he can trust his own senses, whether it might be Satan up there, trying to get his hopes up, just so they can be dashed again, he decides to keep quiet. See if the voice goes away.

He lifts his good hand to shade his eyes, see if he can get a better view of the backlit figure at the top of the well … and a stream of water droplets rolls down his arm and slips off his elbow, making a series of splashes in the water around his waist. The sounds reverberate in the well, carrying easily all the way to the top. He may as well have rung a cowbell.

That was stupid. Now he knows I'm here.

"Hello? Is anybody down there?"

That sure as hell sounded like Amanda.

"Is that you, Squirt?" he croaks. *Please let it be Amanda.*

"*Daddyyy!*" she screams "*Daddyyyyyy! Lindsey, I found him! Help, help!*" In Tim's ears, the sound of her screaming generates a buzzing rattle like a blown speaker, but he doesn't care. It is sweet music.

Lindsey, who had been searching around the old stone foundation for the source of the whistles, joined Amanda at the lip of the well as quickly as she could. Amanda was pinching her nose.

"Dad!" She yelled into the darkness.

"Hi, Princess."

"Are you all right?" Then she got a whiff of the stink, and waved her hand in front of her face. She exchanged a worried glance with her sister.

"No, not really," came her father's weak, disembodied voice. "My legs are broken. I'm gonna need help getting out of here. But I'm so glad to hear your voices. I thought I'd never see you again. He said help was coming, but he didn't say who it was gonna be. I'm so glad it was you. I love you girls so much."

"We'll get help," Lindsey said. "Everything's gonna be okay now, Dad. Don't worry."

Amanda was crying. "Daddy, are you gonna die?" she asked.

"No, honey, not now. You guys saved me. You're my heroes. Where's Kate?"

"We haven't seen her all day," Lindsey said. "We've been out lookin' for you."

"When you see her, tell her I love her, will you?"

"We will. Daddy, what's that smell? It really reeks."

"There's a dead animal in here with me, honey. I think it's a raccoon, or it might be a 'possum."

"Oh," Amanda said. "Nasty."

"We have to go get help," Lindsey said to Amanda. "The fire department, or something. We're not strong enough to get him out of there."

"I'm not leaving Daddy," Amanda stated. "You go. I'm stayin' right here."

"Okay, I'll go," Lindsey agreed. "But stay back away from that hole. We don't need two of us in there."

Amanda backed up a few inches.

"Daddy, I'm gonna go get help," Lindsey said into the well. "Amanda's gonna stay with you. Okay?"

"Hurry," he said. "Please hurry …"

"I will. Bye, Dad. I love you." She turned to Amanda, and met her gaze. Amanda's eyes were wide with shock and worry. They'd found him, but it was not yet time to celebrate.

They gave each other a tight embrace.

They separated, and Lindsey said, "I gotta go." She flitted off through the bracken, back toward the trail.

Jerry watched the developing drama with interest. Apparently, the girls' father was alive. Amazing, but of no consequence.

When the older girl took off to run for help and left the younger one at the well, he knew it was time to make his move.

"Daddy," Amanda said into the dark well. "I was so scared. We knew something bad must've happened, but we didn't know what. And we were afraid when we found you, you might already be dead."

"I know, sweetheart. I was afraid of that, too."

"Daddy? I think I can almost see you down there."

"So proud of you guys ..."

"We worked so good together as a team, Daddy. Whenever one of us was ready to give up, the other one always said we have to keep tryin', and we never gave up, Daddy. We never did, even when we were really stuck on something. We wouldn't have made it without Mr. Leo, though. He helped us a real lot."

"Who?"

"Oh, yeah. I just remembered we're supposed to tell you that Lee—I mean Leo—said you guys are even now, and you can keep the book. He said you'd know what it meant."

No answer came from below.

"Daddy? Did you hear me?"

Still no answer.

"Daddy!"

"You bastard," her father said. "Good one. You really had me going this time. Are you Heckle, or Jeckle?"

Amanda's mouth fell open. "Daddy, it's me. Amanda. Who's Heckle and Jeckle?"

Silence from the well.

"Daddy?"

"If you're Amanda, then what's your favorite song?"

"Huh? It's 'Pieces of Me,' Daddy. You know that."

Her father made a sound like a hiccup.

"Daddy?"

"You really are Amanda?"

"Yeah, it's me, Daddy."

"This isn't a dream?"

"No, Daddy. This is real. I'm right here. Lindsey was here, too. She went to get help."

"He told me you were coming, but I was afraid to believe it."

"Who did?"

"And you said you talked to him, too? But he's dead."

"Who's dead? Are you talkin' about Mr. Leo? 'Cause he's not dead, Daddy. We talked to him a bunch of times today. I told you, he helped us."

"No. Lynch is dead."

"Who's Lynch? Daddy, you're not makin' any sense."

"Nothing makes sense. But never mind, baby. We'll figure it out later. Just keep talking to me, okay? Don't let me fall asleep."

"I can do that."

"Good. Amanda?"

"Yeah, Daddy?"

"I want to tell you something. It's important. Are you listening?"

"Yeah, I hear you, Daddy."

"Okay, listen. If I don't ... if ever there's a time ... I mean, I've always told you that I'd always be there for you. But if something happens ... you know ... someday, I won't be around anymore. But I want you to know that you can still talk to me if that happens."

"You mean, if you die?"

"Yes. You can still talk to me. Know how?"

Amanda felt tears building up, and her throat was all tight. "Are you gonna die, Daddy?" Now the tears began to fall.

"No, I'm not going to die, honey. Not today, anyway. He said it would be a while ... he said ..."

Amanda grew worried after a few seconds of silence. "Daddy?"

"Amanda?"

"Yeah?"

"Sorry. I forgot what I was talking about."

"You said that I could still talk to you if you ... you know, if ..."

"Oh yeah. If I died. And I'm not gonna die, don't worry. But just in case. You can always talk to me because I'll always be inside of you. As long as you're alive, honey, I'm alive too, because I'm part of you. All you have to do ... is listen to my voice in your head. I'll always be there."

Amanda couldn't answer.

"Do you get it, Squirt?"

"I think so."

"You do?"

"Yeah. Because I thought I talked to you last night. You helped me find the clue under my mattress."

"I did? Wow. You know, I think I kind of remember that. But I've had so many weird dreams. It's hard to tell."

"I love you, Daddy."

"I love you too, Amanda. More than anything in the whole world."

"Even more than pizza?"

She was sure she heard her father chuckle at that. "Yes, baby. Even more than pizza."

For the first time today, Lindsey felt lost without a working phone. She could really use one now.

As she pounded up the trail, she made her plan. She would get on her bike, ride over to Virginia Street, and head toward home. If she ran into anyone she knew out on the street, she'd ask to use their phone. If not, she'd continue on home and tell Kate. They'd call the police and Kate could bring her back in the car.

Then she heard a man's voice and skidded to a halt. Not just a man's voice. He had been *calling her name*. Someone had followed them here, and knew her name.

It could only be Lee, or Leo, or whatever his name was. Just when she'd begun to relax her guard with him a little, he had to go and do something weird again.

She froze, thinking, *So this is what it's like to be stalked.*

He called her name again. She moved off the trail as silently as she could, slipped behind the bole of a large tree, and listened.

She remained silent and motionless for at least a minute. But for the birds and the insects, the forest was deadly quiet. Then came the telltale sound of footsteps. Leo was walking again. Coming toward her, or going away?

From the sound, she guessed that he was moving from her right to her left, not toward her or away from her; so she scooted around to the right side of the tree trunk.

He stopped. He must know she was nearby. He was listening for her.

Or he had passed on out of earshot.

Or he had found an area where he could move without creating a ruckus. Soft earth. Stones. The trail.

Lindsey felt an urgent need to empty her bladder. She rested her head against the tree, and resolved to wait one more minute. If she didn't hear any more sounds by then, she would resume her mission. She began counting off the seconds in her head.

She'd reached fifty-five Mississippi when the man's hand snaked around the tree and grabbed her by the upper arm. She screamed and struggled, but could not break free of his iron grip.

19

"I know that brat," Kate said. "That's Grayson Watters, Deanna's younger brother." She pulled the car up to where Grayson rode his bike and opened her window. "Hey, Grayson," she called.

Grayson stopped his bike and looked at her. "Yeah?"

"You haven't seen my daughters today, have you?"

Grayson started to cry.

"Grayson, what's wrong?"

"I ... I ... I ... I didn't mean for it to happen. Honest, I didn't."

Kate's heart skipped a beat. "For what to happen?"

"For that guy to ... to ... you know ..."

Kate threw the car into park and got out. She loomed over Grayson Watters and said, "Grayson, you better start making sense right now. Have you seen my daughters or not?"

Grayson's lower lip trembled. "Y-yes, ma'am."

"When?"

"About a half hour ago."

"Where?"

Grayson pointed. "Right out there in that field."

Kate's knees felt weak. *They were here. They were okay.* "Where are they now, Grayson?"

"I don't know, honest I don't. I ran away, 'cause I was scared."

A shudder of fear rippled over Kate. "Scared of what?"

"See, they were sittin' out in the field doin' somethin', I don't know what. But this big guy with a huge knife came up behind 'em, and I ran. I'm sorry. I think he might've ... you know ... killed 'em or somethin'."

"*What?*" Kate's heart pounded in her chest, and the world spun around her. He'd taken them. The predator had taken her daughters.

Dottie appeared beside her. "Young man, you said you were scared and you ran inside when you saw him come up behind them?" she asked Grayson.

"Yes, ma'am."

"And you haven't seen the girls since?"

"No, ma'am."

"What about the man?"

"Yeah, I know where he is," Grayson said. He pointed across the field, across Route 128, to where Cappie's Bar hunkered like a misshapen toad. Leaning against the front of the bar with a paper bag in his hand was the large ugly man. "That's him right there."

Kate and Dottie regarded each other.

"Let's go," Kate said.

"Lindsey, Lindsey, stop! Calm down. I'm not going to hurt you. My name is George Booker. I'm with the Sheriff's Department."

Lindsey struggled a few moments more before what the man had said penetrated, and then she froze, staring at him, at the uniform, the Stetson. Help was here already. Her mouth fell open.

"OMG," she said. "I can't believe you're here. We found my Dad, he fell into a well and he's hurt real bad, you gotta help him, please, he's right down there, my sister's with him, please you gotta help us."

"Shh, shh, shh," the deputy said. "Slow down. You found Timmy?"

Lindsey nodded eagerly.

"He's alive?"

"Yes!"

"Amanda's with him?"

"Yeah. I told you that. Come on!"

"All right, show me."

Lindsey took off at a dead run back down the trail, trusting that the deputy would keep up.

Jerry stayed back in the trees. *Of all the confounded luck!* He'd been about to take the older girl when he'd seen the police officer coming down the trail. He'd stepped behind a tree and watched as Lindsey hid, but the officer had found her. Now they were going to go back to the other little girl at the well.

Jerry knew he had quite a predicament on his hands. He had missed his chance to take those two girls; that opportunity had dissipated like so much smoke. His objective now was self-preservation. Escape.

First, he had to get out of these woods. How was he going to do that? The police officer was between him and his car, and more would be on the way. If they found either him or his car, there would be hell to pay.

Can't go over it, can't go under it; gotta go around it. He'd cut due west through the woods until he hit Orenzo Mill Road, then walk that road to Cooper Road, and from there, back to his car. Easy. The cop in the woods might hear him start his engine, but Jerry would be long gone before the cop could respond.

He began walking through the woods toward Orenzo Mill, stepping as quietly as he could.

Kate and Dottie first drove out to the end of Horne Drive to ascertain that the girls were not still in the field where Grayson had seen them, keeping their eyes on Leo's figure loitering in front of Cappie's. That done, Kate drove around the block and soon screeched into Cappie's parking lot. She slammed on the brakes, rammed the shifter into park, and was out of the car in less than a second. The car door thunked shut as she advanced on Leo.

When her gaze fell on him, she stopped in her tracks. The wild hair, the beard, the faded black Kiss t-shirt that looked like it might have been on him continuously since the seventies.

"*You!*" she said. "I should have known you were trouble the first time I saw you!"

Leo cowered before her, covering his head with his left arm. "Stop yelling at me. I haven't done anything wrong. I've been good, I swear!"

"What have you done with my daughters? I want some answers *right now!*"

Leo sank lower still, recoiling from her fury. "Stop picking on me. I didn't hurt anybody. I just came over here to make a phone call, that's all. And all I had was a hundred-dollar bill, so I had to go in and break it on something to get change for the payphone, and so I bought a bottle. Just one bottle. To make change for the pay phone. Because I had a job to do, a very important job, very important. You can have the change," he said, extending a wad of crumpled bills toward Kate. "I won't be needing it where I'm going."

Kate shrank back from the proffered cash. "I don't want that," she said. "I want to know what happened to Lindsey and Amanda, dammit!"

"Your daughters are fine," Leo said. "I was just with them. They're my friends."

Kate blinked. "You admit it?"

"Yes, ma'am. I wouldn't hurt them for anything, anything in the world. They were nice to me. At first I thought they were rude, but they're not rude. They keep their promises. And they gave me a hundred dollars."

"What?" Kate turned to Dottie. "This man is delusional. We're not going to get a straight answer out of him." She turned back to Leo. "Are you drunk?"

"No, ma'am. Not yet. But I'm trying." He held up his paper-bag-clad bottle.

"Where would they get a hundred dollars? And why would they give it to you? Are you sure that's what really happened?"

"Yes, I swear. I helped them, you see, so they gave it to me. It was under the rock, and we all thought it was ten dollars, but when I unfolded it I found out it was a hundred. That's why I want you to give them the change back, I don't think they woulda given it to me if they knew it was a hundred."

"We don't care about the hundred dollars!" Dottie said. "We only want to know where my granddaughters are. Do you have an answer, or not?"

"Yes, Miss Dottie. They went to find their Daddy. I told them where to go. I helped them solve the puzzles. I wouldn't want them to lose their Daddy. They're nice girls. I swear I didn't hurt them. I would never do that. I mind my own beeswax. I don't hurt people. I keep my promises. I pay my debts. I help people find the light. Someday soon I'll find it myself. 'For my purpose holds to sail beyond the sunset.'"

"Listen to me very carefully," Dottie said. "Focus. I want to know where—Wait. What did you say?"

"I said, 'For my purpose holds—'"

"No, not that. You called me by name. How did you know my name?"

Leo's eyes flicked from Dottie's face to Kate's, back to Dottie's. "Miss Dottie," he said, "don't you remember me?"

Kate goggled. "You two *know* each other?"

"I'm sorry," Dottie said. "I'm afraid I ... have we—?" Dottie peered at him.

"No," she said, "it's not possible."

Leo nodded. "Many things are possible, Miss Dottie."

Kate realized her mouth was hanging open. She closed it. She watched as Dottie, visibly rattled, stood shaking her head as if in denial of everything that had happened since they stopped the car.

"Listen to me, whoever you are," Kate said, turning back to Leo. "This is very important. Are you listening?"

"Yes, ma'am. But I have to go. They're calling me."

"Who's calling you?"

"The voices. I have one more job to do. I have to go."

"Never mind the voices, damn you. Concentrate on me. We need to find Lindsey and Amanda. They're in danger. It's very important that we find them. Do. You. Know. Where. They. Went."

"Yes, ma'am. They went … they went …" he said, pointing vaguely to the east as his eyes lost focus.

Kate turned to look in the direction he indicated, just as a fire engine came screaming past them on 128, heading in that same direction.

She noticed that Dottie had wandered back toward the car as if in a daze of her own.

"Dottie!" Kate yelled over the noise of the receding fire engine. "Are you all right?"

Dottie gave no answer, did not even turn to face Kate.

"Stay right here," she said to Leo. "Don't you move." Then, with a few loping strides she closed the distance between herself and Dottie, who stood next to the car, facing east, her face drained of all color.

"Dottie," she said. "What's going on?"

Dottie turned slowly to face her. "I wish I knew," she replied.

"Do you know that man, or not?"

At first Dottie didn't answer, only stared. "You might find this crazy, but yes, I think I do. Remember I told you about Timothy's friend, Leonard Lynch?"

Kate nodded. "The one that died, yes. What about him?"

Dottie inclined her head back toward the bar. "That was he."

"What do you mean, 'that was he?'" You told me Leonard Lynch was dead."

"He is dead. He's been dead for over twenty years. There can be no doubt of it."

"Then how could that—" Kate turned to indicate Leo, and found that the man had vanished. "Shit! Where did he go?" She turned in a complete circle, and confirmed that she and Dottie were now alone. "He must've gone back inside. He was getting ready to tell me where the girls were. I'm going in there."

"Kate," said Dottie, placing a hand on Kate's upper arm. "He's not in there."

"Well, where else could he be? Do you think he just up and disappeared?"

"I don't know," Dottie said, "but he did tell us something, in a way. He was pointing over there, in the direction that emergency vehicle went. What do you say we find out where it's going?"

Kate exhaled with exasperation. "Fine. I've no better idea. Let's go."

As she was about to get into the driver's seat, she noticed the crumpled bills lying in the parking lot near the bar. She ran over, scooped them up, and came back to the car.

"This belongs to the girls," she said to Dottie. "But I might put it through the wash before I give it to them."

Kate got them rolling as fast as she could, but the fire engine was already out of sight. They drove right past Amanda's school and through the light at Route 5. Still, they could not see the fire engine ahead of them. Kate floored it.

"Timmy, I called in the fire department," George said. "They should be here any minute. We're going to get you out of there, okay?"

"Thanks, George," Tim replied, his thin voice floating up out of the darkness like a ghost. "Is, um … is my wife coming? I'd really like to …"

"We're trying to locate her. Soon as we do, we'll have her down here. You hear?"

"Yeah … okay. And I need … water … please … so thirsty."

"Sure, I'll try, Timmy. Just hold on now, hear?" Getting Tim out of that well wasn't going to be easy, but George knew they would do it. He had assessed Tim's injuries and informed dispatch within a minute of reaching the well. The man was near death, George knew, and seconds counted now. Next on his list of things to do was to get Lindsey and Amanda to safety, but he didn't want to leave Timmy.

"Listen, girls. I don't think this is the best place for you two to be right now." He held his hand up, as both girls had opened their mouths. "I'm sorry, but I'm going to have to insist. This is a rescue operation now, and we can't have anyone in the way. Another deputy just pulled into the parking lot; I know because I just talked to him on the radio. His name is Alan Curtis, he's an old friend of your Uncle Greg's."

"We met him yesterday," Lindsey said.

"You did? Oh, that's right. Good, you already know him, then. He'll take care of you. Do you two think you can get out there to the parking lot by yourselves?"

The girls nodded. "Yeah, but we wanna stay," Lindsey said. "Can't we stay here with him? I promise we'll stay out of the way."

George shook his head. "No, ladies, you can't." In reality, they probably wouldn't impede the operation, but it was going to be very hard on Timmy and there might be some screaming; also, he probably wasn't going to look too good when he did come up, and the smell emanating from the well boded ill for the condition of his body. George didn't want the girls to be part of that experience. "You guys can say goodbye to him now, if you want, and then I want you to run out to the parking lot. I'm going to stay with him. I promise I'll take good care of him."

Amanda leaned over the well opening a tiny bit. George kept a hand on the waist of her pants, just to be sure.

"Daddy?" she said.

"Yeah, baby?"

Amanda started to cry. "I'm so scared, Daddy!"

"Don't be scared. Everything's ... gonna be fine."

"Okay." She sniffed, wiped her eyes. "Me and Lin have to go now, Daddy. Mr. George is gonna stay with you."

"That's ... that's great, Squirt. See you soon."

"I love you, Daddy."

Lindsey poked her head into the well beside Amanda's. "Bye, Daddy. I love you."

"I love both of you girls ... so much," Tim replied. "Thanks ... thanks for finding me. Hugs ... hugs when I ... get out of here. 'Kay?"

"Okay, Daddy."

Jerry had happened upon a game trail heading in the direction he wanted to go. At first, it had seemed a godsend, but as Jerry neared Orenzo Mill Road, it grew more constricted, began to twist and turn back on itself. The vegetation thickened, lowering his sight distance to a mere dozen feet or so. Fallen trees obstructed his path, forcing him to climb over or stoop under. Briars tugged at his clothing and skin, seeming to be driven by a will of their own.

Jerry pushed on. Sweat trickled down his rib cage, escaped the band of his hat and ran into his eyes. His long pants stuck to him like a second skin. Insects buzzed him, going for his eyes and ears. Never an admirer of forested areas in the first place, Jerry now found this one stifling, claustrophobic. The fetid odor of rotting vegetation grew noticeable, and soon became unbearable. He felt the need to retch.

Judging by the distance he'd already covered, he reckoned that Orenzo Mill Road couldn't be more than thirty or forty feet farther. Yet the confining growth blocked it from his view.

What was that? He froze, listening intently for a recurrence of the sound he thought he'd heard. And there it was. The fall of a footstep. And another, coming from directly ahead of him on the trail ... but out of sight around the next bend.

Of all the ... how could there be yet *another* person in this confounded forest at the same time as him?

Unless ...

Of course. This new arrival was there *because* of him. It was clearly time for a strategic retreat.

Pulse hammering, he turned around and began to retrace his steps as quietly as he could. He would find a place to hide, stand behind a tree trunk as the girl had, and wait for the stranger to pass. Then he would resume his course.

A twig snapped directly behind him. He whirled, and the stranger was there, not three feet away, materializing in his personal space as if out of thin air.

It was all Jerry could do to stifle a scream. He recoiled, and would have fallen on his backside if not for the three involuntary backward steps he took.

Recovering his balance, he locked eyes with the apparition. Wild hair, unkempt beard, old rock t-shirt, rotten stumps of intermittent teeth exposed in a feral grin … and an extremely dangerous-looking blade in his right fist.

The man, leveling a baleful glare at him, said nothing.

Jerry found himself in the grip of a sudden, enervating terror, greater than any mere man, however threatening, should have provoked. It was all he could do not to turn tail and run screaming. Instead, he continued to back up, slowly now. "I'm sorry," he said, "I didn't mean to intrude. I'll just be going back the way I came."

Then, abandoning any pretense of dignity, he spun and fled, glancing over his shoulder once, only to find that the man had vanished as mysteriously as he had appeared. This only amplified Jerry's already unreasoned panic. He continued his stumbling flight, indifferent to the noise he made, the thrashing he took from grasping branches. In his haste, he tripped several times and once fell flat out on the forest floor. Clambering to his feet, he carried on without pausing to brush himself off. When he reached the point where he'd last seen the older girl, he stopped to catch his breath and cast a fearful look down his backtrail.

Nothing. If the man was following him, he was doing so not only silently, but invisibly as well.

But this was no comfort to him. Jerry, an avowed skeptic when it came to things paranormal, now struggled with the idea that this man had already demonstrated the ability to appear and disappear at will.

Under the circumstances, he made a snap decision to return to the main trail. He'd get to Orenzo Mill Road via the school grounds and avoid the woods altogether. It would be a longer walk, but worth it, if it enabled him to steer clear of the freak in the forest.

The idea that there might be more police officers out there never occurred to him.

Alan Curtis, having finished directing a fire engine where to pull up, saw Lindsey and Amanda appear at the entrance to the nature trail. They stopped and looked around, confused. They held hands, and the younger one was crying. He moved to intercept them. They saw him coming, and he extended both his hands to them.

"Hello again, ladies," he said. "Everything's gonna be fine, now."

The girls came to him. "Now, you're Lindsey, right?" he said to the older one. She nodded, and he said to the younger, "And you're Amanda." She nodded, too.

"It's good to see you two safe and sound. A lot of people've been worried about you. Your Mom should be here in a few minutes to pick you up; I sent a deputy over to your house to get her. She'll be here, soon, you foller?"

"You mean our stepmom? Or our real mom?" Lindsey said.

"Sorry, ladies. I meant your stepmom. So, I understand you two found him, ain't that right?"

"Yes, sir," Lindsey said.

"Well, I gotta tell ya, I'm real impressed, because we've been lookin' for him all day long, and we weren't gettin' anywhere, you foller me? But you two little ladies found him, all by yourselves. Shoot, that's good police work. Now why don't we take a seat over here on this bench while we wait for the ambulance to get here? Or would you ladies maybe like to sit in my squad car? Hey, I just remembered I got somethin' in the car I bet you might take a likin' to. Do you girls like kittens?"

Jerry watched the scene from the woods. Thwarted again, this time by a second sheriff's deputy and some firefighters. No matter. Between the knife-wielding terror at his back and the police officer before him, it was no contest. He'd take his chances with the cop.

He cast a fearful glance behind him, half-expecting to see the murderous stranger right on his tail. His entire body twitched as he thought he saw someone slipping behind a tree. But no. It must have been a bit of undergrowth, moving with the breeze.

What breeze? It was still as death in the woods. He shuddered, wiped sweat from his brow, and turned back to the scene in the parking lot.

Talking his way past one officer should be easy. He was just a man out for a stroll on a nature trail, was he not? Perfectly innocent. He could be quite convincing when he was on his game. Best to do it now, before more deputies arrived.

Alan left the girls behind his squad car, playing with the kitten in the grass, while he started rolling out the yellow perimeter tape. He looked up to see a man in dark clothing come out of the woods, ambling along like he owned the place. "Now, where the hell did *he* come from?"

The man took a look at him, waved, turned the other way, and kept walking, away from him.

"Uh, sir?" Alan yelled.

The man turned back to face him.

"Could I talk to you a minute, please?"

Alan and the man walked toward each other until they met in the middle. Alan, with a quick glance, took in the man's muddy clothes, the one pants leg ripped at the knee, the deep scratch on his forehead.

"How ya doin' today, sir?" Alan asked.

"I'm well, thank you. Can I help you, officer?"

"Alan Curtis," he said, extending his hand.

The man gripped his hand, and said, "Barry. Barry Spicer. Nice to meet you."

"My pleasure, Mr. Spicer. Pardon my askin', but didja see a ghost or somethin'?"

"A ghost? What do you mean? Why would you ask that?"

"Just a figure of speech. No need to get ornery about it. It's just that ya look like ya been drug through a field by a runaway tractor. Are ya okay?"

Spicer looked down at himself, seeming to notice his condition for the first time. "Oh … yes, I'm fine. It's just … I was out for my normal walk, and—"

"Walk here a lot?"

"Yes, sir, almost every day. I really enjoy this trail and it's close to my home."

"Which is where, if ya don't mind my askin'?"

"Right over there," Spicer replied, pointing toward the end of Virginia Street.

"You mean on Virginia Avenue?"

"Virginia *Street*."

"Street, of course. That's what I meant."

Spicer nodded, smiling. The sound of more sirens in the distance grew louder by the second.

"What's the house number?" Alan asked.

"Thirty-one ten," Spicer replied without hesitation, idly flicking chunks of mud from his left elbow.

"Okay. Well, ya don't get torn up like this every time ya take a stroll, do ya? I sure hope not."

"No, sir, of course not. But this time I … well, I … this is embarrassing, but I guess I took a little spill. It's those steps back there, officer," he said, pointing back into the woods with his thumb. "Someone really should do a little maintenance on them."

"I'll mention it," Alan said, nodding. The sirens grew deafening, then abruptly cut off as a second fire engine pulled into the lot, with an ambulance right behind.

"Well, as you can see," Alan continued, "we've got sort of a situation here today, Mr. Spicer. I'd appreciate it if you'd go on home and don't come back here until we've got things all cleaned up, you foller me?"

"Yes, sir, I'll do that. It was nice meeting you."

"You, too, Mr. Spicer. And take care of that cut right quick, before it festers."

"Thank you, I will."

They shook hands again and Spicer set off toward Virginia Street.

"Uh, Mr. Spicer?" Alan asked. "Weren't you walkin' the other direction before? When I first saw ya?"

"Yes, sir, I was going to walk around the school, but I thought you'd rather I went straight home instead."

Alan chuckled. "I did say that, didn't I? All right, have a nice day, Mr. Spicer."

Alan felt something latch onto his foot, and looked down to see the kitten attacking his shoelace. At first absorbed in subduing Alan's foot, it then noticed Spicer and went stiff. It scrambled to its feet, arched its back, hissed and spat, and backed up behind Alan's leg.

Alan bent and swept the kitten up in his hand. Cradling it, he turned back to Spicer and said, "I'm guessin' you ain't a cat person. Am I right?"

Spicer didn't answer. His face had gone bone white.

"Mr. Spicer, didja see *another* ghost?"

"I ... I'm afraid of cats."

Click.

"You're kiddin' me. Who could be afraid of a little thing like this?"

"Well, I'm ... actually allergic to them."

"Is that so. Well, to tell the truth, this one acts like she's allergic to *you*. Have you ever seen this kitten before?"

"No. Never."

"Mr. Spicer, are ya sure? Because she acts like she knows you, and when you first saw her you looked like you were about to—"

At that moment, Lindsey and Amanda came around from behind the car to retrieve the kitten. Spicer and the girls came face to face, and all three flinched. Spicer licked his lips, and his hands twitched at his sides.

Alan studied him. "Do you folks know each other?" he said.

"No." Spicer said.

"We saw him." Lindsey said, at the same instant.

"Where?" Alan asked. "In the woods?"

"No, today, earlier, at Wawa. He ... he was ..."

"He was starin' at us," Amanda said. "He creeped us out."

Click.

"They've obviously got me confused with someone else," Spicer said. "I haven't been to Wawa today."

"Mr. Spicer, are those New Balance crosstrainers you're wearin'?"

"Yes, sir. They're a nice shoe."

"Always wanted to get a pair, myself. Mr. Spicer, you wouldn't happen to have any ID on ya, wouldja now?"

Spicer made a show of patting his pants pockets down, then said, "Oh, no. I must have left my wallet in the car."

"In the car? I thought ya said ya walked over here."

"I did."

The firefighters were busy offloading equipment from the engine and the ambulance, preparing themselves for a rescue operation. One of them came up to Alan at that point, oblivious to the fact that he was conducting an interrogation.

"He's back in the woods," Alan said to the fireman. "I got a man back there with him now, but I'll bring him out to show ya where it is." The fireman nodded and moved off.

"Now, Mr. Spicer, you'll have to forgive me, but I'm just tryin' to understand all this. Help me out here. Now if you walked over here, then why's your wallet in your car? Most folks, when they're at home, keep their wallet and other such valuables in the house, you foller me?"

"Well, my wife and I went out to dinner last night, and I take my wallet out when I'm driving because it bothers my sciatic, so when we came home, I guess I left it in the car."

"I see. Would your wife be home now?"

"No, I'm afraid she's gone shopping for the day."

"Uh-huh. How 'bout we call your house anyways, just to be sure. What's the number? I need to confirm that you are who you say you are, foller me? Just a formality."

"Of course, I understand. But I'll give you her cellphone number, that way you'll be sure to reach her."

"That's fine. What is it?"

Spicer gave him a number.

"That's an out of state number, Mr. Spicer."

"Yes, it is. My wife travels a lot for work. That's a company phone, based in Chicago."

"I see. Well, if ya wouldn't mind, could ya hang around right here while I make this phone call?"

"Of course, officer."

Alan stepped a few paces away, waving for the girls to come with him. As they walked, he asked, "Now girls, did ya happen to see him leave Wawa?"

"Yes, sir," Lindsey said.

"Did ya see what kind of car he was drivin'?"

"He didn't drive, Mr. Alan. He walked. He went into the woods behind Wawa. There's a trail there that goes over to the back of Ringgold's."

"And he was carryin' a bag from Justice," Amanda added.

Click.

"Was he, now." Alan called the number Spicer had given him, and got the voicemail of someone named Loretta Spicer. It meant nothing. Then he hailed George Booker on the radio. When George answered, Alan said, "Book, the boys are on their way back there right now. Tell me, from your twenty, how far is it to Cooper Road?"

"About a hundred yards, I guess."

"All right. First I need ya to come back here, Book, and show these boys where to go. Then I want ya to go back with 'em, and take a snoop around back there to see if ya can find a car parked somewhere off of Cooper, foller me? And let me know what ya find."

"Ten-four. Uh, Cap, the victim is seriously dehydrated. Maybe someone could bring back a bottle of water with them."

"Copy that." He signed off and hung his radio on his belt, as another unit pulled in from the Sheriff's Department. It was Todd Newkirk. "About time," Alan said. Then to Newkirk as he pulled up: "Take charge of the perimeter, here, Newkirk. Booker's in the woods, but he should be out soon."

"Yes, sir. By the way, we haven't been able to locate Mrs. Raither. She's not home."

"That's okay. I'll get her cell number from her daughters here. Soon as I'm done with this fella."

"Ladies," Alan said to the girls, "would you mind watchin' this kitten for me for another couple of minutes?" He put the kitten into Amanda's arms and turned back to Spicer, whose eyes darted all around him. "Mr. Spicer," he said. "I wonder if you'd mind goin' for a short ride with me."

"Uh … where would we be going, officer?"

"Just across the road, over to the old Ringgold's buildin'. This won't take a minute. Do ya mind?"

"Uh … well … I really ought to be going home, officer. I'd be happy to help out, but if you could do it without me, I'd greatly appreciate it. I'll leave you my number so—"

"Mr. Spicer, I'm afraid I'm gonna have to insist, now." He took Spicer by the elbow and escorted him toward the back door of his car.

Spicer appeared to cooperate at first, but suddenly, he broke free of Alan's hand and ran. He lit out across the grass, heading for the trees.

Alan shook his head and rolled his eyes. "Newkirk," he said with an air of disappointment. "Take that sumbitch down."

Todd Newkirk had played middle linebacker in college. The NFL had passed him over, but in situations like this, he was a force to be reckoned with. And he didn't mind getting his uniform dirty. He had a good angle, and flattened the sumbitch just before they got to the edge of the forest.

When Alan put "Barry Spicer" in the back seat of his car, the man was in handcuffs.

Kate and Dottie, after coming to the realization that they were not on the trail of the fire engine anymore, had made a U-turn and returned to Sycamore. This time, they had seen a police cruiser turn onto Orenzo Mill, siren wailing, and they followed it.

They did not speak as they pulled into the parking lot, stunned into silence by the scene before them. Police, ambulances, fire engines. Lots of flashing lights. Men and women scrambling around with a sense of purpose, and urgency.

"There are the girls," Dottie said, pointing.

Kate stopped the car and got out. The girls looked up as she approached, and she could read in their faces that they were not sure whether to be happy or frightened to see her. She smiled at them, and their expressions changed to reflect hers.

The girls moved to meet her, and she swept them into her arms, tears springing unbidden to her eyes. "*Finally*, I've found you!" Kate said. "You girls nearly gave me a heart attack."

"I know, we're sorry, Kate," Lindsey said, "but we found Dad!"

"*What?* You did? Where is he? Is he all right?"

"He fell into a well back in the woods. He's hurt, but they're gonna get him out. He's gonna be okay."

The relief that washed over her felt like an ocean wave must feel to a starfish stranded on the beach. She could not speak. At some level, she was aware that she was on her knees, hugging both girls, crying, and that they touched her, said things to her, but the meaning of their words was lost in a swirling sea of solace.

"Mom-mom!" Amanda said, and Kate, gazing at her through blurry eyes, saw the shock in Amanda's face at finding her stepmother and grandmother together. Then she felt Dottie's amorphous presence behind her, and felt a hand come to rest on her shoulder. She turned to look up at Dottie, and opened her mouth, but no words would come out.

"I heard," Dottie said, nodding and smiling, and Kate saw that she, too, was crying.

At long last, Kate regained the ability to form words. "I've got to see him," she said to the girls. "Take me to him, right now!"

"We can't, Kate," Lindsey said. "The police made us leave. They say it's a rescue operation and we can't see him any more until they get him out."

"Tim!" Kate screamed, releasing the girls. She bolted toward the entrance to the nature trail, shouting her husband's name repeatedly. She ducked under the yellow tape and shot through a gap between two fire engines, where a firefighter intercepted her with an outstretched arm.

"Ma'am, ma'am, ma'am!" he said.

Kate came to a stop to avoid crashing into him.

"You can't go through here, ma'am."

"That's my husband in there," she said. "You have to let me through."

"No, ma'am, not right now. We need to keep the area clear."

"Let me through, damn you! Do you have any idea what I've been through the last two days?"

"I'm sorry, ma'am, but I can't. Please stand outside the yellow tape."

"Listen, you. You're starting to piss me off."

"Mrs. Raither," said a sheriff's deputy appearing from her left. She recognized him as Sergeant Booker, the one they'd ambushed at McDonald's. "It's a very delicate operation, what they're doing now. They can't have any distractions."

"But … I have to see him. Can't you at least let me talk to him? Just for a minute?"

"We really can't, Kate. But I promise you, as soon as he's stable, I'll make sure you and your family have a chance to talk to him. I promise. Okay?" He put a hand on her elbow and gave her a gentle turn. Kate acquiesced as Booker put his arm around her shoulders, and they began walking back toward the girls.

"Can you at least tell me how he is?" Kate asked.

"He's alive and he's conscious. That's all I can say for sure. But these people are gonna do the very best they can do for him, and they're very good at their jobs. I've seen them deal with worse situations than this, believe me. Don't worry."

Booker handed her over to Dottie, who had come to the yellow tape to meet them, and she and Dottie trudged back to where Lindsey and Amanda waited.

"You're right," Kate said to the girls. "They'd not let me through."

Lindsey and Amanda glanced at each other and smiled.

"But it's all right," Kate continued. "At least we know where he is. And he's alive. *He's alive!* Oh, God, I was so scared. Thank you, God, thank you! And thank you, Lindsey and Amanda!" She came to them, again sank to her knees in the grass, and wrapped her arms around both girls. "By the way, where'd you get the kitten?"

"It's Mr. Alan's," Lindsey said. "We're just holding her for him."

"Mr. Alan's? He doesn't waste any time, does he?"

"Huh?"

"Never mind," Kate said. "I love you girls. You really did it, didn't you? You found your Dad."

The girls nodded, beaming with pride.

"Why did you keep avoiding me? I wanted to help you. But no, don't answer, it doesn't matter now. You found him and I'm so proud of you!"

Dottie came to them and, much to the girls' surprise, joined them on the ground in the group hug. "Quite the little detectives, aren't we?" she said to Lindsey and Amanda.

Alan walked over toward them, having subdued "Barry Spicer" and gotten him into his car. As he approached, Kate whispered to Dottie, "If he says 'foller me' one time, I'm going to scream."

"I'll join you."

"Kate, Miss Dottie," he said, nodding. "I owe you ladies an apology. Some of the things I said this mornin' were … well, they were downright rotten, to say the least. You ladies were right the whole time. I'm real, real sorry. I knew it didn't feel right even when I was sayin' it, but I wasn't gettin' anywhere and I didn't know what else to do. It took me a while before I came to my senses. In fact, if it hadn't been for these two girls right here, we might still be lookin' for your man, and I'm not afraid to admit it."

"Never mind all that," said Kate. "I need to see him. Can you get me in? Please."

"Now, Kate, ya know I'd do almost anything for ya, but I can't do that right now. The fire department's down there, and they need to be able to have room to work. It's a tight spot your husband's got himself into, but give 'em a few minutes and they'll have him out of there, you foller?"

Kate's and Dottie's eyes met. "Forbearance," Dottie said with a wink.

Kate smiled with one side of her mouth, nodded her head, and turned back to Alan. "May we wait right here then?" she asked.

"Of course. He'll be comin' out to that ambulance right there, so I'll make sure you get a chance to speak to him before they take him off. Now, I've got to take a short ride right now, but I'll be back in a jiffy." He paused, then added, "You should be proud of these two girls, indeed you should."

"Oh, we are. You can believe that."

20

The four Raither girls waited in the parking lot while the firefighters and paramedics worked to free Tim from the well. They spent the first ten or fifteen minutes recounting their adventures of the last two days to each other. It was a time of tears and laughter, of anger and forgiveness, but, above all, of relief and of love.

Lindsey and Amanda apologized all over themselves for having left Kate in the lurch for so long, and in light of the fact that they'd found her husband, Kate forgave them. But she admonished them not to ever pull such a stunt again.

Kate then made hasty phone calls to Darryl and Selena, both of whom, with Brian in tow, soon arrived. There were hugs all around, and from that point on, nothing could dissuade the three friends from waiting with the family.

The emergency vehicles had executed a sort of modern-day circling of the wagons in the parking lot, their bulk screening the entrance to the nature trail from the prying eyes of casual onlookers (of which more than a few had gathered). Tim's loved ones were allowed to cross the tape boundary and wait behind one of the vehicles, so long as they didn't interfere with the personnel. They maintained a safe distance from the entrance to the woods, but kept an open line of sight to it as the sun went behind the trees and cast them in shade, sparing them the worst of the heat of the dying day.

It started with a small remembrance, by Dottie, of the time Tim had broken his arm when he fell out of the cherry tree in the first grade. After

290

that, by mutual but unspoken consent, those gathered around conducted a random-access recapping of Tim's life, interspersed with contemplative silences. They paced, they talked, they complained, they prayed, they held hands, they cried, they embraced, they played with Alan Curtis's kitten.

In spite of these attempts at distraction, Tim's fate was continually on Kate's mind, and looming larger with each passing moment.

"What's taking them so long?" she asked, forty minutes into the wait. "Shouldn't they be out by now?"

"It does seem like it's been a long time," Dottie replied.

"Something must have gone wrong …"

They lapsed into a silence as deep and profound as the grave.

A beat-up old Honda Civic pulled into the parking lot, and Kate leaped to her feet. "Donna!"

Kate's sunburned sister got out of the car and ran toward the group. Kate met her, and engulfed her in a tight embrace, and they cried together with happiness and relief.

"How did you know?" Kate asked.

"Selena called me, and I checked out as soon as I heard. I still have sand in my butt."

Kate dissolved in laughter.

"See what I mean about Kate?" Amanda said to her sister. "She really does love Daddy. And she cares about us, too."

"Yeah, I guess so. She just has a different way of showing it than Mom does."

"Yeah, she's not Mom, but she's okay."

Alan Curtis pulled back into the rear parking lot at Sycamore Elementary. It had been an hour and a half since he left, and the operation was still under way.

He and Todd Newkirk had found Madison in the back room of Ringgold's, and the man known as Barry Spicer had made another ill-advised attempt to escape. Newkirk (the father of a six-year-old girl himself) had been forced to administer a rather severe beating in order to subdue him. Spicer was now in custody at the Detention Center, and things didn't look good for him at all. His fingerprints matched those of Lawrence Kenny, a confidence man, serial rapist, and pedophile, originally from Omaha, Nebraska. He'd been convicted of rape in Kansas, served his time and been released several years ago. Since that time he'd gone off the grid, but they had him now.

In addition to being charged with the kidnapping of Madison Kingsmore, he matched the description for a rape reported that morning at a motel fifteen miles away, for which he would soon be standing in a lineup.

Kenny had lawyered up soon after arrival, and in a bid for leniency, begun leaking details about his activity since his disappearance. Apparently, he'd been kidnapping children all over the country and "selling" them to the black-market porn industry. The feds had been trying to pin down his current employers, a kiddie-porn ring on the outskirts of Boston, for years. He hinted, through his counsel, that he had information on several other missing children. Negotiations were in progress, but even in his best-case scenario, this man would be in jail for a long, long time.

Madison Kingsmore was safe, thanks to the information Alan had gotten from Lindsey and Amanda. She was now being examined at County General Hospital, and was reunited with her family.

Alan parked his car and strode over to where the Raither family was gathered. He exchanged greetings with them and asked about Timmy, but there was nothing new to report.

"You want your kitty back?" Lindsey asked.

"I reckon so," he said. "Think I'll take her home with me. Me and the missus'll give her a good home. Reckon she might do us some good, too." As he accepted the kitten from a reluctant Lindsey, a blue Silverado pickup flew into the parking lot and screeched to a stop. An agitated Greg Raither got out, advancing on the group with an obvious thundercloud over his head.

"Why didn't anyone tell me?" he roared. "He's my brother, you know. I would like to have helped. All these people here, and *no one* called me until a few minutes ago?"

"Calm down, Gregory," Miss Dottie said. "The situation is under control. You weren't needed. As you can see, we have quite a team here, and we've been very busy. I called you as soon as I could."

"Besides," Brian said, "we figured you'd be at church."

Greg glowered.

"I'm sorry, Greg," Kate said. "You're right, we should have let you know. But as your mother said, it's been crazy, and I've not had time to think, let alone make phone calls. Most of us've not even slept. Tim's alive. That's all that matters. Right?"

After an uncomfortable silence, Alan said, "Hey, Greg."

"Alan," Greg said, nodding. "Long time."

"Yep. I need to talk to ya a minute, if ya wouldn't mind. Walk with me?" Alan inclined his head away from the group.

Greg joined him. When they were out of earshot of the others, they stopped, and Alan said, "Greg, I have to ask ya somethin'. You're gonna think I'm plain nuts, but hear me out."

"I'm listening."

"Do you remember Leo Lynch?"

Greg flinched. "Of course," he replied. "Why?"

"Well … I talked to him today."

Greg stared stonily at his oldest friend before replying, "That's not funny, Alan."

"I'm not messin' with you, old buddy. It's God's honest truth. At least, I think it is. It sure sounded like him."

"Ah. This was on the phone, then, I take it."

"Yeah. About an hour ago, back at headquarters."

"A prank. Somebody's idea of a sick joke. I don't appreciate it, and when I find out—"

"Greg. He knew things, you foller me? Things only Lynch could know. It had to be him. He called me from the payphone at Cappie's, to let me know that Timmy was in these woods, and that his girls were goin' to look for him. He's the reason we're all here."

Greg took a deep breath. "Alan, do I need to explain this to you? Leo Lynch has been dead for twenty-three years. They found his body in that house with his mother's, burnt to a crisp. Have you forgotten all that?"

"No, I ain't forgotten, but I ain't so sure anymore about what happened in that house."

"What do you mean?"

"In the first place, now I don't know if you ever knew this, but Mrs. Lynch used to say her husband's death wasn't an accident. Soon as the first deputy got to the house, she up and told 'em that Leo pushed the car onto his Paw."

"*What?* He killed his father, too?"

"Accordin' to her. But Leo's story was different, of course. He said the jack just fell over and the car came down on his Paw while he watched. There was no evidence either way, and Leo stuck to his story, so they had to let him go."

"But he did it."

"Well, personally, I never could believe it myself. It didn't seem to fit, you foller me? You knew him. He wasn't like that. He didn't torture frogs or pick the wings off flies or bully anybody or anything like that. He was nuts, but he was about the most harmless fella I ever knew, except that one time when he pulled a huntin' knife on you and me, and even then I don't think he woulda done nothin'. He was as scared as we were."

Greg nodded. "Yes. And the way he loved his father …"

"Right. But we'll never know for sure. Most guys in the department assume he did it. And after the fire, that just seemed to confirm it. The thinkin' is that he killed his Paw, maybe on purpose, maybe it was an accident; but either way he had somethin' to do with it. Then his ol' lady blamed him for it every day of his life after that, until he finally got fed up with it and took her out, too. Then he burned the house down with himself in it. You gotta admit, it all kinda makes sense, as long as—"

"As long as you didn't know the guy personally, like we did."

"You got it. But here's the thing that's buggin' me today." Alan paused, looked around as if to catch an eavesdropper, and lowered his voice. "I'm not sure he killed his Paw, and I'm not convinced he killed his Mama either."

"Of course he killed his mother. How can there be any doubt?"

"No murder weapon was ever found, you foller me? If he killed her, then killed himself right away, how come they never found the knife?"

"He got rid of it."

"No, he didn't. There wasn't time. If he'd stabbed her, then left for long enough to get rid of the knife, and then come back and set the fire, she would've bled to death. But she didn't, she died of smoke inhalation. That means the fire started either right before, or right after he stabbed her. If the knife was anywhere in or around the house, they would've found it, and he couldn't've taken it anywhere else."

Greg frowned.

"I'm sayin'," Alan continued, "that someone stabbed Mrs. Lynch, and someone lit the house on fire, but I don't think they were the same person. Somebody got outta there and took the knife with 'em."

"How do you know all this?"

"You remember, when I first joined the force, I partnered with Jarvis Mitchell for awhile?"

Greg nodded.

"Well, Jarvis was there. And about the bodies. I'm gonna tell ya somethin' else that *I* ain't even supposed to know, and so the fact that I'm tellin' *you*, well, it just couldn't happen, so of course you ain't supposed to know it either, you foller me?"

Greg nodded again.

"They got a positive ID on Mrs. Lynch. But the kid, Leo, he hadn't ever been to a dentist his whole natural life. You understand what I'm tellin' you?"

Greg's eyes narrowed. "No records."

"None. That body was never positively IDed, Greg. Leo, he went missin' about the same time, so everybody naturally assumed it was him, especially what with his Paw, and that incident that happened on the bus and all. It wrapped things up all nice and tidy, but to this day, we don't know for sure."

"Then who was the other body if it wasn't Leo?"

"Don't know. Nobody else was reported missin' around that time. Coulda been one of her boyfriends, maybe. She had quite a few, remember. Or a vagrant, a runaway, maybe somebody runnin' from the law. Maybe it was the guy that *really* killed Mrs. Lynch. Maybe Leo caught him at it and killed him, then set the house on fire and ran off with the knife."

"Or maybe Leo killed them both."

Alan shrugged. "Possible."

"God in Heaven."

"Heaven ain't got anything to do with it, Greg. I think Leo Lynch might still be walkin' around on Earth."

"But ... but if that's true ... where's he been all these years?"

"Hidin' out, I guess. Homeless. Livin' under bridges. Woods, caves, barns, corn cribs, who the fuck knows? Pardon my French. All I know is, if he's still alive, I wanna talk to him. After all this is over with, maybe sometime tomorrow, I'm gonna go look for him. And the reason I'm tellin' you all this is that I thought you might wanna come along."

No one would ever know what had made Leo Lynch snap that day, what had triggered the frenzy of fire and steel and blood. Yet, in spite of the fact that it had taken place more than two years after Greg and Alan had last seen him, in Alan's deepest heart, he felt partially responsible. He and Greg had never talked about it, yet he knew he shared this burden with Greg, and probably with Timmy, too. It had festered in each of them like a cancer, steering their lives in small but significant ways. It was a large part of what had led Alan to police work. He suspected it was also what had driven Greg to the church, and he knew damn well it had helped Timmy to fall into a bottle.

"It'd be a chance to make amends, Greg. You foller me?"

"Yes. Yes, I do. I guess I would like to go with you, if you don't mind."

Thirty minutes after Alan had left again, there was a commotion at the entrance to the nature trail, and Kate and the others jumped up as Tim emerged from the woods on a stretcher. The paramedics allowed them to approach before they put him in the ambulance. He was covered from neck to toes with a sheet and a light blanket, and his head and face were almost entirely wrapped in bandages. They could barely see him, but they saw enough to know that he was alive, and conscious, and aware that they were with him. Kate mouthed "I love you" to him, and he responded by winking his left eye, the one that wasn't bandaged. He raised his left hand for a weak wave to his daughters.

Later, at the hospital, Kate and the girls received a visit from a tall man with brown eyes and a short, neatly trimmed beard. He introduced himself as Ron Kingsmore, Madison's father. He had heard of what happened to Tim and had left his daughter in his wife's care, to come meet the two young ladies who had been instrumental in Madison's rescue. Kate watched, smiling, as he shook the hands of her embarrassed daughters and thanked them. He then explained to Kate that Madison's injuries were mainly of the psychological variety, and would require a lot of care in the coming months and years, but that she would be able to go home the next day.

"Can we go see her?" Amanda asked.

Kate exchanged a look with Mr. Kingsmore, and as it seemed they were in agreement, nodded her head. Kate stayed with Tim as the girls rode the elevator up two floors to Madison's room.

21

"Poppy!" Amanda squealed.

Kate and the girls, after having spent a few hours at home catching up on some much needed sleep, had wasted no time getting back to the hospital in the morning. As they turned the corner into the waiting room, they had come face to face with Dottie, and Tim's father, Ed Raither, who had abandoned his fishing trip and hopped a redeye to BWI as soon as he heard.

Kate and Dottie then watched in mute fascination as Ed, in a rare display of emotion, swept both of his granddaughters up in one huge bearhug. Somehow, Kate's and Dottie's fingers ended up intertwined as they took in the scene.

"Anything new?" Kate asked.

"The orthopedist was in about an hour ago. Timothy's first surgery is tomorrow. He said Timothy's going to be here for quite some time."

"How long?"

"Weeks, maybe months. After the surgeries, there will be therapy and rehab. Kate ..."

Kate turned to face her mother-in-law. "What is it?"

"He's going to have to learn to walk again."

Kate's hand flew to her mouth.

"It'll be fine, Kate. He's in the best place for it. Just be there for him."

Kate nodded. "You know I will."

"Why don't you three go visit him for a bit? Edward and I will stay here."

———

Kate was encouraged to see her husband awake and sitting up. After the four of them exchanged greetings, Tim flashed Kate a question with his eye, and she nodded, smiling. She slipped over to stand by his side. Then he said, "Lindsey. Amanda. Come over here. I have something for you."

The girls inched closer to their father's bed. He brought a Mason jar out from under the blanket with his good hand.

"You girls earned this," he said.

"What is it?" Lindsey asked.

"It's your treasure, *kunumunu*. This was supposed to be hidden in the wall, but it fell into the well with me. I saved it for you all this time. You solved the whole thing, so now you get the treasure."

Lindsey took the jar from her father, and said, with little affect, "Thanks."

Amanda echoed the thanks, mechanically.

"Well, open it," Tim said.

Lindsey tried, but she was unable to break the seal. She handed it to Amanda, who also made a valiant attempt, but was likewise defeated.

Amanda passed it to her stepmother, who popped the seal without visible effort, and handed the jar back to Lindsey.

Lindsey unscrewed the lid, and took out the envelope within. Amazingly, it was still dry. She handed the envelope to Amanda. "Your turn," she said.

Amanda used her finger like a letter opener and ripped the top of the envelope open. She checked inside. "It's a bunch of papers from … Carnival Cruise Lines?" She removed the papers from the envelope, and she and Lindsey studied them.

"It's a reservation package," Lindsey said, her face lighting up. "We're going on a cruise!"

"*Woo-hoo!*" Amanda cried, then clapped her hand over her mouth, and said, "Oops. I forgot I was in a hospital. My bad."

Standing behind her, Kate winced, but without breaking her smile.

Tim, smiling as well, reached out with his good arm and took his wife's hand. He drew her closer, and she bent down to kiss him.

"Oh, but Daddy," Amanda said, "will you be able to go? With your legs, and all?"

"Look at the date on it, Squirt. It's a year from now. I'll be ready by then. But you guys, I don't know about. Maybe you better start packing now."

22

Lindsey and Amanda met Alan Curtis and their Uncle Greg at their grandparent's house. They were going to see their friend Mr. Leo, and this time they were armed with a veritable feast, as well as clean clothing, shoes, and a bucketful of good intentions. It was just the four of them, as Poppy had refused to leave their Dad's side, and Mom-mom and Kate, after a long day at the hospital, had wanted nothing more than to take glasses of iced tea to Mom-mom's sun room and relax.

Against the dark backdrop of the pines, the afternoon sun illuminated gnats and mayflies as they made their desultory way from nowhere to nowhere. Thomas came running out of the barn to beg for affection, which Amanda and Mr. Alan granted. Jenny and Jill whickered curiously at the four companions crossing the pasture.

The girls chattered as they neared the woods, their excitement mounting. They were eager to fulfill the promise they'd made to help their friend.

As they passed into the trees, the men glanced nervously at each other. Alan knew he and Greg were on the same page. For them, this was about atonement, and they were entirely at the mercy of their former victim. They had no idea what to expect from Lynch. Would he welcome them? Or would he greet them with scorn, fear, resentment, or even violence? Would he even remember them?

"Are you sure this is where it was?" Uncle Greg asked.

"Yes. Definitely," Lindsey said. "It was right here in this clearing. The lean-to was in this corner here—"

"And the campfire was right here," Amanda said, kicking at the soft loam where the fire should have been. "There was a circle of stones and everything. The ashes were still warm."

Lindsey could tell Alan and Uncle Greg didn't believe them. In fact, Lindsey started to wonder herself if they could have imagined the whole thing.

"Now, girls," Alan said. "Are ya absolutely sure? Maybe it was another spot that looks just like this one. That happens in the woods sometimes, you foller me?"

"No," Lindsey said. "It was here. There's no other places like this around here. This is it."

"There were bottles and cans everywhere," Amanda said. "And a milk crate full of junk."

"Well, there's nothing here now," Uncle Greg said. "He must've picked up and moved to another spot."

"He *did* say he didn't wanna get caught down here," Amanda said. "Maybe he didn't trust us not to tell on him."

"I'd think somethin' would be left behind," Alan said. "A man doesn't just pull up stakes and leave no trace like this. Especially when it's been rainin' like it has for the last three or four days. The ground is takin' prints real nice. I see Lindsey and Amanda's prints all over the place, and I see what must be Kate's over here, I guess, but I don't see a *man's* prints anywhere."

"Couldn't he have dragged a branch around and wiped them out?" Uncle Greg asked.

"Just his?" Alan responded. "I don't see how. Besides, that only works on TV. And what about the trash? I can imagine he woulda took all his gear with him, and the lean-to was just a bunch of sticks. He coulda flung 'em all over the woods. But I never met a bum yet that worries about litterin'. They just leave their trash behind. And there ain't a speck of trash here. This place is as pure and natural as it was back in Indian days."

"Native American," Lindsey said.

"Well, remember," Uncle Greg said, "he *wanted* to disappear. He knew we were onto his hideout. He must've gotten fairly good at disappearing over the last twenty-three years. Don't you figure?"

"Maybe," Alan said, frowning. "But the thing that bothers me the most is this campfire ring you ladies mentioned. Where did you say it was, exactly?"

"Right where I'm standing," Amanda said. Lindsey agreed with a nod.

"Right here?" he said, walking over to join her.

"Yes."

"Okay. Now the ashes and stones, he coulda chucked them into the creek. But there'd still be a dead spot here where nothin' grows. These little plants all around here, whatever they are, you can tell they've been here since spring. It doesn't look to me like there's ever been a fire here at all."

Uncle Greg and Alan exchanged a look that Lindsey didn't miss. "We're not making up a story, Uncle Greg. This guy was real. Mom-mom and Kate met him, too. And Kate was even here yesterday! Ask *them*."

"Now don't get your knickers all in a twist," Alan said. "I believe you. Every word. All I'm sayin' is that there's somethin' goin' on here that I don't understand. Maybe somethin' we weren't *meant* to understand."

"You mean like ... you think he's a ghost or something?" Amanda asked.

"There's no such thing as ghosts," Lindsey said.

"Oh, yeah?" Amanda said. "Then how come you won't go down to the haunted house, huh? You're the one that said somebody heard screaming down there, and saw red lightning bugs and everything."

Lindsey saw ... worry? ... in Uncle Greg's and Mr. Alan's faces as their eyes met. "What?" she asked. "What'd we say?"

"Nothing," Uncle Greg said. "It's just ... funny you should bring up that house right now," Uncle Greg said. "It used to be where Lynch ... where Mr. Leo lived."

The girls stared at each other. "That's so creepy," Amanda said.

Uncle Greg sighed, shrugged his shoulders. "Enough about it. Let's go. He's gone, if he was ever here in the first place."

"Yeah," Alan said. "I reckon that's so. I don't figure we'll ever really know the truth."

Uncle Greg stopped moving, and the last word hung in the air like the peal of a church bell while the three Raithers looked at each other.

"Are you girls thinking what I'm thinking?" Uncle Greg asked.

Lindsey was the first to move, taking a couple of steps toward Thinking Rock before the other two followed.

Alan trailed along behind them. "Is there somethin' I'm missin' here?" he asked.

"Maybe," Uncle Greg said. "Maybe not."

Two minutes later, Alan caught up to the three of them standing at the foot of the bluff, looking up at Thinking Rock and all around its base.

"What're ya lookin' for?" Alan asked.

"Not sure yet," Uncle Greg answered. Then he turned to his nieces. "Up top?" he asked.

The girls nodded.

"Why not?" Alan said.

Uncle Greg went first, followed by Lindsey and Amanda. Once again, Alan took up the rear.

Uncle Greg and the girls shuddered as they passed the cave on the way up, as if some evil spirit lurked within its inky blackness. Uncle Greg studied the litter of leaves at the cave's mouth, then continued up the stairs without a word. The rest followed.

Moments later, they all stood at the top. Lindsey was immediately uncomfortable, reeling from the near-sickening dreamlike sense of hyper-reality that held sway atop Thinking Rock.

"It's stronger," Uncle Greg said, looking around. "It's never been like this before."

"Like what?" Alan said.

"It's hard to explain."

"You knew about Thinking Rock, Uncle Greg?" Lindsey asked.

"We all did," he said. "Didn't your father tell you?"

"Not about this," Amanda said. "Poppy told me some things, but Daddy never did."

Uncle Greg nodded. "Your father and I, and Uncle Randy, I think when we grew up, we kind of stopped believing. Like Santa Claus. Dad never did stop believing, though. He kept telling us—"

"That you can always find truth at Thinking Rock," Amanda finished.

"Yes. Exactly. I haven't been here in years. I'd forgotten how it felt … But then, I don't remember it ever being this strong. I'd never have forgotten *this*. It gives me a headache."

"I know, right?" Lindsey said, as Amanda nodded.

"Well, it's a nice view," Alan said, "but I'm blamed if I can see any truth about Leo Lynch up here. That is what we're lookin' for, right?"

Uncle Greg gazed at Alan but did not reply, his mind obviously somewhere else. "I'm thinking it has something to do with that hole," he said. Turning to the girls, he added, "Don't you?"

Lindsey shifted in discomfort. "Do we have to?"

"It looked disturbed," Uncle Greg said. "Somebody's been in there recently. Or some*thing*."

"We did that yesterday," Amanda said. "Daddy hid one of the clues in there."

"He did? And you went in there?"

They nodded, and Uncle Greg looked at them with new respect. "Then why are you afraid of it now?" he asked.

"I don't know," Lindsey said. "It's different now. It's … bad … somehow."

Uncle Greg nodded. "I felt it, too. That's why I have to see." He stepped off the edge and began working his way back down the trail. The others followed, this time with the girls last in line.

Stopping at the hole, Uncle Greg said, "It's too small. Lynch couldn't have fit through that opening."

Alan peered into the hole. The westering sun was shining into their eyes, backlighting Thinking Rock and casting an impenetrable gloom in the cave. "It's darker than a stack of black cats in there," he said. "I don't think a man coulda squeezed through that opening, but it looks like a good place to stash somethin'. I wish I had a Maglite."

"Hold up," Amanda said. "I got an idea." She rummaged in her pack, brought forth Leo's mirror, and handed it to Alan. "Mr. Leo said we would need it one more time. I guess he was right."

"Hmm," Alan said. "Might work, at that." He angled the mirror so that it reflected light from the sun directly into the hole. The four of them leaned forward to see what might be revealed.

Lindsey squinted. She saw ... *something* ...

"It's ... ," Alan said. "I think it's a coffee can." He plunged his right arm into the hole and came back with a rusty can in his hand. Through the rust, along with a picture of an upturned coffee cup, could still be seen the words MAXWELL HOUSE and GOOD TO THE LAST DROP. The seal on the plastic lid was still intact. Alan lifted one edge and peeked inside.

"Arrowheads," he said. "It's full of arrowheads."

Amanda gasped. "Those are Daddy's," she said. "He collected 'em on the farm, and he lost 'em years ago."

"Yes, she's right," Uncle Greg said. "I recognize that can. Timmy accused me of stealing it several years ago. He was really upset about losing them."

"How do you think they got under there, Uncle Greg?" Lindsey asked.

"I don't know. Maybe he hid them here himself and forgot about it. Regardless, I'm sure he's going to be glad to get them back. But it still doesn't tell us anything about Lynch. Was there anything else under there, Alan?"

"Not that I could feel. Let me just have another look, though." Using the mirror, he aimed another spear of light into the hole and said, "Yep, I see somethin' way back there. Don't know if I can reach that far, though. Greg, you got longer arms. Wanna take a crack at it?"

Uncle Greg took a long look, got a positional fix on the object, and stuck his arm in up to the shoulder. "I can't reach it, either," he said in a strained voice. "Wait," he said then, "I just touched it. It moved." He pressed the side of his face hard against Thinking Rock, trying to get the maximum reach out of his arm. His face went red, and his breath came in short grunts as he stretched his body to its limit, until finally he said, "I got it!"

He brought his arm back out of the hole, and in his hand was a moldy lump of rotten tent canvas, wrapped around a thin rod-like object about a foot long. He began to peel off layers of folded canvas, handling the package like the Holy Grail itself. The others watched in silence.

The innermost layer of the canvas was blotchy with reddish-brown stains that had obviously been absorbed from whatever lay within. And when he moved the last fold of canvas aside, they beheld something they'd all seen before, although it was nearly unrecognizable in its current condition.

Uncle Greg rubbed his finger along what was left of the blade, causing large chunks of rust to crumble off and fall to the ground like cornflakes, only to reveal more rust beneath. The deer-antler hilt, apart from a black, crusty substance caked in its grooves, showed no sign of decay. It was that deer-antler hilt that sent a jolt of recognition through each of them.

"What happened to it?" Amanda gasped.

"Time happened to it," Uncle Greg replied. "Time and water."

"Time? What time?" Amanda asked. "Mr. Leo showed it to us yesterday, and it was bright and shiny, right, Lin?"

Lindsey nodded. "Like a mirror."

Uncle Greg shook his head. "Not *this* knife."

"Yes it was, that one," Amanda said. "The handle looks the same."

"You mean it was made of deer antler?"

"I don't know what it was made of, but whatever it was, I'm telling you it looked *exactly* like this one."

"What's that carved into the bottom of it?" Lindsey asked, pointing at the butt end of the knife.

Uncle Greg turned the handle to look at it. The antler's pedicle, where it had once been attached to a deer's skull, served as a sort of pommel. Into that flat surface were carved two nested Ls.

"Hm," he said.

"And those are bloodstains," Lindsey added, indicating the canvas. "And there's more on the handle."

"No," Alan replied. "That'd be rust."

"Yes, of course," said Uncle Greg. "It's definitely rust. Obviously."

The girls looked at each other. Lindsey could tell she and Amanda were thinking the same thing: if the men were determined to believe it was rust, best not to argue with them.

Uncle Greg studied the knife with a thoughtful frown. "How long would you say this has been in that cave, Alan?" he said, handing the weapon to his friend.

Alan took the artifact from him. "I'd have to say a good twenty years, the way it looks. Ever seen a knife like this before, Greg?"

Uncle Greg's and Alan's eyes met.

"Not that I can recall. You?"

"Nope," Alan said. "I don't reckon I have."

Alan handed the knife back to Uncle Greg. "You do what you want with that, Greg," he said. "I never saw it."

Uncle Greg nodded. "I'll get rid of it. It's dangerous to have something like this lying around, where anyone could find it. At any rate, I think we have what we came here for. Let's get back to the farm."

The girls stared at each other in confusion. "We didn't find Mr. Leo," Amanda said.

"We're not going to," Uncle Greg said. "He's moved on. But he left us a message, and we found it."

The walk back to the farm was quiet. The men, striding side by side, went first, Uncle Greg carrying the rusty knife. Neither of them said a word.

The girls trailed behind, also walking side by side. Lindsey bore the can of arrowheads, a treasure of immeasurable value to their father. As she walked, Lindsey tipped the can this way and that, feeling the weight shift back and forth, listening to the soft clunks and scrapes as the stone points slid across one another. She caught her sister's eye, and they favored each other with a smile.

"I'm gonna miss him," Amanda said.

"Me, too," her sister admitted. "But you know what? I don't think we have to worry about him anymore."

"No. I think he'll be fine."

As they broke from the forest and began crossing the pasture toward the Raither homestead, the red sun touched the horizon. Far away in the sky, beyond the sunset, a tiny object twinkled at the very limit of vision.

A sail?

THE END

ABOUT THE AUTHOR

Mark Lee Taylor lives on a fifties-era dead-end street in Maryland, with his wife, two daughters, two dogs, and delusions of grandeur.

Made in the USA
Lexington, KY
12 October 2014